THE BOY IN THE RED BOAT

Michael Seirton

STA BOOKS

Publisher - STA BOOKS

www.spencerthomasassociates.com

ISBN: 978-0-9933957-5-8

Dedication

This book is dedicated to Paul Greaves, my soulmate and mentor, who always made me feel safe and, without whose encouragement and guidance, there would have been no career in Theatre, Film, and Writing.

Respected throughout a long career at The National Theatre, Paul's dedication to his work, good humour and kindness to others less fortunate, will be remembered by everyone, as too will be his love of animals and his passion for finding obscure routes while touring The British Isles. A brave and selfless man whose beautiful spirit took flight in January 2010.

Thank you Paul, for leaving me with so many wonderful memories that began the first day we met at Derby Playhouse, and took the journey of life together.

May God Bless you Paul and keep you safe.

Acknowledgements

To my wonderful mother, Irene Chambers.
I dread to think how my troubled childhood would have ended without her strength of character, perception and guidance. Even now, it seems an extraordinary suggestion that I should apply for work at The Derby Playhouse, given that I was labouring in a scrap metal yard at the time. It was an incredible idea of hers that prompted me to take that first hesitant step towards a career that I never imagined was even possible. My mother bought the green dress - (named in the book,) from a stall holder in the open market in Derby. Needless to say she looked stunningly beautiful, and was naturally the inspiration for Eleanor McKenzie. This remarkable woman will always be eternally beautiful to me, and someone that I am immensely honoured to call both my mother and my friend.

To my Aunt Ruth and Uncle George (Hindle)
With loving memories of a welcoming home in Rotherham, the black-leaded, cast-iron range, producing stacks of Yorkshire puddings swamped in gravy throughout my childhood. The paved blue brickyard, with a row of freezing cold privies, torn-up newspaper threaded on string and, the narrow strip of garden beyond them, with prized chrysanthemums bagged in brown paper against the frost. Sadly this terraced street has long since been redeveloped, but nothing could demolish those vivid images, once again revisited in this novel.

To my Uncle Reg, and Aunt Violet (Chambers)
For caring to take me on holiday, riding pillion behind Uncle Reg with Aunt Vi in the sidecar, (Jack's spluttering combination in the novel,) and later, for introducing me to the Lake District, staying in that neglected farmhouse adjacent to the lake in Hawkshead, both having been reworked into the novel as Moorcroft Farm and The Bay of Dungellen.
Life is richer, for having been related to such wonderful people.

To my friend Stuart Craig – Production Designer
For the opportunity of working on the Richard Attenborough film of 'Gandhi,' and… for the Oscar that came after.
Thanks Stu, for taking that leap of faith in me, and kick-starting my early career!

I offer my grateful thanks Fiona Spencer Thomas, my agent and friend, without whose kind encouragement and suggestions on the manuscript of 'The Boy in the Red Boat,' it might easily have stayed on the shelf gathering dust and might never have been launched.
Bless you Fiona, for having faith in me. xx

To Michelle & Derek Pyecroft (D&G Graphics, Measham)
For all of their help in creating this and other book covers, not forgetting their valuable input into the Bears Adventure Books, - temporarily in hibernation!

THE BOY IN THE RED BOAT

Chapter One

Unbelievable as it might sound, when the sequence of life-changing events first began to unfold three months ago, Jack McKenzie had no idea that 'I' actually existed. At least, not until a letter was mistakenly sent by a young woman temping for the law firm of McNair, Courtney & Fife. The letter was delivered two days later to an address in an obscure back street of a Yorkshire steel town. At the age of twenty-nine, Jack McKenzie lived alone in this dilapidated, two-up, two-down terraced house in a rough neighbourhood of Eastmoor. The year was 1957.

That morning his head throbbed mercilessly from a hangover as he deposited two fizzing tablets into a glass of water. He collected the letters from the patch of worn lino in the front room, closing the door on the incessant barking from the kitchen as he sat down to open them.

The first was a red demand from the gas board, threatening a termination of supply unless the outstanding bill was settled by the end of the week, and the second came from the offices of McNair, Courtney & Fife, postmarked Lochenbrae. He closed his eyes until another wave of nausea passed before he thrust the letter, unopened, together with the gas demand, behind a plaster ornament on the china cabinet. He swallowed the fizzing liquid in a single draught, promising himself that he wouldn't touch another drop for the rest of his life. Well, at least not before the weekend.

Jack McKenzie was tall and lean with dark matted hair. That morning he had shaved badly with a blunt razor blade. The bits of bloodied paper blotting the worst of the cuts in the remaining stubble did nothing to minimise his wild, unkempt appearance.

In the far corner of the bleak room was a portable gramophone. On the turntable was a favourite recording of a waltz, evoking loving memories of his mother, who would dance and twirl him about in her arms. He had been an awkward, gangly boy, briefly transported from a troubled and lonely existence in those happy moments.

After tucking both trouser bottoms into his socks, he lifted his old bicycle through the front door, fingering some recent scratch marks on the faded wallpaper and vowing to be more careful in future. He glanced up as he stepped into the street, fully expecting to see the large, unusual bird somewhere close by. It had been in the area for the past few days, either circling above his house or perched on a nearby rooftop, but never close enough for him to identify its marking, not that he could have recognised anything at all in the dense fog that morning. He could barely see beyond ten feet.

Freewheeling to the end of St Luke's Road, he turned into the main Faversham Road by the corner shop. His breathing became sharper and more rasping as he cycled up a steep incline, damning his pointless existence as the bicycle jolted over potholes. The mist became denser, intermingling with belching volumes of industrial smoke that reeked of soot and iron filings. Pedalling faster, he overtook three cyclists who were also late, but no doubt did not have the pressure of bills to pay. With his rent due by the end of the week, the thought of yet another reduced pay packet made him feel even more nauseous.

Actually, he did have some cash hidden inside the portable record player; thirty-five pounds to be exact. He hated the prospect of using his mother's hard-earned savings and was determined to pay off the gas bill without touching a penny of it.

On his fourteenth birthday she hadn't been at the black kitchen range in the rear parlour. Instead, he had found her slumped in his father's chair, her worn features relaxed as though in sleep but her cheeks and hands ice cold to the touch. It was a traumatic period that put an end to his childhood but one he hoped would reunite her with his father, who had died years earlier in a pit explosion.

After the funeral, Jack didn't finish his schooling. Instead, to avoid being placed in a government orphanage, he found himself a dead-end job stoking the main boiler at the Shackleton foundry and continued to live at the house in St Luke's Road. It was gruelling work for a boy of fourteen. Every day he slaved to earn a tiny wage in a job with no prospects; the same job he still occupied fifteen years later.

For the second time in a week he had the uneasy feeling of being followed as he turned off the Faversham Road, skilfully negotiating the bricks and rubble piled against the skeletal remains of wartime bombing.

At last the embankment appeared through the fog, but his uneasiness persisted until he reached the base of a notoriously hazardous shortcut; a route that crossed a busy railway track but gave swifter access to the foundry gate, cutting twenty minutes off the journey by road.

The railway could be reached by a narrow footpath only accessible via a deep gully. Here mountainous stacks of beer barrels in the brewery yard towered precariously above him. Dismounting by the arched blue-brick wall of the embankment, Jack hoisted the bicycle on his shoulder and began the tricky ascent. As he clambered along the narrow track, a squeal of brakes in the brewery yard caught his attention. The large headlights of an expensive car penetrated the blanket of fog like searchlights. Its powerful engine pulsated with restrained energy. Why would a vehicle like that be there at that unearthly hour, particularly in such a run-down area of town? As he stared at its indistinct shape, the silhouette of a woman passed in front of the headlight beams and paused to peer through the gloom in his direction. He shuddered instinctively, gripping the bicycle, as the hairs on his arms stood up.

He continued his ascent as quickly as he could, stopping close to the railway track for a clearer view of the yard from the higher vantage point. As he expected, the fog was noticeably lighter but, because of the angle of the path, any clearer view of the vehicle or the woman was now obscured by the stacked barrels.

Hearing a familiar sound, he glanced up to see a bird wheeling high above him, shrieking a wild, unearthly cry as it swooped lower in its effortless and magnificent flight through the plumes of belching smoke above the town. As he watched the beautiful shape and noted the markings, he realised it was not unfamiliar and decided to identify it in one of the as yet unpawned nature books in his father's bookcase.

The sound of the works siren made him start and, ignoring the wild shrieks of the bird in his rush to get to the foundry as fast as he could, he stepped out on to the track, careless of any immediate danger. He avoided death by inches as he hurled himself clear of an oncoming train, just as the engine thundered past.

At the end of his gruelling day, the question of Jack's future employment was the subject of a loud and forthright opinion from the foreman. Jack calmed himself by contemplating the two unopened bottles of stout awaiting him at home. But instead of this happy salve, on dismounting at his home he was confronted by a ranting neighbour who threatened him with the painful removal of body parts as she told him how his dog had made off with a chicken carcass from her pantry. For a moment, he wondered if the animal might have returned to its previous owner but discounted the idea almost as quickly, believing that no one other than him would have wanted such a scrawny creature. With stomach churning, he set off in the direction of the recreation ground where he frequently walked the dog, expecting to find him there.

"That flamin' thing ought t'be put down," the irate woman called after him, clattering a baking tray against the yard wall in anger. "An' you along with it, yer bloody half-wit."

He would have apologised had it been any use but since childhood he had been hampered by a debilitating stammer; a condition that had excluded him from any normal childhood existence and made him an object of ridicule. An only child of middle-aged parents, Jack had been cared for better than most until the death of his father when he was eight. This placed the onus of being the breadwinner on his mother, who had never been in robust health. After her untimely death, he had to work a full shift for a minimum wage to survive, pawning whatever he could to avoid eviction.

Three months earlier, on the same wild and stormy night when Jack had seriously contemplated ending his own futile existence, the white dog had appeared. Its large, scrawny frame, sodden and filthy, had pushed open the door, just as he was about to swallow an entire bottle of aspirin. The animal stood hunched against the back door, barely able to stand, a pathetic bag of bones hardly resembling any living creature. Its huge paws were raw and bleeding, as though it had travelled for miles. The sunken, expressive eyes, pleading for food, gave Jack no alternative other than to return the mound of pills to the bottle and, instead, search through the pantry for scraps. More shocking still, when he put the plate down he noticed a decrepit old cat which had slipped in unseen behind the dog and was sheltering against the animal. To have a dog turn up in that dreadful condition was bad enough, but to find a cat too was weird. It was an emaciated creature which he doubted would survive the night, but the peculiarly marked animal had the constitution of a horse and continued to thrive, despite its appearance.

After a long search, he came across the missing dog on a patch of rough ground near the bombsite. It was lifeless, as though on the brink of death, but with no apparent injury. In the fading light, its coat appeared eerily translucent as he gathered it up. Struggling beneath the weight, he made his way home. Each step of the way he regretted that he hadn't purchased an old motorbike and sidecar when he'd had the chance.

He stayed awake with the dog through the night, occupying his time by removing a heavy coin-box from the electric meter on the kitchen wall. He spent an hour prodding the slot with a table knife and eventually slid out five half-crowns. Two hours later he had five more and, by supplementing them with what little remained of the housekeeping, there was now enough to satisfy the gas board – but it would leave him with nothing for food, beer or fags until payday.

By the following morning, with the dog somewhat improved thanks to his care, Jack was able to forestall the gas board's threat of disconnection and pay off some of the outstanding debt, but it made him late at the foundry. As luck would have it, Alfred Dobson, one of the few workers who had ever showed him any kindness, kept the foreman talking, allowing him to slip in unnoticed.

A delivery of coal had been unloaded in the wrong place so Jack's entire day was spent re-shovelling it into its allotted area ready for the night shift. After such a back-breaking day, he barely had the energy to cycle home where, within an hour, he had collapsed on the bed, hardly noticing the lumpy flock mattress and only vaguely hearing the ripping sheet as he tried to get more comfortable, praying for a dreamless night.

All day he worked and at the weekend he would drink heavily and deal with the hangovers that inevitably followed. On the other nights his mind would run free, and those were the times he dreaded most. As far back as he could remember, he had been haunted by a recurring nightmare that always woke him, trembling in terror and sodden with sweat. That night as the white dog jumped up, settling against the crook of his knees, he felt the security he needed to drift off to sleep. Within moments, he was walking through banks of white cloud, with the scent of pine pervading his senses. When the mist cleared enough for him to see, a young, dark-haired woman was standing close by, wearing an exquisite green dress. As she approached him through a shimmering bank of light, the delicate green of the material seemed to be an integral part of the mist itself. In the near distance, he could hear the rhythmic sound of the sea crashing against a cliff, arcing a spray of sparkling droplets that glittered about her as she approached, her arms reaching out to him. On her delicate wrist was a fine, gold bracelet he knew was set with pearls and dark green gems.

Jack's eyelids fluttered over his blank eyes as the magnificent shape of the bird appeared and hovered above the young woman, beating its great wings as she drew closer. Its movement swirled the mist into a spiral until she was enveloped in a cocoon as she reached out to touch him.

The chimes of the clock on the Faversham church had long since announced that he was late for work but he didn't move. He had felt refreshed on waking and had lain, staring at the ceiling; but now he was aware why the bird had seemed so familiar. Was he raving mad, seeing the phantoms of his dreams during his waking hours? Perhaps he really was 'the loony of Eastmoor' as most locals seemed to think.

He stared into his mother's face in the photograph on the bedside table, wondering what she would have made of these magical images that occurred less frequently than the torment of the nightmare. Draped across the frame was a string of glass beads she had used only for best. Beside this was a snapshot of him as a child, seated between his parents, which had been taken in the back yard. The final frame contained a picture of him as an eight-year-old examining a pocket watch with his father, taken only days before his untimely death at the pit. Since then the watch had been wound up each night and placed on the bedside table where he could see it. He was grateful that his parents would never know what little use he had made of his life, or of the impoverished circumstances in which he lived.

Before leaving the house that morning, he flicked through one of his father's nature books until he came upon the illustration of an osprey, identical to the now familiar bird except for its enormous size. It had become a rare species since the turn of the century, after which only an occasional sighting had been recorded in the coastal regions of the Scottish Highlands.

He was desperately late, yet he cycled slowly towards the factory, deliberately avoiding the short cut, as if he wanted a confrontation with the management on bad timekeeping, or in fact anything which might kick start a getaway from his wretched existence. He thought about the woman in the green dress, fleeting images which he recalled in perfect detail: the clarity of her unusual eyes and her lovely face framed by the dark, lustrous hair. Nothing had escaped him. Every feature and expression was perfectly memorised, as too was the shape and texture of that magical dress.

*

In the offices of McNair, Courtney & Fife, Bonnie Jameson deposited a sheaf of neat paperwork into an in-tray on William Blake-Courtney's desk as he began the interrogation.

"You posted it… when?" he asked with disbelief. The damp patches on his shirt spread beneath his armpits as he awaited the dreaded confirmation.

"It was the day after I took over from Amy."

There was a deathly silence as he continued to fix her with his steely blue eyes. "How could anyone make such an idiotic mistake? I thought you could be trusted."

"Is my honesty being questioned, Mr Courtney?" she responded sharply.

"No, not at all, but I find it hard to understand that anyone other than a simpleton would have posted it. Not after my express instructions to the contrary."

"Then you ought to have conveyed that information more clearly to Amy before she took ill. As you know, I typed the letter from her notes and, given those instructions, posting the letter was the obvious thing to do."

"Have you any idea what damage your thoughtless action might have caused my clients? That letter was for filing and should never have been sent. Not under any circumstances."

"Then it might be advisable to deposit only the letters you require for posting into an out-tray, once you have signed them," she responded with defiant calm, pushing her tumbling red hair away from her face as she resumed typing, clacking the keys of the vintage machine with enviable efficiency.

When the door to Blake-Courtney's office had closed, a middle-aged woman appeared from another office to express her concern.

"This incident with Mr Courtney sounds most irregular, Bonnie dear. Is everything settled?" she asked, worried.

"I do believe it is, Mrs McNair."

"He seemed more agitated than usual. Did the correspondence contain anything libellous?"

"Quite the contrary… it was short and said nothing out of the ordinary."

"And has there been any response?"

"Nothing yet, Mrs McNair," Bonnie replied. It had been over a week since the letter was posted and she prayed that, whoever Jack McKenzie might be, he would make contact with the office before long and uncover whatever the new partner was so anxious to conceal.

"Then why is he making such a fuss? This is all very disturbing… I must inform Angus about it once he returns. One cannot be too careful."

*

The first attempt on Jack's life had occurred on the Saturday night, marking the commencement of a disastrous two weeks. It was a lovely summer's evening, marred only by the tang of smoke fumes and the acrid smell of smouldering metal which always hung above the street like a leaden cloak of oppression.

There was an odd, pulsating throb in the air about him as he walked towards the corner shop at the bottom of St Luke's Road. He wondered if a storm was imminent but saw no gathering clouds darkening the horizon. Instinctively he looked up to see if the osprey was circling above but, stare as he might, there was not even a sparrow in evidence. A ludicrous thought. How would people react if they knew he suspected the bird was actually stalking him. How crazy was that?

As he neared Athey's, Frank Wilson, an acquaintance of dubious character, called to attract his attention from the open window of his pre-war Standard saloon, parked on Faversham Road. "Thought any more about buyin' that combination?" Jack shook his head in response, miming the need for cigarettes as he went into the shop.

"He'll do you a good deal, mate," Frank's companion shouted. "Be a sport... we'll give you a lift t' the club, an' talk about it over a pint."

As they waited for Jack to emerge, Frank wound up the window with some difficulty as his companion, Barry, lit their cigarettes. The car quickly filled with smoke, so Frank attempted to crank the window back down again. It jammed.

Jack had been acquainted with both men for years, first at school and then at work, but neither situation was conducive to feeling any sense of trust in their eager proposition. It was perfectly clear they needed to offload Frank's ancient motorbike and sidecar. It was an antiquated machine which he had no intention of buying. However, a lift to the working men's club would be useful, so he played along.

As he stepped into the road, the air filled with an ear-splitting screech from the osprey, which he hadn't seen perched on a nearby chimney stack. Its intelligent head inclined with enquiring, reflective eyes glittering with a magnetic intensity as the awesome wings lifted, quivering in anticipation of flight. What he didn't see, some distance along the Faversham Road, was another parked vehicle that, unlike Frank's Standard, was a gleaming example of the sumptuously modern. The powerful engine of the Sunbeam Talbot pulsated as it sat in neutral like a sleek metallic predator, lying in wait for an unsuspecting victim. As Jack paused for a gap to appear in the traffic, the Sunbeam was eased into gear and moved forward, increasing its momentum until it was racing forward at considerable speed.

From inside his car, Frank peered through a cloud of cigarette smoke as the Sunbeam sped towards them, heading directly at Jack as he stepped off the pavement. Frantically, he struggled to crank open the window but it still wouldn't budge. Instead, the handle came off in his hand and the window jolted down only a fraction. "Watch out!" he yelled at the top of his voice, thrusting his shoulder hard against the door in a desperate attempt to force it open.

At the same moment, a piercing shriek cut the air as the osprey propelled itself towards the intended victim who, until then, had been oblivious to the impending danger. It was hard to define his exact thoughts as he contemplated his death in those split seconds. He was shocked that fate had prevented him from taking his own life only a few weeks earlier and now death was hurtling towards him, in the shape not of an avenging angel but of a piece of machinery, to end the futility of a useless existence in which he had achieved absolutely nothing. What sort of tragic epitaph was that?

His feet were rooted to the spot and his stomach spasmed as if he'd gorged himself on a pound of lemons as the powerful car charged towards him like an ambassador from hell. To close his eyes was impossible. He caught sight of Frank waving frantically and trying to open his car door. In that moment, he felt a violent draught whirling about him from the feathered tips of giant wings that fanned the air as they swooped towards him. His vision blurred as the solid bulk of the bird's huge shape transformed, hypnotically, into a translucent outline.

He heard screaming, but it was not his own, as the jumble of images merged together in a crazy montage. He felt an urgent, tugging sensation as he was pulled upward. His eyes were open wide but he could distinguish nothing as a warm rush of air flowed over the soft down of the bird's feathered underbelly; as it lifted him bodily away from the path of the oncoming vehicle. He experienced an agonising jolt as the charging vehicle swerved dramatically at the precise moment Frank kicked open his car door, directly into the bird's flight path.

There was an ugly crunching of metal and the stench of charred paint as the Sunbeam Talbot collided head on with Frank's door, wrenching the metal from its hinges with a shriek, thrusting aside the stationary vehicle as the unrecognisable twisted remains of the door spun across the road in an explosion of blue and orange sparks.

Cushioned and protected by the injured bird, Jack was deposited sprawling across the roof of Frank's car; every ounce of his breath had been crushed from his lungs, leaving him light-headed but oddly calm.

Frank was deathly white as he clambered through the gaping hole where the door had once been. Incensed and raging he screamed at the gleaming car as it accelerated away and out of sight: "You crazy bastard! I'll get you fer this!"

Jack eased himself into a sitting position on Frank's roof, bewildered and shaken, wondering which, if any, of the recent events had been real. He grasped on to the sloping metal, steadying himself. For some brief, uncertain moments he focused on the bird as it perched awkwardly on a rooftop, dressing its damaged flight feathers, its shape becoming more indistinct with every passing second as it blended into the gathering rainclouds. Then it vanished completely.

"Are you OK, mate?" Barry asked in passing, not waiting long enough for an answer as he joined Frank at the kerbside to inspect the mangled wreckage of the door.

"How the hell did McKenzie get clear of that?" Frank asked him. "I thought he was a goner fer sure."

"I don't know," Barry said, staring at Jack's ashen face. "Come to that, how did he get on the roof of the flamin' car anyway?" He scratched his head in bewilderment. "It's bloody impossible."

"Beats me," Frank answered grimly. "'Ave you seen the state o' this flamin' door?"

"You'll never get that fixed on your insurance, mate."

"That's no good anyway – I haven't got any," he said, kicking the twisted metal. "I can't see any way out of this mess. What can I do, Barry? I've got nowt else... the motorbike's clapped out, you know that," he mumbled so Jack wouldn't hear.

"Then shift the bloody thing fast, an' get this lot repaired with the cash. That daft bugger on yer roof's yer best bet."

"I can't, not after this."

"It wasn't your fault."

"I know, I just feel sorry fer the poor bugger."

Barry laughed. "Save it fer somebody worth a brass fart. Do as I say, an' get McKenzie t' buy that piece of junk while yer can. No other twat's daft enough t' give it a second look. Ask him now while he's groggy."

Although Jack couldn't hear what was being said, he had a good idea, given their furtive looks. He dusted himself down and went on to the club on his own, in no mood to be used.

*

The next morning he rode to work with aching limbs and many conflicting thoughts to ponder. He looked back frequently as he cycled along the Faversham Road, fully expecting the Sunbeam to be tailing him, but he saw nothing. It was a day that had begun like so many others: grey, overcast and chilly enough to button up his jacket. He had cycled past the bomb site and scaled the embankment, crossing over the rail track, but he couldn't shake off the feeling that he was being watched.

He had been hard at work, shovelling coal into the boiler for about an hour, when the incident occurred soon after the day shift began operating the machinery on the main floor. The first indication of trouble was the coarse hollering of male voices and the shrill screams of the women; terrifying sounds that spurred him into immediate action, scrambling over mountains of coal to reach the group of workers staring at the final moments of Alfred Dobson's life. He was a quiet man who had shown Jack kindness and consideration ever since he had started work there as a boy. The spectacle was horrific.

Alfred had been attempting to repair a shredded industrial belt, now flailing wildly, which had dislodged him when the faulty mechanism had cranked into motion. He was now suspended from a girder high above the gnashing jaws of the machine.

The night foreman was struggling to shut down the unit, aided by one of the floor workers as they applied every ounce of their combined strength to the lever in a futile attempt to close it down. The safety device remained jammed and wouldn't budge from the ON position.

With time at a premium, Jack forced his way between the gathered workers and began scaling the nearest post supporting Alfred's girder. His hands slipped on years of oily grime but his determination paid off and he made good progress. He edged steadily upwards, which gave hope to the weakening man. When, finally, he reached the cross-girder a few feet away from where Alfred was hanging, the flailing belt tore some more on its revolving pulley, altering its speed with a severe jolt. A deadly, whip-like section of the belt detached and thrashed randomly across the girder, preventing Jack from gaining any foothold. The flailing strands lashed his bare arms and shoulders until he pulled further back. There was no time to find another route to reach Alfred and he watched helplessly as his grip slackened while he urged him desperately to hold on longer. But it was too late. Jack forced his eyes closed to shut out the final moments of a life, as poor Alfred Dobson dropped from the bar without a sound. He felt the warm splatter of blood over his face as the machinery shuddered to a grinding halt, the momentum almost dislodging his hold on the bar. Nothing was recognisable in the mangled carnage below.

How he got through the remainder of that shift would remain a blur for the rest of his life. The drinking session on his return home began as soon as the club opened and continued until late evening when, hours later, he staggered out into the rain, clutching a bottle of barley wine. By that time he was unable to ride and used his bike only to assist his unsteady progress into St Luke's Road as the deluge worsened.

He barely recognised the bombed-out buildings, or the sound of shattering glass as the bottle spun away from his grasp as he passed out on the rubble. The last sound he recalled was the click-clicking of the bicycle wheel as it spun close to his head. After that, everything went blank as he rolled over, face down. He heard nothing as the louts ran for cover, stumbling over him. He was deaf to their humourless comments and felt none of the insensitive prodding of boots and contemptuous spitting on the rain-sodden clothing of his inert form. Nor did he feel the warmth of their urine as it splattered liberally on the back of his saturated jacket.

He awoke, shivering with cold, in the early hours the following morning and salvaged his bike from the rubble. It appeared to be in much better shape than he was. With aching limbs and a throbbing head he made his cautious way home, jettisoning the stinking jacket on some waste ground. Once inside the house, he began to take off the remainder of his clothes until he saw the reflection of himself in the mirror. At the sight of the vivid red stain across his shirt, he tore at the fabric with frenzied fingers, bursting buttons in his panic and ripping off the blood-stained vest from his trembling body like a man demented. He gasped as he backed away from the image. There was a desperate, haunted look in his eyes, wide and staring at the jagged blue scar running from his left shoulder and across his chest; an old wound, now smeared with the crimson of Alfred Dobson's blood. When he realised the scar wasn't bleeding, he soaped himself down in the old tin bath, slopping the cold water over his body and meticulously scrubbing every inch of his skin until it was red-raw, as if to remove the horror of the previous day. Then he threw all his damaged clothing into the dustbin, dressed and set off once again for work.

*

When he returned home that evening he finally opened the correspondence from the offices of McNair, Courtney & Fife, rereading the contents many times before putting it aside. The letter was short and offered no information other than the fact that he was to receive a small bequest from a distant relative. He was also advised that he must present himself at the offices of William Blake-Courtney in Lochenbrae, a remote town in the Scottish Highlands, before the end of the month, or forfeit his inheritance.

He dwelt on the contents for some time, particularly the paragraph urging him to travel what would be close on two hundred miles, a seemingly impossible distance for him, and for what? A small bequest? He had a job, such as it was, and no transport other than an old bike. What would he do with the white dog and the cat? No one else would look after them, he was certain of that. So he returned the letter to the envelope and placed it next to the clock on the mantelshelf and took another aspirin.

*

That night he was gasping for air as he thrashed about in the bed, fighting the covers, his eyes wide, staring blankly into the nightmare. It unfolded with a burst of orange flames that licked hungrily from the narrow openings of a medieval tower. Sparks erupted from the roof, showering the surrounding trees as the fire intensified, belching clouds of acrid smoke out from beyond the battlements.

Extending from two sides of the tower were wings of living accommodation. Huddled shapes scurried out in an attempt to get the flames under control when a window exploded on the second floor of the western wing.

On the ground, three men worked feverishly at an antiquated piece of firefighting equipment to pump water siphoned from the moat on to the blaze. Suddenly each man stopped what he was doing to stare, mesmerised as, on the battlements, a man had charged out of the belching smoke, his clothes in flames. Without hesitation, he clambered onto the ramparts, launching himself free of the building, his arms spread wide, the flaming garments flapping about him as he fell; a wounded firebird tumbling down through the darkness. His shape twisted hypnotically in a macabre flight of death, each tortuous movement reflected on the smooth surface of the moat below until it was finally consumed in its own image in a plume of hissing water.

Up on the terrace, an elegant woman dressed in a black evening gown had emerged from the shadows. The beaded eyes of a silver fox stole glittered as brilliantly as they had done in life as she leant forward, allowing the fur to slip unnoticed from her shoulders into the darkness. Two diamond clips on her dress sparkled fiercely as she gripped the balustrade, splitting her painted nails as she witnessed the finale of the firebird's descent. As she turned away, her beautiful features, drained of all colour, gave no indication of any compassion or distress, only anger. Her deceptively generous mouth became a cruel slash of scarlet. She strode back into the house.

As the French windows closed noisily behind her, the nightmare ended. Jack sat up in bed with a start.

The following morning he dabbed at the patches of blood oozing from his skin after an excruciatingly painful shave. He must get a sharper razor. Later on he went to the working men's club, where he drank heavily to blot out the memories. His eyes began to glaze over as his mind was numbed enough to diminish the sounds and memory of the sickly warmth of Alfred's blood as it splattered over his face.

Frank and Barry had been hovering all evening. Normally he would have been drinking alone for hours, but on this occasion they had bought him four more pints of black and tan while they expounded the virtues of motorcycling. The drone of their voices became distorted as the glasses emptied and their features were out of focus when they made their abrupt departure from his table.

"You won't be disappointed mate, I promise," Frank said, putting on his jacket. Barry had mumbled something else about Saturday night as he slicked back his hair, adding that Jack needed to bring along cash. Their animated shapes quickly merged, indistinct images in the smoke-filled bar.

When the collection of empty glasses on his table had doubled, Jack found himself staring blankly at the woman sitting opposite, who had clearly been talking at him for some time.

"Got a lot in common, you an' me," she said, reaching across the table for his cigarettes. Inhaling deeply as she lit the first, she dropped the packet into her purse, wheezing into the back of her hand as she chattered on through the smoke haze, the red tip of the cigarette crackling as she puffed away. In contrast to her youthful clothing, she had the voice of an ageing woman and, when she leaned forward into the pool of harsh overhead lighting, her brassy hair appeared even more unnatural. She mentioned a volatile husband who was away on a darts tournament evening and wasn't expected home until the early hours. Jack peered across the table, trying to distinguish a few features beneath the orange make-up, but gave up when once again she wheezed into her hand while lighting up another of his cigarettes. When she upset her drink over her bright pink coat, she cursed like a dockside navvy.

"I've got to get some water on this or it'll be flamin' ruined. Look sharp an' finish that pint... I'm coming back wi' you. I'll sponge it off there." Supporting Jack with one arm, she tottered on ridiculously high heels, struggling to support his weight. The exit door had been left open to let in fresh air. She collided with a table as she passed.

"Watch out, Norma, you'll 'ave me beer over else," a man called after her, steadying his pint as he stood up to wipe the slopped ale from his lap.

"Well if you'd lend a hand instead of watching me struggle t'me car, you wouldn't have wet yer pants, yer geriatric old fart."

The old man stared back at her with unconcealed resentment, steadying himself with the aid of a stick as he sat down. "You daft cow, I can hardly walk myself. Any road, why not get Dennis t'lend a hand?" he added, cackling happily.

Norma propped Jack against the open door in order to catch her breath. "He's got a darts match in town."

"Not from where I'm sittin'!" the old man laughed. "His mate's just come in, so your Dennis won't be far behind."

Norma hurried to haul Jack into the yard, shoving him towards the car. "Get a move on, can't yer? If he catches up now, we're done for."

As the Austin Seven spluttered away from the car park, two men appeared in the doorway, and the older and burlier of the two went back inside to question the old man.

*

Jack gripped the edge of the bed tightly, convinced he was about to be sick from the nauseating waft of stale sweat and cheap perfume coming from Norma as she stripped down to an under-slip. He felt even more ill and the room rotated about him as he stared at the ceiling, stripped of everything but his shirt and underpants. The only light came from a lamp on the bedside table that seared into his eyes. She had deliberately angled it that way. Even so, he could hear her rifling through every cupboard and drawer that might conceal valuables. Yet, struggle as he might to get up from the bed, all he could manage was an unintelligible groan.

"This flamin' thing's stuck fast," Norma grumbled, fumbling to lower the sash window and cursing when it didn't close. "That flamin' dog's shut up fast in the front room, in't it?" she asked, approaching him in a foul, perfumed haze. Blinded by the lamp, he didn't see her lift the treasured pocket watch and beads from his bedside table and drop them into her bag. She snapped the catch shut, before clambering onto the bed and straddling him. Nor did he hear the motorbike grind to a halt outside the house, but Norma did. She froze at the sound of male voices outside. She clicked off the bedside lamp to pass the window unobserved and began frenziedly dressing, all the time straining to hear any other sounds. She heard nothing except for the barking of the white dog. Fumbling in the dark to zip up her dress she stumbled as a man started bellowing obscenities from the back of the house. Moments later he charged across the yard, thundering against the back door with every ounce of his weight. On the second attempt, it split from its hinges in an explosion of wood splinters.

In her panic, Norma crashed noisily into a collection of empty beer bottles as she groped about in the dark, desperate to find the door. When she did, the intruder was already in the hallway, ready to climb the stairs.

"If you're up there, wi' that useless twat McKenzie… I swear Norma, I'll tear yer bloody arm off, an beat yer to death along wi' the bugger," Dennis growled, thudding hard on the front room door to quiet the white dog, unaware that in doing so he had jolted open the latch. The dog scrabbled frantically on the lino at the base of the door, opening the gap further.

Norma skidded on a rolling bottle and slammed hard into the wall. Ignoring her pain and badly winded, she flattened herself against the wall as her husband pounded on the door. Moaning noisily, Jack forced his eyes open to peer unseeing into the darkness of the spinning room. He wondered at the incessant hammering and loud, violent threats.

"I know you're in there, Norma. Open the flamin' door."

The door burst open and the lumbering shape of a man built like an ox crashed through as he reeled across the room. As he caught hold of the bed for support, he saw Jack struggling to sit up. The remains of the door slammed shut as Norma made good her escape, her high heels clattering noisily down the uncarpeted stairs.

Catching his breath and bunching a huge fist, Dennis jerked Jack savagely up by his shirt and punched him in the face. The crunch of bare knuckles hit him repeatedly, the final blow sending him reeling into the flimsy bedside table, which instantly broke beneath his weight. The fallen lamp clicked on beside Jack's head. Dennis hauled him over until he was face up and booted him viciously in the side until his groans ended in mouth-opening gasps for air.

He lay on his back defenceless and beaten, unable to move as the numbness in his face was replaced by unimaginable pain. Dennis thrust his legs wide apart, and was about to boot him where it would hurt most of all when Norma's clattering high heels on the pavement made him rush to the window and peer outside.

"Trev, what are yer doing down there, fer God's sake? Get on after her."

"I can't. I'm 'avin' a piss. Get down here yourself. I'll be a while yet."

There was blood gathering in Jack's mouth as his attacker lumbered past. Norma revved up the engine of her car just as Jack heard a blood-curdling scream as Dennis stumbled at the foot of the stairs. The white dog had launched its attack and taken a sizeable chunk from Dennis's leather pants. The dog was quickly knocked unconscious by a wild swing of an enamel saucepan, the first thing he could grab, spraying baked beans across the kitchen.

The light from the lamp by Jack's head hurt his eyes and, although he wanted to turn away, his body wouldn't respond. The last thing he heard before passing out was the shriek of tyres from Norma's car as it lurched down the road at speed, cornering into the Faversham Road on two wheels as the throaty roar of a motorbike gave chase.

*

As the church clock struck three, Jack's life began to ebb away. Now unconscious, he struggled for breath with the combination of a swollen nose and puffed-up, blood-filled mouth allowing very little air to pass. A storm had been looming for most of the night and only the chimes disturbed the eerie stillness. Jack's inert form was stirred into movement by a cooling draught of air blowing across his battered body. At the open window, the curtains began flapping as the wind intensified. Then came the downpour. His breathing became deeper as, in his semi-unconscious state, he began to transpose the sound of the curtains for the fluttering wings of the osprey.

With an immense effort he reached out towards the sound. Pricked by the remnants of the table, he imagined the talons of the great bird grasping him, gently preparing to transport him away. As another wave of agonising pain overwhelmed him, the only thing he remembered later was a severe tugging at the inner walls of his abdomen and a thread of silver light that whipped sharply past his face as he winced. The pain began to subside and he experienced a sensation of being carried along on the journey to his death. It seemed real as he levitated above his crumpled body in the wreckage of the table. He looked down, watching himself retch and vomit before he was whisked through the open window with the ease of flowing silk, being buffeted gently as he passed beyond the turbulence of the storm.

He was travelling at an immense speed and the rush of cool air felt like morning dew on his face. There was a salty taste in his mouth as, in the firm grip of the osprey, he emerged through a cloud, swooping low above the ocean, gliding on an air current towards a spectacular heather-covered crag. They hovered above the cliff face.

Walking along a narrow path on the cliff top was the woman he had seen before in the green dress. She looked towards him, shading her eyes against the sun, before she moved away from the cliff edge, following a track down a steep incline towards a farmhouse nestling at the base of the crag. There, a strangely marked cat, quite similar to his own, jumped on to the bonnet of a 1920s open-topped tourer parked beside a barn. The woman called out to a young man lounging in the dicky seat. At such a distance Jack was unable to identify his features or hear any of their exchange against the rush of wind as the osprey hovered above.

The man appeared startled but at the same time excited by her words. With all the agility of youth he jumped out of the car and set off towards her, taking a shorter route by clambering sure-footedly up the perilously rugged incline. The fact that he was dressed in a kilt probably aided the speed of his ascent until he reached her. He put his arm lovingly about her waist.

Unlike her companion, the woman was clearly distressed. She buried her head against his shoulder. He, in turn, looked up and fixed his gaze on Jack.

Jack froze in fright and disbelief when he made visual contact with the young man, for he was an exact replica of himself. Everything was identical. The reddish bronze of his dark, unruly hair, the irregular shape of his teeth, even the unusual colour of his eyes were the same. Now Jack could see these details very clearly.

He was suspended in time above them, unbuffeted by the wind, gripped in the strong talons of the bird and secured to its soft underbelly by a glistening silver thread. Except for its enormous size, the bird seemed real enough; its beautiful feathers moving gently in the wind. Only when Jack glanced at his own body, which he could just see at this angle, did he realise to his great astonishment that just the outline of his shape existed. The rest of his former self had transformed into a swirling, translucent mass.

They began a slow descent towards the woman, who was now reaching out to him, her skirts swirling about her in the breeze. The sounds of the ocean surged hard against the cliffs, surrounding the couple with a glittering spray.

He was lowered into the dampness of an incoming mist that rapidly enveloped both him and the couple until they disappeared, along with the surrounding landscape.

*

Jack awoke to the warning growls of the dog and the sound of low voices from the kitchen. He peered through the slits of hooded eyes at the splattering of blood on the linoleum and forced himself up from the wreckage of the bedside table, scarcely able to resist screaming out in agony. Every movement was unbearable. He half expected to see the bird perched close by and was disappointed to find it was not, yet he clung on to the images from the dream to help him through the realities of another day in Eastmoor. He struggled to stand, pushing against the floor with his hand, but was unable to get a grip on the bed with the other, which remained clenched. The white dog was licking his fist gently, until eventually he opened out the palm. A cluster of the osprey's soft feathers drifted to the floor.

Wrapped in a torn, bloodied sheet, Jack made his painful, slow way down the stairs, ready to challenge the intruders in the back parlour, but from the sound of scurrying feet he knew he would be too late and indeed he found the back door off its hinges. What had been a spartan but habitable home the night before had been reduced to something unrecognisable.

Splintered wood dug into the soles of his bare feet, preventing him from entering further. Two sections of the shattered door frame were more or less intact but the smashed hinges remained attached to the door, which had been propped on its side to gain access. The floor was littered with broken china, amongst which pots and pans had been strewn from the emptied cupboards. The curtains from the back window had been removed, as had the hearthrug and most of the plates from the old dresser. Until he had appeared at the foot of the stairs, anything of value was being selectively removed under the supervision of his neighbour, another woman and three boys of differing ages, all of whom rented houses backing on to the communal yard.

Painfully, he blocked up the back door and retreated upstairs where he dozed fitfully in the back bedroom he had occupied as a child for the remainder of the day.

*The next morning he forced himself to get ready for work. He wondered whether to follow up on the letter from Scotland but thought better of it and went out into the foggy street, dreading the inevitable bike ride. Every muscle and sinew tried to resist movement. His mouth, swollen and barely open, took in what air it could. His nose had been rendered useless, the nasal passages completely blocked with dried blood.

No one and nothing seemed to be following him that morning, particularly at such an early hour, and yet the second attempt on his life occurred soon after he freewheeled along the narrow footpath and into the gully. Only then did he experience a real sense of unease.

Almost as soon as he dismounted, he heard the distinct tap of high heels walking purposefully across the brewery yard. An unidentifiable male voice engaged in a low, one-sided argument followed by the sound of the shoes. There was a short silence, before a sledgehammer began thudding the wooden chocks securing the stacked barrels. Jack wrongly assumed it was the early shift engaged in the process of loading.

He was about to hoist his bike up the railway embankment when a loud crash stopped him in his tracks. It was followed immediately by a heavy rumbling. He peered in the direction of the yard but was unable to distinguish anything other than barrels beyond the wire of the perimeter fence. The noise increased and a barrel pitched over in his direction; a menacing object, only halted in its progress by the creaking wire of the fence, which soon bulged under the strain as others followed, colliding with the first.

Terrified, he took shelter in a low drain arch built into the blue brickwork of the embankment wall. From there he watched as the support posts of the fence buckled under the tremendous force and, in moments, the first barrel had crashed into the wall above him, showering him with beer as the wood shattered, while others continued to rumble over the smashed debris, piling around him until, eventually, the avalanche stopped.

When it was over, only the gurgling of emptying barrels broke the silence that followed. He could hear muffled voices from the brewery yard and waited for some time to pass before he heard car doors slamming and the throaty sound of a familiar engine being revved up and driven away. Only then did he crawl out of his shelter, clawing a passage through the wood until he emerged, saturated and reeking of beer. After some searching, he found the mangled wreckage of his bike and abandoned it to trudge through the fog towards the foundry.

*

He arrived at work, late, ill and thoroughly exhausted, yet still prepared to take over from the night shift. He was greeted by a hostile foreman as he began stoking the boiler.

"You've got a nerve to arrive here in that state, you flamin' dummy," he ranted. "Late for work, late an' pissed as usual! What d'yer think this is, McKenzie, a bloody charity fer the likes of dropouts like you?"

Jack supported his weight on the handle of his shovel, gritting his teeth to prevent himself from collapsing. His only refuge from the tirade was to switch off and relive the unreal events of his dream, which successfully detached him from the madness of his useless existence.

"Are you listenin' to me, you flamin' lunatic?" the foreman continued. "Think yourself lucky nobody else wants this bloody job, or you'd be out on your ear. Clean yourself up after you're done here... you stink the flamin' place out."

Crippled with pain and barely able to speak, he handed the shovel to the foreman. "S-s-s-stick it up yer arse, along wi-wi-wi yer bloody job," he stammered, more coherently than he'd managed in years.

"You can't bugger off just like that. Not wi' this lot t' shift… Come back, you half-baked twat! You'll never get another regular job anywhere else."

*

In the offices of McNair, Courtney & Fife, Lorna McNair appeared at her office door in an unusually agitated state.

"Bonnie, would you be a dear and take this incoming call?"

"I apologise if it's Clare, Mrs McNair. I did ask her not to call the office until she arrives at the station on Friday."

"Is your father coming with her?" Lorna asked, her cheeks dimpling at the thought. "It would be so nice to see Ralph again."

"Unfortunately not… You asked me to take a call, Mrs McNair?"

"So I did. Actually, I think it's from that Mr McKenzie in Yorkshire. I can't understand a word he's saying. I'm worried his money will run out before he can tell me what he wants."

Jack immediately relaxed when he heard the younger voice. The lilt of her brogue was soft on the ear and, moreover, she didn't push him into an exchange, which for Jack would have been difficult. Instead, she confirmed that he must present himself at the Highland office in person before the month was out.

"I can't disclose any details of what has been bequeathed in the document, Mr McKenzie, only Mr Courtney can do that," she said. "What we need is your signature in the presence of a witness. Do you have a map of the area? Lochenbrae is not the easiest place to find."

*

His belongings were few, and packing away what remained of the important possessions of his life took less than an hour. It was sad that he had accumulated so little after a lifetime in the same house.

As an afterthought, with the aid of a breadknife he removed a drawing pin from a child's drawing of a cat which he rolled up and packed in his case. Originally it had been framed by his father and hung in a prominent place in his parents' bedroom. Years later the frame had been shattered when a section of the plaster ceiling had caved in shortly after his mother's death.

On closer inspection, he realised the drawing was a likeness of his own cat in every detail, from the unusual blaze of ginger along the spine to the tip of its tail. There was even a ginger patch around its left ear and eye. At some time in the past, the drawing had been stained with blood, but what had caused that he had no idea.

Since the phone call with the lawyers, he had purchased the antiquated motorbike and sidecar from Frank Wilson, paid for with his mother's savings, which fortunately he'd hidden inside the portable gramophone, one of the few things that Norma and his neighbours hadn't stolen. Frank had insisted on fifty pounds for the machine, but Jack offered twenty. Eventually they settled on twenty-five and both men were happy. The gramophone was loaded on to the carrier together with a pigeon basket containing the cat. The machine was old and noisy but, despite Frank's secret conviction that the motorbike would barely get Jack beyond the county of Yorkshire before it conked out, Jack's own confidence in the machine increased with every passing mile.

Chapter Two

With the exception of a flat tyre in the Lake District where he camped out for the night, the journey progressed without further mishap. It would have been hard to express the mixture of conflicting emotions he experienced as he travelled further north. To go such a distance on little more than a whim, leaving behind everything that had been familiar to him since childhood, was bewildering.

He crossed the border into Scotland.

His few reservations fell away at his first sight of the sea from the coast road and he chugged, exhilarated, into the market town of Lochenbrae. The town was situated in an isolated and beautiful coastal region, known more for the migration of birds and the occasional hiker than an invasion of tourists, which most of the townsfolk would have regarded as a threat to their familiar way of life.

Jack had arrived on market day and the square was bustling with shoppers. The faded canvas awnings of temporary stalls obscured the twelve granite columns supporting a medieval meeting house in the centre of the main square. He braked and waited behind a single-decker bus as it unloaded its passengers. A young man clambered up a ladder to the roof rack to remove a bicycle with a buckled wheel. The man crossed the road, carrying the bike on his shoulder, and went into a run-down garage with a solitary petrol pump outside the open doors.

The unbearably hot sun beat down on Jack's flying jacket as he waited. He needed petrol so he pulled into the garage forecourt after the young man. The dog, sitting up in the sidecar, was panting and longing for water, as was the cat who had been unsettled for the last few miles, protesting noisily in the basket.

*

In the office of McNair, Courtney & Fife, Bonnie Jameson went through the filed correspondence on her desk with Amy, whose desk she had been occupying.

"You will find the relevant information in this pile. Everything has been filed alphabetically," said Bonnie.

"When should we expect him to arrive? There's nothing entered in the appointment diary. You know how Mr Blake-Courtney likes everything to be just so."

"Mr McKenzie is travelling from Yorkshire. All I can tell you is that he is expected here today. He didn't specify a time."

"Are you going?" Amy asked nervously.

"I would stay if I could. I'm only sorry I can't be here when he arrives," she answered, consulting her watch. "Clare's train's due in half an hour."

"Couldn't you stay a while longer? The station isn't far."

"I've a call to make before I meet her and the train might be early."

Amy rustled the paperwork uncomfortably.

"Lorna mentioned there was a communication problem… that he seemed a bit odd?"

"It was difficult for Mrs McNair to understand what he said over the phone. Nothing more."

"She couldn't make out a word he said, what with the accent and the stammer," Amy announced. "What will I say to him if I can't either?"

"Just be natural and everything will be fine," Bonnie answered, collecting her bag. "I must get off now, or I'll be late."

"But you've got ages yet. He could walk through the door any minute."

"A stallholder in the market has a dress she's been saving, I promised I'd be back."

"In the market? You mean second-hand?"

"I couldn't afford clothes of that quality anywhere else on a teacher's pay."

*

As Jack waited at the petrol pump for attention, he considered the prospect of leaving the animals unattended in the shade while he found the lawyers' office, which he guessed would be on the far side of the market square. He looked up, recognising the cyclist as he emerged from inside the garage, and walked over to meet him.

"The owner will be out in a minute," he said, making a fuss of the white dog to hide his shock at the sight of Jack's battered features. He covered his reaction well enough. Had it not been for his slight frown, Jack would have been none the wiser. There was no age difference between them, but that's where the similarity ended. There was a clean-cut, wholesome quality about the other man in contrast to his own appearance. His intelligent features still retained some of the innocence of youth while his dark eyes were direct and inquiring. "Phillip Ramsey," he continued in the same pleasant manner. "My bike's got a buckled front wheel which needs fixing, otherwise I shan't make Dungellen by nightfall," he said, staring curiously into Jack's beaten features, as if he expected to recognise something familiar. "I apologise for staring. For a moment I thought... oh, never mind."

Had he been any good at communicating, Jack might well have asked him to keep an eye on the dog, seeing how well it responded to him, but instead he showed him the address of the solicitor's office and mumbled his need to go there.

"I understand; their office is just across the square. I'll be happy to look after these two. It'll be a while before my bike's done," he offered, removing a map from his backpack. "I've a way to go this afternoon and I need to rest a bit before the long ride. It's a bit mountainous up there." Phillip put the cat basket in the shade and settled the white dog next to him as he opened the map. "Good luck with the meeting," he called, as Jack paused while a flock of sheep was herded past. Judging by the amount of horse droppings in the road and the cattle trucks, the livestock auction had been going on for more than a day.

Crossing the road, he dodged a lumbering carthorse, aggravating the constant pain along his side, which now throbbed like crazy with every step. He recognised well enough the curious glances of passers-by thinking how strange he must have appeared. Fortunately, the jostling crowd kept moving amongst the stalls as he made his way towards McNair, Courtney & Fife.

There was no fanfare of trumpets when he first saw the young woman. She was talking animatedly with an elderly stallholder whose pitch consisted solely of a large wicker skip containing clothes and linens. A few unfashionable but high-quality items of clothing were displayed on hangers hooked on to the open lid of the basket, while others had been set out in neat piles on a bedspread laid out over the cobbles.

He was bewitched and couldn't take his eyes from her, needing to absorb every detail of the red-haired girl. There was a natural ease in the way she spoke to the elderly woman. Her engaging smile enhanced her lovely features as she examined her appearance in the long mirror provided, holding a dress against her. He held his breath when he focused on the garment, recognising the exquisite green gown as it drifted about her slender figure. In both style and colour it was unmistakably the same as the one in his dreams, but though the girl and the woman he had dreamt of were very similar in both age and figure, their hair colour was not, this girl's being a tumbling mass of burnished copper.

He tried three times to get closer to hear her voice but was foiled in each attempt by late arrivals from the livestock auction. The fourth time he got close enough to catch the scent of her perfume before he was propelled away by the surging crowd. When he struggled back against the seething tide of humanity, the girl had replaced the dress on its hanger and was purchasing another which seemed more practical. For a few moments she was obscured by a trio of burly farmers, each carrying a large sack on their shoulders and, when they had passed, the dress remained on the hanger and the girl was gone. In panic he searched the crowd for another sighting, wondering, if he ever did find her again, how he could communicate. For if, as he strongly suspected, his wretched appearance didn't terrify the life out of her, he'd then have to overcome his stammer.

He went over to the green dress and pressed the magical garment against his face, catching a trace of her perfume still lingering in the material. His attention was suddenly caught by a dowdy woman heading in his direction, her eyes fixed on the dress, presumably with the intention of acquiring it for herself. As she pushed her way towards him through the crowd, he remembered the many times he had seen it worn by the dark-haired woman in his dreams and wondered, irrationally, how he might feel if it was worn by anyone other than the red-haired girl.

Quickly, he purchased the dress in exchange for two and sixpence and, although he was uncertain how he could find her, he believed he could discover her address somehow and leave the gift for her without giving his name. It would be better that way. It was something he knew she wanted; and for Jack that would be reward enough.

*

Holding the package tightly, he reached the offices of McNair, Courtney & Fife and entered through a classical Georgian porch that gave on to a grand flight of steps. When he reached the reception desk, he was greeted by a nervous young woman with a streaming cold. He thought she should have stayed at home instead of meeting clients. Her eyes were pale and watery and her nose, which she frequently covered with a large handkerchief, was red from blowing. When she eventually spoke, he was under no illusion that she was disturbed by his unkempt appearance and he feared that she was about to have him thrown out or scream for help, until he began to stammer. Fortunately, at that moment Lorna McNair came out of a nearby door and defused the situation, allowing him enough time to formulate his name before she directed him into the office of William Blake-Courtney.

The office, though large, was not furnished in the older style he might have expected. Instead it had been refurbished to contrast with the classical detail of the building in a stark, uninviting Swedish style with the exception of the impressive partner's desk, behind which William Blake-Courtney was seated.

"Yes?" he asked irritably, looking up from a sheaf of papers as Jack entered. "What the devil do you want?" he said rudely. "These are private offices. The farming auction is on the other side of the square." When Jack didn't respond, he stood with his hands pressed authoritatively on the desk as Jack removed his flying hat, revealing the full extent of his injuries. When he hung his jacket on the back of the chair, he thought Blake-

Courtney would pass out, and when he moved the chair closer and sat down the solicitor was almost shouting, "If you don't leave here this instant, I'll have you arrested." He moistened his lips nervously as Jack placed the letter on the desk.

It took a while for Blake-Courtney to fully comprehend once he'd read it. "So you are Jack McKenzie from Yorkshire? Why didn't you say so?" he concluded, lamely. In any other situation, Jack might have attempted a response. Instead he remained silent and let the man's predicament run its natural course.

"I wasn't expecting you here this early with the distance you've had to travel," Blake-Courtney said, looking at the address in Yorkshire. "I'm rather unprepared for our interview at the moment. Perhaps you could wait in reception for a while before we continue. I have calls to make and I need time to sort out the relevant paperwork." Jack remained seated. It was clear to him the lawyer was not trustworthy and he had no intention of going anywhere until he had all the information about his inheritance. After some deliberation, Blake-Courtney removed a thick file of papers from the safe.

"I suspect the bequest will come as rather a disappointment, considering the trouble you have taken to get here this afternoon, Mr McKenzie," he said, without examining the documents. He was fingering the ends of each package with the familiarity of the blind, not once opening a file until he withdrew a slim, folded document from the pile. "Ah, here we have it. I hope your expectations are not high, Mr McKenzie, otherwise it will prove disappointing, especially having travelled so far."

Clipped to the file were two typed letters, which he removed after reading, putting them down near him. Having regained some of his earlier composure, he opened out the main document without a trace of his earlier arrogance, a performance which didn't fool Jack.

"It would appear, Mr McKenzie, that a distant relative has bequeathed you a coastal property some miles north of here. It's nothing to get excited about, I can assure you; in fact the place is literally falling apart and is not even habitable."

Jack was bewildered. There were no family relatives as far as he knew; his parents would have told him if there had been. It had to be a mistake.

"This information appears to have come as a shock. Were you never made aware of this relative?" he asked, his attention transferring to a handwritten letter which included a list. Jack reached across and took the will from the lawyer's hand. It was a beautifully scripted document and there was no doubt that he was indeed the beneficiary. His home address in St Luke's Road was unquestionable.

"This is most unethical, Mr McKenzie. I must insist that you hand back that deed immediately," Blake-Courtney spluttered as he grasped at the air in an attempt to regain the document, but he sat back in his chair as Lorna McNair entered with a tray of tea things. "Not now, Lorna!" he said, unable to control his irritation. "Can't you see I'm in a meeting?"

"Perfectly well, Mr Courtney. However, Mr McKenzie has travelled some distance and must be in need of refreshment. One lump or two?" she asked and stirred in the requested amount.

"The document, if you please, Mr McKenzie." The angry solicitor stretched out his hand but Jack was in no mood to be intimidated. The name of his benefactor was on the document and he wanted to see the signature for himself. She was listed as Miss Eleanor McKenzie, late of Moorcroft Farm and he had no idea who she was, yet he blessed her memory for her generous act. He had a property of his own and could scarcely believe his good fortune. Had he been able to smile he would have done just that as he slid the document across the table.

"By your silence, one assumes you had expected a little more than a derelict farmhouse," Blake-Courtney said with unconcealed satisfaction as he folded away the document, replacing it with one of the typed letters from his clipboard. "However, you are a fortunate young man as I have been given instructions by another client to make you a generous offer on this property, providing you sign over the deeds on Moorcroft this afternoon."

"Mr Courtney, really!" Lorna exclaimed. "This is most irregular."

"It is nothing of the kind and I will thank you to leave this office immediately and allow me to conduct this interview with Mr McKenzie… in private."

It had been a long day and Jack struggled to concentrate in the stuffy office. These were life-changing events and he didn't want to misunderstand anything. He moved away from the desk and opened the sash window, leaning out to breathe in the cooler air.

"What in God's name are you doing, Mr McKenzie? We haven't finished yet. You've said nothing in response to this offer. In fact, you have barely uttered a syllable since you came in here."

"The gentleman has severe laryngitis, Mr Courtney," Lorna interjected, taking the initiative to answer on Jack's behalf. "Mr McKenzie is unable to say anything at the moment," she said, with rather more conviction than she felt.

"Laryngitis! How am I expected to conduct an interview if the man can't speak?"

Lorna glanced at the wall clock as she collected the teacup. "He's been with you for fifteen minutes without there being a problem so I am sure you can continue without any difficulty, Mr Courtney."

Jack took in a deep breath, filling his lungs to capacity with the fresh tang of the salty sea air on that glorious day. Beneath him was an ocean of stall canopies masking the thronging crowds beneath. There was a clear view of the garage, where he could see the dog staring in his direction, and beyond it the waves cresting on a glittering sea. He felt a strong impulse to wave back but thought how ridiculous that would look and, more importantly, the pain it would cause him, so thought better of it. Taking a deep breath, he turned back inside and gave his attention to the lawyer, unaware of the Sunbeam Talbot that had been driven on to the garage forecourt and parked next to his motorbike.

"So, Mr McKenzie, have you had time to consider my client's offer?" Blake-Courtney asked. "I can assure you it is a more than generous amount," he added as he scribbled down on a sheet of paper the figure of four hundred pounds. "Particularly when you consider the inaccessibility of the property, on such a barren piece of land on a very inhospitable coastline."

Instead of responding, Jack's thoughts were elsewhere. Still at the window, he gazed towards a craggy region to the north where he assumed his ultimate destination lay. There his inheritance of the farmhouse awaited his arrival, derelict or not and, since he owned the property, he would stay in that area until he was able to locate the red-haired girl.

"I have the relevant paperwork here," Blake-Courtney continued, unscrewing the cap of his fountain pen and indicating the area for signing. "All I need is your signature in this space to make you a wealthy man. Mr McKenzie?" he urged.

But Jack shook his head. He gazed up into the sky at the circling osprey and would have laughed out loud with happiness, had he been able. He would never return to Eastmoor, whatever happened.

"Is that it?" Blake-Courtney asked. "You would reject such an offer without giving it any consideration at all?"

"Mr McKenzie has decided, Mr Courtney," Lorna intervened. "You must respect his wishes."

"This isn't ended, not yet. I will contact my clients immediately. Given the circumstances, I'm convinced they will submit an alternative, and perhaps more agreeable offer," he suggested, before Lorna ushered Jack out of the room with his belongings, and took him instead into another office.

Three of the walls were fitted with neat glass-fronted bookcases and on the fourth hung two fine copperplate engravings. A bowl of freshly cut flowers stood on a table, filling the room with their scent intermingling with the smell of wax polish and old leather, giving Jack a deep sense of wellbeing; a comfort zone of lost memories making him yearn for a place he couldn't quite remember.

He stood in the doorway, uncertain why Lorna McNair had taken him there, until she spread out a linen-backed Ordnance Survey map on the desk and beckoned him over.

"I thought this would help you find Moorcroft Farm, Mr McKenzie. The village of Dungellen consists of only a few houses and a general store. Please be extra cautious when nearing this sharp bend along the Kenmere road. You can easily miss the turn for Dungellen if you are unfamiliar with the area," she said, adjusting her spectacles and pointing out the route north he must follow.

He would have to travel over a rugged area, following the coast, then take a hairpin bend to access a narrow thread of a road, little more than a cart track. About three miles further on, the track ended at the village of Dungellen.

"The mound you see here is known locally as the Purple Cap," Lorna said, indicating a high section of land where the cliff top sheared away into the sea. "And that is Moorcroft Farm," she continued, pointing to a collection of buildings two miles beyond the village, situated close to the sea. "My husband and I haven't been to the farm for many years. He used to visit the neighbouring estate. However, I do recall it was a pleasant house with a lovely view of the bay."

Comparing his own map to the one on the desk, he could find no indication of a turn-off to the village. It was fortunate the track was marked on the much older print, without which he would never have located the farm at all.

"Why don't you make a copy of the turn? Then you won't get lost," Lorna said, giving him a notepad and pencil. "It wouldn't do for a stranger to get lost after dark. It's impossible to see anything after nightfall. Take these," she said, handing him a bunch of keys with two bulky manila envelopes. "Mr Courtney should have given you the keys to the property. One of the envelopes contains your title deeds; the other comes with the bequest from Eleanor. Please keep the deeds safe until you've read through them, then either return them here or lodge them with your bank."

After sketching out the remote junction, Jack longed to ask if Lorna had actually known the mysterious Eleanor McKenzie. However, because of his current speech limitations, he thought better of it. Time was running out, and he wanted to reach the farm before dusk. He could always return another day when he was more presentable and when the swelling to his mouth had reduced enough to offer thanks for her unexpected display of kindness.

In the forecourt of her local railway station, Bonnie Jameson trudged along with a heavy suitcase, manoeuvring the cumbersome bag into the back of a shooting brake. "Couldn't you at least lend a hand with your own baggage, Clare," Bonnie asked the young woman beside her, who seemed more interested in her own reflection in the car window than in helping.

"I'm not dressed for doing that, otherwise I would."

"You managed well enough getting it along to the station," Bonnie commented as they got into the car.

"Your dad drove me there and helped me on to the train." Bonnie had to brake suddenly as she left the station as a sleek Sunbeam Talbot cut in front of her.

"Did you see that idiot?" She glared after the vehicle, which stopped a short distance away and parked outside the Alhambra Hotel. "I've a good mind to go over there and have a word with the driver." Instead, her attention turned to her faulty ignition, which had groaned sluggishly and refused to restart.

"Why don't you get a new car? There's always something going wrong with this damned thing!" Clare said. Her attention had suddenly been caught by the elegant woman being helped from the back of the Sunbeam Talbot. She was dressed from head to toe in black and was ushered into the grand lobby of the hotel, followed by an accompanying mountain of luggage. "If only Mother had remarried into money," Clare mused.

Bonnie got out of the car with the starting handle, which she carefully inserted beneath the radiator until it locked into the engine. "Clare, I need you to help me with this. When the engine catches, press your foot down on the accelerator. Not hard, but keep it running until I can get in." She coiled back her hair and wrapped a handkerchief round the starting handle, grasped it with both hands and began turning the engine with regular swings.

"Having trouble, Miss Jameson?" William Blake-Courtney called out, tipping the brim of his trilby as he scurried along the opposite pavement with no intention of stopping. Angrily, Bonnie swung hard on the handle and the engine fired up with a roar. She saw Blake-Courtney outside the Alhambra Hotel in the company of a tall, fair-haired young man, who was in animated discussion with the driver of the Sunbeam Talbot. After an abrupt parting, both he and Blake-Courtney entered the hotel.

*

On impulse, Bonnie drove into McIntyre's garage, parked in the forecourt and sought out the ex-land girl owner.

"Hello, Grace. You said to call back if there was a problem?"

"Of course, dear, what's happened?"

"It's the starter motor. It's been playing up all week. Could you take a look before I set off home? If it stalls on the way, I might not be so lucky getting it started. I don't want to break down with a passenger on board."

"I'll do it now. I've just finished welding a makeshift patch on to Andrew's exhaust. There's no one else due for an hour."

"Andrew's here?" she asked, looking about her brightly.

"Well, not exactly. There was an emergency. He dashed off to the market to help a child with a fractured wrist until the ambulance arrives."

"Where's his car?"

"On the ramp," Grace answered, wiping her oily hands on a rag. "He's been gone for some time so he shouldn't be long."

Once her shooting brake had replaced Andrew's black MG saloon on the ramp, she sat on a grassy bank, waiting in the shade for him to return, whilst Clare took advantage of a better seating arrangement beneath the awning of a caravan that doubled as Grace McIntyre's office, which faced the market square. Neither of them noticed Phillip Ramsey when he appeared, shirtless, from the rear of the building, until he turned on an outside tap and filled a bowl with water for the white dog, which actually seemed more interested in Bonnie than the proffered drink.

"Why hello," she laughed as she was greeted by the dog.

"I hope he isn't bothering you?" Phillip asked as she stroked the dog.

"Not at all."

"I can see he likes you." He crouched against the tap to let the water soak into his hair before splashing it over his body. "It's stifling today, don't you think?" The water emphasised the reddening of the taut skin on his back and shoulders.

"You would do better to keep out of the sun. It's quite pleasant in the shade," she said, expecting him to put on his shirt, which he didn't.

"I suppose," he said, fanning himself with his bunched-up shirt. "Unfortunately there wasn't enough shade back there, not for the two of us."

"Then why not wait out here."

"I could, but there's too much traffic. I didn't want the dog running off." He slipped his belt through the dog's collar before he sat beside her.

"Is your car in for repair?"

He laughed pleasantly and lay back on the grass, keeping a tight hold on the temporary leash.

"Actually, it's my bike. The front wheel's buckled."

"You're cycling up here… with a dog?"

"It isn't mine. It belongs to the chap with the motorbike and sidecar, parked over there," Phillip answered, indicating Jack's combination. "I said I'd look after them while he's in town."

"Them?" she asked, distracted by the reddening area on his shoulders.

"There's a cat in a fishing basket. It's fast asleep in the shade," he said. He sat up, wincing as he removed some grass from his back. "Incidentally, my name's Phillip Ramsey."

"You should put something on your shoulders when you get home, otherwise you'll be suffering tonight."

"Home's a long way off. I'm north of the border with a mission, searching for an old house with tall chimneys."

"You're buying a house?"

"No. Well, actually I'm looking for one I lived in with my parents years ago."

Bonnie was about to respond when her cousin, a tall, dark-haired man, strode on to the forecourt carrying a doctor's bag. She smiled and waved.

"Andrew! Over here," she called. "Where have you been hiding? I've called the house frequently but you're never there. I haven't seen you in weeks."

"Sorry Red, these are busy times," he answered sombrely. He watched as Phillip pulled on his shirt. "You should get that sunburn attended to as soon as you can, old chap."

"I will," Phillip answered, buttoning his shirt.

"Have you got anything for it?"

"There's some lavender oil in my saddlebag. That will do the trick." He held back the enthusiastic white dog while the doctor tickled its large ears.

"Surely you could find him some calamine lotion when you get back to Hettie's store?"

"We're not together, Andy. We only met five minutes ago."

"I'm sorry, I thought you had a passenger when you drove past earlier?"

"That was Clare."

He looked about him uncertainly. "Not Connie's daughter? I thought you two didn't get on?"

"We don't." She smiled reassuringly at Phillip as she explained. "Don't be alarmed. It's an ongoing feud. My father re-married and his new wife's daughter Clare has no time for him."

"Then why has she come here? She's never liked the place from what I remember. Ah, seems your car's been done!" Andrew said as Grace reversed it out of the garage.

"All done, Bonnie. There was a loose connection. Nothing more serious and there's no charge for that," she announced as she tied her greying hair back with an old stocking. "It's always a pleasure to see you at any time, dear. Please give my regards to your aunt."

Bonnie smiled, only half-listening. Andrew had left very abruptly and had not offered any help about where Phillip might begin a search for his parents' home. It wasn't like him. Not many people were as familiar with the local area as was Andrew Sinclair.

"He's very grumpy," Clare commented, as they waited for a flock of herded sheep to pass. "Sometimes, I think he's worse than your dad. No wonder he isn't married."

*

Jack made his way back through the market, euphoric with the thoughts of becoming an owner of property. He waited at the edge of the square for the same flock of sheep to pass before he could cross to the garage. He was longing to be on his way to Dungellen and ultimately to Moorcroft Farm.

He saw, but didn't register, the MG saloon as it turned into the Kenmere road just ahead of the sheep, nor did he see the shooting brake which was held on the incline out of the garage forecourt, waiting like himself for the animals to pass.

Revving the engine as she released the handbrake, Bonnie accelerated up the incline and turned on to the Kenmere road. She had to make an emergency stop as Jack, without looking, stepped in front of the car. Startled, he caught hold of the car bonnet for support with one hand. In the other he gripped the package containing the green dress. The buckle from his flying hat swung loosely against his swollen face as he stared through the windscreen, immediately recognising the driver. Bonnie wound the window down to enquire if he was all right.

He could only nod the assurance that he was perfectly fine, mortified to be in such a compromised situation. Unable to speak, he stepped aside so she could drive past. As he did, Clare, who had been staring at him in amazement, burst into fits of laughter.

"Clare, please! Think of the poor man's feelings," Bonnie said uncomfortably. "How can you be so insensitive?" She saw him through the rear-view mirror just standing in the road. A farmer leading three shire horses briefly blocked her view, yet he still continued to stare after the car until they had rounded the bend.

"I wonder if I should go back," she mused. "I might have injured him."

"Don't you dare. There was no bump, only when he pressed down on the car. The man's either the village idiot or an axe murderer on the loose from the local asylum."

"Now you're being foolish. He must have been in an accident to get those injuries. Didn't you see his face?"

"See it? It was horrible! Could you imagine meeting up with that on a dark night? How Mother would have laughed if she'd been in the car."

After driving some distance in silence, Bonnie reduced speed at a fork in the road where a barrier blocked off the coastal route, diverting them on to the other that veered sharply inland, away from the coast. She could no longer see the sea, nor did she see the sleek Sunbeam Talbot parked under the trees.

Bonnie continued to drive in silence for some time before rejoining the Kenmere road. "Why exactly are you here, Clare?" she asked. "You don't like being away from the city. You never have."

"It's Mother. She asked me to come."

"Why? Is Connie ill?"

"Not a bit. Quite the contrary in fact."

"So is this visit about my dad?"

"Well... sort of."

"Either it is or it isn't. Can't you be honest with me for once, Clare? What's this all about?"

"Since you ask, he's been quite obnoxious with Mother. Very offhand in fact. You can cut the atmosphere between them with a knife. They barely speak these days. Mother's at her wits' end."

"That is totally out of character for my dad, but if it's true he must have good reason?"

"There was a misunderstanding which got out of hand. He's been raging at the apartment for weeks. Now he's threatening divorce. You can imagine Mother's feelings. What if the bridge club hears about this before she can make him see reason?"

She grabbed the dashboard at the squeal of brakes as the car slowed abruptly.

"What the hell are you doing?" she protested. The car had slowed to a walking pace at a bend, before Bonnie turned off sharply into a narrower lane which was little more than a track. "How does anyone find this place?" Clare snapped.

"Fortunately, not many do. You were explaining what happened."

"There's not much to tell really. Mother went dancing one night. What's wrong in that?"

"That depends. Was she alone?"

"Well, not exactly. She bumped into an old friend and they had dinner afterwards."

"Hardly a reason to talk of divorce," Bonnie answered, as they drove into the village of Dungellen.

"The trouble is, Mother missed the last bus home and stayed overnight at an hotel."

"This old friend you mentioned? It wouldn't be Lionel Travis by any chance?"

"Actually, it was. But they had separate rooms. Nothing happened. She was adamant about that."

Bonnie crunched the gears as they approached a bend. "And you believe her? This is almost a repeat of what happened last time. No wonder my dad's furious."

"You must do something, Bonnie. He will listen to anything you say. You know he did well marrying Mother. You can't deny that and we manage very well on what his employer left him. What if he goes ahead with the divorce and doesn't settle anything on Mother?"

"Settle what? After Connie's reckless spending there's probably nothing left"

They drove past the cricket green and out of the village.

"What would we do if he gave up the apartment in town and moved back here to work on that estate he's forever going on about? Mother couldn't abide staying here for longer than a week. Come to that, neither could I!" she concluded vehemently.

"Daddy couldn't do that even if he wanted to. It doesn't exist any more," Bonnie answered as she pulled up outside her aunt's store.

"What beats me is how anyone in their right mind could ever consider living in this wretched place for so long!" She stared bleakly at the rugged landscape, shadowed by the dominating peak of the Purple Cap, which blocked out any view of the sea. "And who would come back here through choice?"

*

When Jack walked on to the forecourt, he found the garage doors closed and Phillip waiting patiently with the white dog and basket and the repaired bicycle propped nearby.

"I don't suppose you've heard of a place called Dungellen?" he asked, opening his own map, more detailed than Jack's own, but which still didn't show the turn-off or the village. "It's got to be somewhere close to the Bay of Dungellen but I can't find a route in."

Jack showed him the drawing he had made in Lorna's office when he had marked the location of Moorcroft Farm.

"Wow… This is some coincidence. Are you going there too?" he asked, as Jack got the dog to leap into the sidecar. He then tied the cat basket on to the carrier.

"I… I…" he stammered. "I… l-live there." He was wondering how far the girl in the shooting brake had travelled along the Kenmere road before she turned off.

"Any objections if I pitch a tent there for a couple of nights?" Phillip asked, and smiled broadly when Jack shook his head.

"N-none at all."

As he started up his antiquated machine, he hoped Phillip would do just that. He felt at ease in the company of this young man, who was of a similar age and who seemed both honest and sensible, but most of all because he wasn't bothered by Jack's speech defect. He was a stranger who had been accommodating with his dog when he needed it most, and for that he was grateful.

As he drove along the coastal road, he fancied it was the most pleasurable ride he had taken. It became much hillier when he got clear of the town and in some parts it seemed dangerously near to the cliff edge, where sections of the safety wall had fallen away into the sea. About three miles beyond the town he pulled up at a fork in the road where a neglected stretch of the track continued to follow the coast. The other, which branched inland, had been sealed off with a 'road closed' barrier. Oddly enough, an AA patrolman was accelerating towards him along the same stretch of road at an alarming speed, waving furiously as Jack depressed the clutch and continued on.

When he passed the brow of a hill, he felt he was being watched. There was a concealed place off the road, amongst trees, where he caught the flash of reflected sunlight from a chromium-plated radiator grille, but before he could brake the road pitched down a steep incline which required his full concentration. He manoeuvred the heavy bike past a rock fall and rounded a sharp bend in the road that veered away towards the cliff edge. Taking a deep breath, he grated the gears down into third as he was confronted by another steep incline, at the bottom of which most of the road had crumbled into the sea. There was no barrier to prevent any unsuspecting motorist from hurtling over the edge. Beyond and to the side of the collapsed road was a bog and some lethal-looking rocks. He had the choice of the bog – or hurtling over the edge!

He slammed on the brakes while grinding the gears into second, which reduced his speed with screeching machinery and burning rubber. Just as disaster seemed to have been averted the rear brake cable snapped, lurching the combination towards the cliff edge, restrained only by the front brake, until that lever too went slack in his hand. Using every ounce of his strength, Jack steered the heavy bike away from the gap in the road, praying the bog would jam the wheels and prevent him from crashing into the jagged rocks beyond.

Churned-up mud and clumps of grass stopped the squealing machine with such a jolt that it flung Jack and the white dog clear, but not the strapped-down suitcase and his cat, now yowling noisily in the basket. He was making sure both animals were uninjured when he saw the AA man drive cautiously down the hill on his patrol bike and park a short distance away.

"Are you OK?" he asked. "God knows which idiot swapped the road signs around back there. They ought to be jailed for life. I tried to attract your attention when you drove past, but you didn't see. This section of road's been impassable since last winter. Lord knows why the council haven't sealed it off properly."

Jack shrugged, more relieved that he was alive than anything else. Beyond that, there was no conversation as the AA man tied a rope to the rear of the combination, and with Jack's help pulled it clear of the mud with his own powerful machine.

"Take it easy, mate, while I have a look at this bike of yours," he said, offering him a hip flask. "Have a swig of this. It'll make you feel better. You've had quite a shock."

With the exception of the brake cables there was little damage and it took less than fifteen minutes to fix the bike. "It's odd, both cables snapping like that," he said after fitting new ones, but once he had examined the old ones his attitude changed as he offered them for Jack to inspect. "Blimey, mate, take a look at these cables: they've been half cut through! Take them with you and report this to the police as soon as you can." He scribbled his name and patrol number on a page from his notebook. "I don't want any payment for doing this, pal, you've got enough to worry about. You're lucky to be alive."

The old machine struggled up the hill at the end of the tow rope. There the two men discovered that the diversion barrier had been replaced across the coastal road.

"The whole scenario gets crazier by the minute," the bewildered patrolman said. "You can rest assured, Mr McKenzie, I'll be reporting all of this to head office when I get back."

*

With his mind on the recent incident, he missed the turning to Dungellen at the hairpin bend and drove on for more than a mile before he realised his mistake and turned back. From the Kenmere road he drove very slowly, as he was beginning to enjoy every mile of the picturesque landscape before he reached the village.

On the approach, the white dog became alert and interested in the surroundings for the first time since they had set off from Yorkshire. The cat too had begun clawing at the basket in an attempt to get free, yowling its objections loudly in protest.

Set in a prominent position, high on a rock, was the church. Opposite was a pond and the village green, around which was a variety of cottages, some with stone roofs and picturesque gardens, others with fruit trees and vegetables. At an isolated one of these, an arthritic dog barked, waking an elderly woman resting in the porch. The vintage motorcycle spluttered along the narrow track, which widened out to accommodate an avenue of stately gnarled limes overhanging the dusty road, forming a lush canopy. Through the trees, dappled sunlight created a sight worthy of any aspiring poet. The air was heady with the scent of honeysuckle and roses. It was a place seemingly divorced from the harsh realities of modern-day living. A cameo of the past, where tranquillity reigned and which to Jack, after the hardship of his life in a steel town, seemed untouched by the energetic pace of progress.

On the outskirts of the village he rode past an ancient copper beech shading a derelict cricket pavilion by a neglected pitch. Beyond was a line of cottages at the beginning of a crumbling dry stone wall that seemed to Jack to go on for ever, and which he assumed belonged to an old estate. The wall ended at a Jacobean gated arch. Beyond the grand, rusting wrought-iron gates was a magnificent expanse of parkland. Chiselled into the upper section of the arch, crafted centuries earlier, was a weathered heraldic crest segmented into three parts. On the lower, right-hand panel there was a sleeping animal carved into the stone, so worn it was impossible to identify. Similarly on the left there was another creature, more feline in shape, which again, through years of erosion, was impossible to distinguish. In the upper panel there was barely nothing except the outline of a bird, its wings poised in preparation for flight. Intrigued by the upper section, he switched off the ignition and scaled the wall to examine it more closely. It appeared to have been partially erased, which was odd as it had been chiselled from the same block of granite as the other worn figures.

From his vantage point on the wall, he had a clear view of the lush park, beyond which he could the graceful curve of the drive, which, like the gateway, was overgrown. Instead of leading to any grand house, it curved on through a wide avenue of trees as the land sloped down until it disappeared from sight, revealing the glittering sea and the Bay of Dungellen.

Rising up to a considerable height on the left of the drive was the Purple Cap, which formed a natural barrier to his own property. Even though Lorna McNair had spoken of the landmark with great affection, he had been totally unprepared for the wild expanse of rugged beauty. It was an inspirational sight, enhanced by the late-afternoon sun slanting across a field of bracken and heather. He blessed the memory of Eleanor McKenzie for her generosity to a complete stranger and for bringing him to this enchanted place; not just for an afternoon, but for the rest of his life.

Instinctively, he looked up and again saw the familiar shape gliding above him with such grace of movement. He went back to the motorbike and lit up a cigarette, watching mesmerised as the bird drifted slowly earthward, spreading the fearsome extent of its talons in preparation for landing. Blinking hard, he shaded his eyes from the sun's glare as it temporarily blinded him. He felt a connection with the rush of air from the great wings beating rhythmically in the bird's final descent as it settled on the carved granite arch of the gate.

When he could see clearly he rubbed his eyes in disbelief. There was no sign of the osprey perched on the apex of the arch as he had expected. Instead, there was a perfect replica of the bird cut into the upper section of the heraldic shield, where moments earlier there had been nothing.

With misgivings about his sanity he set off down the road, thinking perhaps that the beatings had affected his brain. He had driven less than half a mile when he pulled into a gravelled area outside Hettie's store and parked up. He jotted down a short shopping list of essentials he would need to supplement what he had brought, to avoid the inevitable problem of verbal communication. He was hoping to explore his new home before dark. Making sure the package containing the green dress was secure inside his jacket, he made his way up the worn steps into the store.

*

A clatter of dishes announced that dinner had finished in the back parlour as Bonnie cleared them away into the kitchen where her aunt was busily washing up.

"Did I mention a Mr Kincaid called here just before you arrived?" Hettie said, filling the bowl with a kettle of hot water.

"No, you didn't. Who is he? A lost hiker?"

"Oh no, dear," Hettie laughed. "His shoes were much too nice and very expensive. Do you not find it odd how much you notice about a person on the first meeting?"

"Sometimes," she responded absently.

"What was extraordinary were his laces, tied in neat bows which were perfectly even."

"Some people can be weird. How did he get here, by car?"

"I suppose he must have. I didn't notice."

"And you say he was here just before we arrived? I don't recall passing anyone on our way here. What did he want anyway?"

Hettie refilled the kettle that hung on a bracket over the fire in the cast-iron range.

"He offered to buy the Cap," she answered, gazing through the window at the rugged outline darkening against the setting sun. "Why would anyone want to buy such an uncharitable mound? It doesn't make sense, Bonnie. The Cap could be of no value to anyone."

"He said nothing about buying the shop? Only the Cap?"

Hettie squeezed her niece's arm affectionately. "That could well have been his next question, but he'd be wasting his time. I wouldn't sell either."

"Good for you, Auntie! Neither would I."

Chapter Three

Jack entered the store to the accompaniment of a jangling bell attached to the door announcing his late arrival. Inside, there was enough light to see everything on display. There was an extraordinary cross section of provisions and hardware. A cluster of tools and gardening equipment was arranged alongside an assortment of old-fashioned wallpapers and the appropriate borders. Nothing appeared to have been overlooked in the requirements of any villager unable to travel into the nearest town. There was even a space allocated for haberdashery and rolls of cloth. It was a store he would have attributed to earlier times. Perfect for any local shopper, but confusing to a stranger like himself who needed to find something in a hurry amongst the organised clutter.

He had found a bottle of milk, a packet of tea and a hurricane lamp and had his back to the counter examining a claw hammer, which wasn't on his list, when he heard the light footsteps of a woman approaching from the back room. She addressed him from a section of the counter designated as a post office.

"Can I assist you?" she asked, in a kindly way, as she closed the post office door. "There is so much in here that I hardly know where to look myself at times."

He trembled as he caught the delicate fragrance of her perfume. He clutched the package containing the dress tightly and turned, hoping it was the same girl from the market, yet dreading the likelihood that it was.

"Oh my God… it's you!" she said, unable to conceal her surprise, expecting him to respond, which he didn't. Instead he stared back at her like a cornered animal. "How did you know where to find me?" Bonnie asked as her aunt scurried to join her.

"Who is it calling at this hour? Mr Kincaid?" Hettie asked, halting in her tracks when she saw the state of his battered face. Her homely features expressed concern as she peered above her spectacles. "What are you thinking of, Bonnie? Have the laddie sit down. Dearie me," she wittered on. "Whatever happened to you?" She switched on the light for a closer inspection as she urged him to sit on the bentwood chair next to the counter.

"This is the man I told you about, Auntie. The one I almost ran over in town," Bonnie said.

"You did this to him? Dearie me, Bonnie, what are we to do? Did you inform P.C. Perkins about what happened?" she exclaimed.

"N-n... no" Jack protested. He tried to stand, but was held down by Hettie's firm hand. "Sh-sh-she didn't," he stammered awkwardly, shaking his head.

"Leave him alone, Auntie, you're upsetting the poor man," Bonnie said. "I stopped in good time. The car didn't touch him." Her lovely eyes sparkled briefly as she began to question what had happened. "I didn't injure you, did I?"

Had she been responsible for anything, he would have forgiven her, and he was convinced that his heart would burst through his chest if she looked at him in that way a moment longer.

"N-n-no," he floundered, shaking his head.

"Whatever have you been up to, laddie?" Hettie asked, clucking about him like a mother hen with a lost chick. "Get me the bottle of witch hazel from the bathroom cabinet, Bonnie, and bring a fresh roll of cotton wool from the top shelf."

By the time Bonnie returned, Hettie had persuaded him to remove the cumbersome flying jacket, but not the package that he clasped against him, more for security than anything else. He was embarrassed when Hettie said her niece should soak the cotton wool in witch hazel and bathe his face.

"I'm going into the kitchen to heat up some stew. He looks as though he hasn't eaten in days. And, young man, take off that silly hat and let my niece see what she's doing."

For the best part of fifteen minutes he was subjected to the most excruciating pain, despite her light touch, but he would rather have died than let her know.

"Please tell me if this is hurting," she kept asking, dabbing each swollen area, uncertain of the truth of his denial. He continually shook his head to indicate that it wasn't hurting. She took extra care with the severe gash to his left eyebrow. "This cut and the one on your cheek should be looked at professionally. They might need stitches. I have a cousin living nearby who's a doctor. He would see you tomorrow if you're not passing through?" she suggested, searching his swollen face for any indication of agreement. "Forgive me for staring," she continued with a trace of embarrassment. "It's just that your eyes are very striking. The colour is so unusual." The gentleness of her smile made him melt, more so when eventually he summoned the strength to look directly into hers.

"How silly is this? Here we are and I don't even know your name," she said.

As if to reassure her, he reached forward and removed his wallet from the inside pocket of his jacket, which lay on the counter, and removed his identity card. For a second he was unsure of the reaction when she examined his name with open amusement.

"This is too much of a coincidence. You can't be the Jack McKenzie? Not from Eastmoor?"

His lips parted to form a tortured smile when he realised exactly why her voice had sounded so familiar.

"How's the laddie doing?" Hettie asked, as she scuttled out of the parlour.

"We're almost done," Bonnie answered, gently bathing the swollen mouth. "How about you?"

"Clare's dragging herself away from the mirror long enough to bring the soup through when it's hot," she said, switching on an overhead light to examine Jack's scribbled list. "You must help me get this order together when you're finished. I don't want him going out there when it gets dark. Do you have far to go, laddie?" she asked, while examining Jack's list of provisions. It was the same scrap of paper he had used to jot down the directions.

"Moorcroft Farm…? Are you the new owner?"

"This is Mr McKenzie, Auntie," Bonnie said, disposing of the cotton wool.

"I thought you hadn't met the young man until this afternoon?" Hettie sounded curious.

"It's all very odd actually; like one of your mystery books. I posted Mr McKenzie the letter which caused so much annoyance at the office two weeks ago, and we spoke on the telephone about him coming up here earlier this week."

A clatter of broken china came from the parlour as the door was pushed open. "Sorry, Hettie," Clare shouted. "Can Bonnie get more bread from the kitchen? I couldn't balance the plate." She emerged from behind the counter carrying a steaming bowl on a tray and, looking about her, asked, "Who is this for anyway?" as her eyes became accustomed to the dim lighting in the shop. When she caught sight of Jack, she gasped, her mouth

70

gaping like a landed fish, before shrieking, "Bonnie, it's him, that Neolithic creature from the market! What's he doing in here?" She concluded by cackling with laughter, an unnervingly penetrating sound which drove him to the brink of despair.

His gut constricted with revulsion, not only at the sound but because he was the object of her abuse from which there was no escape, and also because Bonnie had been witness to such a hideous display of character assassination. The situation only continued to worsen as Clare squealed theatrically and dropped the tray as he staggered to his feet. He was unable to stand properly, his limbs having stiffened from sitting in the same position too long, yet he was determined to put as much distance between himself and that excruciating laughter as he could. How ironic it was that he had travelled so far from his persecuted existence in Yorkshire only to be confronted by the same ridicule in such a remote place as Dungellen.

"For God's sake, Clare. Do shut up," Bonnie snapped angrily, seeing Jack preparing to make a bolt for the door.

In the general confusion and his haste while grabbing his jacket and holding the package he neglected to collect his wallet. Faced with the prospect of never seeing Bonnie again, he thrust the package towards her. "I... I..." he faltered, "I... I got th-th-this f-for you," he managed to blurt out with more coherence than he could have hoped for, considering his embarrassment. She looked puzzled.

"Please, Mr McKenzie, you mustn't leave. Not like this." She put out her hand, restraining his arm.

Instead he pulled away, unable to face her. He had to get clear of the nightmarish sound of her friend's laughter, pushed open the door and stumbled down the steps. He kick-started the engine and drove away from the yard without a backwards glance at Bonnie or her aunt, as they watched him from the open door.

He had gone barely a mile before he braked sharply and threw up in the hedgerow. The anxiety had really got to him. When the nausea had passed, he drove a short distance until he saw the rocky outline of the Cap, and beyond it a spectacular view of the glittering bay. Half a mile on, the road ended abruptly at a neat little gate hung between two granite posts which bordered the carefully attended gardens of a large house. He knew this would not be his unoccupied property so he turned back to the base of the Cap and stopped at a rotting five-bar gate, which collapsed on broken hinges when he attempted to open it to drive through. A rutted drive to the farm pitched sharply down towards the bay, avoiding the track obstructed by rocks. He slipped the engine into a low gear and the machine spluttered down the hill.

He could see no evidence of any farm. The obnoxious lawyer's talk of his inheritance being only a ruin became more and more feasible until at last some chimneystacks appeared above the trees as he drew closer to sea level. When he rounded the final bend his delight and amazement grew as he took stock of a substantial gable-ended farmhouse built of irregular blocks of hewn granite.

As Lorna McNair had told him, the doors and windows were boarded up to protect against the weather. They had been for some time by the look of the neglected yard and outbuildings. Yet, when he inserted the ridiculously large key she had given him into the lock, the door opened effortlessly on oiled hinges.

In the village store, Hettie Jameson was closing up for the night when she found Jack's wallet and shopping list on the counter.

"Bonnie dear, can you hear me?" she called up the stairs. "Mr McKenzie has left his wallet behind. Would you be a dear and take it over in the morning. I'll pack some provisions to send as a peace offering. God knows, it's small compensation for Clare's rudeness."

"I'll be down in a moment," Bonnie responded as she gazed at the green dress she had laid out on the bed. "How is it possible that he could he have known about this?" she asked herself, as she gathered the vaporous material in her hands with near reverence.

*

With his animals fed, Jack scoured the outbuildings for any tools, having discarded the hammer during his hasty getaway, and came across a workshop which contained a well-organised chest with every item greased to preserve it from rust.

Armed with a crowbar, he removed the wood covering the kitchen window to reveal the intact panes of glass. As the sun was setting, he decided against taking down any more until morning when he could examine the interior of his new home to his heart's content. However, he did peek into a good-sized living room where monochrome shapes of furniture, shrouded in grey dust sheets, gave him cause to contemplate why Eleanor McKenzie, his generous benefactor, had chosen an unknown, distant relative from a back street in Yorkshire to inherit her estate. As an afterthought and without opening either, he put both manila envelopes out of sight, high on a shelf. He intended to examine the contents the next morning.

There was an unusual stillness in the air as he set off to walk the dog, passing the rusted shell of a vintage car with its dicky seat open. Curled up on the bonnet, next to the windscreen, was his old cat, purring contentedly like a tractor. There were nagging, familiar images which he couldn't quite recall. Why wasn't he surprised to see that car abandoned there, even though he was confused as to why it was a rusted hulk?

Despite his experience on the coast road and the unfortunate incident at Hettie's, he thought this had been one of the most pleasant days he could remember as he strode confidently away from his new home, glancing back every so often to reassure himself it wasn't a dream.

At first, he thought about following a narrow footpath to the summit of the Cap, but instead chose to leave it until the following morning when he could view everything with fresh eyes. Pursing his lips together, he made an attempt to whistle happily, but still found it too painful.

At the base of the Cap there was a two-storey stone barn, which he intended to explore in daylight. Inexplicably, he felt this old building held the key to something important and he needed plenty of time to explore it. As he continued his tour, he didn't notice Phillip Ramsey parking up his bike and knocking on the kitchen door of the farmhouse behind the barn.

Jack followed a sloping track down until he reached the bay, where the tide had receded, exposing a vast beach of golden sand. It was a flawless evening with the orb of the sun immense as it sat on the horizon. The sky was cloudless, with the exception, that is, of a dark and compact cloud formation, which appeared to be drifting gradually towards the bay.

Ahead of him, the white dog took full advantage of his new-found freedom to crunch on shells and charge after a flock of squawking seabirds, catching none. There was a sudden and glorious gust of wind which blew back his hair and billowed out his shirt. Liberated by the wild beauty of his surroundings, he strode happily towards the sea, which seemed a mile distant, his footfall not making a sound on the sand to break the perfect silence.

When he had covered a good distance he stopped and looked sharply about him, convinced he had heard a boy's voice, but there was no one in sight. Nothing at all, except acre upon acre of pale, unblemished sand. He was thoroughly confused by the sound and looked around again, knowing there was nowhere to hide. It didn't make sense. It had been a day of extreme emotion and now all he wanted was to enjoy the tranquillity of the evening and walk along the beach with his dog.

"Is he here yet?" the disembodied voice of a boy asked, making Jack spin around. He was convinced he would see the boy who had spoken, but there was no one about. What the hell was going on?

The cloud formation had darkened ominously and was approaching the bay rapidly as Jack crossed a high ridge of sand with the sea a few feet beneath. He crouched with the white dog against the lapping water, preoccupied with thoughts of Bonnie and wondering if he would see her again.

Suddenly he was buffeted by a fierce upsurge of wind as it whipped across the surface of the water, forcing him to climb higher up the sandbank to the top. When he turned back to face the water, he discovered to his amazement he had been cut off from the mainland by the incoming tide, with its cresting, white-capped waves where previously there had been only sand. He was now stranded on a sandbar, a good quarter of a mile beyond the rugged cliffs of the Purple Cap.

As an intense vacuum of bitter wind whipped about him, he was in a quandary about the white dog, which he feared would never manage the rough crossing with its long fur, if indeed he could manage such a swim himself. Looking up, the evening sky was obscured by a mass of dark, swirling clouds, rumbling with thunder, casting an eerie green light about him.

He was unnerved by the increasing threat as the storm broke in a torrent of ice-cold rain, lashing across the water with such force that it was hard to draw breath. He was angry at his own stupidity at being so far out, especially at the end of the day. His only alternative was to trek along the narrowing strip of sand, running parallel along the cliff face of the Cap where it then curved inland, disappearing into what seemed to be a hidden cove.

He almost leapt out of his skin when the boy's voice called out, "Look over there! I can see him!" It sounded much closer than before but now the words were distorted in the increasing wind. Jack was in no mind to question disembodied voices, being more preoccupied by other, more threatening events around him as he bent double against the gale. He was battling along the sandbar when an unnatural, eerie glow began pulsating beneath the surface of the sand at the pressure of each footstep, tracking his progress in the impressions.

Now too desperate to be scared by anything, he forced himself slowly forward. The storm was real enough but the wind was so fierce he could only breathe when he turned away. He was soaked through to his skin, which confirmed that the experience was no dream. Steadily, he progressed along the sandbar, passing a stretch of cliff which rose from the sea on his right until, just when he thought he couldn't continue any further, there was a violent crash of thunder. Terrifying bolts of lightning seared through the blanket of rain directly ahead, exploding in his path and spearing the sandbar with such repeated ferocity that it formed a fearful portcullis of energy. He knew he must reach the coastline. He became angrier than he had been in years, shielding his eyes from the glare of the flashes as he got closer, with the accompanying blast of heat scorching his face as the thunderbolts continued to strike the sand. Despite the treacherous conditions and with grim determination he never faltered in his approach while protecting the dog as best he could.

Just as the heat became almost unbearable the lightning changed direction, now stabbing the turbulent water on either side of the sandbar just enough to allow them safe passage. The further he progressed along the narrow ridge of sand, the lower it sank until he was sloshing through the water up to his ankles so he could use only the pulsating sand beneath his feet for guidance.

He passed through an arch of exploding thunderbolts and emerged into comparative darkness, where the icy rain was so painful that he could only squint to see the way ahead. By this time, bent double against the merciless wind, he was dragging the frightened dog which was in danger of being swamped by the rising water. Its long, saturated fur was dragging it down so, with superhuman effort, Jack lifted the animal from the water and staggered on, determined not to put it down until he had passed the far side of the Cap. It was then that some even more surreal events began to unfold.

He was completely exhausted when he realised that the rain had stopped, but this was not the case on either side of him, where it was still sheeting down, but only directly ahead where the droplets were suspended in mid-air. For a few yards there was no rain at all, as though he had been contained in a vacuum, but when he continued the curtain of suspended droplets began spreading into each other, until they merged into a pane of solid water, creating a barrier between him and any access to land beyond.

Cursing the elements, he put the dog down and charged headlong into the translucent wall, where he sank into a jellied, rubbery mass from which he bounced back. Twice this happened, by which time his energy was thoroughly depleted. He could have wept in frustration. He was too exhausted to look about him when he heard voices whispering nearby.

"Doesn't he know what to do?" the boy asked.

"Be patient, he will," a woman answered. "He must make his own way here."

Exasperated, Jack swung wildly at the barrier using the edge of his hand and sliced effortlessly through the thickness of the 'wall', tearing open a narrow section to reveal beyond the calm clarity of a summer night. After a few moments the tear had resealed itself.

Placing both hands together as in prayer, he penetrated the mass easily by diving through it and ripping open a gap large enough to pass through. Moving quickly, he gathered up the dog and edged into the rapidly resealing gap by kicking and stamping his way through. He staggered out the other side and waded through the water until he reached the bank, where he sank exhausted on the grass, watching with glazed eyes as the storm drifted back out to sea, illuminated by diminishing lightning flashes.

Reaching out, he stroked the dog, reassuring himself that it was still breathing. Looking about him in the gathering darkness he could make out a line of trees close to the base of the Cap. The rough outline of the cliff face appeared softened by the onset of night, and the lulling sound of the crashing waves caused his eyelids to droop.

From where he lay, he could now see a boathouse outside which he could just make out a moored boat. Connected to the staging was a walkway leading up to three terraced gardens, each surrounded by a substantial fence interspersed with a series of urns with an abundance of trailing flowers. Lush foliage and well-established trees flanked the wide steps between the terraces.

He had been stroking the animal when he realised the long fur was now perfectly dry. He pushed his fingers into his own hair to discover that it too was no longer wet; neither was his previously sodden clothing.

He lay back as the unnatural cocoon of the storm disappeared beyond the horizon and, with one hand resting on the dog for reassurance, he allowed his eyes to close, fully expecting to wake in his own bed with a massive hangover, surrounded by the depressing familiarity of Eastmoor.

Chapter Four

When the cloud formation drifted from behind the Cap and came into full view, Bonnie could barely comprehend what she was seeing. A funnel of swirling energy, so violent the thunderbolts seemed to electrify the downpour of rain, zig-zagging orange and green flashes, all contained within a cylinder. There was no sign of turbulence elsewhere in the bay, yet it continued to drift at speed towards the horizon.

When she came away from the window she studied her reflection in the mirror thoughtfully, hardly seeing the green dress, which fitted perfectly. Suddenly the door swung open.

"You look nice," Clare announced grudgingly. "Where on earth did you buy it?"

"Don't you ever knock?" Bonnie responded icily.

"Why? Is there someone in here I shouldn't see?"

"Of course not," Bonnie replied, more interested in the meteorological phenomenon that was now close to the horizon and barely visible.

"I say. This material is incredibly fine. It's extraordinary."

Instead of answering, Bonnie opened the window wide and leaned out.

"Have you seen what's been happening in the bay? There was the strangest cloud formation I've ever seen. Look, you can still see it. Over there," she said, pointing.

"You can be so infuriating at times, Bonnie Jameson. Just like your father. I'm interested in the dress you're wearing, not an account of the weather."

Enviously she examined the soft, gossamer fabric which floated about her fingers like a delicate green mist.

"I know you didn't buy this. It would cost too much. Anyway, you'd never be that extravagant, not for a dress. Someone bought this for you, didn't they? Don't deny it, your face gives you away."

With flashing eyes, Bonnie lost any fascination with the passing storm to confront her stepsister.

"So tell me, why wouldn't I buy this?"

"Unless you've come into money, you could never afford such a luxury. Not on your wage."

"I didn't buy it," she answered calmly, unhooking the fastenings and stepping carefully out of the gathered material which she then put on a padded hanger and hung on the wardrobe door.

"It was Andrew, wasn't it? He's rich enough."

With mixed emotions, Bonnie contemplated her inquisitive sibling in the mirror as she tied back her hair. "Why is this so important?"

"Because…" she faltered. "Because I've never seen anything so beautiful. Damn it, Bonnie, why won't you tell me?"

"Very well. But this is an end to your questions. It was Jack McKenzie."

"Who?" she asked, startled. "I've never heard of him. Your dad's never mentioned him, not once, and you tell him everything. Where's he from? How long have you been going out?"

"We're not. I've only met him twice and you were with me on both occasions."

"Where was this, in Edinburgh?"

"No. He stepped in front of my car at the market. The man you ridiculed here tonight. Now get out of my room, Clare. Please go. I don't want you here."

Any further exchange was interrupted by Hettie calling from the hall.

"Bonnie dear, can you come down? Mr Kincaid is here again. He would like a word with you."

When Bonnie appeared at the back porch, she was quite unprepared for the elegant man who was waiting outside in the gloom. "How do you do, Miss Jameson?" he said with careful deliberation, endeavouring to conceal a surge of personal interest. "Please forgive me for calling here at this late hour but, since I spoke on an important issue with your aunt earlier today, I wondered if you would allow me to explain my proposition in more detail, perhaps over dinner?"

There was nothing about him that suggested anything other than good breeding, yet she was unsure of what might be going on behind his pale, slightly hypnotic eyes. Instead of agreeing to his offer she looked at the time on her watch. "Some other time perhaps. This has been a long day for my aunt and we are entertaining," she said, relieved that she hadn't agreed. There was something about his reaction, more calculated than genuine, that made her uneasy.

"A guest, so far from town?"

"A relative, Mr Kincaid, as it happens," she responded, watching his reactions carefully. There was barely a flicker in his eyes as she spoke, but she saw a perceptible gleam of interest.

"I understood that your aunt was unmarried and that you were an only child."

"You seem remarkably well informed."

He smiled disarmingly. "Before entering into any legitimate proposition there is inevitably an amount of research. You must forgive me for the zeal I have for correctness, if you find it offensive."

"Surprising, I suppose."

"Then the assumptions are correct?"

"I'm not prepared to discuss our business on the doorstep with a complete stranger, Mr Kincaid. Now, if you will excuse me, I must get inside."

"My apologies to your aunt for detaining you and I look forward to renewing our acquaintance some other time," he said amiably. "When you might consider another invitation for dinner?"

"There wouldn't be any point. My aunt is passionate about retaining ownership of the Cap and has no intention of selling."

"Never underestimate the power of money, Miss Jameson," he responded, returning to his vehicle.

"I never do and fortunately neither does my aunt," she called after him, adding, "Your car appears to have been damaged, Mr Kincaid. The money you mentioned might be better spent on having it repaired."

"Everything is in hand, Miss Jameson, never fear. I'll call by again tomorrow. Perhaps take you out for a spin?"

*

Jack awoke. The air felt warm and soft on his face as he gazed into a canopy of stars, but he could barely see anything in the darkness. At first he considered making his way to the boathouse, but the thought of rowing past the Cap in the boat was not an option, not without his neighbour's permission. Stumbling along behind the luminous white coat of the dog, he reached the staging and climbed to the lowest section of terraced gardens, tripping on the broad steps as he became disorientated by a swarm of fireflies which danced about in the inky darkness.

When he reached the second terrace, he could make out an Italianate colonnade of pale columns, evenly spaced between sections of a stone balustrade that followed the gentle curve of the terrace. Set on either side of the remaining steps to the final level were the huge trunks of grand firs of unimaginable height. At the gated entrance, beyond which he assumed lay the house, there were two more firs and a manicured hedge of yew. The hefty wrought-iron gate swung open more easily than he expected given its weight. From inside the building there were soft, welcoming lights burning at two of the windows on the ground floor. At one he could make out the shape of a woman peering into the darkness, framed by the heavy curtains.

Until his eyes refocused in the gloom he couldn't see the white coat of the dog, and blundered headlong into a rose bed. In such darkness it was impossible to gauge where the path would be. Uncertain, he stumbled towards the house, his trousers snagging on bushes as he crashed into them, snapping off blooms as he freed himself and fell on to the grass.

Unable to access the grand terrace of the house, he groped his way into a small courtyard. A door opened, streaming light over the cobbled area as an old man came out with a bucket, which he filled with coal from a bunker. Not wanting to alarm him, Jack waited until he was finished before he showed himself. When he did, the man glanced in his direction but didn't react to his presence. Instead, he picked up the scuttle and shuffled past him. As he entered the house, the old man left the door ajar, allowing Jack to follow him inside. He entered an echoing corridor with a wide flagstone floor and heard voices chattering beyond an oak-panelled door. He emerged into a large kitchen with a high, vaulted ceiling.

He found the old man seated beside an iron cooking range that would have dwarfed his own back in Eastmoor. It was a welcoming space, where copper pans and racks of dried herbs hung above a wide, scrubbed table where a matronly woman rolled out pastry whilst talking with the old man. At the sink there was a thin, younger woman with colourless skin and saucer-like eyes, whose hair, like the older woman's, was covered by a starched linen cap. Both wore long service dresses protected by equally long aprons.

Jack cleared his throat noisily, expecting at least someone in the group to notice him. Instead, the conversation continued as though he didn't exist.

"You can't be serious, Mr Ross? At the end of the month?" the older woman enquired.

"It will be a party of six, Mrs Jennings," Ross answered, inserting a taper into the fire grate. Neither of them was paying attention to the young maid, who craned her neck to see into the darkness beyond the window.

"Listen! There it was again," she said urgently, quite oblivious to the white dog as it padded over and sniffed about her ankles. "Didn't you hear anything? It was much clearer that time."

Old Ross packed more tobacco into his pipe, and lit it. "I might be getting on, lassie, but there's nothing wrong with these eyes. You can take it from me: if there was anything out there tonight, I'd have noticed." Saying this, he shook open a newspaper for emphasis.

Jack circled the room, passing each of the occupants in turn, expecting them to take notice of this stranger amongst them. First he confronted the maid, who looked directly at him but registered nothing. Instead, her attention was elsewhere as she caught her breath, turning about to stare searchingly out of the window once more.

"There's someone out there, watching. I just know it!"

"Come away from the sink, Dora. You're imagining things." But Dora shook her head.

"Whoever it was, was staring at me," she said as Jack continued on around the kitchen. "Closer this time. Nearer the house!"

When he stood beside old Ross, he too looked up without reaction. Muttering about his need to change an overhead bulb, he shifted his position to a better angle to the fire to get more light, before re-immersing himself in the newspaper. Jack moved on. "What's wrong with the electrics in here tonight?" the old man said crossly, moving back to his original position. "The blasted thing's gone bright again."

Finally, Jack approached the kitchen table. Mrs Jennings was preoccupied with her baking and, like the others, didn't react to his presence. In frustration, Jack touched her lightly on the arm.

"Is that window off its catch, Dora?" she asked, glancing up. "I felt a draught just then and I don't want the cake ruined when I open the oven."

"It's shut fast, Mrs Jennings," Dora replied, checking the window catch as Jack touched Mrs Jennings for a second time.

"Well, it's coming from somewhere. I felt it again, just then."

Jack was accustomed to being deliberately excluded from any conversation in Eastmoor, but to have no reaction at all was bizarre. How could he be an observer amongst this domestic activity without being acknowledged? Was everything he was experiencing a dream? Yet the aroma of baking assured him otherwise.

Dora leant across the Belfast sink, standing on tiptoe to peer into the darkness.

"I can't see anything. Whatever was out there, it's gone now," she said, drying her hands on her apron.

"What did you see exactly?" Ross asked as he attempted to relight his pipe.

Dora looked at Mrs Jennings for support. "I think it was a man, but it was hard to make out properly."

"Well, make up your mind. Either it was or it wasn't," he mumbled, emptying out the tobacco on to his newspaper with his penknife. "What was he doing? Hiding?"

"It was more like floating," she said hesitantly, "like mist. Out near the dovecote."

He grunted, refilling his pipe with tobacco, and thrusting a taper into the fire. "That lassie's away with the fairies, Mrs Jennings. Make no mistake."

"Leave the girl be, Mr Ross. You should know Dora well enough by now. She sees things."

"There was a dog too… I saw it clearly, closer to the house."

"And also floating, no doubt?" Ross chuckled and lit up his pipe.

"Well, yes, but I recognised it from when I first came here."

He grunted. "Now I've heard everything! How long do you think they can live?"

"Leave the girl be, Mr Ross. Who knows what goes on in this place?" the cook answered as she chopped up a mixture of dried herbs.

Uncertain of how to proceed, Jack stood beside a large dresser as the activity continued around him. He moved a blue china bowl from the back of the dresser into the centre. His hunger pangs worsened as Mrs Jennings sliced into a succulent pork pie, which she garnished with sliced tomato and a sprinkling of the chopped herbs.

"Dora, have you been moving things on the dresser?" she asked, returning the blue bowl to its original position to put down the platter. But Dora wasn't listening. Instead she was straining to hear the whining of the white dog as it fixed its attention on the pork pie.

"Surely you must have heard that, Mr Ross?" Dora asked, without a glance at the animal but looking instead into the darkness outside.

"Come away from the window, dear, you've been there long enough," Mrs Jennings urged. "I'm running late; I need help preparing supper."

Unable to ignore the plate of food any longer Jack removed a slice of pie, still fully expecting a blast of abuse from the cook, which never came. When he glanced up again, it was too late to shout a warning as Dora blundered into the dog. Incredibly, instead of falling over as he expected, she passed right through the animal in a swirl of vapours, as if her skirts were made of mist, which made him begin to wonder if the entire sequence of recent events was the result of a drinking session in Eastmoor. However, if that ruled out the seeming reality of the girl at the local store he had no desire to wake up.

"Mr Ross! How could you?" Mrs Jennings said indignantly and very close to Jack's ear. "You've taken a slice of pie off the plate without asking. Just look! You've ruined the arrangement. How can I present this to my lady now? It was ordered for eight o'clock sharp." She glanced at the wall clock. "And it's five past already."

"I've done no such thing, woman," Ross responded defensively, folding away his newspaper.

"Well if you haven't, then who has?"

From deep inside the house a door slammed, attracting Mrs Jennings' attention and making her stare intently at where Jack was standing, rubbing her eyes. "D'you know, Mr Ross, if I didn't know better, I could have sworn there was someone leaning against the dresser a moment ago."

From the corridor outside the kitchen came the sound of running feet, which stopped abruptly at the sound of a wooden box clattering to the floor and the contents scattering. "I'll be there in a minute!" a boy's voice called out. "If anyone finds any pencils out here, Mr Ross, they're mine."

When she heard his voice, Mrs Jennings beamed like the sun and took a rice pudding from out of the pantry. "There," she said happily.

"You'll be the ruination of that boy, Mrs Jennings," old Ross said, attempting to conceal his own pleasure as he rocked in his chair, puffing contentedly on the pipe.

"Should I tell the young master what I've seen?" Dora asked.

"Better not, pet," the cook assured her. "That child's had enough upset. He doesn't need to imagine noises in the night when he should be asleep."

By the reactions from everyone in the kitchen, it seemed as if the light of awareness had been switched on when a boy of about six years old appeared in the doorway rubbing his knee, clutching a box of pencils in his other hand. He was an odd little thing, with pale, tissue-like skin, compelling eyes and dark, rebellious hair. There were blue ink stains on his fingers and hands and a smudge of the same on his cheek.

"What have you been doing?" Mrs Jennings murmured affectionately, wetting the corner of her apron in her mouth to rub hard at the smudge until it was almost gone. "There, that's better," she said, straightening the crumpled collar with busy fingers until he squirmed free.

"Hello, sorry I'm late," the boy said, looking calmly into Jack's eyes as he reached and took hold of his hand. At his touch, Jack felt a fierce jolt of energy surge along his arm, crackling with such force he was certain it would scorch their flesh, and yet the boy wouldn't let go. His dark eyes paled with each surge of energy and his ashen skin became more translucent with each jolt, as though his life's blood was draining away. His sensitive features reacted in agony as the energy level increased in a series of vivid blue flashes, but Jack could do nothing to break free. Their hands were welded together as if an electrical transfusion was being passed from the child's body into his own.

"Let go of him!" Mrs Jennings suddenly shouted in alarm, reaching out to separate Jack's hand from the boy's, but jumping back, repelled by a flash of energy. "Mr Ross! Do something about this intruder. He's trying to kidnap the master," she concluded, now brandishing the rolling pin.

Jack could do nothing but stare back into the depths of the boy's unfathomable eyes as the flow of energy eased off as suddenly as it had begun.

"There's nothing to worry about, Mrs Jennings," the boy reassured her, letting go of Jack's hand, leaving his fingers tingling. "See, it's all over."

"Put that thing down before you do any damage, Mrs Jennings," Ross said, putting on his spectacles and standing hastily. "Look at him… the boy isn't afraid."

"Who are you?" she demanded crossly, "and what on earth is that dog doing in my kitchen?"

"A dog, Mrs Jennings? Where?" Dora was alert and peering across the table. "I told you I heard something."

"Never mind that, Dora. I want an explanation from this… this person. Who are you, and what are you doing here?" Mrs Jennings demanded as Ross joined her and removed the offensive weapon from her grasp.

"I… I…" Jack began awkwardly, but he was not concerned about any of them or their sudden interest, only for the boy, whose face was like chalk, his previously energised hand now lifeless and cradled in the other like a dead bird. Instinctively, Jack reached out and grasped the immobile hand between his own until he felt renewed warmth.

"I think we are entitled to some kind of an explanation, young man," Ross said, taking the initiative from Mrs Jennings' prodding elbow.

"He's expected, Mr Ross," the boy answered. His colour was becoming more normal and his eyes were darkening.

"I-I-I…" Jack stammered, attempting to speak, feeling oddly reassured by the clasp of the small hand which still clung to his own.

"What's your name?" the boy quizzed. "Mine's Duncan, but you must know that if you came here to find me."

Unexpectedly, both Mrs Jennings and Dora bobbed in deference to a person who had come up behind Jack and the boy.

"M'lady," Ross said. "I believe this would be the gentleman you were expecting?"

"Indeed. Welcome to Dungellen Hall, Mr McKenzie," she said, as he turned to face her. "Madeline de Beaufort."

For some inexplicable reason, he half expected to be confronted by the woman in the green dress. Instead, he was greeted by a grey-haired woman with gentle features and a smile very similar to the boy's. There was no doubt she was somewhat shocked by Jack's battered features, a reaction she would have concealed admirably had it not been for her glistening eyes as she reached up, lightly touching his injuries.

"You dear boy. What dreadful things have happened to you out there?" At first he thought she was about to say more, but instead she addressed her attentions to the old man. "Our guest must be very tired after his long journey. I will take him through to the main house."

"Mrs Jennings has food prepared as you requested, M'Lady. Where will you be dining? In the great hall?" Ross asked.

"Not tonight, Mr Ross. The drawing room will be more relaxing," she answered, stepping into the light where Jack could see her better. There was a familiar grace about her which was hard to define. She was beautifully dressed in a gown which reflected more elegant times that suited her perfectly.

"Will you take tea, M'Lady?" Mrs Jennings asked, all trace of her rebellious attitude gone.

"For myself. I imagine Mr McKenzie would prefer something stronger after such an arduous journey. Come now and follow me, both of you," she said walking ahead of them. The pale amethyst drops of her earrings glittered hypnotically. The Louis heels of her shoes clipped briskly on the stone floor and then deadened into the deep pile of richly designed carpets in the acre of space that was the main entrance hall. In awe, Jack could scarcely comprehend the size of the stone fireplace in which a log fire was crackling.

Hung high on the walls were embroidered, armorial banners, most of them faded with age and near rotting. On each was the heraldic design replicating the one carved above the gateway he had passed on the Dungellen road. Opposite the main entrance was a grand staircase that divided at a half landing beneath a magnificent stained-glass window, on either side of which was a spectacular display of battle-scarred broadswords, mounted beneath an armoured breastplate that reflected the light from the many flickering candles. In stark contrast, there was the heady scent of honeysuckle and wild flowers mixed with roses and ferns coming from an urn placed between the rich, loose folds of the window hangings.

On either side of the long corridor leading to the drawing room hung a collection of landscapes. In truth, Jack would have appreciated more time to examine at least two of these artworks in closer detail as they seemed vaguely familiar. Instead, he was pulled along by the child, who followed Madeline de Beaufort as she walked on ahead.

Absorbing as much detail of his surroundings as he could, he trailed his fingers lightly over the polished wood of ancient furniture, wondering what he was actually doing in this extraordinary house. Were they confusing him with someone else or was he expected as the boy had suggested? As the thoughts passed through his mind the boy squeezed his hand reassuringly as if Jack had spoken aloud. He said nothing.

They caught up with Madeline as she opened a sturdy oak door, revealing a spacious and beautiful panelled room. Before long he was seated in a comfortable chair opposite the woman and her grandson, relaxing in front of a crackling log fire in the medieval fireplace. Against the panelled wall behind him was an exquisite cabinet fitted with marquetry doors, which caught his particular attention.

"I see you are as fascinated by the craftsmanship as my late son. It was a particular favourite of his," Madeline said.

"Mine too," Duncan added. His remarkable eyes sparkled with enthusiasm. "Look at the bird. It sees everything."

Madeline ruffled the boy's hair affectionately as she spoke. "The marquetry was done by an ancestor. As you see, he took the craft of inlaid woods very seriously. It is a lovely example of Queen Anne, wouldn't you agree?"

"It's… b-b-beautiful," he stammered, but speaking more easily than he expected under the circumstances. His attention was focused on a perfect replica of an osprey in flight, so intricately worked in different wood veneers that the flight feathers appeared to be quivering in the wind and, as the boy mentioned, the eyes did seem unnaturally alive and watching his every movement. There was a timeless quality about the old house which made it a perfect retreat for anyone jaded by the frenetic pace of modern life. It was an estate where, in different circumstances, he would have enjoyed working, and remaining for an eternity.

Idly he fingered a cluster of periodicals in a magazine rack, searching for a newspaper but finding nothing. In an edition of *Country Life*, the property advertisements showed photographs of houses which he imagined could only exist in literature, offered at ridiculously low prices which Jack knew had gone out with the ark. Most of these detailed a mains water supply and electricity as added extras, which seemed to be of more interest to prospective buyers than the acreage included.

"Those magazines belonged to my son," Madeline said unexpectedly. "John had a passion for the past." By some trick of the light her features seemed more youthful than they had been when he had first met her. By marked comparison the boy was fading noticeably, appearing frail and exhausted in sleep.

After he had eaten the plain but wholesome food Mrs Jennings had prepared, and basked in the warmth from the fire, Jack struggled to keep awake, closing his eyes for what he thought would be a few moments during a lull in the conversation. Instead, he drifted into a dreamless sleep lulled by the rhythmic ticking of a long-cased clock. It was all so far removed from his neighbour's blaring radio against a thin partition wall and noisy squabbling children, or worse still, his drunken ravings which shattered any hope of peace and tranquillity in the evening.

He awoke with a jolt, expecting to be in Eastmoor and late for work. A standard lamp with a beaded shade had been switched on beside the sofa where Madeline had been nursing her grandson. Now she was engaged in working an embroidered cushion. Duncan, who had changed into a pair of silk pyjamas, was fully alert and staring at him intently. The white dog was asleep and twitching at his feet.

Jack might have laughed at the way the boy seemed to observe his every reaction had his face not hurt as much, and particularly when he remained focused longer on some specific object. There was an exquisitely carved cow on a small plinth which held Jack's interest and, in particular, the four impressions cut into the base towards which the animal's head was turned. He awaited the boy's unnerving response to his thoughts, as if he had spoken them aloud.

"There used to be a calf in that space. That's why the cow's head's turned towards it."

"Darling, you mustn't keep doing that," Madeline said, stroking Duncan's cheek affectionately. "It can be most off-putting for anyone if they don't know you as well as I do. Jack is a guest in our home. Give him time to accept the oddity of your ways, and don't stare so much."

In truth, Jack didn't mind the boy watching him so intently. There was no trace of ridicule, only the natural curiosity of a child unused to outside influences. Presumably his battered face and shabby clothing were as acceptable to Duncan as was the rarity of such beautiful surroundings to himself. He felt strangely comfortable in their company and so much at ease in the great house that everything seemed as natural as breathing.

"Jack, please forgive my asking this favour so soon after your arrival but time is of the essence, and I wondered if I could impose on you over the coming weeks to help my estate manager maintain the grounds? Ralph would be so relieved if you would agree as another assistant will not be available to replace Ambrose for at least a month and there is so much catching up to be done. For one man single-handedly, however willing, this would be impossible."

"You will help, Jack, won't you?" the boy urged.

Surprised by the unexpected offer, it was nevertheless, heaven sent. Could she have guessed that he was almost broke and desperate to find work?

"We know about things," Duncan whispered, staring knowingly into Jack's bewildered face as he snuggled against Madeline. "Can Jack and the dog stay here, Granny? We'd be safer if they did."

"If… that would be agreeable to Jack? A man's presence in such a big house would be most welcome until more staff are engaged."

It was decided. Jack would remain on the estate for one month before taking up residence at Moorcroft and Dora, not Jack, would collect his old cat and clothing early the following morning. He was not surprised to discover that preparations had already been made for his stay.

"Has Dora made up the bed in John's room, Mr Ross?" she asked when he entered.

"Indeed, M'Lady. The room was aired first thing this morning and the bed made up, as you requested. Would there be anything else before I turn out the lights?"

"Please convey my appreciation to Mrs Jennings for the excellent pastry. It was delicious."

"And what of the dog, ma'am? Shall I take it to one of the stables?"

"I think not; my grandson would be most unhappy if you did. It can stay in the house. He will feel safer that way, having it nearby."

"And what of the young master, M'Lady? Should I carry him upstairs?"

"I suspect Mr McKenzie will oblige me this evening, Mr Ross," she answered with a smile.

There was something very comforting about the boy clasping Jack around the neck when he lifted him gently off the sofa. However, he was more concerned about the strange lethargy of the boy's limbs than his own recurring pains. With an attentive grandmother at his side, he carried the boy up the wide staircase which opened to the left on to a broad landing that revealing a corridor with recessed doors on either side. At the far end was a massive oak door hung on forged strap hinges. It was set in a wall of chased granite, a medieval structure on which the east wing of the house had been constructed centuries later. Illuminating the area to the left of the door was an oil lamp on a highly waxed table. To the right was placed an elbow chair with a carved heraldic back.

The white dog, which had been trotting ahead, disappeared into a room on the left of the medieval door.

"This one's mine," the boy whispered into his ear sleepily. "You're over there," indicating the room the dog had entered.

The boy's room was quite small compared to the other rooms in the house. Against the main wall was a four-poster bed which was accessed by three upholstered steps. Opposite there was a leaded window overlooking a sweeping drive, now perfectly illuminated by the moonlight. This made no sense to Jack as there had been no moon visible when he arrived. On the window seat was a stuffed elephant wearing a pair of blue pants, a one-armed bear sitting on a pile of colouring books and a galleon in full sail spanning the wide windowsill. There was a miniature log cabin surrounded by Indians on horseback adorning the nearby bookcase.

"Goodnight, my darling. Sweet dreams," Madeline said, kissing the boy on the forehead.

"Can Jack stay until I go to sleep?" he asked drowsily.

"Not tonight, sweetheart... he's only across the hall."

*

Jack was tired to the point of exhaustion when he entered the bedroom and, unable to find any light switch, groped around in the dark until he found the bed, undressed and was asleep before he had pulled up the covers.

That night he had a most restful sleep as his body seemed to float on a mattress of air. The sheet wafted about him like a cloud when he turned over, his eyes briefly flickering open to see the silvered rays of moonlight.

He awoke in a four-poster bed between a set of fine linen sheets, as crisp and pressed as if they hadn't been slept in, to a chorus of birdsong intermingling with the calming sound of the sea. The barley twist mahogany bedposts tapered upwards to support an embroidered canopy, from which hung four drapes of rich Venetian brocade. In daylight he could see the room was spacious and beautifully furnished with a collection of antique furniture, selected for practicality and comfort. Alarmed to hear the door open, he sat up too quickly. The pain was a sharp reminder of the beating. Old Ross entered.

"Your bath is ready, Mr Jack. Fresh clothes have been laid out in the dressing room as m'lady requested."

"W-w what?" he stammered.

"The maid has taken your clothes away to repair, if she can. They were in a bad state and barely wearable. I trust you will find the alternatives laid out are to your satisfaction. The Laird was similar in build to yourself and they should fit nicely," he said, holding out a long dressing gown with a monogram on the pocket. "I would suggest you take your bath soon, Mr Jack. The water is at a perfect temperature."

The scale of his altered situation in less than a week hit home as he slid into the luxurious hot water in a vast enamelled bath, wondering how long he could soak his aching frame. A time hadn't been mentioned for when he should start work, so he clambered out of the water much earlier than he would have liked and towelled down. He found the clothes laid out, and every item fitted perfectly, with the exception of the tight waistband on the Laird's trousers which he had to fasten lying flat on the bed. However, when he caught sight of his new reflection in the cheval mirror, he felt infinitely better.

From the dressing room window there was a spectacular view. He could see the boy playing on the upper terrace of the gardens with the dog. There was something alarming in the way he clambered about, oblivious to the danger of falling or the vast drop to the lower level if he missed his footing. Jack caught his breath as he saw him scramble on to the ornamental balustrade where he balanced precariously along the slender strip of capping with the bravado of someone crying out for attention.

Unable to shout any warning, Jack bolted from the room and expertly negotiated his way through the maze of corridors until he was outside and running barefoot across the lawn. He heard the distressed cry of a young woman calling to the boy, looked around but could see very little of either the house or the terrace, as his line of vision was blocked by a long yew hedge. Through the overhanging branches of a cedar tree he glimpsed a young couple, clearly agitated. It was hard to distinguish the features of the woman or the dark-haired man who was restraining her. The only impression he had as he turned away and continued running was that they were about his age.

"G-get d-down!" Jack called urgently as he got closer. "It's loose." While never being more sure of anything in his life, despite the realisation that he had no way of knowing that it was the case, he was certain of the boy's imminent danger, which spurred him on even more.

"Granny won't listen unless I do this," he cried, balancing along another section before Jack reached the spot. He scooped him off the parapet just as the boy lost his balance and nearly toppled when a section of loose capping crashed over the edge, shattering into pieces on the stone bench immediately beneath.

He was relieved to have saved him, but totally unprepared for the tremendous jolt of energy which passed between them, increasing tenfold when he held the child closer. "Y-y-you daft young bugger." Jack brushed the strands of dark hair away from the boy's eyes, which again paled noticeably with each surge. "Why is this happening between us?" he thought.

"You couldn't stay here if it didn't," the boy responded weakly.

Madeline appeared from beyond the yew hedge at a fair speed for a woman of her advanced years. Duncan buried his head against Jack's shoulder as his grandmother came closer. "Make her listen, Jack," he pleaded. In those few moments everything about him had been transformed. He was no longer a wild, energetic boy; instead he had become listless and was trembling uncontrollably. His features were as pale as death, and his eyes wide and staring. "Don't be upset, Jack, when they come for me. I won't be afraid... not to die. Only sad because I can't stay here in Dungellen any longer."

Ignoring his own severe pain, Jack hugged him tighter, unnerved by the icy coldness of the boy's skin and the abnormally slow beat of his heart. "I won't let anyone take you from here," he whispered, unaware that he had spoken without a trace of his stammer. "You won't die, I can promise you that." He felt sickeningly helpless, unable to do anything as the boy shuddered, his slight body stiffening as he attempted to move. The grip of his hands about Jack's neck slackened. He realised that he must get the boy to a doctor immediately, remembering that the girl at the store had mentioned one who lived close by.

"No, Jack... you can't," Duncan answered, in a voice barely audible. "No one can help. Only you."

"I don't understand."

"It happened before. In a dream. You were there," he said to Jack as Madeline arrived.

"I couldn't keep up. I'm sorry," she said, holding on to Jack's arm for support while she caught her breath. She peered down at the shattered capping from the parapet on the stone bench beneath them. "How can I thank you enough for getting here in time? He is all I have."

"I... I..." Jack began, wanting to do more as she examined Duncan anxiously.

"He will soon be unconscious if we don't get him back inside the house. You must help me get him back there immediately. He needs complete rest now where it's quiet. That will restore some of his energy," she said, patting Jack's arm reassuringly. They walked back through the gardens. "There is no need to worry so, my dear. My grandson suffers with a rare complaint, which in time he will grow out of."

They passed through the ruin of a Gothic building close to the house and Madeline rested against what Jack thought might once have been an altar. An old chapel maybe? She took the child from him.

"I have no idea what possesses him to perform such wild acts. His father was never as rebellious as a child... Not like this. Why would you do such a dangerous thing?" she murmured, pressing her lips lightly on his forehead

"Please don't let them come here," he said, struggling to stay awake.

Attempting to conceal her distress, Madeline straightened his collar with trembling fingers. "Hush, my darling. Rest. You know I would if it were possible. No one can alter their destiny. This has to be."

While Duncan rested, at Madeline's insistence Jack breakfasted with her in the morning room. It was a light and airy space of considerable charm. The wainscoting was painted a delicate grey and the walls above were papered in the palest design of blue on an ivory ground. It was a room at peace with the environment, with lovely arrangements of wild grasses and glistening ferns and an intoxicating scent of the wild roses and pale freesias in a vase. The table centred in the bay window was set with the most delicate blue-and-white hand-painted china on a crisp linen cloth. It was a lovely beginning to any day as the sunlight filtered through the gathered folds of pure Chinese silk curtains, complementing the fronds of two sprawling kentia palms.

"My son's clothes fit you well," Madeline remarked as she buttered her toast. "I hope during your stay here you will oblige an old woman by wearing whatever Mr Ross lays out for you each day. It would be a great pity if John's clothes were never worn again." He had seen her son's wardrobe in the dressing room and he was pleased to agree, even though he was unused to such fine attire.

After breakfast, he was taken on a short tour of the grounds, where Madeline indicated the areas most in need of attention.

"Ralph, of course, will arrange everything," she said as they emerged from the house and strolled along a wide terrace which ran its entire length. "But before he does, I wanted to give you a personal view of our precious gardens. My daughter-in-law adored this particular aspect and I thought you would appreciate them too. They were very formal before she came here and, as you see, she altered my opinion and refashioned them into what you see here today."

Looking at the gardens with fresh eyes, he admired the companion planting amongst the established trees and shrubs, unobtrusively introducing many seemingly random walks between banks of delphiniums and hollyhocks and arbours of pale roses that revealed different aspects of the old house. He longed to find a vantage point where he could absorb the design in its entirety.

There was a loud clatter against the French windows as Duncan emerged, scattering his pencil box across the flagged terrace as he disentangled himself from a lace curtain. He was clutching a sketchbook and seemed more energetic than ever.

"Can't you walk like other boys of your age?" Madeline asked, helping to untangle him. When she released him, he searched about until he had collected up his pencils. "Now what are you looking for? Haven't you found them all?"

"Yes... but not all of my pen nibs. I need them for writing."

"Perhaps that is a blessing in disguise," she answered laughing, examining his hand. "Just look at these fingers, darling. I can hardly see them for ink stains. Why have you brought all of these things outside?"

"I thought we could draw something?" he suggested eagerly, pushing a clutch of pencils into the pocket on his shirt.

"No sweetheart, you can't... What have I told you? You should stay in bed after these attacks. It isn't good to be racing about so soon."

"Sorry, I forgot. Can I draw the dog if I'm quiet?"

"Well, just this once. Mind that's all you get up to. No more climbing along walls."

"Is the Red Fox not coming today?" he asked, scribbling on his pad with great concentration.

"He'll be arriving shortly. He had things to do first." Madeline smiled apologetically at Jack. "He's asking about Ralph, our estate manager. My grandson is very fond of him. You will understand why he calls him the Red Fox when you meet him."

During a tour of the grounds Madeline pointed out a rickety weathervane at the end of a long barn that was in need of attention. The magnificent dovecote that Dora had mentioned the previous night also badly needed repair. It mystified Jack how relaxed he felt in her company, and he was finding it hard to believe she was just a temporary employer and not a companion. Perhaps the most outstanding quality he admired was her tact. Her questions were so perfectly phrased as to require little response, thus minimising his speech impediment. When she took hold of his arm over rough ground, or trod cautiously down the steps on the way to a lower terrace, it felt as natural as if he had been assisting his own mother.

"Look, Granny… there he is!" the boy called excitedly.

"Ah yes, I see him," she answered, as a man with pleasant features and hair the colour of a fox appeared, pushing a wheelbarrow. Now Jack understood the name perfectly as the boy went racing off towards him, the dog bounding along at his side.

"Foxy… I'm over here. Wait for me."

When they caught up with him, Madeline introduced them immediately. "Ralph, my dear, this is Jack McKenzie. The gentleman we were expecting."

Ralph was barely a year older than Jack and yet he seemed perfectly suited to the position of estate manager. His handshake was firm and decisive. His amiable face winced a little as he smiled, exposing a broken front tooth.

"I hadn't expected you in so early," said Madeline. "Not until this afternoon."

"The appointment with Sam Grainger's been put off until next week, ma'am. His missus said he's got a bad fever. Doesn't want me to catch it in case I pass it on to the wee lassie."

"A wise decision," Madeline answered thoughtfully. "Then I shall arrange to get you some oil of cloves to tide you over."

"It's not painful no more," he said, tapping the broken tooth with a finger. "I reckon it died on Sunday night. I've had no pain from it since."

"Ralph!" she chided knowingly.

"I only get the occasional twinge now an' then."

"I'll send out for the tincture anyway; there is no sense in being uncomfortable."

She returned to the house. The remainder of the day was spent working in Ralph's company, always with the boy close by. Soon Jack was straddling the barn roof, re-attaching the weathervane, and in the afternoon he made a good temporary repair to the dovecote.

"Nice to see the lad with the dog again," Ralph said. "Like bacon an' eggs them two were."

Why hadn't Duncan mentioned having had a dog? Unless, of course, something terrible had happened, Jack thought. When he looked at the boy, he was staring back at him in the oddest manner. And then he ran off.

It was remarkable how flexible Ralph was with the boy. Always firm, but considerate, never patronising. It was an education for Jack to see how Ralph watched over the boy, as a shepherd might guard against an unseen predator, never allowing his wild exuberance to endanger his safety. A perfect father figure.

"Our little turnip head's a bit on the wild side when the mood takes him. Best keep an eye on him when I'm not around, Mr Jack," he said, hoisting the squealing boy aloft, carrying him along on his broad shoulders.

Chapter Five

Phillip Ramsey shivered as he crouched against the smouldering fire, which had died out while he was taking an early dip in the bay. With only a towel resting lightly on his sunburned shoulders, he blew with desperation into the smoking twigs, hoping to re-ignite the flames, when a black MG saloon freewheeled to a stop next to Jack's motorbike.

"I didn't expect to see you here," Andrew announced as he got out of the car. "What on earth are you doing at this hour with nothing on? Is this some weird ritual?"

"The fire went out." Phillip responded, his teeth chattering.

"If you're as cold as you look, get some clothes on first. That would be a start."

"Was there something you wanted?" Phillip asked moodily, grabbing his pants.

"The owner... that isn't you, I take it?"

"Obviously not," he muttered, struggling to retain his balance as he tugged his underwear over wet skin. He toppled on to the tent, yanking out a guy rope. "Bugger!" he yelped, holding his shoulder in pain.

"Here," Andrew said, offering his hand, and staring at Phillip's sunburnt shoulders. He pulled him to his feet. "Sit down, and let me take a look at that."

"There's no need. It's nothing to bother about."

"Just sit down, will you? I won't be charging you for a consultation!"

"Glad to hear it. I'm skint anyway," he answered, wincing badly even though Andrew's fingers had barely touched his sensitive skin.

"I thought you were going to put something on this burn yesterday?"

"I was, but I forgot to pack the oils," he responded.

Andrew took his doctor's bag and removed a tube of cream. "This should ease the pain. You'll feel the benefit very soon," he said as he applied the salve. "Now, if you do own a shirt I would suggest you keep it on and not wander about half naked."

"What is it with you?" Phillip asked tersely. "I told you I was OK, and I was... perfectly, before you arrived. I wasn't dressed because it was so bloody painful, and there's nobody here except me!" he said with some relief as the cream started to take effect. "You didn't need to bother. I could have managed it myself," he added, ungraciously.

"You wouldn't have been able to reach. Second-degree burns can lead to serious complications if they are left unattended. I'll do this again when I've finished my rounds."

"There's really no need to make another visit."

"I must. This will need more than a single application before it begins healing."

"So why are you here at this ungodly hour?" Phillip grumbled, easing on a shirt.

"Jack McKenzie," he responded, prodding the smouldering embers with a stick. "Is he about yet? I was told he'd been injured... quite badly."

"I haven't seen hide nor hair of the bloke since I left Lochenbrae yesterday, although I must admit he was in bad shape when he gave me the address for this place."

"When was this?"

"Yesterday, late afternoon. At the garage."

"And you haven't seen him since then?"

"No," he answered with a shiver. "I don't suppose you've got such a thing as a firelighter in the car?"

"Have you checked the kitchen for dry sticks and newspaper?"

"There's no sign that anyone's lived in that place in years."

"This is very strange. He called at the local store last night, and that's less than a mile away," Andrew answered, peering into the kitchen. "Maybe he never made it this far if he was in such a bad state. I might take a walk back to the store, in case he's collapsed in a ditch along the way."

"He did make it this far. The combination near the house belongs to him... the engine was still warm when I got here," he said, as Andrew retrieved a foot-pump from the car and began pumping air into the embers, which soon ignited the flames.

"Then where is he now?"

"Search me," Phillip answered, putting a saucepan of water on to the fire. "Tea?"

"I can't, I've other calls to make. When he comes back would you let me know? If you turn left at the gate, I live at the next house along. It's at the dead end. You can't miss it," he said, climbing into the MG before roaring up the steep drive and out of sight.

Bonnie had just finished loading the basket attached to the handlebars of her bicycle when the MG pulled up outside the store. "Andrew... you're early. I was just on my way to the farm to see how Mr McKenzie is."

"Then I've prevented you wasting your time, Red. He hasn't been there all night."

"Why ever not? Did he come to your house by mistake?"

"I haven't seen him."

"Then how can you be so certain? He drove off towards the farm, and he didn't come back this way. We'd have heard the motorbike if he had."

"Well I can assure you he isn't there... but I can tell you who is. That young chap from the garage you were talking to yesterday."

"Phillip Ramsey? What's he doing there?"

"Camping by the sound of it. He seemed genuine enough. Said he'd just missed McKenzie when he got there."

"Oh dear. What if he was caught out on the Cap during that freak storm? Anything could have happened."

"What storm?" he asked, registering surprise as he looked at the dry surroundings. "There wasn't even a breath of wind yesterday in town and Lord knows we could do with some rain up here."

"That's just it. I never saw anything like it before, and the oddest thing is, like you, no one else did either. Only me. Auntie Hettie was sorting out in the storeroom and Clare, well she couldn't be bothered to look."

"And this happened yesterday?" Andrew was thinking. "Before seven thirty?"

"About then, I suppose. Why? Did you see something after all?"

"I did notice some blue flashes on the horizon which didn't resemble any weather conditions I'd ever seen. Not up here, or anywhere come to that. I can tell you, if it was a storm it was the freakiest storm I've ever seen. There was something else, though, which struck me as peculiar."

She looked at him intently, answering almost before he had finished. "The bird?"

"Yes. Then you saw it too? It was hovering on the far side of the Cap. Quite extraordinary how it seemed to evaporate into the sky. One second it was there, crystal clear, and in the next moment it was gone without a trace."

"What kind was it?" she asked, needing confirmation. "I couldn't tell for certain."

"It was an osprey, I'm almost certain."

"That's impossible. There hasn't been a sighting of an osprey in these parts since the last century."

"Eighteen-eighty-five to be precise. But I have to agree, although while it might have looked like an osprey it was far too big. You know, I've read about something which fits this bird's description perfectly, in a book of myths and legends your dad gave me one Christmas."

She was silent for a time and removed Jack's wallet from the basket. "What shall I do about Mr McKenzie?"

"Nothing for now. There's no point involving the constabulary if he's only been gone for one night. Give it a couple of days first. He might be away with friends or relatives."

"He doesn't know anyone, Andrew. He's not from around these parts."

"If he inherited the farm from Eleanor, perhaps he's visiting distant relatives?"

"That's a bit unlikely, considering."

"But a possibility, nevertheless," he said as she mounted the bicycle. "Now where are you going?"

"I'll drop these off with Phillip at the farm, if he's going to be there for a while. Mr McKenzie might return home at any time and he didn't take his supplies."

On her return to the store, Bonnie sensed an atmosphere. This was immediately confirmed by her aunt Hettie, as she abandoned her pastry-making to confront her.

"Clare's been on the telephone for almost an hour, ever since you left, Who is she calling? Has she no idea of the cost? I'm not made of money!"

"Connie, I would imagine. There's trouble brewing with my dad."

"He was a fool to have married that woman. I warned him what he was getting into, but he wouldn't listen. Said you needed a mother. I agreed with that in principle. But not her!"

"Yes, Auntie, you did say."

Hettie fussed with her pastry, rolling the same piece time and again in an agitated manner, straining to catch any of the hushed conversation from the hall. "If there is a problem, why is she here and not in town with her mother trying to patch things up?"

Ignoring the comment, Bonnie replaced Jack's wallet on the dresser. "Mr McKenzie wasn't at the farm. Apparently he hasn't been there all night."

"Clare's got a lot to answer for, behaving like that. He was probably hiding when he saw you cycle up."

"Andrew hadn't seen him either."

"Well, he can't have gone far, dear. Call by again this afternoon when the sun isn't quite as hot." Hettie opened the hall door a fraction wider, attempting to eavesdrop on the muted telephone conversation.

"I wish you wouldn't do that, Auntie," Bonnie protested, but Hettie ignored the comment.

"She can't be talking with Connie. If she were I'd hear every word and I can't hear a blessed thing! Mark my words, Bonnie. That girl's up to something or I know nothing about folk," she said, removing some brochures from the pocket of her apron which she offered to Bonnie. "Why else would she bother coming up here? And why bring these?"

Bonnie studied the brochures curiously. "I don't understand, Auntie. What are you doing with these? Details of terraced houses for sale in Edinburgh? Some of them look quite squalid."

"I came across them on her dressing table this morning… I needed to dust."

"Honestly, how could you?" Bonnie said. She folded up the papers and took them upstairs. A few moments later she returned empty-handed. "Prying into Clare's things like that."

"They were left out for anyone to see."

"In the spare room? You never go in there when anyone stays."

"I have to keep this place clean," she qualified guiltily. "What have you done with them?" she asked, just as the receiver clicked down in the hall.

Later that afternoon, once Bonnie had departed for Moorcroft Farm, Hettie had serious cause to reflect on the earlier conversation with her niece.

"Has anyone been asking for me?" Clare asked, fingering through a stack of knitting patterns on the shop counter.

"No, why? Were you expecting someone?" Hettie answered. She was referring to a list whilst packing a selection of groceries into a small box.

"Not particularly. I just wondered, that's all."

"I didn't think you knew anyone this far out of town, except us?"

"I don't, except for Andrew, and Bonnie's welcome to that cold fish," she answered, searching the shelves for alternative reading material. "Don't you have anything with fashionable clothes, instead of a pile of dull catalogues full of beastly underwear?"

"There's more demand for flannelette in these parts. If you want anything more stylish, there are some nice knitting patterns."

Quite deliberately, Clare placed the brochures she had been concealing in front of Hettie. "By the way, I brought these for you to look at. I misplaced them earlier, otherwise I would have given them to you sooner. I found them on the floor near my dressing table," she said, pushing them closer.

"Why bring these to me? Are you and Connie moving?"

"Not in the least. These are for you," Clare responded, setting out the property details with great care, seemingly unaware of Hettie's confusion at the direction the conversation was going. "You really ought to sell this place now you're getting on."

To cover her shock, Hettie pondered over a selection of cheeses in a cabinet before taking a piece of cheddar from under a muslin cloth. "Why on earth would you imagine that?" she asked.

"Well, since you ask, Mother and I were led to understand that you had sole ownership of this property, but that isn't the case at all, is it? Apart from which, it would certainly help ease some of the tension between Mother and Stepfather if you did."

"How in the world did you come by that information? My brother would never have discussed our joint interests with anyone other than Bonnie. I know him too well for that. It was never made common knowledge."

"Well, don't you think it should be? Mother has been tied to that man for eight years, making do on what little he earns from that pathetic job with the council."

"And what of the apartment he bought at Connie's insistence? Does that count for nothing?"

Clare propped four brochures next to the cheese slicer, preventing Hettie from cutting up the cheddar with the wire. "Not since he's been holding out about the investment in this place. You would do well to consider these properties, Hettie. With your share from this place, and the surrounding land, you would do very nicely from a quick sale."

"The property was left to us as security in old age, but on the understanding it would never be altered or sold."

"Was that ever put in writing?"

"There was no need. We gave our word."

"Well, values change, Hettie, and so must you. It's time to move on."

Hettie's eyes flashed angrily as she pushed past the younger woman. "I can't imagine why Connie put you up to this ridiculous proposition. Is this another scheme of hers to make money?"

"I haven't mentioned anything about this to Mother. Not yet anyway. I thought I'd wait until I got your reaction."

"Well, now you have. I would never consider selling my home. Or the Cap. Neither would my brother, and that's final."

*

That night Jack slept like the dead and dreamt of the Purple Cap rising out of the mist as he stood in a swirling carpet of fog that clung to his legs. As he entered the boathouse to untie a red boat from its mooring, he froze as he realised he was kneeling in a pool of blood. Inside the boat there were crimson handprints, and more blood had pooled in the bottom, but there was no trace of an injured person anywhere.

On his way to breakfast that morning he made a wrong turn and found himself wandering aimlessly through a labyrinth of pale corridors. Eventually he came to an area of bare granite, which he assumed had once been part of the exterior wall. At the end was a door that opened into a room filled with light.

He entered and discovered a beautiful winter garden with a staggering collection of exotic plants. Luxuriant, drooping palms grew on either side of four pathways intricately inlaid with Italian mosaic, as was the central dais which accommodated a concert grand piano, covered with a dust sheet.

Georgian arched windows along two sides of the garden gave a spectacular view of the Purple Cap and the bay beyond. Strategically positioned on the other walls were long gilded mirrors that reflected the beauty of the exotic plants. Above the piano, and suspended from a domed roof, was an exquisite chandelier that completed the picture of style and grandeur.

"What is this place?" he wondered, gazing at the reflection of the exotic interior in one of the long mirrors.

"Granny calls it our winter garden." Duncan's uncanny response broke into his thoughts as the boy, who seemed to have appeared from nowhere, caught hold of his hand. For a time they wandered through the tropical maze together. A mild charge of energy passed along Jack's arm and continued throughout his body. It gave him the feeling that he was undergoing some sort of transfusion. It was a strange idea, and yet he did feel quite different. More at peace with himself as the reassuring pressure of the boy's hand clung on to his own, they inspected every inch of that enchanted place before stopping at a marble fountain in a corner overlooking the Bay of Dungellen. He lifted the boy on to his shoulders for a clearer view above the palms.

"That's all ours," the boy announced with pleasure, pointing out to the bay. "Daddy sailed there a lot. He took me out with him once." He touched the swollen area around Jack's mouth. "Does it hurt much?"

"No, not much," he answered, surprised again that he spoke without a stammer, and that the injuries had eased enough for him to smile.

Still holding the boy aloft, he took stock of his own reflection in one of the mirrors. He was barely recognisable in the soft linen shirt and grey flannel trousers that had once belonged to Madeline's son. The swelling, not only about his mouth but also on his cheek and jaw, was noticeably reduced, as too were the scars on his eyebrow. Considering the short time since the incident, it was truly remarkable.

"You look nice like this," Duncan said into the reflection, before struggling to get down.

During that second, Jack gazed back into the fathomless wisdom of the boy's eyes, but was blinded by a beam of sunlight that reflected off the bay, leaving him unable to focus. When he could see again, Duncan had clambered on to the dais and now stood in front of the piano, plonking out an unrecognisable tune and grinning from ear to ear at the racket.

The piano was undeniably the focal point of the place, which made him wonder who had been the player? No sooner had the thought occurred to him, the hairs along his arms crawled as the boy spoke.

"Mummy... she liked this room best of all."

It was a great boost for Jack's confidence to find Duncan waiting for him outside his dressing room door before they went down for dinner and, without fail, Duncan would scrutinise the way he had dressed. On one occasion, he simply had to turn down a crumpled collar before retying the bow tie in the way his grandmother expected.

"When will you mend the broken latch on the dining room door so we can use it again?" he asked, pausing to stare at the loose cuffs of Jack's shirt, saying, "You can't go down like that."

"Hang on." Jack returned to the dressing room, where he opened a carved box on the chest by triggering a hidden catch, and removed a pair of monogrammed cufflinks. "How the hell could I have known how to do that?" he wondered, as Duncan fitted the links into the shirt cuffs.

"You know everything," the boy said, and took Jack's hand.

"Do I?"

"You don't understand. Not yet, but you will. That's why everything seems so odd," he said, laughing. "A bit like me I suppose."

"Not all the time. You're just strange now and again. That's all."

"It wasn't a prank when I asked you to repair the catch. It's very important. Mummy's waiting and I miss her."

He had no idea why the boy was so insistent but it was obviously causing him a great deal of distress. "I will see what I can do, very soon," he answered. He wondered why he could master a conversation with the boy and with no one else. "I must get him to let go of my hand when we reach the foot of the stairs," he thought, wondering if the experiment would work.

"Why do you want me to let go?"

"If you hold on too long, you'll get weak…" Jack thought, but didn't speak, continuing the experiment. "Because I don't want you to get ill again."

"I won't, I just need to hold on until we get there. We mustn't separate," Duncan said, and they walked clasping hands until they reached the double doors opening on to the great hall.

Every time he entered that awe-inspiring space he felt honoured to be allowed to spend time in a house steeped in so much family history. Momentarily, he was distracted by a slight movement in a darkened area of the minstrels' gallery, where he saw the slight figure of a young woman wearing a green dress, who seemed to be looking in his direction.

"My grandson informs me you have kindly agreed to repair the lock on the dining room door," Madeline said, as they sat down to eat. "It would be a blessing if you could. Mr Ross has such a task keeping this large hall warm enough to dine in during the long winter months. To have the use of the dining room for the evening meal would be ideal."

*

In the back parlour of the village store, Bonnie handed her aunt a cup of tea, successfully masking her own concern. "Would you like me to arrange an appointment with Mr McNair?"

"There's no need, honestly. I feel a fool now for mentioning this to you. Your father would never go back on his word about selling this place, even if Connie has eventually got to know."

"Did Clare mention how she found out?"

"Not a word. That's what I find so annoying. I did ask but she wouldn't say. It puzzles me how she came by the information. Only your father, myself and Angus McNair knew about the gift. There wasn't another soul involved."

"There is a new partner in the firm, Auntie."

"Mr Courtney wouldn't say anything, surely?"

"To be perfectly honest, I think he would. Judging from his cloak-and-dagger antics with Mr McKenzie, I wouldn't put anything past him."

"By law, he couldn't give out information like that."

"If it wasn't you or my dad, that only leaves Mr McNair, and I can't imagine he would breach client confidentiality. Mr Courtney on the other hand does have some peculiar ideas of what is ethical and what is not. Take the incident of the Jack McKenzie letter as a prime example."

"You told me about it, dear."

"I told you of my altercation with Mr Courtney. I was careful not to mention anything to you about the contents of the letter."

The evening began quietly enough, but with no enlightenment as to where Clare had got her information. Just as Bonnie and her aunt were waiting for her to join them at the table, there was an authoritative rap on the back door. Bonnie went to answer it and was confronted by the immaculately dressed Edmund Kincaid.

"Please forgive the inconvenience, Miss Jameson, in calling by at this late hour, but it occurred to me as I was nearby that I might entice you out for a spin on such a perfect evening?"

"Thank you for the considerate offer, Mr Kincaid, but I cannot accept. My aunt has dinner prepared, and we are about to sit down." She was interrupted by Clare's unexpected and immaculate presence as she joined them in a cloud of perfume.

"Why ever are you dressed up like that?" Bonnie asked, staring at her.

"Do I need a reason? It's what is expected in the city at the weekend, or have you been away so long you've forgotten?" She responded without taking her eyes off Edmund.

"And what about your companion? Is she unavailable too?" he asked.

"I can't speak for anyone else, Mr Kincaid. However, I must stress that we are about to sit down and eat."

"If you wait just a moment, I'll get my coat," Clare said, unhooking a small jacket from the hall stand.

"But Clare… Auntie has gone to a lot of trouble preparing our dinner."

"I did say earlier, I wasn't hungry. Her cooking is much too bland for my palate."

"Well, at least tell her you're not staying."

"She's barely speaking to me as it is. It's better if I go out this evening with Mr Kincaid. You can smooth things over before I get back. You do it so much better."

As the big car pulled away from the store, Clare opened her purse and removed a small box.

"Edmund, is there any need to continue with this secrecy?" she asked, slipping a sparkling ring on to her finger, examining the brilliance of the stone in the fading light.

"It's more diplomatic to keep it this way for the time being. We did agree it would be more sensible if we did that. You know how people find fault with everything. Some might consider our chance meeting more than just a coincidence."

"Darling, how could they? It was fate that you called at Mother's apartment by mistake. If I had returned home after you had arrived, instead of a few moments before, we would never have met."

Edmund rested his hand lightly on hers. "We both know it was destined to happen, but who else other than you and I would believe in the coincidence, or that we were unaware at the time of the other connection."

"Or that we were so perfectly matched?" she said, snuggling against him, still examining the ring. "I can hardly believe we met only three weeks ago? Oh, darling… I'm dying to tell them. What harm could it do? They're almost family."

There was a distinct change to his mood as he ground the engine into a lower gear on the approach to a sharp bend. "Trust me, Clare, this is all for the best. They will find out soon enough, and from what you tell me, Connie may not be related for much longer, which would also divorce your own association with them."

"What if Bonnie had agreed to your suggestion? Would you have taken her instead?"

"There would have been no choice. You should have opened the door as we planned."

Instead of responding, she examined the glittering gem in the street lights as they drove into Lochenbrae. "It looks frightfully expensive, Edmund."

"You're worth it, darling."

"I must get it insured, the moment we get back to Edinburgh."

"No… you mustn't do that," he said nervously. "I'd feel it would somehow detract from our commitment."

"But what if I were to lose it?"

"Then I shall buy you another," he answered amiably, as he pulled up in the car park of the Alhambra Hotel. "Incidentally, were you able to speak with the aunt?"

"With difficulty. She was very frosty, and barely glanced at the brochures."

"There was no headway then? You will try again as soon as you can? Make her see reason before you return home?"

"I will try, but she can be so obstinate. Sometimes I'm convinced the old biddy doesn't care for me at all. Everything she does is centred around her niece."

"Then you must try harder. Remember, darling, our future prospects depend on the outcome."

Clare took his arm as they went into the hotel. "Why is this so very important, Edmund? You never did say."

"My parents are expecting to move into a property near Hettie's store which once belonged to that same estate. Until that and the surrounding land is secured, they won't move out of my apartment which, although spacious, isn't large enough to accommodate the four of us. Now you understand, darling, how imperative it is we make the purchase," he reassured her, escorting her into the restaurant.

It was later that evening, when Edmund had returned from making a telephone call in the foyer, that the atmosphere became noticeably brittle. The duty manager of the Alhambra Hotel wore an ill-fitting uniform and frequently attempted to ease the restricting starched collar away from his reddening neck. He nervously approached an angry Edmund Kincaid.

"I do apologise for the inconvenience, Mr Kincaid. The internal phone has been checked, as you requested. Unfortunately, the line has been engaged."

"For the past hour?" he retorted. "That's highly unlikely."

"I can assure you, sir, that is the current situation," he said, offering Edmund a message pad and pencil. "If you would allow me to suggest. I propose that if you indicate on the pad that you need to use the telephone, the concierge could take it up to your parents' suite and slip the note under the door."

"That won't be necessary," he said, standing abruptly. "It's rather late and I have a guest who needs to return home."

"I didn't know your parents were staying here," Clare interrupted, expressing her surprise.

"What if they are?" he responded, glowering at the manager.

"Perhaps this would be the perfect opportunity for an introduction to my future in-laws?" she said, flashing the glittering diamond on her finger. "I don't need to get back so soon, Edmund, honestly."

"Some other time... I'll call them on the way back."

"Why not ring them from Hettie's?" she asked brightly.

"Darling, that wouldn't be practical, would it? And I strongly advise that you remove the ring before we set off."

"Just let me wear it a while longer, darling. I'll take it off as soon as we enter the village."

The narrow streets were pitch black as they drove through Dungellen. The arcing beam of the headlights scanned the cluster of cottages like a searchlight.

"Any ideas where the call box might be?" Edmund asked, peering through an open window towards the cricket pavilion.

"It's further on, I think," Clare answered, buttoning up her neat but quite impractical jacket against the night air.

"How much further exactly?" he asked, checking his watch as they passed beyond the last cottage. "If I don't place this call soon, we'll be at the store, and then what?"

"There! There it is!" she cried out, as they drew level with a telephone box. With a squeal of brakes, Edmund turned off the road and parked close to the gated entrance to Dungellen Hall. Unprepared for the jolt of stopping, Clare instinctively grabbed the dashboard, narrowly avoiding banging her head against the windscreen.

"Sorry, darling," Edmund said. "Are you hurt?"

"No... I wasn't prepared for you to react so fast. I didn't expect you to stop without any warning." He got out of the car hurriedly, giving her a reassuring smile as he entered the dimly lit kiosk.

Her imagination ran riot as she stared into the darkness. Twisting the ring absent-mindedly she wondered why he had baulked at telephoning from the store, which was no more than a mile ahead. Unless, of course, he had reason not to be overheard. Thinking this must be the case, she watched him as he gestured in her direction through the condensation on the windscreen. He was agitated and scowling, until he saw her and turned away abruptly.

A broken nail had snagged on her bolero jacket and she began to search vainly through her purse for a nail file. In desperation, she clicked on a map light, thinking she might find what she needed in the stuffed-full glove compartment, which sprang open as soon as she released the catch. She stared at the package that fell on to her lap as, with mounting curiosity, the damaged nail forgotten, she undid the neat ties, glancing nervously towards Edmund's back inside the booth as she unfolded an intricate plan of the village and surrounding area.

Outlined in red was a vast tract of land encompassing the entire bay, Dungellen Hall and its extensive grounds. The Purple Cap was also included, along with Hettie's store, ending at the furthermost boundary of Moorcroft Farm, which skirted Andrew Sinclair's property on the peninsula. It was marked 'Pending negotiation at a later date'.

Outlined in detail on an accompanying drawing was the staggering concept of an ambitious holiday camp, where a vast activity centre with multiple dining facilities supplanted Dungellen Hall, and row upon row of identical chalets and three enormous swimming pools had replaced the extensive gardens. Moorcroft Farm had fared no better, having been replaced by the construction of a brash and ugly entertainment hall, roller-skating rink and amusement arcade. Where Hettie's store now stood was a shopping arcade and cinema constructed of sections of new-age sectional concrete, moulded in the shape of rough-cut planks.

Given her limited sensitivity, this proposal to create such an ugly blot in that remote part of the Highlands seemed more ludicrous than offensive. She considered the continental shrubs which thrived in Dungellen because of the Atlantic Drift, and how warm the sea had been when she swam there as a child. It was an area that at one time had been likened to the French Riviera. The coastline a few miles on either side was less sheltered.

She looked up with a start as the door was yanked open and she clutched the drawings against herself protectively.

"What the hell are you doing... rifling through my papers?" Edmund shouted, wrenching her bodily out of the car. She was too shocked to protest as the neat stitching of her jacket tore open and the sleeve came away in his hand while she clung on to the plans for grim death.

"I wasn't prying, Edmund, honestly," she shrieked as he struck her hard across the face.

"Let go, damn it! Give me those plans, you cow. I'll not ask you again. Hand them over," he snarled, before he hit her again. The ring twisted as she slammed hard against the car, the misshapen shank gouging a deep groove in the layers of immaculate paintwork, but still she refused to release the papers.

"Don't you dare touch me again... you... you rotten bastard!" she screamed, struggling to get free and stumbling against the car as he bunched up his fist.

"Then hand them over... and do it now," he shouted menacingly.

With the accuracy of a scrum half, Clare jerked her knee viciously into the soft and unprotected area of Edmund's groin, which felled him at once. Groaning in agony against the car, he was still able to pin her beneath him before she could move away.

"You bitch!" he gasped, salivating on her face as he attempted to re-bunch his fist in preparation to thump her. "I'll make you regret that."

In sheer terror, Clare bit deep into his earlobe, then, with the same instinctive accuracy, jerked her knee savagely into his crotch yet again, struggling free and disappearing into the inky blackness as Edmund sank in agony to the ground.

His mouth was wide open and gasping for air like a landed trout. His eyes screwed into slits in excruciating pain as he attempted to stem the flow of blood gushing from his ear with one hand and clutch his genitals in desperation with the other as he curled into the foetal position, alternating his agonised groans with threats of slow mutilation when he found her.

After some time, when he had partially recovered, he staggered to his feet, grasping hold of the car for support, and reached inside for a torch. He shone the beam in every direction in the hope of locating the missing drawings but, like Clare, they were long gone.

"Darling, come back!" he called desperately. "I didn't mean to hurt you, I swear. I love you. Please forgive me. I don't know what came over me… it was pure madness," he yelled, swinging the beam of light in every direction until the battery began to fail and the light dimmed.

Bonnie had been lying awake for two hours when she heard the car draw up outside the store. She rose and slipped on her dressing gown.

"Go back to bed, dear," Hettie called from the bottom of the stairs, her greying hair curled up with strips of rag. "It's time to nip this in the bud. What will the locals think? Staying out until this hour, for goodness' sake… it's way past midnight."

"I'll make a hot drink," Bonnie said, going into the kitchen as her aunt opened the front door.

"Oh, it's you! And you're alone. Where is Clare, Mr Kincaid?" Hettie asked, suppressing her alarm as she peered into the gloom.

"Clare insisted on coming on ahead. I only called by to see if she got back safely," Edmund blustered, seemingly at a loss for words.

"On her own, at this time of night? How? You didn't allow her to walk home in the dark? The girl isn't used to it up here. It isn't the same as in a city. There are no street lights," Hettie said. "You'd better come inside and tell me exactly what happened."

"We… There was a minor misunderstanding," he answered, entering the kitchen, registering Bonnie at the cooker.

"A misunderstanding; what do you mean 'a misunderstanding'? Where… in town?" Bonnie asked.

"Not far from here actually. Near a telephone box outside the village."

"You allowed her to go off on her own? At night! What were you thinking? That's a mile away. She couldn't walk a quarter of that distance in those shoes," she answered, removing the kettle from the hob.

"I couldn't stop her. She was quite determined."

"She could easily have lost her way. If there was any trace of moonlight she would stand a chance of finding her way back, but not on a night like this! I would find it hard myself and I've lived here most of my life," Bonnie exclaimed.

"I tried to stop her. You must believe me. I've searched everywhere for over an hour and can find no trace of her anywhere," Edmund said as he grasped the back of a chair for support. "Would you mind if I sat down? I took a bad tumble in the dark," he said, exposing a bloodied hand. "It's black as pitch out there."

"You can't simply abandon her, Mr Kincaid," Bonnie said furiously. "You must come with me and search again. Clare will be terrified. She hates the dark."

"I can't. Not until I've rested. It's exhausting stumbling around with no clue where you are."

"So imagine how Clare feels. Well, I'm certainly going. Which direction was she headed in?" she demanded. "I need a starting point."

"She ran off towards the Cap. I couldn't see a thing. Not even with a powerful torch."

"You mustn't go up there, Bonnie. It can be treacherous during the day. At night, it would be suicidal," Hettie said, catching hold of her arm urgently. "Stay here, please," she urged as Bonnie abandoned the boiling kettle.

"I can't just sit around as though nothing's happened."

"What are you doing?" Edmund asked with alarm as Bonnie picked up the telephone.

"I'm calling the police station. Sam Perkins needs to know about this."

"You won't get through, dear," Hettie said, replacing the receiver into the cradle. "Mrs Harris doesn't open the switchboard until seven. You can call through then, if she isn't back."

"I must do something, Auntie," she said, looking suspiciously at Edmund. "What happened to your ear?"

"I… I snagged it on some brambles in the dark… searching for her."

"You should have it seen to. It could turn septic," Hettie said, busying herself with a bowl and a packet of salt from the kitchen cabinet. "I'll put some of this in hot water you can bathe it with cotton wool. That should stop any infection. If Clare's wise, she'll wait until it's light before making her way back. We can't do anything until then. Bonnie dear? Now, where are you going?" she asked as the girl hurried past.

"Upstairs… I need to get dressed."

The door had barely closed when Hettie concentrated her attention on Edmund. "Perhaps you would tell me exactly what's been going on now that my niece is upstairs? And don't avoid the issue by saying it was nothing more than a misunderstanding. Clare is not the type to walk away from any argument. Quite the opposite actually, and particularly as she has a phobia of the dark."

Edmund clutched his genitals with both hands and crossed his legs, leaning himself forward. "Could I trouble you for a glass of water, Mrs Jameson?"

The measured tick of the wall clock seemed excessively loud in the silence. It continued until she handed him the glass. "Well, Mr Kincaid?"

"I left her in the car when I stopped to make a telephone call. When I got back, she was going through some private papers." He was thinking fast, and took his time drinking the water.

"And this... misunderstanding? How did that come about?"

"There is more to this than I've let on, Mrs Jameson," he said intently, taking control of the conversation. "And whatever I impart this evening must be kept secret at all costs."

"Go on."

"I have recently acquired some devastating information in the form of a proposal for a radical change to this area. Therefore I entreat you to reconsider my offer to purchase the Cap." He sat back in an attempt to alleviate the pain in his groin, with a dribble of water running down his neck and into his collar as he attempted to appease the old woman by swabbing the damaged earlobe.

"You are very insistent about this, Mr Kincaid. You already have my answer on the subject, so why continue. Why is the Cap so important to you? Indeed to anyone? But, more importantly, how would that affect Clare?"

"She ran off with the proposal, which cannot be seen at this stage. Not by anyone."

"And what is your part in all this?"

"I am to inherit the neighbouring estate with my parents, who are strongly advocating change to the area… whereas I am not. Therefore, Mrs Jameson, if I were to re-purchase the land, in my name, I would be the majority shareholder, and nothing could go ahead without my full approval. Which, I can readily assure you, would never happen."

The conversation ended abruptly as Bonnie appeared, fitting new batteries into a clip-on lamp. "I've put money in the till for these, Auntie." She stared at Edmund's cleaned earlobe. "Are those teeth marks?" she asked accusingly, scrutinising his ear before he covered it over as she passed. "They look very much like it to me."

"Where are you going, dear?" Hettie asked, with mounting concern.

"Into the village, to see Constable Perkins."

"You must allow me to take you," Edmund offered. He stood up too quickly and doubled over in pain.

"Do sit down, Mr Kincaid… you're in no condition to drive anyone," Hettie said, filling a glass with water and offering him two aspirins.

*

Dawn was barely breaking when Phillip Ramsey peered groggily out of the tent at the sound of pounding fists on the farmhouse door. He wondered if his eyes were deceiving him when he saw the sobbing and dishevelled figure of a young woman pleading for it to be opened. In a moment, torch in hand, he was out of the tent, the laces loose on his plimsolls and pulling on a sweater as he ran to the distraught woman. When he touched her lightly on the shoulder she broke into a series of ear-splitting screams. Her appearance was wild and manic as she faced him, exposing a blackened eye and a bruised cheek, the twigs and bracken caught in her hair giving her a savage, demented appearance which caused him to wonder if she had escaped from a local asylum.

"Please... there is no need to be frightened," he said, pointing to the tent. "You woke me. I'm camping here."

"Why won't they let me in?" she cried, hammering on the door. "I want to go home."

"There's no one here, only me," he said, uncertain how to deal with the situation. "I could make you some tea?"

"Tea! After what I've been through? How can you be so bloody stupid? I need a stiff drink. More than one, if you've a bottle. Not tea, for God's sake," she screeched as she began thumping on the farmhouse door again. "Why will no one come out?"

"No one's inside," he answered patiently, and gave up trying to lead her away, which in truth was like wrestling a wild boar. She was a pitiable sight. Both hands and arms were scratched or bleeding. Her clothes were filthy and her stockings torn and drooping about her ankles on shoes that had lost their heels. Stuffed into the waistband of her dress was a wodge of grubby, folded papers.

He felt helpless being in such an unpredictable situation. "There is nothing to fear. Not from me. I want to help you, that's all."

Clare seemed to be reassured by his sincerity and tugged the papers free of her waistband. "Then take these, and swear you will keep them safe," she said, thrusting Edmund's drawings into his hand, collapsing just as he reached out to catch her.

Her eyelids flickered open and she stared at him blankly "Where are you from?" he asked. "Please... you must tell me your name and what you can remember about what happened last night."

"Take me home," she demanded hysterically, gripping his hand with fingers of iron. "And hide these plans away where he can't ever find them." she sobbed, throwing her arms about him.

For a moment he deliberated the best course of action, supporting her weight as well as he could until they reached Jack's combination, where he lifted her bodily into the sidecar. After retrieving the ignition keys from the kitchen table, he fired up the engine and revved the machine hard up the steep drive.

As Andrew had intimated on the previous day, his house was only a short distance away and, at six thirty in the morning, Phillip could only hope the doctor was awake.

Unlike the approach to Moorcroft Farm, the curving drive had been well maintained, while on either side were wide terraced lawns and rockeries, well stocked with a multitude of tropical plants. The glistening expanse of water beyond gave one the impression of approaching a villa on one of the great Italian lakes.

The house was large, with a green tiled roof. It stood higher than Moorcroft Farm which gave the owner an unbroken view over the bay. Getting no response to his insistent knocking, Phillip ventured down to the beach where he found Andrew Sinclair and explained the predicament as best as he could.

"And you've no idea who she is?" he asked, stooping to grab a towel and wrapping it about his waist before going up the steps into the gardens. "How bad is she?"

"A hysterical mess. She has a nasty black eye and some cuts and bruises on her face. From what she said, I gather she's been out all night."

"What is it with Moorcroft Farm and these goings-on?" he asked, shaking his head. "Nothing out of the ordinary has happened here in years, and now this. One smashed-up person gone missing and another smashed-up person wandering all night on the Cap? How did you find her?"

"She was hammering on the farmhouse door less than half an hour ago," Phillip said. "I thought it best if I brought her over directly."

"Good man. And what about this fellow McKenzie, was he involved in this?"

"Not that I'm aware of. There hasn't been a sign of him or his dog since the storm."

"You saw that? And the bird?"

"I saw that too."

"This is all very odd. And the woman… she said nothing about what happened?"

"Not a word. She tended to scream mostly, to be perfectly honest."

"And have you reported this to the police?"

"I've no idea where to find them," he said, as Andrew grabbed his shirt off a garden seat and tugged it over his head, staring towards the cliffs off the Cap.

"This woman can have no idea how lucky she is to be alive. Anyone could have tumbled over that cliff in the dark, and she wouldn't be the first." Andrew said, as they neared the house. "What the hell was she thinking, wandering out there at night? Was she hiking?"

"I wouldn't have thought so. She appeared to have been quite well dressed, or would have been last night. The truth is, she did look familiar, but I can't remember from where exactly."

"You remembered me easily enough," he said wryly.

"Only because you were so bloody rude."

Andrew ground his teeth with irritation at Phillip's response. "And where is she now?" he asked, letting the comment go as he missed his footing and stubbed his bare toe on the upper step.

"In the sidecar. We're parked out front," he answered.

"Then go ahead and get her inside. I need to put some iodine on this split toe," he said, hobbling over the gravel. "The front door's open. Take her into the first room on the left. I'll meet you there."

"My God, it's Clare!" Andrew exclaimed as he padded into the room in his bare feet. "What the hell were you doing out there on the Cap at night?"

Backing away nervously, Clare caught hold of Phillip's sweater and stepped behind him, whimpering. "Why was he so beastly?"

"I think she's intimidated by you," Phillip said.

"Don't talk rot. I've known her for years. Who are you talking about, Clare?" he asked, as he opened a medicine chest and removed a syringe. "I don't want to take any chances, so I need to give you an injection. This won't hurt, I promise."

"He called me a cow!" she announced wildly. "Why would he do that? He was in love with me."

"People say things they don't mean when they're angry," Phillip answered, removing the shredded jacket to expose her arm for the injection.

"There, that should do the trick," Andrew said. He applied a plaster and examined her hand. "Your hand's swollen. What have you done to your finger?"

"Oh no! It's been squashed!" she cried frantically, screwing at her finger to release the ring.

"Here, let me take a look," Andrew said, examining the band carefully. "This is bad: it's been restricting the flow of blood."

"Can't you cut it off?" Phillip asked as Andrew walked away.

"My finger?" she screeched. "You want him to chop off my bloody finger. Just like that?"

"I meant the ring!" he responded, trying not to laugh. He took a firm hold of her wrist as she squirmed, protesting loudly when Andrew appeared with a pair of small cutters.

"You can't damage this, I won't let you. It's an engagement ring and worth a small fortune."

"Would you prefer to lose this finger? Or even a hand? Either is possible if I don't remove this piece of worthless junk," Andrew said coolly, with just the faintest hint of a smile at Phillip.

"Junk! It's the real thing, you bloody moron!" she shrieked.

"Look… there are scratches all over it. Now let me cut through this band before the finger goes septic," he growled back and he cut through the metal with a steady hand, and gave her the twisted shank when he was finished.

"You think this isn't gold?" she asked. There was a low rage in her voice.

"It's worthless. You wouldn't get threepence for the scrap value. Take it to a jeweller if you think I'm wrong. Whoever the blighter was who gave you this has taken you for a prize chump."

Clare lurched to her feet unsteadily, her face bleached white with anger. "And the diamond, what's that… glass?"

"Or something very similar. Where are you going?" he asked, as she tottered unsteadily towards the door. "You must rest. The sedative I gave you will begin working very soon. After that I'll run you home."

"I can't go anywhere just yet. I need the loo," she answered tearfully, allowing Andrew to guide her towards the bathroom.

When he returned alone moments later, he sat in the chair opposite the younger man.

"It's a nice place you've got," Phillip began. "Do you live here alone?"

"Most of the time... Why do you ask?"

"On the way in, I was impressed with the grounds and how nicely they are kept. In fact, I noticed quite a few plants I've only come across in the south of England."

"Do you know much about gardening?"

"Not as much as I'd like to. I tried for a place at an agricultural college a while back, which came to nothing because I couldn't get a grant. That's another reason for coming this far north. I thought there would be more opportunities for securing some interesting work."

"I'm not sure I understand. I thought you said yesterday you came from these parts?"

"Years ago, but I can't remember whereabouts. When Dad died I was taken into care at an orphanage in Kenmere until my mother remarried. All the better memories I have from these parts are a bit of a jumble before that."

"If you were at Kenmere for any length of time I can understand why."

"Did you know it?"

"Only by reputation, and that wasn't good. So where did you grow up? In the south?"

"In Dorset, but I never settled. Not properly anyway," Phillip answered, gazing out of the window at the rugged landscape. "It was nice enough, but too soft and placid for my taste. Not wild and exciting the way it is up here. Like that freak storm when I arrived."

"Any more thoughts on the house with the tall chimneys?"

"How did you know about that?"

"Bonnie mentioned it the last time we spoke."

"Did she? Well, since you ask, nothing yet, but it's early days, so I'm not giving up."

"I've got an Ordnance Survey map knocking around the place somewhere. If you're still around when I come across it, I'll drop it by the farm." Andrew was sifting through his mail. "I'll make some breakfast before I take Clare back. Don't feel obliged to hang around if you have something else to do."

"Actually, I'm enjoying the luxury of a chair after roughing it for a couple of weeks on the road. I didn't realise how much, until now." He relaxed back into the armchair and stared at a painting above Andrew's head. "That's nice," he said, squinting to see it better. "Did you paint that? It's very well done."

"Unfortunately not. I can't paint a thing, though I've tried often enough. That's a favourite of mine. It was done by a friend up from Harrogate. The only thing missing is the boat, and Steve wouldn't have known about that."

"The boat? Where is this place? It captures the tranquillity of a boathouse perfectly."

"It's not far from here, on the far side of the Cap actually."

Phillip looked about him thoughtfully. "I don't suppose you could suggest anywhere locally where I might rent a place for a couple of months while I go job hunting? This chair's got me yearning for a drastic change of lifestyle." He laughed. "The thought of spending another night in that tent gives me the creeps."

Andrew put aside the mail abruptly. "Where has she got to? Surely she can't still be in there. I'd better go and see."

"I should give her a bit longer. She's probably trying to make herself more presentable."

"OK, I'll give her another five minutes." He drummed his fingers lightly on the arm of the chair during the brief silence that ensued. "I've a place at the back which might have been suitable for you. Unfortunately, it's full of easels and stuff and I've nowhere else to put them," he said with a shrug, then got to his feet. "Clare's been too long in there. I really must take a look."

He had been gone for less than a minute when he called for Phillip to help in the bathroom where Clare was lying face down on the floor, her clothes covered in vomit.

"Let's get her out of these clothes and wash her down," Andrew said, supporting her weight as he turned her over. "Are you OK with that?"

"Just tell me what to do," Phillip responded, unbuttoning her blouse even as she vomited over him. "Don't bother about me. She's the one who needs help. I'll get cleaned up afterwards," he said rather weakly.

They stripped the girl of her stinking clothing, filled up the bath with warm water and gently lifted her into the bath where Andrew sponged her down. When he had finished, they wrapped her in a towelling dressing gown.

"Thanks. I can get her from here into the bedroom," Andrew said, lifting her up bodily as though she was no weight at all. "You'd better get cleaned up yourself. I'll dig out some clothes which might fit," and he carried Clare through to a bedroom.

"We're hardly the same size," Phillip called after him, smiling wryly.

"Not mine, some that belonged to my artist friend. He was about your build."

"Won't he be needing them?" Phillip emptied the bath and set about cleaning himself up.

"Not for some time."

When Andrew reappeared with a pair of corduroy trousers and a shirt, the bathroom was sparkling and smelling of disinfectant. "Sorry I've taken so long to get these, but I needed to sit with her until she settled and then I couldn't find where Steve had packed his clothes."

"That's all right. I kept busy anyway."

"What on earth have you been up to in here?"

"She'd been sick everywhere. The place stank and needed a good clean."

"Well thanks, but you needn't have tackled this on your own. I've been thinking. If you don't mind roughing it for a while, I could make up a bed in the studio for a couple of weeks or until you get settled. It's clean enough and dry and has a separate toilet. You can use the bathroom in here and of course have full use of the kitchen. I'm out most of the day anyway."

"Thanks. I'd like that a lot."

*

"Sit with me up front" Andrew said, as Bonnie helped get Clare into the back of his car. "It's a long drive to Edinburgh. If you stay in the back you won't be any use. She'll sleep most of the way," he said, starting the engine. "Did Connie report the incident to the police?"

"No. Not when she knew Clare was safe. All she wanted to do was berate my dad. He filed for divorce at the weekend."

"And not before time after what you told me. It can't be that much of a shock to her. I've seen it coming a mile off. What baffles me, though, is how she continues to put herself before anyone else at a time like this," he said, as he took a sharp turn onto the Lochenbrae road.

"I called them anyway," she answered quietly, as the sleeping passenger shifted her position. "Edmund won't get away with abandoning her like that. Anything could have happened to her."

"Better not say any more in case she wakes. She doesn't need to relive the ordeal," he said as they continued south on the road towards Lochenbrae in comparative silence.

"Andy... what about Jack McKenzie? Shouldn't I report to Constable Perkins that he's gone missing? I really am worried about him, but Auntie says I should wait."

"So do I. Give him a few days longer before alerting Sam. If this McKenzie fellow is with that white dog he won't come to much harm. It would be embarrassing if you reported a missing person and he returned to the farm having been away visiting, or exploring the area."

"I hope when he does return that he stays there. It would be nice to see it occupied again."

He readjusted his rear-view mirror to deflect the strong rays of the sun and noted the car that had been tailing them for some time, before he spoke. "I hadn't been down to the old farm in years until this morning. I'd forgotten what fine buildings they are. In fact a group of people have shown an interest in that site recently."

"Auntie said nothing about any strangers being up here."

"She wouldn't have seen them and neither would I if I hadn't been swimming. They arrived by boat, and looked like they had surveying equipment with them," he answered, checking his rear-view mirror again.

"You must be mistaken. Jack McKenzie is the last person who would bother with any survey."

"You seem very sure about this."

"I am. Lorna McNair said she had never seen anyone so altered by having somewhere of his own to live. Moorcroft Farm was his home. Do you know anyone who would bother having a survey done 'after' they've moved in, because I don't?"

"Well, I was swimming, so it was hard to see accurately." He accelerated as he rounded a bend and turned off along a narrow side road.

"Andy! Where are we going? And so fast!" she said, struggling to steady Clare and prevent her from toppling on to her side.

"Just leave her where she is and let her sleep. She won't wake again until we're close to Edinburgh," he answered, adjusting the rear-view mirror again.

"Why did you turn off the road like that? And why keep looking in the mirror? You've been doing it for miles. What's going on?"

"I'm positive we've been followed for most of the way," he said, as the Sunbeam Talbot sped past on the main road. "I wanted to see who it was." Andrew stopped and switched off the engine.

"It must be Edmund Kincaid. I recognise the car."

"Then why's he been following us?" he asked as Edmund's car pulled over and stopped, a good half mile ahead.

"He's more likely to be going home to his apartment in Edinburgh."

For some time Andrew watched the Sunbeam Talbot, which made no attempt to restart. "You never mentioned Clare was engaged."

Bonnie stared at him in amazement. "You can't be serious. Do you imagine she could be at my aunt's for more than ten minutes without announcing the fact if that was the case?"

"Nevertheless, she insisted she was when I needed to cut off the ring. I got the impression it was this Kincaid fellow she went out with that evening."

"Edmund!" she responded, as the man in question got out of his car and assisted a woman from the passenger seat, both of them shielding their eyes from the glare as they looked back along the road. "That's impossible. They'd never even met before that evening."

The pair got back in the car. Andrew turned on the ignition and reversed the MG further along the track until it was well concealed behind the hedge. Shortly afterwards, the Sunbeam stopped opposite the turning then drove on.

"Does Kincaid have Clare's address?" Andrew asked. "I'm not sure if we should take her back after that."

"How could he know?" she asked as he pulled on to the road, accelerating towards Edinburgh.

*

The following morning, Bonnie arrived at Moorcroft Farm to discover Phillip Ramsey dismantling the tent and making good the campsite.

"You're leaving, and so soon?" she said regretfully.

"I'm not going far. Your doctor friend offered me the use of his studio for a few weeks until I find a place of my own."

"You plan on staying up here indefinitely?"

"I'd like to, if I can get a job to tide me over. Failing that, I'll go back where I came from."

She helped him roll up the tent and pack up his few belongings. "No news on Mr McKenzie then?"

"Not a sign of him yet. When he comes back I must thank him for allowing me to camp here."

"It's most fortunate that you did. I'm very grateful for everything you did for Clare."

"Anyone would have done the same," he answered awkwardly. "How was she when you took her back?"

"Glad to be back home, I think. She always thought of Dungellen as being one of the wildest places on earth," she answered with a laugh.

"And you?"

"I love every inch of this area. I can't imagine living anywhere else."

"It's the devil of a place to find. If I hadn't known where to turn off the road, I swear I would never have found it." Phillip was about to tie his tent on to his bike when he went to his rucksack and removed a set of plans.

"I clean forgot about these papers she gave me. Ought I to post them on?"

"It depends how important they are, I suppose," Bonnie answered, taking the plans from him. "She needs complete rest for the next few days, so I shan't bother her with these until I go over next week. Where did she get them anyway? All she had with her that night was a purse."

"Wherever she got them, they must be very important because she was holding on to them like grim death when I found her. Keeping them safe was all she cared about," he said, as Bonnie started to unfold them on the ground.

"Oh my God... these must be the papers she ran off with. This is why Edmund was so anxious to get them back."

Thrusting the tumbling red hair away from her eyes she systematically examined every detail of the proposal, intermittently exclaiming her outrage and disbelief at the proposed annihilation of Dungellen.

Chapter Six

Every day spent working at Dungellen Hall seemed like a holiday to Jack. It was a perfect time to be outdoors and he embraced each new morning with fond thoughts of Eleanor McKenzie, who had been so instrumental in bringing such a change to his life.

He had been making some minor repairs to the lead guttering at the end of the house, and needed to enter a rear door for access to another part of the roof. He became aware of the hushed voices of a man and woman engaged in a light-hearted conversation in the winter garden. He had every intention of continuing with his work until he heard a hauntingly beautiful melody being played on the concert grand. It was a hypnotic sound that transfixed him and left him wanting to hear more. Although his knowledge of music was limited, he could tell that the player was an excellent pianist. Drawn by the magical notes he approached the entrance cautiously. When he could see a reflection of the interior in one of the long mirrors, he paused, not wanting to interrupt the pianist, who continued playing softly.

When he stepped into the garden, the sun illuminating the dais briefly dazzled him but in the reflection of the long mirror he could see a dark-haired young woman in a green dress seated at the piano. He felt certain too that there was a young man leaning on the instrument opposite the woman, but when his vision cleared the images vaporised into the lush foliage surrounding the grand. He felt a little alarmed as, although he was no longer able to see the pianist in the reflection, the keys still appeared to be moving. Was it his imagination or a trick of the light? But he was convinced of one thing. The music had been real. He glanced upwards as the shadow of a large bird flew overhead, and he saw the osprey swoop low towards him before it swept high above the Cap and out of sight.

As the week passed, he gradually began to accept the odd happenings as everyday occurrences in Dungellen and, by the following week, he had ceased to question anything. He had also given up all thoughts of venturing as far as the store in search of the red-headed girl. It could wait until his employment had ended. But inevitably something always happened to prevent him from leaving.

During that second week he spent two full days making good the barn roof, and another finishing the repairs he had started on the dovecote, which Madeline really appreciated. His skill in blending the comparatively new lengths of wood with the old was greatly admired by Ralph and the boy.

There were times when it was difficult to avoid calling Ralph 'Foxy', with Duncan referring to him in that way so often. Jack found he needed to stop himself on more than one occasion, which Ralph took in good part, seeming almost pleased at his mistake. Before long, the two men were working together in perfect harmony, during which time the bond between Jack and the boy had made them almost inseparable. Yet he could never shake off the feeling it was the boy who was in control.

"I didn't know you were married, Ralph," Jack said, noticing the wedding band on his finger as Ralph lifted the boy from his shoulders.

"I was until three years ago," he answered, dangling the squalling boy above a steaming compost heap before he deposited him on a wooden shelf inside the potting shed. "Now then, my little turnip head, let's get these geraniums re-potted."

The boy beamed and set out a row of terracotta pots, putting a handful of stones in each. "What's next, Foxy?" he asked, as Ralph removed a tray of sturdy plants from a cold frame.

"When Jack's made up the mix, you can trowel some of that into each pot. By then I'll have these little beauties ready for you."

"You want me to plant them?"

Ralph laughed, his eyes twinkling. "Well, yes. Unless you want them for lunch," he said, pricking out the seedlings. He paused when he noticed Jack observing them closely.

"You've got a nice way him, Foxy. If I'm ever lucky enough to have children, I hope I can be the same with them."

"It comes with practice," he answered, showing the boy how to set the first young plant. "My wife died having our little girl. She's a bright little thing for a three-year-old and she needs lots of attention… which I can't give her and that's a dilemma."

"Who looks after her while you're here?"

"My sister. She's got a place in the village and takes good care of the wee lass, but the strain is showing, combined with taking over a small business. I can't expect things to continue for much longer. It would be unfair of me to expect any more. The child needs a mother."

The graceful shape of the osprey cast a shadow over Ralph as it swooped low and settled on the ridge of the walled garden, from where it peered down on their industry.

Jack knew he had pried enough into another man's life by the ensuing silence and Ralph's furrowed brow. Occasionally, when he glanced in the other man's direction, he would find him staring back, not angrily as he might have expected, but curiously, with no trace of resentment.

During that week, Ralph re-introduced him to the game of chess in the potting shed whenever they took a break. To begin with Jack found it difficult, never having played since his father died, but Duncan, who was inevitably nearby, would offer advice whether he wanted it or not and which, surprisingly for a six-year-old, generally proved to be right.

*

At the start of Jack's third week at the estate, Madeline had retired to her bed with a severe migraine and didn't make an appearance until late the following afternoon. On the same day, Ralph had an appointment with old Mr Grainger for the tooth extraction and aired his thoughts about what Jack should be getting on with in his absence.

"That lad never stops mithering when he wants something. If he's mentioned that perishing lock on the dining-room door once, I swear it's been a hundred times since you got here," Ralph said, pressing his painful tooth.

"I did promise I would fix it. Would you mind?" Jack asked, sympathising with Ralph's unhappy condition.

"Then get it done. Today if you can. It could take a time – those doors are old – but I doubt I'll be back until morning. Old man Grainger's a decent chap. He said he'd take the tooth out but it could be hit and miss in that makeshift place of his."

"I imagined he'd have a decent surgery the way you talked about him?"

"In town, yes, but that's closed for another month for renovations. I can't wait, and this tooth is driving me mad."

"Where is he doing it?"

Ralph laughed nervously. "In the garden shed."

"I thought all that went out with the Middle Ages."

"It sounds worse than it is and I can't complain, the old boy's doing me a favour, and the shed's where he stores his old equipment. Ambrose, who worked here before you came, had a tooth removed in the same place. It seemed to bleed a lot, but he didn't feel anything when he pulled it out."

In the afternoon, armed with a toolbox and a heavy mortice lock with a huge key that looked as though it had gone out with the ark, Jack made his way to the dining room. It was located in a part of the house he hadn't been in before, which made him wonder why that particular room was so important to the boy. With the curtains drawn the room was in darkness, and as he was unwilling to open them without permission he had to rely on the light from a nearby table lamp to examine the door. Within an hour the old lock was replaced with the new one and worked perfectly.

As Ralph had predicted, he didn't return that day. Madeline hadn't put in an appearance so Jack was debating whether he might take Duncan along to the kitchens where they could eat with the staff. However, that thought was soon dispelled when the boy appeared in his room excited and glowing with anticipation.

"I've asked Granny if it's OK, and she said, yes, so I've told Mr Ross we can eat in the dining room tonight."

"Wouldn't it be better if we ate in the kitchen? Just for this evening?"

"We can't do that. Granny's getting dressed to join us there," he said, grabbing Jack's hand and tugging him towards the stairs just as the lights flickered and dimmed, then went out.

"Oh bother. Now you won't see anything."

Carrying an oil lamp he'd found in the kitchen, Jack conducted his small charge to the dining room.

"Slow down, Duncan. I don't want to drop the lamp with you tugging at me. Why are you so excited?"

148

"Mummy's in there," he answered promptly, squeezing his hand. "She's been waiting for ages. And don't worry – she'll like you if I do."

Jack was unsure what to expect when he entered the room, illuminated by the candles of two enormous silver candelabra positioned on a wide tapestry runner down the centre of a highly polished table. He stared hypnotised through the flickering flames as the indistinct figure of a woman seated at the head of the table moved the nearest candelabra aside so she could see him clearly.

"Thank you for restoring the lock in here. It doesn't stick at all and the door opens perfectly," Madeline said. "I always had the fear we would be shut in here for days on end if it jammed again."

He had to admit to feeling some disappointment that she was sitting there alone, after all the talk of the boy's mother.

"I do apologise for our having to eat by candlelight. Unfortunately the generator appears to have a mind of its own these days."

"Would you like me to have a look and see if I can do anything to help?" he asked.

"Tomorrow perhaps, if Mr Ross is unsuccessful this evening."

She had barely finished speaking when a standard lamp in the far corner of the room flickered on momentarily, revealing, above the fireplace, a heavy gilded frame surrounding the portrait of an elegant young woman in a green dress. The portrait had the boy's undivided attention, before the light bulb popped loudly, and went out again.

"Did you see her look at you, Jack?" he asked excitedly. "She was staring straight at you when you came in. Mummy knows you're here!"

"That's quite enough, darling," Madeline said. "Eat your food. Mrs Jennings has taken a lot of trouble for you tonight. Eat up, before it gets cold."

Like the boy, Jack was fascinated by the portrait and hoped that the generator would work long enough for him to examine the painting better and see more than a darkened figure. The meal was predictably well cooked and enjoyable but nothing like the ones his mother had made on a smoking range with a very restricted budget. His favourite meal had been, by necessity, well supplemented with a stack of flat Yorkshire puddings smothered in a generous helping of gravy to eke out the thin slices of beef, topped by a good spoonful of boiled cabbage. This evening he was dining on salmon baked to perfection with a dressing of mixed herbs, wrapped in a delicate folder of leaves. It was accompanied by out-of-season new potatoes, baked celery and leeks and a salad of apples, grapes and a fruit which had the taste of a dessert gooseberry, with onions soaked in vinegar and a mixture of chopped nettles and other leaves which, although familiar, were not easily identifiable.

When the meal ended, as though on cue, the generator kicked into life and the room was lit suddenly by the soft glow of table and standard lamps. One of which perfectly illuminated the portrait.

For a long time he studied every detail of the painting, unable to say anything while absorbing each aspect of her lovely face framed by dark hair which had been drawn back and coiled at the nape of her elegant neck. The clarity of those eyes was fascinating: eyes which, as the boy had said, appeared to be gazing directly into his own. It was a three-quarter portrait, in which the subject was seated in a high-backed chair. Her slender hand rested on the arm, exposing a delicate bracelet of pale emeralds and pearls. She wore no other jewellery except for a very beautiful engagement ring. Everything about her was familiar, but it was the soft folds of the ethereal green dress that identified her clearly as the frequent visitor to his dreams.

"Who is she?" Jack whispered as he got unsteadily to his feet, taking comfort from the energy of the boy's tightening grasp.

"Duncan's mother… it was painted on the day of her engagement."

"Then why do I know her?" he challenged hoarsely.

"She was Eleanor McKenzie before her marriage. She was the owner of Moorcroft Farm." Madeline spoke quietly as the lights flickered and the room was again plunged into darkness. After that, no more was said. Jack was content, for the time being at least, to know it was Duncan's mother who had initiated his journey to Dungellen; the instigator of his life-altering experience.

Later that evening, as Jack carried the sleeping child to his room, he hugged the boy tightly, vowing to protect Eleanor's only son from whatever dangers might be lying not far ahead. Dangers which he felt were, perhaps, his own reason for being here now.

Although he wanted to bring up the subject of Eleanor McKenzie over the following days, and even though the opportunity presented itself many times, something would invariably occur which allowed Madeline to evade the issue. His time on the estate had extended well into three weeks and he was happier than at any other time in his life. Yet, as he observed his employer closely, he came to the conclusion she was unwell but doing her utmost not to show it. More worrying still was the continuing drain on the boy's energy whenever they were together, which was most of the time, so much so that during the latter part of the week there were occasions when Duncan needed to be carried.

"What do you think is the cause of this?" Jack asked, as Ralph took the boy from his care, affectionately draping him across his shoulders, massaging him on the back like a baby. "He should see a doctor," Jack continued. "This isn't normal for a boy of his age. It's as if all that vibrant energy he has every morning gets punctured when he is near me. Why do I affect him that way, Foxy? Surely you must have noticed?"

"It's nothing to worry about, Mr Jack. My little turnip head is prone to having these turns. He will grow out of them," he answered. They passed through an arch in the garden wall where they had been working that afternoon. "This one will pass soon enough and we'll get our boy back." As if to confirm Ralph's theory, Duncan's eyes fluttered open, and slowly his cheeks flushed with colour.

"Foxy… why is it he reacts so differently in your company? Look at the lustre in his eyes and the flush to his cheeks now you're holding him."

"Don't be too harsh on yourself. It was bound to happen; he's been around no one other than the mistress, the servants and me. You're more of a stranger than I am. I've known him every day of his life."

"I can't help feeling I'm in some way responsible. Would it be better if I went away? If I go back to the farm?"

"Is that what you want?" Ralph asked, the sun reflecting from his fine gold wristwatch as he shaded the boy's eyes from the brightness.

They had stopped and were now sitting on a grassy bank with a perfect view over the gardens. Dappled sunlight filtered through the trees, whose branches moved in the gentle breeze. Below they could hear the soft sounds of the ocean. The air that afternoon seemed to be alive with birdsong and the intoxicating scent of flowers. It was a perfect retreat for anyone needing to re-align themselves with nature. Jack felt an overwhelming sense of peace, a tranquillity he wanted to retain for the rest of his life.

"No… that's not what I want," Jack finally replied.

"That's not what turnip head wants either," Ralph answered simply, easing the sleeping child from his shoulder and passing him over to Jack. "Take him from me. He's fast asleep and breathing normally. That sickly phase has gone. He's well again. You won't wake him."

*

At the start of the fourth week, just five days before visitors from Edinburgh were expected, Madeline had again been taken ill with an acute migraine that kept her in bed for two days. It was during this period that Ralph mentioned the boy's inability to swim and, when the morning's work was finished, the two men decided to teach him.

Jack was amazed to discover just how warm the sea was and spent a full hour in and out of the water close to the boathouse, keeping the boy afloat until he could manage a reasonable dog-paddle with his support.

"What's that?" Duncan asked, tracing a finger along the savage blue scar that ran from Jack's shoulder down across his chest. "Does it hurt?"

Jack hesitated as he looked at the hideous scar, then said, "Not a bit."

"Blimey!" Ralph spluttered, emerging from beneath the water and clinging to the pier next to him. "That must have been agonisingly painful. When did it happen?"

"I couldn't say. I don't remember anything," Jack admitted, somewhat foolishly.

"Something like that? I find that hard to imagine," Ralph said, heaving himself out of the water to sit on the other side of the boy. "How could you not remember something so serious?"

"I don't know, but I'm glad I don't," Jack mused, tracing his finger along the jagged blue line.

"I suppose that does make some sense. So… what shall we do with Turnip here? He's looking much too dry," Ralph laughed as he stood up, lifting the boy up by his elbows and dropping him into Jack's waiting arms as he stood in the water.

They had towelled themselves dry and were half dressed when Madeline hailed them from the lower terrace, and came down the steps to meet them.

"I'm pleased to see you're well again, ma'am," Ralph said, helping her from the final step to the uneven ground.

"Thank you, Ralph, I feel so much better today," she answered, which belied the ghostly pallor of her features. "When I saw you enjoying yourselves from the upper terrace, I thought how pleasant it would be to have a picnic together. It is such a glorious day. I'd almost forgotten how beautiful it can be to breathe in this delightful air. We are so fortunate to be allowed this special time here."

Jack wasn't looking at Madeline when she spoke, but her words were not lost on him. When he looked up, he thought how intently she was looking at him. There was a group of ancient willows up high on a grassy bank, their leaves falling close to the water's edge. It was not far from where Jack had emerged from the storm on that fateful night, and he couldn't help but reflect on the changes which had happened since then. He felt the pressure of Duncan's hand gripping his hand tightly.

"I want to show you my secret place," Duncan said, lagging behind the others. Ralph was helping Madeline on to the grass where Dora was setting out a picnic. "No one else knows about this except me," he whispered, his engaging little face becoming serious as he tugged Jack towards the base of a specific willow, where years of erosion had exposed a web of twisted roots, each one as thick as a man's arm. Between these was an opening large enough for Jack to crawl through after the boy. Once settled beneath the tree, he rested his back against a bank of earth and wondered how on earth the boy had found such a place.

"It was Daddy's secret first. He came here too, when he was small," he responded as naturally as if Jack had voiced the question. "I've got something to show you," Duncan went on, beavering into the soft earth until he uncovered a tin box, out of which he removed a grubby handkerchief bearing his father's monogram. "It's very special. No one knows it's here. That's why it's safe."

"It's the silver penknife, isn't it?" Jack answered impulsively, staring fascinated at the wrapped object. Before he knew what was happening the boy had scrambled out of the hideaway, and when Jack emerged he found him clinging to his grandmother, sobbing.

"What have I done?" Jack asked anxiously.

"You knew what it was," the boy said tearfully.

"It was just a wild guess, nothing more," Jack said, genuinely concerned, as he sat beside Ralph in the hope of support. "I didn't mean to upset you... honestly."

"He means it, Turnip. Mr Jack wouldn't say anything unkind," Ralph said, taking hold of the boy's arm reassuringly.

"You see, darling? Ralph agrees." Madeline was drying his tears. "Come now, sweetheart, this isn't the way to behave in company. Why don't you show them what you have there, I'm sure they would love to see it."

When Duncan dutifully unwrapped the handkerchief, Jack felt a creeping shudder of recognition tingle along his arms as he saw the silver penknife glinting in the sun. "You see Darling, that wasn't so very hard, was it?" She smiled gently, her normally fresh complexion looking ghastly in the sunlight. "Are you going to put it back again?" she asked. Ralph helped her to a shadier spot where she arched her back against the tree, filling her lungs to capacity like a drowning man about to submerge for the last time.

The boy came to Jack and put the knife into his hand. "I'm sorry. I thought you were cheating, and I want you to have it," Duncan said earnestly. But instead of putting it into his own pocket, Jack folded the blades away, re-wrapped it in the handkerchief and returned it to the rusty container.

"You are very kind, but I can't accept. This belongs to you and no one else, but I will help you bury it again, if you like?" At this suggestion, the boy's face relaxed considerably.

"Can we? Just you and me? And you won't tell anyone else where it is?"

"You have my word."

It had been a delightful afternoon, first swimming and afterwards enjoying such amiable company for the relaxing picnic. Perhaps his only regret was that his own parents could not have been a part of this idyllic time. It was so far removed from the industrial grime where that kind and dutiful couple had tried so hard to give him a sensible start in life. They would have loved to have been there.

After they had packed the remains of the picnic into the hamper, Jack helped Madeline to her feet. She appeared to have recovered and commented on how delightful it was to hear him speak without a trace of a stammer. He had been aware of the change happening, which until then he had only noticed during his conversations with the boy, or occasionally with Ralph. He experienced a tremendous surge of wellbeing as for so many years he had been unable to convey even the simplest of thoughts without fear of ridicule.

"You see? Nothing is impossible here." As she spoke, she staggered momentarily and though her frail body made contact with his arms he felt no spark of warmth.

Subconsciously, he was aware that she, like the boy, had interpreted his thoughts, but he was more concerned with the state of her health than anything else. "May I walk you back to the house?" Jack asked, expecting her to take his arm as she had done on other occasions, but instead she took hold of Ralph's for support, saying the oddest thing.

"I shall go with Ralph. You must take my grandson with you. Be with each other for as long as you can. Our precious time here is fast running out."

He looked into the sky, expecting to see gathering storm clouds, but there was nothing but clear skies. Duncan was putting away the records they had played during the picnic. He struggled to carry them with the portable gramophone.

"Here… let me help," Jack said, offering to take the record player from him.

The boy's face was straining with the effort and yet he persisted. "I can't do that. I've made a bet with myself that if I carry them as far as the house, you will stay here for ever."

"Then let me carry you. That way we both do what we want," Jack said with a laugh.

"I s'pose," he grumbled, allowing Jack to gather him into his arms and carry him up the steps, the same steps he had clambered up in the dark on the night of his arrival. Ahead of them, a skylark fluttered out of the undergrowth and spiralled above them, its lilting song a perfect comment on the day.

As Jack tracked its flight, he saw the osprey swoop low over the Cap and, with outstretched wings, glide on an air current towards the house. He felt a cold shudder run through him when he saw the complete view of Dungellen Hall for the first time since his arrival. At the centre of the building was a weathered, medieval tower. On either side of the tower were extensions, later additions to the living accommodation, all of which were an exact replica of his recurring nightmare. It was a shock to recall the dream in such perfect detail. It caused him to speculate why he hadn't previously associated the nightmare with the Hall, unless of course, this entire facade could only be seen from this particular place.

"Wouldn't you have come here, if you'd known about all this before?" Duncan asked, with childlike directness.

Drenched in sunlight, the building offered nothing dark or brooding and had an entirely different ambience. For a moment he was stumped for an answer as he took in every enchanting aspect of the place. He felt as free as the wind as his crisp linen shirt lifted slightly on a sudden breeze, ruffling his dark, shining hair like a caress. Then, Jack McKenzie allowed himself to smile. Without the swelling, cuts or bruising to his face, he was without question an exceptionally handsome man. "I'm only grateful that I found my way here and that I met you in Dungellen. I wouldn't alter that, not for anything in the world."

Chapter Seven

If anyone had asked, Jack could never have fully expressed the sublime contentment he experienced being on that estate. Without exception, every room, stairway and corridor of the rambling old house exuded charm. The faded collection of Venetian drapes hanging in deep folds in rooms enriched by linen folding panels, a random collection of antique furnishings from different periods, gave every area a feeling of comfort. It was exactly the way a home should be; a home to enrich the daily life of any growing boy.

The grounds of the estate, which ought to have employed an army of gardeners, had in fact benefited more from there being only two. He loved the hint of neglect and, where herbaceous borders had replaced the more formal rose beds, this only served to add to the romance of those enchanted gardens. It was an artist's paradise from any perspective. There were bowered pathways of cascading blooms, where the intoxicating scent of old roses hung like a heavenly cloud for anyone passing beneath. An elongated pond reflected the arched boughs of drooping willows where the ground dropped away to the first terrace.

By late afternoon, and with nothing else to be done until Ralph returned the following day, Jack changed into a pair of grey flannels that Ross had laid out in the dressing room, which, to his surprise, fitted perfectly about the waist. With these, he wore one of the fine linen shirts in which he felt so at ease. A month earlier, he would never have considered wearing such clothing.

He had wandered on to the terrace at Duncan's request and was sitting on the flagstones awaiting his arrival, his back resting against the hewn granite of the old house. Through the open French windows, the gathered silk of the sunscreen billowed out in the breeze and he heard the clatter of running feet. Duncan pushed his way through, dropping his pencil box, which scattered across the terrace.

"Can we draw the cat?" the boy asked eagerly, referring to Jack's old cat which was sunning itself on top of the balustrade. "We can make a nice picture for Granny. She's not very well today and it will cheer her up." So they sat side by side and began to draw. "You will come back again, Jack? Promise me that," the boy asked unexpectedly, finishing his drawing with a flourish.

Jack was unprepared for the directness of the question and his distress was physical as he remembered that his time on the estate was limited to only a month and that it would come to an end the very next day. There had been no talk of any replacement for Ambrose and he had assumed, wrongly it appeared, that his time might be extended.

"I won't be far away. The farm's only a short distance from here on the other side of the Cap."

"Will you take the dog too?" he asked. "I don't like it when he isn't here."

Before answering, Jack looked guiltily at the dog, which was watching them with coal black eyes, as if it could understand every word. "If he will be happier here with you, then of course he can stay."

"But if he isn't? Will you bring him back here to see me?"

"Of course I will, or you can play with him at the farm."

He was unsure if the boy had heard anything he said, as he appeared to be listening intently to something else on the other side of the house. It was then that Jack too heard the sound of a car approaching the main entrance, then tyres crunching on gravel, followed by an eerie silence when the powerful engine was switched off. When he looked at Duncan, the boy was trembling and had a desperate look, like that of a cornered animal.

"They're here," he said, in a highly agitated state. "It was no use, I couldn't stop them."

*

A gleaming black Daimler with white-walled tyres and wide running boards had pulled up outside the main entrance to the house. An immaculately dressed adolescent boy of about twelve got out of the passenger seat quickly. He examined the bright red smears on the front bumper, radiator grille and nearside headlamp, then wiped all traces of the blood from his fingers on a white handkerchief. Then followed the chauffeur, who set his peaked cap at a more jaunty angle to emphasise better his rugged features. His perfectly tailored uniform accentuated his lean, muscular frame as he reached inside the passenger seat to retrieve a rigid bouquet of flowers. This he handed to the boy before opening the rear door of the saloon.

"Where in God's name is everyone?" asked a rich, husky voice as the chauffeur took a gloved hand to help a woman out of the car. "Surely Madeline was sent the date we were arriving?" she continued, uncoiling herself from the back seat and displaying her long, shapely legs before adjusting the length of her figure-hugging dress to a more appropriate level.

"The telegram was sent. I drove your husband's secretary to the main post office myself."

"Peters can be such an idiot at times. I can't understand why Hamish ever employed the likes of him. Anyone could do his job blindfold."

"But no one else is quite as in with the planning officer as is Peters. In that respect, your husband chose wisely indeed," he responded, his hand resting lightly about her waist as she faced him.

"And what of your own position, since you decided to remain in our employ?" she asked, as she re-aligned the angle of her hat, an exceptional creation of stylish proportions.

"Speaking personally, I find myself ideally suited," he answered, lowering his voice as Ross opened the door. "The fringe benefits are quite unbelievable."

"Phyllis, how are you?" Madeline asked as she emerged to greet her. "We were expecting a party of seven for the weekend. Are Hamish and the others not coming?"

"Yes, but later. Unfortunately Sir Nigel declined at the last moment. His private secretary, Vernon Lyle, will travel up from London instead. Hamish has arranged to collect him from the station in Edinburgh and will drive him here." she explained. She took the chauffeur's arm for support to climb the stairway to the grand entrance. Her footwear was stylish, but quite impractical.

"Edmund? How tall you have grown," Madeline addressed the sulking boy. "How long is it since you were last here?"

"It's been almost two years. I came up with Mother for the funeral," he said in a flat, monotone voice before thrusting the flowers towards her. "These are for you."

"How thoughtful," Madeline answered, accepting the stiff floral tribute.

"Is it the same room as before?" he asked, not hiding his boredom as he strode past.

"Can you remember where the room is?" she answered, calling after him.

"How could anyone forget?" he retorted.

Choosing to overlook his bad manners, she responded pleasantly enough. "Good. I have placed you all together in the guest wing."

"He is so excited being here," Phyllis said, as the two women came face to face, exchanging no expression of warmth in their greeting. "I had expected Duncan to be here this afternoon. I expect he's altered considerably since we last met?"

"In many ways, yes he has. He's becoming more like his father every day."

There was a noticeable stiffening of Phyllis's normally supple figure. The collection of rings on her slender fingers glittered brilliantly as she adjusted the clasp on the mink cape draped about her shoulders.

"How fortunate that is for you, Madeline," she responded to the gathered audience, gripping the chauffeur's arm tightly. "What a tragedy it was to everyone who knew that darling man. I feel John's loss acutely. No words could express my sorrow in bringing you the tragic news of the fall."

"Would you care for some light refreshment before you retire to your rooms?" Madeline asked. "Dinner will be served in the main hall at seven, which will give you all time enough to freshen up."

"That would be perfect. I have to get out of these rags and languish in a tub of hot water for an hour after such an arduous journey. Davis, be an angel and bring up the wine-cooler from the car and then run me a bath while I get Ned settled into that lovely room."

There was an uneasy stillness in the air, as if a thunderstorm was imminent. For several minutes Duncan had been sitting opposite Jack as if carved in stone. Every speck of natural colour had drained from his face.

163

"It's all over now," he said with calm resignation, his usually clear, light voice dropping an octave lower. The depth of his eyes transcended anything natural as he faced Jack.

"What is?" said Jack, loosening his collar in the stifling heat.

Instead of answering, the boy continued to stare without blinking for a long time and, perhaps by some trick of the light, it seemed to Jack that these were not the eyes of a child which looked into his own, but those of a troubled young man.

"I can't talk with you again like this. Not when it's over," Duncan said in a hushed tone as his voice deepened even more. "Not for a long time. Maybe never."

Jack blinked repeatedly to clear his vision as the area immediately surrounding them became distorted, but it did nothing to remove the heat haze rising between them. He felt as bilious as if he was adrift on a storm-tossed sea and there was tremendous pressure at the back of his eyes which made him press hard against his temples with the palms of both hands, convinced he was about to faint.

The heat became sweltering and he could see nothing for the brilliance of the sun, which had intensified until it almost blinded him. It was impossible to take his eyes off the boy, who seemed to be altering from his childish shape with every intake of breath.

The sun was infinitely hotter than at midday and his shirt was saturated with sweat. He felt giddy, even though he was sitting, and reached out a hand to steady himself, thinking he might pass out. Pressing down hard on the slabs for support, he found nothing solid beneath his palms to brace him. It was as if he had been disconnected from reality, and his body went rigid as though clamped in metal bands. In the same moment that he glanced away from Duncan, he felt an irrational sensation of tumbling through space until the boy regained his attention by calling his name.

When he looked again into Duncan's eyes the dreaded nausea returned in fearful waves. Every breath became agonising and the air being sucked into his lungs felt as sharp as if it had crystallised in his throat. He could only watch with a trance-like fascination as the child commenced a slow, painful transformation. His small body was jolted savagely by each surge of power, as the blistering rays of the sun seemed to illuminate every particle of his human form, crackling with energy and sparking so violently in its brilliance that the boy virtually disappeared.

Eventually, the light dimmed into a swirling mass of vapour and Duncan's childlike features twisted in torment as they very slowly matured into those of a young adult. The boy's body and face were systematically transformed until a clear outline of a young man remained. Vaporous fingers reached towards Jack and brushed over his head and face until they rested lightly against his temples.

At the spidery touch, his breathing became so intense and laboured that he wanted to scream, but the rising bile in his throat threatened to choke him whenever he opened his mouth. He feared he was about to die if he didn't get away, but he was unable to move until the shape of the man began to evaporate into the sun. Then, in the distance, he heard Ralph's voice reassuring him that he was safe.

Everything within his vision was jumbled and the estate had become a bizarre, distorted image, as if he was staring into the crazed varnish of an old painting. The billowing clouds above the Cap slowly fractured into segments and separated like splintering ice. The leaves on the graceful willows, which hitherto had shivered with every passing breeze, became static and the trees themselves seemed to hover above the earth in a blanket of ground mist.

His head was swimming and the heat was unbearable, making it almost impossible to breathe. As his nausea worsened he began retching and closed his eyes tight shut at the very moment he passed out.

When he regained consciousness, he found Ralph kneeling against him, cradling him like a doting parent and bathing his face with cold water. "You're safe now, there's no need to fret. Let's get you out of these messy clothes and we'll have you right in a jiffy." He removed Jack's shirt, rolled it into a bundle and handed it to Duncan, whose image was no longer distorted, but was clearly a troubled six-year-old who was staring at Jack wide-eyed.

"Ask Dora to give these clothes a good soak, Turnip. And see if you can find him another shirt on your way back."

"Is he going to die, Foxy? Like Ambrose did?" the boy asked, as Jack's eyes flickered and became more alert, focusing on him.

"There's nothing to fear, Mr Jack," Ralph said reassuringly. "You've been out in the heat too long. It's given you a bit of sunstroke," he explained as Jack shuddered involuntarily at the memory of the hallucination.

"You can't let him go back, Foxy. Not before it's time," Duncan whispered anxiously, clutching the shirt tightly against him.

"He's made of stronger stuff than that. Like you and me. Now be off to find Dora before that mess of his spoils your own clothes."

Feeling as weak as a newborn, Jack had to avert his eyes from the intense scrutiny of the boy.

"Foxy, I didn't expect you back here today," Jack said, in an effort to cover his embarrassment.

"I had to run an errand. Mrs Jennings needed a few groceries for tonight's dinner and asked me to collect them from the village store."

At the mention of the store, Jack longed to ask what Ralph knew about the girl with red hair and if, by chance, she had mentioned him. Instead, as his strength gradually returned, he enquired about the guests from Edinburgh and said how fortunate it was that it was Ralph who had come to his rescue and not one of them.

"I saw things happen, Foxy, right before my eyes, and I have no logical explanation for any of it. What I saw… was so weird."

"I'm not surprised. You've been peaky all day. You did too much strenuous work in the heat and that can make the mind of any level-headed man wander. So take my advice next time, and wear a hat when the weather's like this."

Later, in the privacy of his bedroom and having given his firm assurance to the boy that he would be dressed for dinner at seven precisely, he searched for the cause of the sharp pain in his outer thigh and found a rusted pen nib, one of those which had been scattered over the flagstones two or three weeks earlier, which had pierced the fabric of his trousers when he had collapsed. It was now firmly stuck in his skin.

In the dressing room where Ross would normally have laid out a shirt, tie and trousers for dinner, he discovered a silk dress shirt with a wing collar, a bow tie and – even worse – a tartan kilt. When Duncan came into his room half an hour later, Jack was still searching for a pair of trousers. "I can't go downstairs wearing that," he protested. "What will everyone think?"

"Nothing. Why should they?" the boy answered. "I'm wearing one. It's tradition."

"It's not the same for me. I'd feel like a girl," he blurted out, red faced.

Laughing, Duncan expertly unfolded the kilt. "You must wear this tonight. It's the clan tartan. Granny expects it."

"Can't you say I've got a headache or something?"

The boy shook his head firmly. "There's nothing wrong with you, and there are visitors waiting in the great hall. Granny expects this of you."

When he was finally dressed, he walked along the hallway like a man in a trance, unable to disassociate himself from the swinging motion against his bare knees. The kilt was heavier than he had expected and, apart from the draught about his knees, it felt surprisingly comfortable. He felt quite at ease with the garment by the time he entered the dining hall.

Madeline was waiting in the warm glow of a crackling fire. The fine strands of diamonds about her slender throat enhanced the simplicity of her elegant gown. She looked magnificent and seemed only half her age. She smiled at them.

"How very nice you both look. Come where I can see you more clearly. Sit here beside me." She indicated the chairs either side of her at the table, which had them seated in a row opposite the main door.

It was hard to see the door clearly beyond the brightness from the candelabra and Jack was about to ask why the fire had been lit on such a warm evening and why there were no lamps alight when Duncan peered at him from the other side of his grandmother in the way which Jack had come to expect.

"Mr Ross is having trouble with the generator tonight," he said. "The fire gives more light."

"Be a dear and open the French windows, Jack," Madeline asked. "It's getting too smoky in here. I must arrange with Ralph to have the chimney swept."

Jack had just returned to his seat when the main door was thrust open and young Ned entered.

"Mother will be down in a moment," he said, without joining them at the table. Instead, with his usual expression of total boredom, he slumped into a wing chair near the fire, his long legs dangling over the arm. "Mother's complaining that you simply refuse to organise a shoot."

"That would be my prerogative, I think."

"But why ever not? There's so much game roaming about up here, you wouldn't miss a hundred or so. We ran over at least a dozen pheasant on the way in," he announced, obnoxiously. "Mother's convinced that's why Sir Nigel backed out of joining us this weekend. You can have no idea what consternation that caused."

"When I misguidedly arranged for a shoot on the last occasion your parents were here, Ned, the grounds were littered with dead and wounded birds. Your mother's aim is much too accurate for sport, whereas your father's is not. Personally, I don't see the justification in killing for sport and I don't understand the appeal that pastime has for your mother."

Unconcerned by the rebuke, Ned continued to lounge like a sloth in the chair, and started to comment on the furnishings.

"Why does everything in this place seem so dull and old-fashioned? Why don't you get rid of the clutter and spruce the place up for visitors?"

"This is our home, Ned, and we enjoy it this way. Compared to life in Edinburgh, I suppose it must seem rather old-fashioned to an outsider."

"The thing is, you haven't got a radio anywhere," he stated with an air of incredulity. "How do you keep updated on the news and world events?"

"We muddle through well enough," she responded. "Why not sit at the table, Ned? Dinner will be served shortly." She indicated a seat opposite Duncan.

"I'll wait for Mother," he answered, looking about the great hall with despair. "My parents are quite right about this place. This crumbling pile you live in is cocooned from any normal contact with reality. Why would anyone, given a choice, prefer to spend so much time here, wallowing in the past? It doesn't make sense."

"We do see other people," Duncan cut in tartly, "and if you dislike it like it here so much, why bother coming at all?"

"Duncan! Mind your manners. You should know better," Madeline reprimanded.

"It was Mother's decision, not mine," he answered, peering across the table towards Jack's silhouette, which he was unable to see clearly beyond the glare of candlelight. "Do you ever see anyone from outside Dungellen?" he asked Duncan. "Geriatric staff and villagers don't count." He turned expectantly towards the door at the sound of a woman's high heels clipping sharply along the flagged corridor.

"Sometimes we entertain ghosts," Duncan responded, laughing at Ned's reaction. "They can be a lot more interesting than an influx of people from the city. Actually, there's one of them at the table with us tonight!" he concluded, victorious as Ned scrambled from the chair and backed towards the door, beyond which the footsteps had stopped.

As Ned yanked fearfully at the door handle, Jack got to his feet in an attempt to see beyond the candles. As the door swung open and Phyllis entered, his stomach turned and his breathing became shallow and gasping, making him grip the edge of the table for support. The light from the mass of candles on the candelabra had intensified and their heat was scorching his eyelids as he stared in her direction. He expected to discern more than just her silhouette, but failed to distinguish anything other than a dark figure.

"Darling, whatever is the matter? You're trembling all over," she asked, as Ned pressed his head against the perfect curve of her breasts. Two diamond clips on her sheath-like black dress glittered brilliantly as she pushed him aside to continue her dramatic entrance. "Is there no electricity in this part of the building, Madeline? You really should consider moving to the city before this draughty old pile crumbles about your ears and buries you alive!"

"Mother, don't go in there!" Ned cried, clutching at her arm in an attempt to pull her back.

"Darling let go. You'll bruise Mummy's arm," Phyllis said, as she disengaged him with a hand glittering with an array of rings. "What has come over you this evening? You're behaving like a petulant child. What will Madeline think of you?"

"My grandson's been filling his head with ghost stories."

"Is that what's affecting him? Ned always had a vivid imagination. He's too sensitive for his own good at times."

But Ned wasn't to be dismissed so lightly and took her arm again, urging her to leave. "Come away, Mother. It's true what he says. There's one over there," he said, pointing in Jack's direction. "Look, he's been watching me all evening," he whimpered hysterically, tugging at her waist until Phyllis slapped him sharply across the cheek.

Seeing Jack's indistinct shape beyond the flickering candlelight, her reprimanding mood altered and her posturing quickly switched to affected elegance, bordering on the theatrical. "I do so apologise for Ned's behaviour this evening, Madeline. You didn't mention you were entertaining other guests. Had I known, I would have worn a more appropriate gown and not this old thing," she announced, smoothing out imaginary creases from the immaculate garment. Her beautiful voice was husky and sensual as she purposely moved clear of the candelabra so they could see each other clearly. She froze. "Oh my God! It's impossible! You're dead! You went over the cliff."

A look of amused satisfaction flickered momentarily in Madeline's eyes.

"Allow me to introduce Jack McKenzie. He is staying here for a while."

"Why? Why have you come back?" she hissed.

Had he heard the question, he couldn't have answered as his mouth was as parched as the Sahara, and there was a severe pounding in his ears and pressure pulsating behind his eyes. He was certain his head would explode, until Duncan took his hand reassuringly. He rallied as his knees were about to buckle. In moments, Madeline had taken him by the arm and, supporting his weight, led him on to the terrace. Gasping for air in the pitch darkness, he filled his lungs to capacity while he held on to the balustrade to prevent himself from falling over.

"Who is that woman?" he asked hoarsely.

"An actress who married Hamish, a second cousin of my husband. Hamish and Ned are the only blood relatives we have."

"Why has she affected me like this, Madeline? Why?"

"Déjà vu, my dear; everyone experiences something like that at one time or another," she said affectionately. "You look dreadfully pale. Let me get you a brandy from inside. Wait here; there's no need to come with me."

How long he waited for her to return he had no idea, but he took full advantage of the darkness. He felt enclosed in the safety of the night. A breeze wafted over him like a caress, carrying with it the heady scent of honeysuckle, calming his anxiety. In the distance he could hear the repetitive breaking of waves against the rocks at the base of the Cap. It steadied his nerves better than any brandy could, and yet he couldn't bring himself to go inside and hear again that beautiful voice.

Raised voices sounded from the great hall and he moved away until he was out of earshot. For a moment he imagined he saw two lovers walking hand in hand through the gardens, but he couldn't be certain without moonlight. Duncan, who had been at his side unnoticed, once again answered his thoughts.

"I saw them too."

"Is there magic here in Dungellen?" Jack asked. "Everything about this place is so perfect."

"Only Granny could tell you that. It's a trade secret," he answered, handing him a glass of brandy. "She said to drink this down in one gulp and you'll feel better."

"I don't need that. I'm fine again now," Jack said, hoping the boy wouldn't notice how badly he was trembling.

"No you're not. Hold the glass with both hands and you won't spill any." Duncan waited until Jack had drained the glass. "You needn't go back in there while they're arguing. You can reach the stairs through the library but be careful, there aren't any candles lit," the boy said.

Before Jack entered the library he saw the boy pull aside the curtains to go into the great hall. As he did, a broad shaft of light projected into the rose gardens, giving him enough time to glimpse the lovers watching the boy enter before they concealed themselves in the foliage. What had caught his interest in particular was the now familiar green dress the woman wore. The young man's features were concealed by the clusters of rambling roses swathing the lattice columns of the pergola, as were hers

He had been unnerved by the outburst of the woman at the dinner table, but since then he had had time to consider her initial reaction. She had mistaken him for someone else. However, what disturbed him more was Duncan's reference to him as a ghost. Had he merely been teasing the obnoxious Ned? It was impossible to tell.

Deep in thought, he entered the dark library, blundering into the furniture as he made cautious progress towards an area on the opposite wall where he assumed the door would be. Banging into an occasional table, he sent everything on its surface crashing to the floor, amongst which was a gilded table lamp, which clicked on as the shade twisted against the switch in the collision.

After righting the table and replacing the lamp, he looked around the room. Positioned above a reading table was a large gilded frame containing a fine portrait of a young man which he was shocked to realise it was him. He examined it minutely and saw there was not one detail of the man's features that differed from his own, even down to the clan tartan he wore.

He sat staring at the portrait until he fell asleep. When he awoke, the house was deathly quiet. The air was heavy as though in anticipation of a violent storm. Anxious for the boy's safety, he looked into Duncan's room to discover he was sound asleep. With the white dog close at heel, he went to his own room and lay on the bed fully dressed. He was sure something dreadful was about to happen.

*

A few miles away, the large headlights of a Bentley saloon car pierced the darkness like a knife as Peters, the chauffeur, swung hard on the wheel to negotiate the sharp turn off the Kenmere road before accelerating towards Dungellen.

"You failed to mention how very remote this property is, Mr Kincaid. Sir Nigel will not welcome the news that it is so cut off from everything… normal," Vernon Lyle commented, clutching a portable typewriter against him as he peered into the inky darkness and squinting at the cluster of quaint cottages and the cricket pavilion as they drove through the tiny village.

"It's hardly Baden-Baden I grant you, Lyle. However, all that will alter with an injection of capital from Sir Nigel. After that, you won't recognise the place."

"But with the talk of unrest in Europe, wouldn't you consider a venture of this magnitude to be rather … whimsical?"

"For a personal secretary, Lyle, you do offer your opinion more readily than I would expect."

"Sir Nigel has insisted on my involvement if he is indisposed," the secretary answered as the vehicle turned off the road through the elaborate gates and on to the sweeping driveway. He looked enquiringly at his companion when Peters switched off the engine so that the vehicle could coast silently down the avenue of trees towards Dungellen Hall.

"An elderly relative will be asleep and it would be most inconsiderate to wake her at such an unearthly hour," Hamish Kincaid said by way of explanation, as he clipped off the tip of a broad Havana cigar, which he then lit.

"This would be Lady Beaufort you speak of, who owns the property?" Lyle enquired, squinting hard through the passenger window to better see the ancient house.

"Actually, no longer. It is now held in trust for her only grandchild."

"This contract must be done legally, Mr Kincaid, with witnesses. Sir Nigel cannot afford to have a whiff of scandal. We must adhere to whatever was agreed in the earlier discussions. There is no room for any errors at this stage; not with so much at stake. Where is the boy now?"

"In the chapel of rest… until the burial," he answered, through a cloud of smoke. He tapped Peters on the shoulder, telling him to switch off the headlights, and the phantom vehicle continued its approach in darkness.

"Dead?" Lyle was shocked and adjusted his spectacles to examine his companion as best he could through the smoke haze.

"Sadly, yes. He's been sickly since birth and he died in his sleep."

Lyle struggled with the information. "And when did this happen? Recently?"

"This evening. My wife telephoned tonight with the sad news, prior to our departure," Hamish said as the car pulled up outside the main entrance. "I didn't mention it before because there was nothing we could do. However, in some respects it is fortuitous that his death has coincided with the arrangements for this weekend. Once the formalities are over, the only signature you will require for the document will be mine. I am the sole beneficiary."

When Lyle stepped out of the car, he took some time to take in the elegance of the building before he followed Hamish up the steps. "It seems a tragedy that this fine building is to be demolished after so many centuries; so much history will be gone when it is only a mound of rubble."

"That's progress, Lyle. It's time to move on. This mausoleum has dominated the landscape for long enough," he said in a lowered voice as Davis opened the door. "Are you coming inside the house, Lyle, or will you be gawping outside until dawn?"

"This is such a magnificent building, Mr Kincaid. I do wonder what will become of the present occupant when this has gone."

"Lady Beaufort is a resourceful woman and will do well wherever she chooses to settle... as long as it's a considerable distance from here. Mr Lyle, it's time you came in," Hamish said tartly, exchanging a knowing glance with Davis, who immediately ushered the inquisitive secretary inside.

"Show Mr Lyle to his room, Davis, then join me immediately afterwards with Peters in mine. We must act quickly before dawn. There isn't a moment to lose."

*

The night air was as still as death with no sound coming from the house. Jack lay on his bed, still convinced something dreadful was about to happen. He had heard Madeline coughing in her own apartment at the end of the long corridor an hour earlier. After that he had heard nothing.

Some time had elapsed when he sat up abruptly, straining to hear a repeat of a floorboard creaking on the stairs, but heard nothing more. Then the clacking of a typewriter began some distance away in the guest wing.

Unable to relax, he went to the window seat and gazed out over the gardens, now shrouded in a gathering mist. From his restricted viewpoint, the main structure of the house, which projected at right angles to the wing he occupied, presented an eerie spectacle.

It was the white dog, bounding down the hall at great speed, which alerted him to the sounds of a struggle coming from the boy's room. Jack was barely a yard behind the animal as he reached Duncan's bedroom door and saw the dog felled by a savage blow to the head as Davis, with great accuracy, swung a warming pan at the snarling animal as it sprang at him. Fortunately an oil lamp had been lit in the corridor, which, though balanced precariously on a table, gave Jack the advantage as he gripped Davis about the throat and dragged him away from the door before punching him to the floor with a single blow in his haste to get into the room. As he barged inside, Hamish Kincaid was pressing down hard on a pillow in an attempt to suffocate the life out of the struggling boy trapped beneath. When he saw Jack he exclaimed in horror.

"What the... what's this? How can you be here? You're dead!" and he backed away from the child. This gave Jack a perfect opportunity to vent his rage on his bigger opponent, forcefully punching him in the face. Kincaid retreated from the bed and out onto the landing.

"Get away from here, Duncan! Find Madeline and warn her!" he called as the boy ran out of his room. But Duncan saw Phyllis, fully dressed, barring any access to the stairway and he altered course and ran into Jack's room.

Unnerved by the sight of her, Jack didn't see the punch coming and was sent reeling by the force of Hamish's huge fist thudding into his chest with brutish ferocity, slamming him hard against the table. The lit oil lamp fell, shattering its porcelain bowl on the floor, showering burning oil on to the heavy curtains. The remaining oil pooled on the carpet and immediately caught fire. Fending off a renewed attack, Jack was unable to control the spreading blaze. Through the suffocating smoke he saw Madeline brandishing a broadsword in Phyllis's direction, enabling her to edge slowly towards Jack's bedroom and her grandson.

Keeping her distance until Madeline had retreated into the bedroom, Phyllis deposited the contents of a vase of flowers over Davis's unconscious face and yanked the disorientated chauffeur to his feet, urging him to do something.

"Davis, for God's sake, don't just lie there as if nothing's happening. Do something. If this place goes up in flames, we're ruined. The valuables in this dump are worth a king's ransom. You have to save them."

"What d'you expect me to do?" he answered, looking about in a daze.

"Put the fire out, you bloody idiot. There isn't a script for this. Think for yourself, damn it. We're not on stage now. Use your imagination and do something constructive!" she screamed irrationally, slapping him hard across the face.

Staggering against the wall, Davis pulled off his tight-fitting jacket in an attempt to blanket the fast-spreading flames.

"You bloody fool! That won't do any good now the fire's caught hold," she rasped, grabbing Lyle by the arm as he attempted to pass by with his typewriter clutched tightly against him. "Here… take this man with you and find Peters. At least he knows where the fire equipment is kept, and be quick about it!" she said, backing away from the flames as the slugging between Jack and Hamish Kincaid continued.

Although Jack was nearing exhaustion, weakened by the superior strength of his opponent, he had delivered a fierce attack on the burly man. Kincaid had blood streaming down his face, mainly from the savage blow that had split an eyebrow, causing him to swing blindly, and his nose was bleeding and swollen as was his mouth.

Although Jack had suffered badly from the force of those massive fists, his face and body had somehow been miraculously protected from his opponent's fury. His strength almost gone, he staggered into the smoke, catching Hamish off guard and sending him reeling into a suit of armour. As the clattering metal fell into pieces, the big man grabbed hold of the broadsword and slammed the flat of the blade against Jack's legs in a ferocious strike. It would have shattered his unprotected knees had the blow not been cushioned by the mysterious protective cocoon. Nevertheless it still sent him crashing to the floor. As he struggled to get up, Hamish brandished the sword menacingly above his head in readiness for a downward strike, which Jack knew would inevitably cleave him in half, cocooned or not.

"Get the boy, Phyllis. Now, while I finish this blighter off!" Hamish shouted above the roar of the inferno, as a landing window imploded.

Jack knew then why he had come to Dungellen, and that he couldn't allow this to be his final moment on earth. Somehow he had to save the boy, even as Hamish prepared to end his own life. Yet there was no avoiding that horrific downward swing. Not with the flames blazing out of control on either side. Nor could he protect himself against with a piece of the armour, now engulfed in the flames. Momentarily crippled by the excruciating pain in his knees, he could only watch transfixed as the knuckles of his aggressor's hands whitened from the tightening grip.

Through the smoke, he heard Madeline screaming out for him to do something and defend himself. Her cry spurred him on and he stumbled blindly towards Hamish, grabbing his crotch and squeezing hard on his unprotected genitals. Without releasing his grip, and still on his knees, he forced the man towards the door to the tower, at the same time taking himself away from the intense heat of the consuming flames. A final desperate hand squeeze before he released his grip had Kincaid screaming in agony as Jack scrambled painfully to his feet, narrowly escaping mutilation as the sword dropped from Hamish's grasp.

As Hamish staggered backwards, Madeline wrenched open the ancient door into the tower. "Force that monster in here," she coughed, choked by the smoke as Hamish charged at him. With a lucky punch, Jack sent him reeling through the doorway and, in an instant, Madeline had slammed the door shut after him, locking the retaining bar into position. "That will hold him until the police arrive and we have them all removed," she said. She looked about her for Phyllis, who was now noticeable by her absence. "Where did she go?" she asked, her voice trembling. "You must find her before something terrible happens to Duncan."

"Where is he?"

"Hiding in the shrubbery, waiting for you," she answered. "You must go to him now. Go quickly. He has the dog for protection until you get there."

"I can't leave you like this. Not with the fire out of control. We must put it out," he said, with the intention of helping as Ross and Mrs Jennings arrived with buckets they filled from his bathroom. Dora too appeared through the smoke.

"There is no time. It's almost dawn. We four can get the fire under control. You are needed elsewhere. It is vital you save my grandson. Without him, Dungellen will be destroyed and the spirit of this place lost for ever. Promise me that, whatever happens during the next few days, you will never lose faith in him or Dungellen. Promise me now that you will find him again. It's imperative."

"I can promise you that, if nothing else," he answered solemnly, finding it pleasantly reassuring when she kissed him lightly on the cheek as they parted. Anxiously he searched the shrubbery where Madeline had said Duncan would be hiding.

Close to the ornamental pond at the base of the tower, Peters, with the help of Davis, manhandled an antiquated piece of firefighting equipment to where Lyle had laid a length of canvas pipe in the water. He trained the hose on the building where smoke and flames belched out of elongated arrow slits, as Peters and Davis began pumping the handles on either side of the equipment, forcing a jet of water at the flames.

Searching the length of the terrace Jack found the boy crouching in the shrubbery near the dining room, still in close proximity to the blazing tower, but where he could easily be seen by any of the three men. He made Duncan promise that he would remain hidden until he saw the coast was clear, then to make his way to the boathouse to crouch down in the red boat until Jack collected him.

Taking as few chances as possible and with the white dog close at his heels, Jack skirted the house with great difficulty as he found it almost impossible to penetrate the dense banks of mist. It took infinitely longer than he had hoped, but he managed to avoid being noticed by any of the men. Making his way to the back yard he grabbed the clothes that Dora had hung out to dry that afternoon. After a few unsuccessful attempts, he bundled them into a shape that might resemble the boy at a distance, thus creating a diversion to enable Duncan to escape through the mist along the narrow track.

He was about to emerge in full view of the men when they stopped pumping and stared at the ramparts, where Hamish's burly figure had charged through the belching smoke, his clothes alight as he emerged, transforming him in moments into a flaming mass. Aghast, Jack watched open-mouthed and unable to move, staring in horror as the nightmarish sequence of events he knew intimately began to unfold exactly as they had done so many times in his dreams. He shuddered as the blazing figure leapt on to the battlements, knowing instinctively this was the end of an era as the 'firebird' launched away from the tower. The awful sound roared menacingly as the flaming body of Hamish Kincaid made its rapid descent through the darkness and, immediately beneath, the reflected image of the spectre tumbled towards the still waters of the moat.

Jack's mouth was parched when he noticed Phyllis on the terrace only a few feet away from the hidden boy. The diamond clips on her dress glittered brilliantly, reflecting the glow of orange from the flames. Her beautiful features were a mask of calm detachment. Her serenity expressed no emotion as she saw her husband hurtle downwards. When Jack caught sight of the boy, his white face was upturned towards the horrific sight and, his eyes reflected the flaming image as it plunged ever lower. Jack knew he must act immediately, as he braced himself for the inevitable splash as the fireball was swallowed up in a great hiss of steam as it hit the water. Yet when it did happen, as he knew it would, his legs wouldn't move. All he could do was stare at the now submerged man and wait, breathless, for the continuation, which had never figured in his dreams.

When the three men had dragged Hamish from the water and laid him on the bank, Madeline arrived to help Ross remove the burnt clothing. She looked relieved when a small car appeared through the gloom and drove across the lawn. It stopped nearby and a woman with a young boy of about twelve got out. She was carrying a doctor's bag.

"I saw the flames from over the Cap. My God, Madeline, what happened here?" the doctor exclaimed, kneeling next to Hamish to examine his wounds.

"I think his back is broken. There's no movement in his legs. Oh, Helen, he's in such pain. I wouldn't wish this on anyone!" Madeline exclaimed.

"How did the fire start?" Helen asked. "What's been going on here tonight?"

Madeline knelt beside her. "This man came here tonight with the sole intention of killing my grandson. A lamp was knocked over in the struggle."

"And where is Duncan now?" the doctor asked, looking about her with alarm. "Is he injured?"

"No. He's safe, and in hiding for the time being."

"And the fire, can it be put out?"

"It's already extinguished in the main house but we can't do anything with the tower. It's burning out of control, but at least it's contained and the house will be safe."

"If only we'd been nearer, Andrew and I could have helped," she said, making Hamish as comfortable as she could.

"Helen, there is something I need your help with and it must be tonight. I know it must seem a strange request with all this going on."

"Anything, my dear. What is it?"

"Because of what happened last night, Helen, I must add a codicil to my will to protect Duncan's inheritance."

"Is that really necessary?" Helen asked. "Angus McNair would have made sure your existing will was iron-clad."

"After what happened tonight, added precautions must be put in place to block any loopholes. Where this property is concerned, the Kincaids would try anything to get possession. Hamish wasn't alone in this... there was Phyllis too."

"Even so, given the injuries he's sustained, that man will be hospitalised for a considerable time yet."

"Maybe Hamish will be out of action, but not that unscrupulous wife of his; that woman is capable of anything. The only way I have of protecting my grandchild is by making sure neither of the Kincaids can harm him. If I stipulate a delay of a few years after my death before the details of my will and Eleanor's own wishes are put in motion, the Dungellen estate will be protected until Duncan reaches adulthood. By then he will be better prepared to protect himself against any attempts on his life."

"I do understand, Madeline, but you have been through a terrible ordeal tonight, so you're coming home with me... no arguments. I will call Ralph as soon as I get you home. Rest assured he will come over here immediately. You can work out any details of the codicil tomorrow, but only after you've had a complete rest."

"You are very kind, my dear. What I would ask of you is for your input on the correct wording of the document, but you must also promise me that whatever we discuss is kept strictly between ourselves. None of the details in this codicil must be disclosed to anyone and the contents of the document must be kept completely secret."

"Of course, Madeline, I promise. I will say nothing to anyone. All I want is to help you in any way I can."

"Then would you agree to be one of the witnesses?"

"Of course, that goes without saying. Who will be the other signatory? Ralph? He would be ideal, particularly as he is a close friend of the McNairs."

"Ralph would be perfect, but even he cannot know the content."

"I can arrange that easily enough and then you must rest. You're exhausted," she said. She spoke swiftly to the young boy who had been helping with the bandaging. "Sweetheart, you must help get this man to a hospital immediately. If we don't he could die of shock."

"I could call the hospital if you like, but I don't think they're connected to the exchange from here. What would you like me to do?" Andrew asked urgently.

"Take the car and drive home. Make a call to the hospital from there. If no one answers at the exchange, keep ringing until they do. Tell them it's an emergency. They will understand. Hurry now, there's no time to lose. Just remember what I taught you about driving the car, and take it steady along the top road. On the way back call by the store and collect Ralph. We need him here as soon as possible. He needs to know about the fire and will organise everything here for Madeline."

Lyle, who had been left to his own devices, had moved nervously away from the smouldering man and all the activity surrounding him, and was now wandering aimlessly around the lawns in search of the abandoned typewriter. Madeline's attention was elsewhere as she caught sight of Jack breaking cover, followed by the white dog. The bundle of clothing was clutched under his arm as they ran towards the terraced gardens, and ultimately towards the sea, Peters and Davis in hot pursuit.

"Who are those men, Madeline?" Helen asked. "Where are they going? Surely they should be fighting the fire and not racing away."

Glancing back, Jack could see the two men and the shadowy figure of Duncan, who clearly hadn't done as he'd been told. Instead, he had managed to avoid the ever-encroaching mist and scrambled on to the terrace. Jack gaped at the unnatural vision of the building, now seemingly detached from the earth and rising from a pulsating cloud of energised fog. The only avenue he could pursue was a narrow pathway through the mist leading from the tower, through the gardens, to the boathouse and ultimately the sea. Under other circumstances he would have turned back, but the situation was now out of his control and, with no chance of finding another route or escaping his eager pursuers, he continued to distract them as planned and followed the white dog into the almost impenetrable mist, missing his footing and stumbling. The thick wall of fog bounced him aside like rubber with the same force as the membrane he had encountered on the night of his arrival.

As he followed the dog down towards the sea, the mist became turbulent on either side as it closed in on him, sealing off the pathway. Between the swirling grey layers seethed an open wound of orange and red gases that closely resembled molten lava and gave off a searing heat. He was sweating profusely. The fumes choked him as he attempted to breathe. He staggered after the white dog along the now illuminated track. The wispy tendrils that snaked out from either side wound around his legs like bindweed, then began intertwining with each other slowly, stitching the opening together.

When he finally reached the beach, Jack looked back to see that the two men had closed the gap between them, seemingly unhindered by the hellish mist beneath which blinding flashes of light had begun to explode. He raced after the white dog, which by now was splashing into the bay along the already submerging sandbar.

In the distance, Peters glanced at his wristwatch anxiously, searching the sky above the Cap where it was beginning to lighten.

"Come on, we still have time if we act now," Davis said, urging his companion along by the arm until they reached the boathouse. Between them they untied a small boat with an outboard motor on the stern. Davis fired it up as Peters clambered aboard, pulling the oars inside to allow them more room to manoeuvre.

"I can see them over there. They've not got far," Davis cried, squinting towards the Cap where Jack, the white dog and the bundle were floundering in the deepening water that now covered the sandbar.

*

With the exception of Madeline and Jack, no one had seen Duncan as he crept through the shadows of the terrace and disappeared into the dining room. There he climbed on to a chair beneath his mother's portrait, which was considerably taller than him and weighed more than a six-year-old boy, and reached up in a futile attempt to take down the painting of Eleanor McKenzie. He turned quickly at the sound of high heels that clipped briskly in his direction before stopping at the open door.

"I thought I'd find you in here," Phyllis said. Her graceful figure, in silhouette, blended into the shadows as she stepped into the darkened room, though the glittering diamond clips on her dress gave away her position as she approached. "What are you doing? Get off that chair before you injure yourself, and come with me. It isn't safe to be inside the house until the fire is out," she said. Her charisma was hypnotic. "Take my hand. I will look after you."

The boy scrambled off the chair and pushed it to form a barrier as Phyllis lunged at him, her fingers grasping in the dark, clawing at space as Duncan dodged out of her way. He paused just long enough to grab his drawing of the cat that had been left on the buffet. Phyllis clutched at his shirt, tearing off the sleeve as he escaped on to the terrace.

"Come back, you little swine!" she shrieked, blundering into the upturned chair in her pursuit, snagging her gown. When she emerged on to

188

the terrace, there was no trace of the boy, only swaying shrubbery close to the balustrade, which she failed to notice.

A loud explosion sounded inside the tower as a floor gave way in a vivid display of sparks through a shattered window. In the west wing where the fire had first started, wisps of smoke signified an end to the smouldering as Ross emptied a bucket of water on to the last of the embers.

Above the Cap the sky was just beginning to lighten and in the near distance came the urgent clang of an ambulance as it drove at speed through the village. A motorcyclist raced ahead to catch up with a police car. All three vehicles drew up in front of the house. In an outburst of pure rage and frustration, Phyllis picked up a piece of the broken balustrade and hurled it into the shrubbery. She didn't hear the muffled scream that occurred simultaneously with the collapsing roof of the tower. The shower of sparks illuminated the area where Hamish was moaning in agony as he was placed on a stretcher and lifted into the ambulance.

"Is there anyone here who can tell me what's happened?" a reporter asked as he abandoned the motorcycle, flashing his camera towards Madeline as Helen helped her to a bench.

"Please go away," the doctor said crisply. "This is neither the time nor the place."

"It will only take a minute," he persisted, then squirmed like a rabbit as Ralph grip caught hold of the reporter's collar and marched him away.

"If I see you bothering anyone again tonight, I'll smash that bloody camera over your head and take great pleasure in doing so. Have you got that?" Ralph growled, thrusting the man aside as Phyllis made her dramatic appearance through the French windows, a glamorous, tragic beauty ready for her sufferings to be recorded for posterity. In anticipation, her gown had been hastily dusted with a generous sprinkling of ash. The clinging material had been torn just enough to reveal an enticingly shapely leg. Appearing bewildered by the appearance of the two men, Phyllis clutched at the doorframe for support, fumbling to tidy the tumbling hair around her shoulders as she fixed her tearful eyes on the estate manager.

"Ralph, thank goodness you came," she gasped, pressing her curvaceous figure against him with a smouldering look. Instead of helping her, Ralph pushed her unceremoniously in the direction of the reporter.

"I've a mind this woman could answer every question you might ask about what happened here this evening. If you can see beyond her performance."

"Careful, Miss, you could injure yourself in the dark," the reporter said, studying her closely with ever-widening eyes. "Don't I know you from somewhere? An actress? I say, aren't you… Aren't you that actress who was involved in a scandal up here a while back?" the reporter said excitedly, looking around urgently. "Jeffery. Over here!" he called to a man who was re-parking the motorcycle. "You'd better get a shot of this, Jeff. What a scoop this will be. Finding a star like Zenobia here in the Highlands. I can't believe our luck." He smiled delightedly as the first of many flashbulbs popped in Phyllis's direction.

*

Blood oozed through Duncan's fingers as he staggered out of hiding, his hand pressed tightly against his chest, his eyes wild and staring. He could see nothing of his grandmother as she helped tend the twisted body by the tower. Deeply traumatised, the child staggered precariously in the swirling mist, and reeled blindly from the track as the nearest section of the banked-up mist sucked him closer. Stumbling away from the intense heat, he missed his footing on the steps and went sprawling down to the lower garden. He righted himself and staggered towards the lowest level. Immediately ahead strands of vapour from either side of the narrowing pathway writhed until they made contact, pulsating with a fierce energy as the banks began drawing together. He whimpered fearfully as he tried to fight free of the grasping, snake-like tentacles that grabbed at his bare legs, tripping him over time and again until his knees were raw and bleeding, until at last he arrived at the relative safety of the beach. Once clear of the danger, Duncan staggered along the boarded walkway to reach the little boathouse, where he sank to his knees against the red boat. Crying from the agonising pain of his ripped shoulder, he managed to release the mooring rope. Then, in a heroic effort to stand, he stumbled forward, lost his balance, missed his footing and crashed over the side of the boat where he landed face up on the bottom. There he lay, dazed, his eyes staring blankly at the rafters of the roof passing overhead as the boat drifted from its mooring. There was a wild screech from the osprey which swooped low over the boathouse as the red boat drifted silently into open waters, unnoticed by the two men who were intent on cutting off Jack's route to the Cap.

The water had risen up to Jack's waist. He was supporting the struggling white dog and still clutching the bundle of clothing when he saw the motorboat bearing down on them, blocking any chance of escape.

The first rays of the sun dazzled Jack as it rose unnaturally quickly over the Cap, exactly at the moment when Peters cut the engine. The athletic Davis grabbed an oar and raised it above his head in readiness as the boat drifted nearer to him. Jack frantically tried to avoid the crushing blow by submerging, releasing his hold on the white dog in the process. Afraid it would drown, he surfaced, grabbed hold of it once more and braced himself for the inevitable strike to his head. Holding the dog tightly, he waited, eyes closed, for what seemed an eternity for a neck-shattering jolt of pain which never came.

When he opened his eyes again, the boat had disappeared without trace. There was nothing to be seen except a small boat in the distance, almost on the horizon. It was so far away that he knew it could not be the one containing his assailants. Apart from that, he saw nothing.

The mist that had drifted out from the estate swirled around him in a great gust of wind. It spiralled through his wet clothing, like a vacuum siphoning out every trace of air, threatening to suffocate both him and the dog. Then he felt mild, cool air enter his lungs as the now familiar soft down of the osprey's underbelly brushed his head lightly, hovering inches above him. Gradually, the beat of the enormous wings cleared a passage through the mist and he could make out the hazy grey outline of the Cap. He stood stock-still in the water, unable to move as the bird's talons gripped him gently and the wind increased tenfold as he was lifted clear of the water, still clutching his faithful dog.

The rhythm of the osprey's wings neither faltered nor increased as, below, the cresting waves gelled into a grey and blue haze. Suddenly the bird was flying faster and his cheeks contorted like rubber as he passed through a kaleidoscopic tunnel of blurred colours. Despite travelling at such great speed, the dramatic outline of the Cap ahead of him never seemed to get any closer and, just when he thought he wouldn't be able to endure the pressure of the wind any longer, the tunnel of colour began to pale until it was colourless. Then the mist thinned and disappeared altogether as the wind subsided. At last, Jack relaxed and began to breathe normally. His feet trailed along the surface of the water until they reached the sandbar, where he was lowered gently and released with the dog, still holding on to the bundle of clothes. He watched as the osprey flew at speed towards the Cap and, with a wild cry, veered towards open water, swooping low above the sea towards the tiny red boat on the horizon.

Chapter Eight

Jack stepped forward with the uncertain tread of a child. His throat was parched and the back of his eyes ached unbearably. For a moment, the blurred impression of his shoes appeared segmented, like the juddering images of multiple exposures on film, the disconnected pieces then merging together as he slowly gained access to the foot of the Cap's cliffs. Aided by a low tide, he clambered along the rocky base until he reached the balustrade on the lower terrace and saw, finally, the boathouse, where he expected Duncan to be waiting.

Squinting hard, with the morning sun full in his face, Jack scoured the area for any sign of his pursuers before making his way towards the boathouse. The nearer he got, the more neglected it appeared. Increasing his pace to a sprint, he ran past the curved balustrade of the terraced gardens, his heart pounding as he reached the boarded walkway with its decaying timbers, which less than an hour earlier had been perfectly sound. He had to balance precariously over rotting and missing floorboards to access the tumbledown building. The nightmare of its crumbling interior made him catch his breath with disbelief as daylight streamed through the broken roof and walls. The flaking paint on the intact areas gave no indication of the neat and orderly interior he had repainted less than a week before. As he trod cautiously, his foot skidded on the accumulated slime of years of neglect, and he was only saved from toppling into the water by a pile of washed-up debris.

Furthermore, there wasn't a single boat moored on the rotting posts; most importantly, the red boat was missing. None of this made sense! The boathouse, which until that morning had been well appointed and perfectly safe, had become a scene of neglect that appeared to be in grave danger of crashing about his ears.

He scrambled outside and his fear of what might be awaiting him at the Hall increased with every step as he climbed the disused and almost inaccessible steps to reach the lowest terrace, now strewn with decomposing storm debris. At the next level, the remains of a fallen tree blocked any reasonable approach to the steps. He managed to scale the trunk, followed by the white dog, and force a passage through the tangle of briar on the final level, before reaching the gardens.

He pinched his arm more than once to see if he was indeed awake, as he stared open-mouthed at the unimaginable transformation of Dungellen Hall. A flock of jackdaws, disturbed by his unexpected arrival, circled noisily above the remains of the tower, reduced to a shell by the fire. There were smears of blackened granite above the medieval arrow slits but they appeared more weathered than he would have expected from just the intensity of the fire. A sturdy tree, long established, was growing inside the hollow interior, its mature branches sprawling through a jagged hole in the granite wall.

The inexplicable havoc caused in his short absence from the now ravaged gardens made him sick with every step he took. He forced a pathway through the neglect, where it was hard to differentiate between what had once been lawns or flowerbeds. Only the rotting posts of the rose walks gave him any sense of what had been where in those once glorious gardens. He felt a piece of wood give way underfoot as he waded through a bank of stinging nettles. It was a decayed piece of the dovecote he had so painstakingly restored only a week earlier.

When he finally reached the long terrace, he was desperate for any sign of life. He had expected to enter the house, but every door and window was boarded over.

"Duncan? Where are you? Ralph...? Anybody? Please answer me!" Jack cried out in desperation. He looked for a way in but found none, at least not until after he had searched for an hour and discovered a window frame leading to the winter garden, through which he clambered.

Fighting his way through the tangle of bramble and thistles, he stood on an exposed section of the mosaic path, the greater part of which was hidden beneath a thick carpet of ivy and moss. It was heart breaking to witness how such hideous neglect of that beautiful place had annihilated every aspect of its former unique enchantment. Where clusters of flowers had hung from trailing vines, only dried strands supported clusters of skeletal leaves and brittle clumps of shrivelled flowers. Where a covering had fallen away from one of the long mirrors, a wasps' nest was attached to a corner of blackened glass. The other mirrors were covered over with sheets and layered in dust.

Searching aimlessly amongst the tangle of vegetation, now a haven for mice, spiders' webs and dust and just a few straggling plants that continued to struggle for life in the rock-hard soil, he made for the door. It was locked, making it impossible to gain access into the main house. The dais where the concert grand had once stood was bare and there was no sign of the magnificent piano anywhere, damaged or otherwise.

What the hell had happened here? What had become of everyone he held dear? Was he mad? It had to be a dream. Nothing made sense. Numbed by the transformation, he wandered about the devastated area in a daze. In an attempt to restore a sense of normality to his situation, he re-attached the hose of the sprinkler system and, with a superhuman effort, turned on the water, inhaling the damp, intoxicating aroma as the flow of water from the antiquated irrigation unit began penetrating the parched beds.

On some of the crumbling vines he found dried up seed-pods in which a few seeds remained. He started searching for the catalogued seed trays which Ralph had shown him only a few days earlier. These he came across more by luck than judgement after heaving a dead palm from a mound of rotted foliage, Beneath it was the storage cabinet. The weight of the fallen tree had crushed the legs of the unit but fortunately its sturdy oak had sustained little damage, and the drawers slid out easily.

After that, he spent a good two hours labelling the seeds he had been able to remove from various plants, the names of which he could remember. Ralph and Madeline had been very specific in naming each of the categories of plants and he blessed them for having allowed him to share in their mutual interest. After he'd scribbled down the names with the stub of Ralph's old pencil, he ran his fingers lightly across the chewed-up end and slipped it into his pocket as a keepsake. How he wished his friend would appear at that moment to help him to understand the complexities of what had been happening.

*

Jack returned to Moorcroft Farm via a narrow pathway leading over the Cap that was dangerously close to the cliff edge in places. It was evident that someone had been using his motorbike during his absence, but it caused him no concern as it had been left in good order. He found some food on the kitchen table and realised how hungry he was. Before he ate, he found something for the dog and it was only then that he remembered that the last time he had seen the old cat was in Dora's arms on the night of the fire, and wondered where it was now.

By lunchtime most of the cladding over the windows had been removed. As he was working on the far side of the building, he had no idea that anyone had arrived and when he came around the corner with a hammer and an armful of timber he collided with Bonnie.

"I'm so sorry!" Jack exclaimed, dropping the wood with a clatter as he caught hold of her arm to steady her from falling. How ironic it was that the first person he should meet would be the local red-headed girl of his innermost thoughts. Seeing her so close and vulnerable caused every other thought to be driven from his mind.

"You can let go of my arm," she was saying. Her cheeks flushed with the nearness of him. "I'm perfectly able to stand."

He had half expected her to smile but she didn't and he stepped away. "I didn't intend any offence," he sighed.

"And there was none taken," she answered quickly, seeming more sure of herself with a little distance between them. "I heard banging. I was looking for someone... I hadn't expected anyone else to be here."

He hesitated before responding because her manner was so cool, although he was curious to know who she had been expecting if it wasn't him, when the white dog bounded over to greet her, diverting her attention.

"Would you tell me where I can find Mr McKenzie?" she asked.

"Mr McKenzie?" he repeated, not understanding and feeling like an idiot.

"Jack McKenzie. I have something which belongs to him." She held out his wallet.

"That's mine!" he exclaimed with surprise, reaching out as she hastily withdrew her arm. "Where did you find it?"

"I'm afraid there's some misunderstanding. You are not the person I'm looking for."

"You said Jack McKenzie. Well that's me. Have you forgotten?"

"Forgotten?"

"I'm sorry. Of course you wouldn't remember me, why should you? It was a month ago when I called by your aunt's store." He was aware of an icy coolness between them. Was it something he'd said, or done?

"I would remember if I'd met you before," she responded, just a little too quickly, flushing crimson. "I don't remember you at the store, nor anyone else come to that. No strangers have visited Dungellen in months. Not until last week actually."

"But you have my wallet. Surely you can't have forgotten?"

"This wallet, which you claim belongs to you, was left there two nights ago."

"That's impossible. It's been a full month since I was there."

"Two nights and one day to be perfectly accurate. You can take my word for it. Mr McKenzie left in a hurry. That's why I came here yesterday, and again today."

He was shocked. Admittedly she did seem genuinely angry and yet, had it not been for her extraordinary story about the dates in question, her honesty would not be in question.

"Why would you say such a thing? I'm Jack McKenzie, and I've been working away for a month. I was in the store with you that night, and that's my wallet in your hand."

Her eyes widened a fraction as she brushed away the tumbling red hair from her face, coiling the glistening auburn tresses behind her neck. "Working? And just where exactly, because it certainly wasn't in these parts or my aunt would have heard."

"Not far away actually. On the large estate just over the Cap."

"Dungellen Hall?" she exclaimed. For a moment he imagined she would burst into laughter but instead she turned away coldly, replacing the wallet in her pocket as she remounted her bike. "You're a fool playing these silly games, and I won't be a part of it. Say what you like!"

"What are you saying? I don't understand?"

"The Dungellen estate hasn't been worked since the great fire when I was a child."

"I wouldn't lie about something so important!" he protested. "I am Jack McKenzie."

"Oh, for goodness' sake, where is he?" she demanded, her eyes flashing angrily. "The genuine Mr McKenzie has to be here somewhere. That dog belongs to him." As she received no immediate response, Bonnie pedalled away until she was out of sight, leaving Jack baffled and unhappily aware of her apparent immense dislike for him.

He realised that he hadn't settled up for the groceries she had delivered the day before, which set him thinking. It was inconceivable that the girl had been lying. Why would she? Yet, if it had indeed only been two nights as she had said, then where exactly did that leave him? Admittedly, everything he had come to love about the estate had altered so drastically as to be beyond comprehension. Also, his physical appearance had changed markedly over the past four weeks, and if she only remembered him as he had looked when he first arrived, battered and bruised, that still didn't answer the questions. How could anyone explain the devastation of the estate, the last four weeks and Bonnie's talk of just two days?

After he had cooked a meal from the food Bonnie had delivered, he knew he must make a visit to Hettie's store early the next morning. He wanted to repair some of the damage caused between him and Bonnie, a prospect that cheered him the more he thought about it; that was until he remembered his current financial situation, which as he recalled, amounted to the princely sum of 12*s* 6*d*. Instead of enjoying the first night in his own home, with much to occupy his mind, he spent restless hours lying awake in a comfortable bed, wondering more about what could have happened to his cat, and what employment he might be able to find in such a remote area in order to feed himself and the white dog.

The next morning he unpacked a rucksack of his old clothes, which he decided against wearing, choosing instead to wash through the clothes he had worn the previous day and wear the ones he had brought with him from the night of the fire, wrapped in the boy-shaped bundle.

Before he set off for the store, Jack opened the manila envelopes, the first of which contained the deeds to his property. In the second there was a serious amount of money. Four hundred and fifty pounds to be exact, bound together in bundles of five-pound, one-pound and ten-shilling notes, which gave him cause to bless the unaccountable generosity of Eleanor McKenzie and vow he would never rest until he had found her only son and returned him to the estate where he belonged.

Although it would have been infinitely more convenient to ride the motorbike to the store for the few groceries he needed, he decided against it to avoid more accusations from the girl. The store seemed more spacious than he remembered it on the evening he arrived and he was nervous of meeting the girl again. How would she act? He had no idea how he might begin the conversation which, as it turned out, never occurred.

"My niece isn't here." Hettie answered his enquiry with interest, eyeing the crumpled shirt as Jack packed away the provisions into a rucksack. "Who should I say was asking after her when she returns?"

"It's better if I don't say. Not until I've had the opportunity of speaking to her again. I'll call in some other time soon. I shall be in these parts for a while," he answered amiably.

"Are you staying in the village?" she asked curiously.

"More or less," he answered evasively. "Incidentally, your niece kindly delivered some supplies to the farm for Jack McKenzie. How much does he owe you?"

"Oh good. He's returned home then," she answered brightly. "We were quite worried about him you know. Going away like that, just after he arrived."

"When was that exactly?" he asked casually enough, not wanting to attract more interest in himself as, clearly, she too didn't recognise him.

"It was only a couple of days since. It was an upset caused by a visiting guest you see, which made us more concerned for his whereabouts. Where did he go exactly?"

Paramount in his mind was relief that the girl had been telling the truth, but he felt uneasy enough when he realised that his time spent on the estate could not be accounted for.

"You were saying?" Hettie asked, jogging his memory.

"He was away visiting friends. I'm sorry you were worried."

"There's no need. He seemed a very nice young man. I do hope he will call by here himself. How is he?"

"Much better in himself."

"The poor dear. It will be some time before those cuts of his heal, if they ever do."

*

202

Calling the white dog, Jack forced an opening for him in the briar growing around the gated entrance to the estate, before clambering over the high wall. There was a breathtaking view of the bay as he ambled along the sloping drive through an avenue of stately limes, the girth of each trunk much larger than any he could ever recall. A slight breeze rustled the leafy canopy overhead in a gentle whisper as if welcoming him. The pattern of dappled sunlight changed shape as he rounded a curve in the drive and Dungellen Hall appeared ahead. It was undoubtedly the most exquisite house imaginable and, as he walked on towards it, he prayed that it would be as he first remembered and that Duncan would appear, running towards him.

Apart from a herd of startled red deer and a squawking flight of pheasants, nothing in the vicinity of the building moved – except that is, for the osprey. It had appeared from nowhere, swooping low and winging its hypnotic flight towards the Hall, startling a cloud of jackdaws that fluttered clacking into the air in fright, circling over the house as the osprey alighted on the burnt-out tower.

Jack roamed about aimlessly, desperate to find a way in. There had to be a clue somewhere as to what had caused such an inexplicable transformation. All points of access were boarded over. With renewed energy, he scoured every inch of the overgrown shrubbery where he had last seen Duncan in the hope of finding a trace of the boy, but there was none. He couldn't have dreamt it. His friends and all the bizarre events were too real and too recent. Dejected, he sat on the steps of the terrace for a long time, wondering what to do next. The sun was high and the temperature became increasingly hotter. Unbuttoning the neck of his shirt he rolled up his sleeves and the realisation occurred. The shirt was the one Dora had laundered. It was an item of clothing he would never have purchased himself back in Eastmoor and, even if he'd had the sort of money to buy such fine linen, he would never have known where to shop, therefore he must have been in the house. That was an irrefutable fact which made him consider what other confirmation he might find.

Locating the precise spot where Ralph had ministered to his nausea and removed his shirt took surprisingly more time than he expected, considering the recent events were still so fresh in his mind. There were three massive buttresses braced against the main wall and it was the central one of these which helped him locate the boarded-up windows of the dining room near to where he had been sitting with the boy. Heaving aside a fallen bough, he reached the flagged area but it proved an impossible task to identify the exact spot. It was difficult to identify as it was covered in a tangle of weeds that had sprouted through the gaps in the flagstones, and the surfaces on most of those supported a lush growth of moss and lichen.

He'd been searching a specific area for over an hour when he paused to take a well-earned break and found a sheltered corner against a buttress out of the sun, where no moss or weeds were growing and where, unlike anywhere else, a mound of dried leaves had clustered together over the years against the granite blocks of the medieval pier.

Resting his back against the support, Jack idly gathered up a handful of the leaves, which crumbled to dust between his fingers. He pondered his search. It was a daunting task when he considered that the extent of the paved area would be in the region of four hundred square feet. From where he sat, the French windows were at least twenty feet away.

He shifted his position to allow the white dog more room to stretch out, and that was when he caught sight of the unusual impression in the stonework where two initials had been carved. The letters had been worn away over the years and it was hard to distinguish them exactly, but what did make his pulse race was that it had been the last thing he remembered seeing before he had passed out.

Crouching against the mound, he sifted carefully through the leaves from years past until he found an item of great importance. It wasn't what he was looking for, but what a find. He held up Ralph's precious wristwatch, astounded that a man with such an orderly mind would have lost such an important item. Indeed, had it not been for the fine workmanship of its silvered dial, he would never even have recognised it as Ralph's most treasured possession. The gold case and linked bracelet which he'd held in such high esteem were badly tarnished and Jack could only assume that his friend must have removed the watch for fear of damage during the violent struggles, from what he could remember of that evening.

To his immense surprise, the watch began ticking after he'd clipped the bracelet on to his wrist, and he felt a pricking sensation in his eyes as he dwelt on the possibility of never meeting Ralph again. As an afterthought, he searched again through the leaves close to where he had discovered the watch and, in no time at all, found both the monogrammed cufflinks, proving beyond any doubt that he had been there before. But how long ago? From the state of the place it must have been years.

When he surveyed further the terrible disorder of the estate, an estimate of years didn't seem such a wild assumption and, with the discovery of the cufflinks and Ralph's watch, he had no real trouble accepting the only explanation possible of what must have happened to him. He had actually experienced something he never thought possible. He had, indeed, travelled back in time; but if so, how far back in time? This presented a more urgent dilemma. How could he find the boy if he hadn't a clue what the year had been and how old would Duncan be now? Deep in thought, he contemplated the situation.

With a sharp intake of breath he stood up suddenly, balancing precariously on the worn granite to see further, as he had caught the briefest glimpse of russet hair beyond a yew hedge, but now it was obscured. In a matter of seconds he was down the steps and running towards the entrance of the walled garden, calling Ralph's name. When he reached the open gate, he was about to call again when he hesitated. Had he been mistaken? Uncertain, he made his way through the tangled briar by following a narrow but well-trodden path towards the potting shed and a wave of happiness warmed his heart with the hope of meeting Ralph again. He once more caught sight of the burnished hair through the bushes and the white dog charged past him.

When he entered the clearing he was stunned to find not Ralph but Bonnie, and in a place where he had least expected to see her. She was sitting in the place he had so often occupied himself in the past weeks, and it wasn't until she looked up and their eyes met that her lovely face hardened into an expression of immediate suspicion. As he approached, her slim body stiffened noticeably beneath her light cotton dress.

"What are you doing here?" she demanded, in a way that immediately put him on the defensive.

"I was enjoying the day. There's no harm in that, is there?"

"That would depend. Who are you here with?" she asked suspiciously.

"No one except my dog. I came here alone."

"I heard you calling to someone. Don't deny it."

"Why should I? It's simple enough. I mistook you for someone else."

Next to her on the bench were an empty satchel, three classic novels and a notepad in which she had stopped writing when he arrived. "Someone from the village?"

"I believe so," he responded lightly, successfully concealing the embarrassment he felt at being in such close proximity to her, and he leant casually against the wall. For a time, neither spoke as she made a fuss of the white dog.

"Who are you exactly?" she asked, with unusual directness.

"You know who I am," he answered with sincerity. "You must remember that evening at your aunt's store."

Again she didn't respond immediately, but instead she flicked through the pages of notes with increased irritation.

"I know who you're not!" she retorted, glancing up from the page and closing the notebook. "What do you take me for, a fool? You were never there. I met another man and no, I don't remember you at all!"

"But you must," he protested, desperate not to panic. With no one around to interrupt them, he had a golden opportunity to present his case and make her understand his situation. "There was an unpleasant woman with you that night who seemed to find me highly amusing?" It was a question half asked and it was difficult to keep the bitterness from his voice as he spoke. He could see he had touched a nerve by the way she gathered the tumbling hair away from her shoulders and into the nape of her neck. Even so, she was far from convinced.

"Whatever game this is you're playing, you might as well save your breath. I have good cause to remember Mr McKenzie; good cause indeed."

He could see that she didn't like it when he stared at her for too long, but it was very hard to do otherwise. Another thing he found disturbing was that, although he was much more presentable than he had been when they first met, her attitude towards him had become one of marked dislike, rather than any of the gentleness she had displayed towards him at her aunt's store. And for the briefest moment he regretted the disappearance of his habitual stammer.

"Because of the embarrassing stammer?" he asked.

"What do you take me for?" she protested. "I would hope I could see more of a person than a speech defect."

"A defect is hardly the word to describe that impediment," he responded irritably, wishing he hadn't been so riled by the attack. It was as if they were speaking about a third person and yet he was standing opposite her. "Why won't you believe it's me?"

"You wouldn't understand if I told you and, yes, he did have a stammer. A very bad one, come to that, but that was no act. He was genuine."

"In other words you think I'm not?"

She stared at him calmly. "You seem to be managing perfectly well without any trace of a stutter. You might have at least assumed one to appear more credible."

"Why can't you try to see that I'm telling the truth? OK, I know this must seem impossible for anyone to imagine but I swear I lost it, and I don't know how."

"Just like that; a speech impediment, gone in two days? If it wasn't so preposterous, it would be downright laughable!" she rallied, packing away her notes.

When she voiced some of his own reasoning aloud, it did indeed sound like a ridiculous suggestion, but he had to keep trying. He had to convince her he was telling the truth. If he wasn't able to confide in someone else soon he would go insane, which the girl probably suspected he was anyway.

"I explained that it didn't happen overnight. It took a while. A month, to be perfectly accurate," he said, hoping that she would at least hear him out.

Instead she remained silent until she had packed away her books then said, "Even so, it would have taken a small miracle to achieve that level of success, if what you suggest could happen."

"I know," he answered. There was no doubt she was more irritated by the suggestion than even remotely convinced but, since he himself could scarcely comprehend what had happened, or how long a period he had been away, it was unlikely anyone else could.

"Incidentally, what are you doing here? No one bothers to come to this place any more."

"Well you do," he retorted, close to frustration.

"I spent a lot of my childhood here and it is very special to me. That's why I come here alone," she said with emphasis. "This is not a place for strangers."

"I did work here, you know, and that's God's honest truth," he ventured, in a botched effort at breaking the ice.

She was staring at him, challenging. "Where then exactly?" she asked.

"I generally made myself useful doing odd jobs where they were needed. I worked for a time in the gardens."

Looking about her at the devastation surrounding them, she gave a brittle laugh, stood up and gathered up her belongings. "I really must go."

"But you've only just got here. Can't we just talk a while? Let me convince you that I'm telling the truth."

"There is nothing you could say which would ever convince me. I have absolutely nothing to say to you," she answered, gripping her bag tightly. "Can't you see by looking around here at the grounds exactly how ludicrous you sound?"

"Something happened to me, I don't know what exactly. I think that perhaps… perhaps I went back in time. I don't know for sure."

She wasn't laughing as she referred to the volume by Jules Verne in her bag. "That's what comes of believing what you read in fiction. I don't," she said, moving away. "Now I really must go."

"Wait! Please, don't leave yet. I need someone to believe me. Help me understand what's happened here."

She was running out of patience and was determined to end the exchange and leave. He had to stop her. There were important questions he needed to ask.

"If you would excuse me!" she said, as he barred her way on the path.

"What happened to the boy?" he blurted out, unable to contain his concern any longer.

"What boy? I've no idea what you're talking about. Now let me pass. You're blocking my way."

"Duncan, the boy who lived here? If you've been in these parts most of your life, you must know something," he said in desperation. "What happened? Where did everyone disappear to?"

"This boy you mentioned?" she asked, staring at him with uncertainty. "Why are you asking about him now, after all these years?"

"I have my reasons" was all he was prepared to say, unless she was more forthcoming.

"Duncan? Everyone knows he died in the fire."

"That's impossible! I arranged to meet him at the boathouse at dawn. The fire was almost out by then."

"WHAT?" Her response was scathing as she forced her way past. "This is absolutely ridiculous."

There was a bitter taste in his mouth and he felt sick to his stomach. It was impossible to accept. Duncan couldn't be dead. Whatever she'd gathered from local gossip, it had to be wrong. "He was in danger, but not from the fire. There were people there that night who wanted him dead. The worst thing is that I left him waiting for me to return, and when I did…" His eyes were prickling when she turned to confront him at the gate.

"You're telling me you were there at the fire?" Her cheeks flushed with anger. "How insane are you? That fire happened years ago!"

He was perspiring badly with the sweat streaming down his face, as every hope of finding the boy safe disappeared. Although he had accepted, by his own reasoning, what must have happened, to hear it confirmed, even indirectly from another source, made him shudder at the prospect of his insanity. He grabbed hold of a rotting compost frame as he felt his knees buckle beneath him, steadying himself for support as he stumbled away from her, gasping for air.

"What's wrong with you? Are you drunk?" she asked, depositing the satchel on the ground as she came to him and caught hold of his arm.

"No, damn it, I'm not!" he retorted weakly, attempting to shake off her arm. Fortunately her grip held him steady as he tottered. In moments she had him sitting, with his head unceremoniously thrust between his knees.

"Just remain where you are for a moment and the dizziness will pass. We can continue the argument when you've recovered," she concluded, with the vaguest hint of a smile.

He saw the gliding shape of the osprey blend into his own shadow as he stared at the ground. His eyes ached unbearably and his head pounded as though it would explode. Flashes of brilliant colour had begun to blank out every semblance of reality as he toppled forward, sprawling on the ground, battling every inch of the way against being returned to the past.

Hampered with drastically impaired vision, he grabbed a handkerchief from his pocket and wiped the stream of blood from his nose. Lodging the material hard against his nostrils, he forced his head back. His left temple throbbed mercilessly each time he coughed, which he did frequently. There was someone close against him who was supporting his hand, which was pressed against his nose. Eventually, when the jabbing flashes of colour had eased, he could clearly see the osprey circling above him. Only then did he voice his immediate fears.

"Where am I?"

"In Dungellen. Can't you remember?" the girl asked softly.

"I didn't go back again?"

"You've had a nasty fall."

"Did I go back?" he insisted in barely a whisper as he opened his eyes. He was seated on the ground, his back pressed up against the compost frame where the girl had positioned him. There were streaks of blood on his shirt and the monogrammed handkerchief clutched in his hand was sodden.

"You've been here all the time," Bonnie reassured him as he looked at her intently. "You can give me the handkerchief now. The bleeding's stopped," she said, removing the blood-stained material from his hand. "I'll wash this through when I get home."

"I have to find him. He can't be dead," he persisted weakly. "When was the fire?"

"You're ill. These hallucinations you've been having, they're not real. You have to see someone who can help."

"What I need more is information about when it happened. If you know anything, please, you must tell me."

"The fire was years ago. It's hard to remember when exactly," she said, removing a thermos flask from her satchel and pouring out a cup of coffee. "All I can do is repeat what my aunt told me. It was the same year that Elgar and Gustav Holst died, sometime in the thirties, before war broke out. Here, drink this," she urged, closing his fingers around the Bakelite cup. "This will make you feel better. Have you eaten anything today?"

"Nothing. Not since last night."

"A good enough reason to make you feel faint. I've got sandwiches. We can share those too, if you like," she said, as a peace offering. "Who are you really?"

"I've already told you. You know who I am."

For some time neither of them spoke, each engaged in their own thoughts.

"If, as you insist, you are Jack McKenzie, then who was the man at my aunt's store?"

His full awareness was returning and Jack knew he had to tread carefully with his answer, otherwise she would have bolted from the gardens and the delicate balance of their communication would be lost.

"It's pointless me saying. Why do you ask so often?"

"You wouldn't be interested," she answered, pouring more coffee into the empty cup.

"Is this because of the green dress?"

She was on her feet at once, her eyes flashing with resentment at the intrusion into her private thoughts. "How do you know about that? I haven't even mentioned it to my aunt!"

Instead of looking at the girl, he tried to focus on the osprey, which had perched on a section of the tower projecting above the garden wall. His head was spinning as he braced himself to stand and face her, but he found it impossible. He had to answer her question, and would be damned if he did, yet damned if he didn't. There was an unpleasant taste in his mouth as he drank the remainder of the coffee, which helped clarify his thoughts. There were no blinding flashes of colour as there had been before, but he was scared nevertheless that he was about to be transported away from reality before he could resolve the disappearance of the boy.

"Haven't you got anything to say about that?" she persisted.

"I know it once belonged to Eleanor McKenzie."

"How could you possibly know that? She died before I was born," she said incredulously, looking anxiously at him. "Enough of this. You must wait here while I get a doctor."

But he wasn't interested in anything other than the truth, now that he had her full attention. "There was a portrait of her which hung in the dining room. She wore that dress for the sitting."

"You know all of this, and yet you cannot account for the year?" she retorted, unable to help herself.

"Why would I have asked? I assumed it was still 1957."

"There must have been papers delivered to the house; you would have noticed something in the news items, or maybe have glanced at the date."

"I didn't see any."

"Then what about a radio? A house of this size could have afforded one at least," she said, waiting for the response which never came, except for a shake of the head. "There must have been one of those. Everyone listens to the news."

"There was none there."

"How very convenient. You must think I was born yesterday, expecting me to swallow such a preposterous story. So what did they do in the evenings for entertainment? They must have done something?"

"There was a gramophone with plenty of records. Oh yes. A grand piano." He could tell that her interest was alerted, and wondered why she might assume he'd been trapped by this information.

"A grand piano? Are you sure?"

"It was a concert grand. A Steinway actually," he answered, calling her bluff accurately.

"Where was this kept? In the drawing room I suppose?" she asked casually enough, but with her eyes fixed on his as she awaited confirmation.

"If they kept one there I never saw it. The one I mentioned was kept in the winter garden, on a central dais."

He had shocked her, and it registered clearly.

"How on earth could you have known about that?" she enquired, wide-eyed.

"I was there, remember," he answered, panting for breath as the dizziness returned.

The continuing nausea he felt frustrated him and made him intolerant of the ongoing suspicion. "If that doesn't satisfy you, then why not ask something which you think I couldn't have known about. Something more personal." He was taking a tremendous risk, realising he could never have all the answers, but he needed to gain her trust, and even partial acceptance of what had happened. He attempted to stand but stumbled badly and clutched on to the compost frame for support. He waved her aside as she stepped forward to assist him. "I can manage." After that he remembered nothing.

When he finally opened his eyes, she was stooping over him, coils of her russet hair, trailing like wandering spiders across his face.

"You need help. Keep still, and don't try to get up. I'll only be gone a while. I need to make a telephone call from the lane."

He heard the hasty retreat of her step and the subsequent sound of bicycle tyres on a gravelled path. He didn't attempt to move. Instead he watched the osprey launch off the tower and swoop low in his direction as the waves of nausea increased before he rolled onto his side and began retching. He felt the earth shudder beneath him like intakes of breath. Flashing colours leapt with increasing pain behind his eyes until he was barely able to see. The last thing he remembered was the osprey, hovering above him, blocking out the sun, and he passed out.

Chapter Nine

Through a dull blur, he felt strong hands lifting him up and the sensation of being carried. The white dog barked continuously as it trailed behind.

"Open the door, Phil and help me get him into the back seat," Andrew said urgently. "And watch his head on the frame."

"What shall we do about the dog?" Phillip asked

"The barking has stopped, hasn't it?"

"Yes, but we can't just leave it here," he responded, as Jack was jolted into the back seat.

"We won't, but let me attend to this chap first. Any idea who he is, Bonnie? You didn't say."

"I'm not sure. It's all a bit confusing," she answered cautiously, mounting her bicycle. "I'll ride on ahead and meet you at the house. I think the dog will follow."

"I recognise that dog!" Phillip exclaimed, as the white dog raced away from the house. "Look, it's heading for the Cap."

"I'll come back and find it later," said Andrew as the animal disappeared amongst the bracken.

"I'm sure it belongs to Jack McKenzie."

"Has he come back?" Andrew called after Bonnie as she increased her speed to get up the incline of the drive, but was unable to interpret her answer. "Who is he, Red?" he asked, catching up with her at the gated entrance to the estate.

"I've already told you. I don't know," she said evasively.

"I must have a name for the report. He must have told you something. Come on, out with it. I've known you long enough to see when you're concealing something."

"He claims to be Jack McKenzie!"

"That doesn't make sense. I thought you said McKenzie was badly injured?"

"He was in a really bad state. I met him too," Phillip concurred.

"What else, Red? Are you holding something back?" Andrew persisted, his car crawling alongside her as she cycled along the road.

"I'm only repeating what he told me. I know it isn't him."

"And? What else! I know there's more."

"Oh, very well. This man, whoever he is, has a fixation that he's been working at the old Dungellen estate for the past month."

"What? That place has been closed since the thirties!"

"He insists it was an operable estate while he was there and that he stayed in the house during that time."

"What? What the devil is he about, talking such tripe?"

"You asked what I knew about him, and that's it."

Andrew drove the short distance to reach the house in silence, debating the situation and what to do next.

"Just look at that!" Phillip said with astonishment as the car pulled up outside Andrew's home, indicating the white dog, waiting on the doorstep. "How on earth did it know we were coming here?"

"Never mind that, let's get this chap inside, where I can make a proper examination."

Later, when Andrew had removed the empty water glass from Jack's hand, he eased him back in the bed where he lay exhausted, staring blankly at the ceiling, his entire body shuddering.

"I'm baffled by this... I really am," Andrew announced. "You seem perfectly normal in every respect and yet..." he trailed off, tapping the stethoscope and re-applying it to several areas of Jack's chest, listening intently. After a time, he took hold of Jack's wrist and searched for a pulse. Throughout, his concentration was intense. "This is barmy!" he muttered, removing the stethoscope. "And how do you feel in yourself, old chap?"

"Much better than I was earlier."

"Incredible," he muttered, with a shake of the head. "I'll let you rest now. Is there anything you want from the kitchen? Incidentally, these dropped out of your pocket when we carried you in." He put the cufflinks on the bedside table.

"I'd like to get back to the farm if that's OK with you."

"It's better if you stay here tonight. I must get you to the Infirmary for tests, as soon as possible."

"Please don't. I can't leave Dungellen. Not yet, or I'll die," he protested weakly. He wondered whether, maybe, this was his body's self-correcting process.

"What do you mean? Is someone trying to kill you?" the doctor asked, but Jack was already asleep.

"It was very kind to let a stranger have your bed, Andy," Bonnie said, laying the table. "Where will you sleep?"

"The sofa's OK for tonight."

"You can't do that," Phillip protested. "You must have my bed in the studio. I'll take the sofa."

"There's no need; it's only for one night. I won't be crashing out for a while yet; I've got some research to do on his condition," he answered, searching the bookshelves until he found the volume he sought. "I need to get him into the hospital tomorrow for tests."

"Why? I thought he was recovering? Is he really ill?" Bonnie asked, concerned.

"Not in the normal sense, no, but he's defying every law of nature. By any normal standards, that man upstairs ought to be dead," he stated, examining the index of the volume.

"You can't be serious!" Bonnie retorted. "Except for the dizziness, he seemed perfectly normal."

Andrew sat back in his chair rubbing the stubble on his chin. "There's more to it than that. There's nothing wrong with my stethoscope and yet I can barely detect a heartbeat. His pulse would probably be no better… if I could find one, which I can't," he added, turning to a page on the habits and habitation of British wildlife. "If I didn't know better, I would say all the symptoms indicate he is in a state of hibernation."

"Andrew, honestly…! How can you say such a thing?"

"I know it sounds idiotic, but I have no other explanation, which is a good enough reason for him to see someone else immediately."

"Where will you send him? To the Royal Infirmary?"

"That's what I thought, but not now. He needs a lengthy examination by an expert; a specialist in mental breakdowns. The best man for this condition is in Kenmere."

"At the asylum! He isn't crazy. I'd know if he were," Bonnie exclaimed.

"I haven't done this without some consideration. Based on his unusual condition and, given his conviction he's been working on the estate for a month, it all suggests he's delusional. Something has to be done, and soon if we're to help him."

"I didn't repeat what he said so that you could use it against him!"

Andrew was genuinely concerned by the situation, and exasperated by his own inability to diagnose Jack's illness. "I not conducting a personal vendetta against the blighter. I just want to do the best I can. I only want to help the poor chap."

"Then let me try. What more could any psychiatrist know about the history of this village than I do? You know they will only ask random questions and show him weird diagrams on boards. Well, I can do better than that. I know all the details about village life in Dungellen. Who lived here and what the conditions were in the early days at the old Hall. After all, Dungellen is all he talks about."

"And Jack McKenzie."

"He's convinced of it."

"All the more reason for him to be examined by a professional. The poor chap's psychotic."

All I'm asking for is a chance to prove that he's not in need of such drastic measures."

"Very well, but not until morning when he's more rested. Question him then if you insist, but on the clear understanding that if you've made no headway by lunchtime, I shall drive him to Kenmere in the afternoon."

Jack felt unnaturally tired when he awoke after a fitful night's sleep in a strange bed. His body ached unbearably when he swung his legs out of the bed, gasping for breath. At first he was unable to stand, and when he did he experienced a severe tingling sensation in his feet as he made his way unsteadily to the window, which he thrust wide open, breathing in the air deeply.

It was a glorious morning and he longed not to feel so lethargic. The sunlight was raking across the craggy magnificence of the Cap. He leant forward to see more of the cliff face, beyond which lay the old Hall.

There were hushed voices downstairs, which had him scouring the room for any sign of his clothes, of which, except for his underwear, there was nothing.

On the far wall was a washbasin, with a mirror which he took advantage of, examining his reflection for any remains of the vicious attack back in Eastmoor. With the exception of a healed scar on his eyebrow and another, barely discernible, on his chin, there was none. Oddly enough, he also discovered there was no reason to shave that morning, exactly like the day before, which, for a man who normally woke with a heavy stubble, he found quite astounding. He was so immersed in the examination of his appearance that he didn't hear the door open, and was unaware that anyone had entered until Andrew spoke.

"I didn't expect you to be up just yet," he said. "You're not well enough to be to be out of bed. I looked in on you a few times during the night and you were very restless. Come away from the window and sit on the bed. I want to listen to your chest." He connected the stethoscope to his ears. "How are you feeling now?"

"I can't find my shirt or trousers anywhere."

"I meant, your health."

"I'm well enough to go home, I've taken up too much of your time as it is."

"Not necessarily. There's a dressing gown in the wardrobe. You can wear that for the time being. I couldn't let you go yet anyway. You were very ill yesterday, and your clothes were a bit of a mess. They've been washed and won't be wearable for a few hours yet."

222

"I've thought of that," Bonnie said, attempting to suppress a smile as Jack grabbed at the bed sheet to cover the scar on his chest.

"Red, can you leave us please. I need to check him over."

"I'm sorry, I didn't mean to intrude. I thought he would need a change of clothes," she said, placing them neatly piled on a chair. "I called at Moorcroft Farm on my way here and collected them."

"My clothes?" Jack asked, uncertain where she would have found any, except in the battered suitcase he had brought with him from Eastmoor.

"I don't know who they belong too," she said evasively. "I got them from a chest of drawers in the bedroom. I just hope they're your size." From her bag she took out a Fairisle cardigan and hung it on the back of the chair. "You might be needing this, if it turns cold."

"Thanks," he replied feebly as she began to leave.

"It was no trouble. I'll make some tea and bring you one up once you're dressed," she said, more for the benefit of Andrew than Jack. After that he was subjected to an intensive examination.

"There's no alteration whatsoever from last night," Andrew said, handing him another of the fine linen shirts from the pile of clothing. "Here, put this on, and tell me exactly how you've been feeling since you woke this morning, and don't miss out a thing! Starting with the first thing you remember."

Throughout the time it took for Jack to give a full account of his symptoms, Andrew was like a bloodhound on a trail, asking every conceivable question ranging from his normal sleep pattern to the lack of stubble on his face.

"What do you think is wrong with me?" he asked.

"I'm not sure. That's what we're trying to find out. There is a real problem in here," he said, tapping Jack on the chest as he buttoned up the shirt. "I'm wondering about this scar tissue. It could be related to your present condition, but then again, perhaps not. How did it happen? Did you have a fall climbing?"

"That's odd; Ralph asked me the same question last week on the estate," he answered, without thinking.

"Sorry, I think I misheard. Who did you say asked you?"

"It doesn't matter, you wouldn't know him. It happened a long time ago." For a moment he thought Andrew was going to question him further but after some deliberation he altered his course of enquiry.

"I would have thought that you, like myself, would need to shave at least once a day?"

"Normally I do but, since I got back, I haven't needed to touch a razor." He floundered again, aware of the interest in the other man's eyes, but Andrew chose not to pursue the slip. Instead he rubbed the growth on his own chin ruefully as he prepared to end the interview.

"I would count that to be something of a blessing. Anyway, thanks for your patience. I'll send up tea and biscuits."

Jack drummed his fingers on the broad wooden arm of the reclining chair as he waited for Andrew to return. More than anything, he wanted to get back to the farm but he didn't feel up to the walk. What he needed was a burst of energy. The mere effort of dressing seemed to have wasted every ounce he had in reserve and so, as he waited, he endeavoured to formulate a plan of how to locate Duncan.

Instead of Andrew returning, it was Bonnie who brought in the tea, which made it extremely difficult for him to concentrate on anything once she had entered the room. He found it hard to attempt a conversation, except for the obligatory "thank you". However, contrary to expectations, instead of there being an uncomfortable silence between them, he felt the semblance of a truce as she sat on the window seat opposite. This gave him time to observe her closely, as something she saw outside had caught her attention.

"Andrew, can you come here for a moment?" she called. When he came into the room, she said, "Look over there, on the Cap. What's that glinting? Are they binoculars?"

"I thought we agreed you would talk to him?" he enquired, in a lowered voice.

"I will in a moment, but I want your opinion on this."

"Why the concern? It isn't unusual for hikers to be wandering about over there."

"Yes, but why are there two pairs of them, both trained on this house?"

He peered over her head, his hand rested lightly on her shoulder with an intimate familiarity. "I can't see anything out there. Show me where exactly."

"Oh bother! Now they've gone," she said.

"One of them hasn't," he responded, staring at the area she had indicated. "They could be birdwatchers, of course, hoping for a sighting of the osprey."

At the mention of the bird, Jack wanted to join them at the window for an opportunity to see again what he had begun to regard as a phantom of his unstable imagination. Since the first sightings in Eastmoor no one but himself had seemed to notice, or comment, on either the rarity of the species or its remarkable size. However, since both Andrew and Bonnie had passed comment on the bird, it caused him to wonder if either of them had been witness to the storm.

"It was around here on the night of the storm."

"Yes, we both saw it that evening. Fortunately it must have avoided the eye of the storm otherwise it wouldn't be out there now," Bonnie responded, facing Jack. "It would be horrible to think it had been caught up in that freak weather. I can't imagine anything could have survived such a force. Thank God it was so isolated and didn't come inland."

Andrew picked up the cufflinks from the table as Jack attempted to do something with the sleeves of his shirt. "Here, let me help," he said, inserting them into the cuffs, and consulted the time on his watch. "You've got an hour, Red, and no more, otherwise I'll miss any chance of an interview with Adrian Moore."

"Why? Have you called him already?" she demanded.

"I needed to make an appointment."

"Which I hope you can cancel?"

"Yes, if I have to," he replied. "One hour is all you get. No more."

Jack felt something important had just passed between them that related to him, thus alerting him to retain concentration. His limbs felt like lead, and an invasive tiredness threatened to envelop him in waves of darkness. But he refused to submit and forced his aching limbs into action.

"Do you think you should be moving about yet?" the girl asked, expressing concern.

"I need air. Would you mind opening the window?" For the first time since he had been brought to the house, he observed his surroundings and he took great comfort in the old world charm he saw. He assumed the furnishings had changed very little since the house had been occupied by Andrew's parents. Arranged on the dressing table was a collection of framed photographs, one of which caught his attention. It was Helen as he had seen her at the fire, her arms clasped about the young Andrew.

Although he had limited vision through the window, he could sense the osprey was near, just as he had in Eastmoor. He closed his eyes as Bonnie opened the window. "Is that any better?" she asked.

He felt an invigorating rush of cool air over his face, reawakening him. "I need to get away from here as soon as I can."

"You can't just leave here like that. Andrew won't allow it. Not until he's satisfied with your condition."

"You don't understand. I must get back to the farm, it's imperative," he said restlessly, breathing deeply. He was feeling better. His limbs were less achy and his mind was clear for the first time since he'd woken. "What did Andrew mean when he said he'd give you an hour?"

"He wants you examined by a specialist."

"A specialist in what exactly?" he asked, and from her delayed response he knew precisely. "Dependent on what?"

"This is so embarrassing! I'm sorry. I've repeated everything you told me. Andrew wanted all the scraps of information I could give him," she said as he walked past her. "Now where are you going?"

"Back to the farm. I won't get better if I stay here. This 'condition', as Andrew calls it, will only get worse," he answered instinctively, urging his knees into action, walking, as best as he could, to get a clearer view from the window. "I need to get closer to the Cap, that's where I can breathe properly. This house is beyond the boundary."

"Of what?" she asked, bemused.

But he didn't answer. Instead, he looked searchingly about the room where someone might hide, but saw no one other than the girl, yet the message had come through as clearly as if Duncan had spoken, urging him to get away. Fainter, but he could hear the voice nevertheless. "I'm sorry, you wouldn't understand if I told you. I must ask you, is there anyone else in the house, other than the three of us?"

"No one except Phillip Ramsey, but he's not here at the moment. He's out running. He set off before I arrived. Don't you remember him from yesterday?"

"Should I?"

"He helped Andrew bring you here."

"Ah, he's the artist?" he answered, studying the broad, impressionistic strokes of paint expertly applied on a nearby canvas.

"That was someone else."

He could see the osprey clearly, circling above radiating bands of mist, which encompassed the Cap like the rings of Saturn, before it swooped low above the cliff top with a wild cry and dropped from sight to where he knew the farm must be.

"Did you see that?" she exclaimed.

"The osprey? Yes I did, and that's where I'm headed too," he answered, consulting the timepiece on his wrist. "I must get going."

She was clearly troubled by his decisive mood, and did her utmost to prevent him leaving. "Don't go without drinking your tea. I brought two cups," Bonnie insisted, pouring out the steaming liquid. "Sit over here on the window seat if you need air," she said, fumbling for something in her bag. "You must allow me to return this item to you," she said, handing him the laundered handkerchief.

"Thank you; there was really no need," he answered, taking the neatly pressed item from her.

"The monogram is beautifully worked. My aunt was particularly enthralled. She adores this fine work," she said carefully, making herself comfortable in a chintz-covered easy chair. "Before you were taken ill, we had been having a rather heated conversation," she said, pushing her hair away from her shoulders.

"Ah yes… I remember it well," he responded with the glimmer of a smile.

"You were insisting that I asked you some detailed questions about your time on the estate. Why was that exactly?"

"To prove I had been there. It was unfortunate that I passed out when I did," he answered, placing the handkerchief on a small table between them.

"Would you mind if I asked those questions now? We've got less than an hour."

"If you're prepared to keep an open mind, I don't mind at all."

At first, he didn't think she would ask him anything at all until her eyes flickered towards the dressing table. "That handkerchief I returned. Where did you get it?"

"I forget exactly. Why? Is this important?"

"My aunt seems to think so. She embroidered the one you have with five others as a gift set one Christmas."

"Could she be mistaken?"

"Not about her own work. So where did you get the one you have?"

"The same place as these," he answered, fingering the gold links in his shirt cuffs, thus allowing her to make a comparison.

"They are the same," she said warily, examining the blackened surface of the gold. "Why are they so grubby?"

"I found them again, yesterday. Just before you arrived in fact. I've had no time to clean them. The monogram's clear enough, isn't it?"

"Yes, it is," she answered doubtfully. "Although the same cannot be said for the explanation."

This was not going to be an easy interview but, after the heated confrontation of the previous day, he hardly expected it would be smooth sailing. But to be challenged even indirectly, and so soon, didn't bode well for the next hour.

"Before we make a start, would you mind if I asked about the watch you're wearing?"

"Not at all... do go on," he responded, displaying the blackened timepiece.

"I'm sorry, I was mistaken. I shouldn't have asked. I suppose one gent's watch is very much like another, except perhaps the shape. It was that which intrigued me."

"I suppose," he answered, wondering why she was behaving so oddly. "It belonged to an old friend. I'm keeping it safe until I meet him again."

For a moment he thought she was going to pursue the same line of enquiry, but instead she consulted the time on her own watch and settled back in the chair. "We should get on with this if you don't mind."

"I'm ready," he answered drowsily.

"During the time you supposedly worked there, was the boy ever taken ill?"

"Yes he was. Often."

"Then you would have met the family doctor? What was his name?" she asked, averting her eyes from his intense scrutiny, not wanting to give anything away.

"The only doctor who ever attended the house during that period was a woman. Her name was Helen, I believe."

After this, the change to her line of questioning would, to anyone other than him, have been barely perceptible, as she raised the next issue. "What about naming the dentist? This village is too small to accommodate one but

I'll give you a clue. The surgery we attended was in Lochenbrae," she said, searching his features for any trace of scheming. "You can't answer that, can you? Why don't you admit to this game?" she announced, expecting no response.

"Sam Grainger was the dentist," he answered. This shocked her considerably and yet, as quickly as the time it took to draw breath, she continued with the interrogation.

"I must hand it to you, your research so far has been faultless, but not enough to convince me. So let me ask you this. If you worked on the estate as you say, who did you replace?"

"All that he said was Ambrose. He never mentioned a surname, only that he was very ill and had moved down south with his family."

"He? And did this 'he' give a reason why Ambrose had travelled such a distance?"

"It was for hospital treatment," he answered, which seemed to satisfy her for the moment. Yet she was planning something else, which could only be a trap.

"And who, exactly, was the person who told you this?" she asked, looking away. "Didn't he have a name too?"

"It was Ralph, the estate manager."

"Didn't 'Ralph' have a surname?" she persisted.

"That was never mentioned."

"How very convenient," she answered, challenging him with flashing eyes. "And that's all you know about this man you supposedly worked with so closely for almost a month. Can you tell me nothing else; something personal?"

He was on rocky ground, and she was expecting more. "There had been an accident during a local cricket match which damaged a front tooth," he answered, indicating his own.

"And you saw this happen?"

"No, the accident occurred before I arrived."

"I see. Anything else?"

"It was giving him a lot of pain and he had it extracted while I was there."

She stared at him intently as though trying to peer inside his head. "And exactly how did he travel to the surgery in Lochenbrae? Did he drive, cycle, or maybe catch a bus? Take care what you say, I do know the answer to this one!"

He could hear Andrew moving about downstairs and wondered how close he and the girl were. "It was none of those. The surgery was being renovated so he had it removed in the village."

For a brief moment she appeared taken aback by the response "You couldn't possibly have known that," she exclaimed, wide-eyed.

"I could if I was there," he responded more confidently. "In fact, it was taken out in old Mr Grainger's potting shed. Where he'd set up a temporary surgery."

"Who are you? A private investigator?" she asked, in a display of temper. "No one could have known that. Not even me. Not if my aunt hadn't said," she announced, getting out of her seat and pacing around the room in agitation. "You can be quite infuriating, Mr whoever-you-are."

"I'm only answering as truthfully as I can," he responded.

She sat at the dressing table and stared back at him through the mirror, gathering up her mass of hair as she deliberated the next question. "Then answer me this if you can. Since Duncan spent so much time in this man's company, how did he address him? Was it Ralph, or was it something else?"

"He called him the Red Fox, but 'Foxy" usually," he answered, smiling gently at the memory.

She was so shocked by the response that she abandoned any further management of her hair. "That's impossible! You couldn't have known about that," she exclaimed, just a little too sharply. Her features drained of colour. "No one could."

As much as he loathed pressing home the advantage, it was time to assume more control. "And yet I do, therefore if I'm not telling the truth, how do you account for it?"

"I can't. Not yet anyway," she answered, conjuring up another way of bringing him down. "Well, if you are so very clever, what was his pet name for the boy? Ralph must have had one."

He could feel his heart racing as he confronted her, looking deeply into her beautiful eyes, which barely flickered. She didn't look away or avoiding his gaze as another girl might but challenged him every step of the way.

"See! You haven't a clue, have you? So why not end this charade and tell me who you really are?" she concluded, though with much less conviction. "You can't answer that question, can you? No one could and that exposes you as the charlatan you really are!"

"Actually, it was 'Turnip Head'," he answered, more calmly than he felt, expecting another attack, but instead he was rewarded with the glimmer of a smile.

"What? Don't be silly. Of course it wasn't. It couldn't be. Not that."

By receiving such a complete rejection, he knew at once that he had called her bluff and she had no idea of the answer. "If I'm wrong, then prove it, by telling me your own version." He was irritated by her continuing obsession with proving him wrong, and damned if he would concede on anything he knew to be correct. Why did she refuse to meet him halfway, and not consider that what had happened to him could possibly be true? "You don't know the answer yourself, do you?"

It was obvious she was floundering, from her inability to either confirm or deny his answer as she spun round to face him, her cheeks flushed and her eyes blazing. "It just escapes me for the moment but, whatever it was, it couldn't have been Turnip Head!"

"And why not? The boy was only six at the time."

"It's just too silly."

"It was nothing of the kind!" he answered vehemently. "It was the name Ralph tagged him with and, whether you choose to believe me or not, the boy loved him. I was there, remember. I saw them together and you didn't," he said, unable to curb his annoyance. "Anyway, if you're so sure I'm wrong, why not prove it. Ask your aunt; she might know. If not, there must be someone who does!"

"There is no one who could answer that, even if I was prepared to ask. Not up here, there isn't, anyway," she answered with considerable agitation. "I don't know why I've put up with this charade for so long. I refuse to listen to any more of this. I wish I hadn't intervened. Andrew can do what the hell he likes!"

"Are you behaving like this because you don't believe me, or because you're afraid you just might?" he challenged, struggling to his feet to confront her. But she was already gone.

As he passed the open window, he felt a warmth from the radiating bands of mist which encompassed the Cap; a life-force which he needed in order to breathe normally and focus on the task of finding the boy.

As he passed out of their range onto the landing, it was hard to put one leg before the other, but by this time he was so furious with the girl that he pushed himself to the limit and made steady progress down the stairs. With clenched teeth he prevented himself from crying out at each torturous step, and eventually reached the hall where Bonnie was in deep discussion with Andrew.

"What did he have to say?" he was asking.

Her features were troubled, but there was doubt in her eyes as she expounded her views in no uncertain terms. "Plenty, since you ask. I can't believe a word he had to say. The man's a liar. He's the worst kind of impostor!" she announced, refusing to look in Jack's direction as he made his way past them to the front door.

"Where are you going, old chap?" Andrew asked, lightly restraining him by the arm.

"Since no one will attempt to believe me I'm going where I hope to uncover the truth."

"In my opinion, what you believe to be the truth extends from an overactive imagination. It's impossible to separate the two unless you reject the conviction you were at the estate on the night of the fire," he suggested, not unkindly. "Be sensible, old chap. It isn't possible. The disaster you think you witnessed happened twenty-odd years ago."

"Even so, I was there. I saw how the blaze started. Everything that happened that night!" he said with conviction.

"That's impossible. How could you when I'm much older than you? I was a schoolboy back then."

"Yes, but you were old enough to drive. It was your mother who attended the wounded man that night, and I saw you drive away in her car to get help. Helen called after you to take care driving along the top road.

How would I know that if I wasn't there?" he announced. "I'm not mad, unlike everyone chooses to think, and I don't need a psychiatrist."

As if he'd been doused in cold water, Andrew stepped away.

"I need to get away from here and get closer to the Hall," Jack continued. "That's where I should be if I'm ever going to get well. Not here, or worse, being locked away in an asylum where they'd throw away the key," he concluded, whistling the white dog to heel.

He then made painful progress along the coastal track until, nearing the farm, his stride became more natural and, at last, the pain became non-existent as he scrambled over the rocks and walked past the old barn with no trace of a limp.

Chapter Ten

Bonnie cycled only part of the way back to the store and walked the remainder, debating at length on her conflicting emotions, one of which she expected to be resolved soon after confronting her aunt for the relevant information. The jangling shop bell and Hettie's perceptive look did little to induce any sense of calm as she greeted her.

There was a small pile of ironing neatly folded on the sideboard in the back parlour, on which Hettie placed the final pillowcase before she dismantled the ironing board. "Bonnie dear, has anyone upset you?"

"It's nothing really. There's been a slight misunderstanding which seems to have taken a wrong turn."

"Who with?"

The tick of the wall clock seemed louder than usual as she pondered on an answer, uncertain of how much to divulge. "You wouldn't know him, Auntie, and to be perfectly honest, I wish I didn't either. What I can't understand for the life of me is why someone with any modicum of intelligence can persist with a lie when the truth is so blatantly obvious."

"It wasn't your cousin, then?" Hettie said, putting the ironing board into a closet beneath the stairs.

"Of course not. Andrew can be irritating at times, but he doesn't lie," she responded.

"Well, since you called me from the house, what else am I to think?" she said. She angled a clothes airer across the closet door to give her niece access past the sofa. "Unless it was the lodger in the back studio. I heard from Mrs Broughton yesterday that he was boarding someone else. I would have thought he would have learnt his lesson since the last episode.

Heaven knows what your Aunt Helen would have thought if she could see what he's doing to your mother's old home!"

"You will choose to listen to an old gossip like Emily Broughton! You should try calling on Andrew yourself; you would see it's as well cared for now as it was when Mother and Aunt Helen were alive."

"I'm only thinking of Andrew's welfare," Hettie protested, fussing with a tablecloth and setting out plates. "This young cyclist could be anybody. He could be a thoroughly bad lot, for all we know."

"Well take it from me Auntie, he isn't. He's very respectable. In fact, Andrew told me the reason he came up here is to trace his family's origins."

"Respectable, is he?" she answered with interest. "And was he the person who upset you?"

"No, he wasn't," Bonnie said attempting to repress her exasperation. "It's no use asking me anything about this other man. I have no idea who he is, nor would I want to, come to that," she said, filling the kettle. "I'll make a pot of tea. Are there any biscuits in the tin?"

"There's not one in the house. Mrs Pritchard bought up every last one for the church bazaar. I'm waiting for a fresh delivery, but there are a few crumpets left in the pantry," she replied, and unhooked a toasting fork beside the fire. Bonnie took the crumpets off the shelf and drew up a chair as her aunt speared the first of three crumpets.

"I know what this other man said must have been bothering you, dear," Hettie said. "Why not tell me about it while I toast these?"

"Very well. Can you remember Duncan's nickname?"

"I don't think he had one. If he did, why would I remember such a thing? It was so long ago, dear. It couldn't be that important, surely?"

238

Bonnie fiddled with the edge of the tablecloth, debating just how much to tell her aunt. "Curiosity, more than anything else."

"Dora might remember something." She was examining the light toasting of the crumpet before repositioning it over the fire. "He was a spirited boy, and a great favourite with Mrs Jennings. You should ask her."

"This man knows so much about everything connected to the estate with such accuracy. How can that be?"

"There was a lot written about the tragedies that dogged the Laird's family. I've probably still got some of the newspapers tucked away in the attic. A lot of my generation would have kept them so it wouldn't be difficult for a stranger to come by such information," she said, removing the crumpet, replacing it with another.

"Perhaps the bigger issues, but not the smaller ones. They wouldn't be newsworthy."

"Ralph could answer your question about Duncan," she said, with some reservation, as Bonnie poured out the tea. "However, I think it would be most unwise to ask him. I'm certain that's why he never came back to Dungellen after the fire. I've never seen anyone so affected by grief."

"You think that's why he left?" Bonnie asked with renewed interest.

"That fire was a tragedy. It just about broke his poor heart when they couldn't find any trace of the boy, which is the reason he took up with that awful Connie as soon as he arrived in Edinburgh. It was an attempt to forget. He never did say, but I'm convinced of it," she said, spearing another crumpet.

"Then, if he wouldn't mention anything to you before he left here, how could anyone else know what he called the boy?" Bonnie poured more tea as her aunt removed the final crumpet and placed it with the others on a plate.

239

"There's a chance that Dora or Mrs Jennings might remember. Why is this so important, dear?" she asked, buttering the crumpets. Bonnie had added two spoonfuls of sugar to her tea, slopping tea into the saucer as she stirred. "I haven't seen you this upset in years?"

"Why do you say that?"

"Well, for a start, you don't take sugar!" she answered. She went over to the wall telephone and unhooked the earpiece.

"Well, since you ask, it's what this man says about things; personal things that no stranger could know. Apart from that he can be infuriating. I don't know why he bothers me so. He really is of no importance."

"Then it's time I made this call and informed the police about what's been going on," Hettie answered, as a woman's disembodied voice asked for the number Hettie needed. "I need to speak with the duty constable, if he's at home, Alice. If he isn't there, his mother can pass on the message," she said. Bonnie covered the mouthpiece with her hand.

"You can't do that," she whispered in alarm. "It's too drastic. There was nothing sinister about him, Auntie. It was only what he implied which had me confused."

"Hello, Mabel dear, I do apologise for the call," she said, firmly removing Bonnie's hand. "The dress patterns you ordered arrived yesterday and I wondered... oh, is he? Yes, and a quarter of backgammon and a tin of Bournvita? Yes, I'm writing it down," she said, scribbling on the notepad attached to the telephone by string. "I'm sorry, dear, the biscuits haven't been delivered yet. Yes dear, a bag of broken ones, when they arrive. There are never many chocolate ones amongst them. Yes, I will... and a quarter of aniseed balls. Very well, dear, they'll be ready for Sam to collect this afternoon."

"Thank you, Auntie. This man's been unwell. Andrew's very concerned about him and I could... well, I suppose I could have been more understanding," she said, tying back her hair and putting on a cardigan.

"Where are you going now?" her aunt clucked nervously.

"I'm taking your advice and calling on Mrs Jennings at the cottage," she announced as Hettie followed her into the store. She collected two packets of cream crackers from the counter, together with a blue bag of sugar, three bananas and a tin of condensed milk.

"Would you deliver these if you're going there on the bike, dear. Dora forgot them when she took their order yesterday."

*

For the first time since receiving his inheritance, Jack took immense pleasure in wandering through each room of his new home, removing dust covers from the furniture as he went. Everything was appropriately placed to suit the proportions of each room, and yet it wasn't until he lit the fire that evening and took time to lounge in the comfort of a winged armchair that he noticed the familiar marquetry of a cabinet against the far wall.

Eagerly he switched on a standard lamp and in no time at all discovered it was the same as the one he had admired on his first night at Dungellen Hall. It was a find that prompted him to examine other pieces in closer detail, which he also identified as having come from there. He made a thorough examination of every item of furniture in the farmhouse and soon realised there was not a single piece amongst the contents of the house he hadn't seen previously. It was a very comforting discovery, considering his current situation. It seemed as though every one of his immediate needs had been accommodated, with great thought and in extensive detail.

Every item of clothing and linen was at hand, aired and ready to use. From the neatly pressed sheets and folded towels to the contents of the chest of drawers, linen press and the wardrobe, situated in the principal bedroom, which contained all the clothes that had once belonged to Duncan's father, and which he himself had worn during his stay at the Hall.

Apart from all this, there were beautiful, deep-pile carpets laid out in the rooms, all of which were lit to great effect by a recognisable selection of standard and table lamps. In the kitchen, there was an assortment of Mrs Jennings' prized cooking utensils, a collection of Madeline's crested bone china and a drawer full of useful crockery. There was everything one might need, down to a packet of soap flakes and a bar of Fairy soap.

Oddly enough, there were no adornments on any of the furniture, which at Dungellen Hall, had been such an integral part of each room. Nor could he find any of the exquisite Venetian hangings, with their rich hues and intricate woven designs that conjured up images of marauding pirates and traders from the Orient. Without any hangings at all, the windows of the farmhouse contrasted starkly with the comfort created by the other furnishings. Neither was there a single mirror, engraving or painting of any kind, hanging on the bare walls, their absence spoiling Jack's fond memories of that idyllic time.

That night he slept like a child, awaking rested and thankful not to be in Eastmoor. With the complexities of past and current events, he couldn't have imagined that another three weeks would pass before it would be safe to venture beyond the energy field at the farm, which was in fact keeping him alive and stable.

But Jack was impatient to resolve what might have happened to Duncan on the night of the fire.

He needed to do something. Anything. It was impossible to think indoors. He needed air.

Emptying his rucksack of provisions, he found he had enough to keep him going for a few days, making a return to the store unnecessary, even though he longed to see Bonnie again. He hoped that a lapse of time before they saw each other once again might temper any antagonism, heal the breach and resolve some of their differences. Even so, he doubted he would ever convince her of the truth of what had actually happened.

He stepped outside intending to explore the interior of the barn, but with the promise of such a glorious morning ahead he chose instead to sit in the rusty car with a tin of metal polish and a cloth, to examine the etched wording on the back of Ralph's watch. After he had polished up the gold case, the blackened grooves of the engraving became clearly visible against the gleaming surface of the gold. Inscribed was a perfect dedication to his friend:

To a treasured friend and companion.
Sincere wishes on your twenty-first year.
John de Beaufort, Laird of Dungellen. May 1923

Naturally, his first instinct was to put the watch in a safe place until he returned from a walk over the Cap, but because Ralph's treasured possession had been concealed for so long, he was loath to hide it yet again, so he clipped the bracelet over his wrist. He set off along the twisting path leading to the heights of the cliff top, happy in the knowledge that, whatever had happened to his friend during the intervening years, there remained a link between them. He was thrilled to have the watch as something more tangible than a memory.

Glancing up he saw the osprey wheeling above before it dropped down towards him at a terrifying rate. The spread of its huge wings swooped low over the path, skimming inches above the white dog, which trotted on as if nothing unusual had occurred. Looking back, he watched a runner following the coastal track from the doctor's house until he disappeared amongst trees on the approach to Moorcroft Farm.

The path was much steeper than he'd imagined and the force of the wind did nothing to help the ascent. He grasped on to any handholds he could as he stumbled upwards until he reached the dizzy heights of the cliff top. As he approached the edge, the unnerving shrieks of the osprey seemed to increase. He peered cautiously down the sheer drop at the heaving waves crashing over a projection of jagged rocks thrusting out from the water. He stepped hastily away from the edge for fear of being blown over.

Sitting on a low rock he couldn't help but consider how much of this life he would have missed had he been stupid enough to have swallowed that handful of aspirin in Eastmoor, when his future had seemed so utterly bleak less than a month earlier. Now, instead, he could look out over a breathtaking, glittering expanse of sea, capped with the foam of cresting waves, beneath a sky of cerulean blue, and he thanked God for allowing him the opportunity.

When the wind had eased into a gentle breeze he made his way towards the uppermost height of the Cap, a spectacular formation of rock from the top of which he hoped to see the ruined tower of the Hall and the grounds. He continued along the clifftop path, and as he got nearer to the rock he noticed a section of the path had crumbled away. He gripped tightly onto the white dog's collar. Still watching him from above, the osprey hovered on currents of air, screeching until Jack diverted from the path and away from the cliff edge .Now he was approaching an abbey-like formation of rock on which the osprey had perched and was peering down at him from the highest point.

It was difficult to see anything properly with the sun shining full in his eyes, but Jack got the impression there were mounds of floral tributes gathered against a darkened opening, like a religious shrine. He thought he could see Ralph stooped inside the opening, against the back wall, but the sun was too bright to see clearly. Increasing his speed and shading his eyes as he got closer, what he thought was the shape of a man turned out to be the irregular back section of a cavern. It had been gated over with wrought-iron railings, similar to the railings on the estate.

Nor were there mounds of floral tributes gathered against the railings as he had imagined, except for a solitary bouquet of freshly gathered wild flowers, which had been arranged with care in a pewter vase against the back wall of the shallow cave. Immediately above this, chiselled into the rock face, was the Dungellen crest, beneath which was an inscription: 'One day he will return again to Dungellen and release the spirits from this sacred place."

Scaling the difficult ascent above the shrine, he wasn't able to stop with any degree of safety until he had reached the top, from where there was a clear view of the estate. Staring down on the bizarre transformation, he felt hot tears stinging his eyes as he scoured the neglected grounds for any semblance of the gardens as he remembered them so vividly. Yet there was no dereliction on earth that could entirely destroy the enchantment of that remarkable place. Even the tangle of briar and ivy that sprawled in a mass of green across the ruins of the tower could only contribute to the bewitching elegance of a bygone era.

Instinctively, he crouched as he caught the flash of binoculars trained in his direction, and he shuddered at the sight of the Sunbeam Talbot parked, semi-concealed, a little way from the Hall. After a lengthy time of waiting he saw two figures emerge from the trees, one of them pushing a stooped person in a bath chair. At such a distance it was impossible to identify anyone before they got into the car and drove away, largely obscured by trees.

When he climbed down, there was not a breath of wind, and he found the white dog panting in the shade of the shrine.

"Come on, Spud," he urged, walking ahead in the direction of Moorcroft. "Let's get you back and feed you."

He had been following the track for a short distance when the sight of the clusters of heather on the rocks tugged at his memory. He then recognised it as the route Eleanor McKenzie had walked as he had dreamed of her so often in Eastmoor, the woman in the green dress. This in turn brought back the memory of the kilted young man who had scaled the Cap to greet her. The hairs on his arms stood on end as he recalled looking into the face of that man who looked so much like himself. As he gazed down on the barn, he determined to explore the interior after he had eaten.

For a time he searched through the house to find a suitable key to unlock the heavy padlock on the barn door, which he eventually located. It was hidden inside a secret compartment in the living room bureau that Ralph had shown him during his stay at the Hall.

Once inside the barn the air was cool and the interior dark. The ghostly shapes of shrouded furniture stacked orderly on top of each other. Each piece carefully covered over, unfortunately blocking out most of the available light. Jack uncovered two dust sheets and found more of the gleaming antique pieces he recognised from Dungellen Hall.

Not having any means of illuminating such a vast area, he made his way up a flight of steps, lit by a shaft of sunlight from the floor above. He assumed there would be light to examine whatever was stored there, if anything, and he was not disappointed. Stacked against the nearest wall to the steps were a dozen huge laundry hampers fastened down with buckled leather straps. On the far side were eight, readily identifiable shapes of long-cased clocks, well protected beneath the draped folds of white dust covers. At either end of the top floor there were metal-framed windows illuminating the entire area of the top floor. Along the centre was an undulating ocean of sheets covering what he could only assume were four orderly avenues of framed artworks.

Before investigating any of these, Jack clambered over two of the wicker hampers and unbuckled the nearest. As he creaked open the lid, he thought he heard the white dog bark, but after listening for a moment longer paid no further heed and removed the protective sheet inside the lid to uncover the sumptuous Venetian drapery which had once hung against the long windows in the drawing room at the Hall.

Breathless, he sat on the edge of a hamper and contemplated the amassed furnishings from the Hall, wondering why so many treasures had been stored in such an unlikely place as Moorcroft Farm. He was about to climb down when he froze, momentarily, at the sound of the barn door creaking open. He moved quietly to the head of the staircase and peered down.

"Hello? Is there somebody up there?" a woman called out of the gloom, a voice he knew immediately.

"I'm here," he responded as Bonnie stepped into the light where he could see her better.

"What are you, an antique dealer?" she asked quizzically, as he came down to meet her. "I've never seen so many beautiful pieces of furniture in one place."

"Nor I," he answered, as she replaced the protective cover he had removed from the table beside the door.

"They're not yours?" she asked with increasing curiosity. "Then why are they here?"

"I wish I knew the answer to that one."

"You don't know where they came from?"

"I didn't say that," he answered, then realised the error, no doubt unleashing more questions, which would inevitably end in another dispute. "I was investigating the top floor to see what was there."

"What? There's more upstairs?" she asked in amazement.

"There are a few clocks, and some hampers of curtains. But most of what's up there appears to be paintings."

"You mean prints, surely?"

"Take a look, if you want to see for yourself," he answered, stepping aside.

"Are these steps safe? It's very dark in here. I can hardly see where I'm going." She paused on a lower step where he caught the delicate scent of the perfume she had worn when she had tried on the green dress.

"Take my hand; you won't fall if I hold on to you," he said without thinking, and it wasn't until he felt the light touch of her hand holding tightly onto his as she stumbled in the gloom that he realised what he had done.

"How amazing. There are so many things up here," she announced, as a cloud of dust billowed up when he moved a covered chair to give her more room to stand and look about her. "What is in those hampers?"

"Drapery, I think. I was opening the first when you arrived," he answered, clambering up to reach the open hamper, where he lifted up a curtain for her to see.

"That is beautiful!" she gasped as he allowed the exquisite material to fall in sumptuous folds over the lower baskets. "I've never seen material like it. Where on earth did they come from?"

When she posed the question, he answered truthfully, agonising at the inevitable outcome as he did. "They were hung in the drawing room at the hall."

"When you were there, no doubt!" she responded cynically.

"Yes, as a matter of fact... they were a particular favourite of Duncan's."

"Oh, not that again!" she announced, turning away from him as if she was about to leave. She then seemed to think better of it, staring instead at the vast quantity of picture frames, hidden beneath the dust covers.

"Would you care to see them?" he asked cautiously.

"Only if you don't give me your own version of events."

Without uttering another word, Jack carefully folded away the material into the hamper, after which he got down and removed the nearest cover from the artwork, raising a cloud of dust.

"Let me help," Bonnie said, taking up the edge of the sheet opposite him. "If we fold the dust sheet inwards, together, there will be less chance of us suffocating if you intend removing them all."

They revealed a row of carefully stacked frames. "There are some lovely frames amongst these. Have you any idea what's in them?" she asked, with the hint of a smile.

"Perhaps some of them, but not all," he answered, eyeing the many frames uncovered beneath the first sheet. "It was the pictures which caught my interest. Not the frames."

"How can you persist with such a monstrous lie?" she challenged, as they continued folding the sheets amid a haze of rising dust. "Judging from the amount of grime which has gathered on these sheets, they haven't been uncovered in years!"

His heart raced with the opportunity she had unwittingly offered. "Then why not test my knowledge?"

"What? You're actually claiming to identify all of these?"

"Of course not. I didn't go into every room of the Hall and study each of the works in detail. Do you think I'm barmy or something?" he responded, then laughed at the obvious irony. "If you go along the rows I'll suggest the ones I might know. Then you take them out and see if I'm close."

Despite not wanting to be cajoled into good humour, it was impossible not to give a companionable response. "This situation is becoming quite idiotic, you know! Most people would have had you dragged away from here in a straitjacket ages ago," she answered with the glimmer of a smile.

"Well... where do you want to start?" he asked, as they folded away the last dust sheet.

"Very well," she answered, taking up the mental gauntlet, and strolled along the first row until he asked her to stop.

"This one?" she queried, taking hold of an elaborate frame.

"Not that... the next one along, with the ebonised frame," he re-directed her, as she stooped to remove one of the framed works. "There should be four of them in the set," he said, as she took hold of the ones he indicated, displaying only the back of the picture towards him while she examined

250

the composition. "If they are the same ones which hung on the staircase, they are a series of Highland engravings by Landseer."

"They are," she answered after viewing all four, and glanced at him with some apprehension, awaiting further instruction. "What next?"

He felt better now the challenge was under way, but was all too aware that he couldn't risk any mistakes. He scrutinised the frames beside her. "Sorry for taking so long… I need to be certain what they are, before I say anything."

"Take as long as you want, but don't cheat by looking at them, except from the back."

After some consideration he indicated a frame he thought he recognised from the morning room. "Try me with that one," he said, but changed his mind when she lifted the frame clear of the pile. "I'm sorry. I can't be certain about that one. Would you try another?"

"This is beautiful. Out of interest, what did you think it might be?" she asked.

"Maybe a study in pastel of three horses' heads in a manger. I think there was a pigeon there too, but I can't be certain. The one I was thinking of was hung over the buffet in the breakfast room."

"Then presumably you would know who the artist was? If you had seen it so often?" she challenged, returning the frame carefully to its position in the stack. But he could tell by her guarded reaction that he had been right.

"It's a work by Herring and there was a water mark on the right-hand corner where it had been exposed to damp."

Without giving him the satisfaction of a response, she waited for him to suggest another work. "What about these?" she asked, pausing against a pair of elaborate frames which he didn't recognise at all, but further along there was one which he did. His skin tingled at the memory of it.

"Not those. Can you put them back and try the large gilt one near the back of the second row? I do recognise that one for sure."

"You can't expect me to lift that without help!" she exclaimed. "I'm not an Amazon!"

He couldn't help but laugh at the remark that eased the tension between them. "I wasn't expecting you to."

"Then what do you propose?"

"If I only look at the back when I lift it for you to see. You judge the content for yourself!" he said, gently easing out the elaborate frame to avoid damage, keeping the face of the canvas turned away from both of them. "Do you remember that day I first saw you in the market?" he asked, but she chose not to answer. "That was the day I saw this too!" He lifted the portrait of Eleanor McKenzie to face her. "She is wearing the same dress you were trying against you, and that I gave you that night in the store." He could see that she had been considerably shocked by the revelation, but she still grasped for a more logical explanation.

"How could you have known about this painting?" she asked with astonishment. "It must have been stacked away undercover for years. You couldn't possibly have seen it!" she announced, more in fright than with any acceptance of his claim. It only served to re-ignite his frustration with her.

"Then perhaps you can help me to understand this one over here!" he called out, striding over to the final stack from which he produced another equally large framed painting, the front of which he kept turned well away from them both. "I would very much like to hear your opinion on this one because I have no answer for this myself!" he concluded, acknowledging his own defeat as he turned it to face her.

"It's you!" she exclaimed in astonishment. "The features are exact in every detail."

"I knew that already! But who the hell is it? I don't know, because it certainly isn't me... I've never been to Dungellen in my entire life. In fact, I didn't even know about its existence until I received that letter from your office. And yet it had already been painted when I began working here. How scary is that?" For a moment they both stared at his image on the canvas in complete silence.

"What are you going to do with them? Cover them over?" she asked, reopening the conversation.

"I won't leave either of the two portraits here. The woman's especially. She was Duncan's mother, and I owe it to him to keep it safe."

"How can you be certain that's who it is?"

"If I told you, you wouldn't believe me," he answered, not expecting her to respond, which she didn't. "It was painted for her engagement; see her ring? She was still Eleanor McKenzie and lived here. This is where her portrait should rightly hang until it can be returned to the Hall." He could see she was clearly troubled by something else, but decided against questioning her about it.

"Even so, this doesn't prove you were at the Hall all those years ago... I want to believe you, honestly I do, but I can't. The idea that anyone can travel through time might be credible in a novel. But not in the reality of everyday life," she said. There had been a sadness in her voice, and as he accompanied her down the steps he took hold of her hand until they emerged into the sunlight.

Outside they perched on a wall opposite the barn. "Then let me prove you wrong and meet me in the grounds tomorrow. Allow me to prove beyond any shadow of doubt that I really was there!" He spoke with more conviction than he actually felt.

"If you like," she answered. "But it can't be too early. Auntie Hettie and I must attend an appointment with Angus McNair in the morning about some projected development which will affect the entire community if it is allowed to go ahead."

He was unnerved by this information, which he thought might be the possible cause of her distress, but thought it better to leave any questions until the following day. "You've grazed your knee," he remarked, changing the subject as she inched down her skirt to cover the wound.

"It's nothing really. I stumbled earlier. It was quite windy on the Cap."

"Were you at the shrine today?" he asked, and she nodded. "It's quite remarkable. Who is it dedicated to?" he enquired, wondering if she would take offence if he offered to bathe the graze for her.

"I thought you would have known that, since you seem to have the answers to everything else!" she retorted instinctively.

"Well I don't," he responded more sharply than he had intended at her barbed comment. "It was an innocent enough question, I would have thought."

For a moment she was silent. "I'm very sorry, that was rude of me. It's dedicated to the memory of John de Beaufort, Madeline's son. He died in a fall over the cliff where the path has eroded."

"And you put the flowers there?"

"It's a commitment, but not an unpleasant one. I've been doing it since I was a child."

"Why? What's your connection with that place?"

"My father worked every day for two years chiselling out the de Beaufort crest. He would settle for nothing less than perfection."

"The inscription too?"

"He worked on it every time he brought me back from Edinburgh. The carving was his personal tribute."

"It's remarkable workmanship. I've never seen anything to match it. For a local stonemason, he is an exceptional craftsman. The carving is beautifully done."

She smiled affectionately. "I agree with you on that, but a stonemason he was not. He's just an ordinary man like any other, who loved working the land."

"What was he then, a local farmer?" he asked, wondering about the lack of agricultural land in the district.

"Not at all. My father was employed at Dungellen Hall as the estate manager," she answered, staring at him unflinching. "You've actually mentioned him more than once in your accounts of being there… His name is Ralph Jameson."

Long after she had gone, as he transferred some of the stored items into the farmhouse, he could scarcely understand why he hadn't asked more questions about her father. There was no doubt that she had told him the truth about her relationship to Ralph. That in itself was enough reason for her to resist Jack's account of how well he had known him, considering that at the time Bonnie would have been a child. However, there were two reassuring things which had arisen when they had parted. The first was her assurance that she would meet him on the long terrace at about eleven o'clock the following morning. The other, and perhaps more important, was that they had parted on agreeable terms which gave him good cause to speculate that, after their recent findings in the barn, she might be more inclined to believe his claim of having travelled through time.

Later that morning, Bonnie leant her bicycle against one of the two shop windows and went up the steps, so deep in thought that she didn't notice the bike falling over as she entered the store.

"Thank goodness you're back, dear," her aunt exclaimed.

Her own thoughts abandoned in moments, Bonnie was at her side and assisting her into a courtesy chair situated at the counter. "Auntie, has something happened? You're all of a quiver!"

"I've had some worrying news from your father, my dear. Constable Perkins would like a word with you as soon as he can. He's waiting in the parlour."

"That can wait until you've told me what's happened. Is Daddy ill?"

"No, dear. He's perfectly well. There's been an incident at the apartment in town. The place had been ransacked when he returned there to collect his belongings."

"The flat always looks a mess when Daddy's not there," Bonnie answered with some relief. She reached beneath the counter to retrieve a bottle of brandy and poured a generous amount into a tin mug which she handed to her aunt. "There has to be more to it than that, Auntie, to involve the police. Did Constable Perkins mention what this is really about?"

Instead of drinking from the mug, Hettie handed it back to her niece. "I don't need this, dear. Pour it back into the bottle; it's too expensive to waste. I kept this bottle aside for the Christmas pudding and mince pies. A nice cup of tea will serve just as well." She got to her feet. "We can't keep poor Sam waiting on his own any longer."

"If he's here on official business, Auntie, you shouldn't use his Christian name. You never did that with his father."

Once inside the parlour, whilst her aunt occupied herself making the tea, Bonnie riddled the ash from the grate and put more coal on the fire, as a diversion from the silence from PC Sam Perkins, who could only stare in acute embarrassment into the interior of his helmet. He was barely able to communicate with Bonnie at all until Hettie returned with three cups of tea and a plate of freshly baked oatcakes.

"Now Bonnie's joined us, do continue telling us what happened, Constable Perkins. You were suggesting the burglar didn't take anything of value from my brother's apartment?"

"It seems they were disturbed before the robbery could take place. We've been informed by your sister-in-law how she had returned unexpectedly from a shopping expedition to the sales in town, to discover the apartment door open, where an unidentified person was inside, apparently searching indiscriminately through every drawer and cupboard."

"And where was Clare while this was happening?" Bonnie asked, expressing her concern. "What was Connie thinking? She ought never to have been left on her own in her present condition."

"According to my notes, her mother said the young woman you mention was in bed at the time, terrified out of her wits," the constable answered, consulting the report. For a few moments the exchange ended as Hettie urged him to sit with them at the table. This allowed Bonnie time to reflect on the information.

"There can only be one explanation for this," Bonnie confided with her aunt, in a voice barely audible, as Sam Perkins stooped to retrieve his pencil from the floor. "Andrew insisted we were being followed on the afternoon we drove Clare home."

The constable's head reappeared, clunking on the edge of the table. "Have you any idea who the intruder was?" Bonnie asked.

257

"There was no positive identification from either relative. However, we do know this was no ruffian off the street, but a well-dressed woman whose features were concealed beneath the veil of her hat. Unfortunately, there is no other description... except," he said, his voice trailing off as he read the relevant section of his notes, "it says here your stepmother gave the officer a detailed account of the hat. Even suggesting the name of which milliner was responsible!"

Hettie poured out more tea, adding three teaspoons of sugar into the constable's cup. "What I don't understand in all of this, Sam, is why on earth didn't Connie apprehend the intruder? That woman's as strong as an ox for all of her idiotic airs and graces!"

"Which is exactly what she did, Miss Jameson, but foolish nevertheless since the burglar came armed with a gun," he responded, drinking his tea.

"A gun?" Bonnie gasped.

"A gun, which was fired during the altercation with your stepmother when she cornered the woman in the back room."

"Well, good for Connie! Was anyone injured?" she asked.

A glimmer of a smile flitted across the constable's pleasant features as he smoothed the neat parting in his hair. "It would appear the only damage caused... was to a large collection of your stepmother's hats."

The telephone on the wall rang, and Hettie crossed to answer it.

"What? All two dozen of them?" Bonnie exclaimed, barely able to contain her delight.

"Your father counted forty-eight hats," he answered, looking directly at her for the first time, flushing bright crimson as he did so, and quickly examining the interior of his empty cup. "That is, of course, if you were to include the one she was wearing, plus three others in hat boxes, recently purchased, which were subsequently trampled beyond recognition during an ensuing affray."

Hearing this, it was hard for Bonnie not to smile. "And yet the woman escaped?"

"Unfortunately, yes. She got clean away without a trace."

"Given this situation, and with my father having moved out, what will they do, Sam? Two women can't be expected to stay in that place alone after this. It wouldn't be safe."

"I would assume an incident of this nature would warrant more than a basic investigation by the Edinburgh police force. Unfortunately, this is all the information I have," he answered, folding away his notebook which he placed in his inside pocket. Hettie hooked the earpiece on to the wall telephone and rejoined them.

"That was Ralph with more information. He saw them off on a train to Broadstairs, less than an hour ago," Hettie informed them. "He couldn't stay talking. He's back at the apartment packing their belongings, which he will send on this afternoon."

"Did he say anything else?" Bonnie asked.

"Only that Connie won't be returning, and he'll stay in town until he's got the apartment back in good order to hand over the keys to the estate agents."

"Why Broadstairs of all places?" Bonnie asked, puzzled.

"He mentioned they were moving in with a friend of Connie's. Lionel something or other? Ralph sounded very angry about it. I can't understand why he would take such umbrage. It seems a kind offer to me, considering the situation?"

"Well, for what it's worth, if it's Lionel Travis, it's no kind offer!"

"It can't be him, Bonnie dear… they haven't been in contact for years."

259

"Clare says different and I believe her. Personally, I think they deserve each other. How long Connie's attachment will last after Lionel's money runs out is anyone's guess. Fortunately, my dad won't be involved by then."

*

Jack felt uneasy as he waited for her to arrive. He had a strong sense that something was about to happen, but was unsure of what exactly. The sun was warm, but not blisteringly hot as it had been at other times when he was about to be challenged by the unknown, and the air, although still, wasn't static, unlike on previous occasions when he was about to be transported into the past.

When he got to his feet he had the distinct impression he was being observed and it wasn't until he walked further along the terrace that he again caught the flash of binoculars from a lower section of the Cap. Concerned about Bonnie's safety, he checked the time on Ralph's watch. She was later than expected and he hoped she would cycle, do as not to attract the attention of prying eyes, if indeed that is what they were.

He moved to another part of the terrace to wait and sat with his back resting against a buttress to contemplate exactly what else he could do to persuade her of the truth of his story. He knew he had invited her that morning under false pretences, having exhausted every conceivable avenue of proof. He tried to imagine how life would be in Dungellen with the continuing rift between them widening; or worse, if she persisted in regarding him as a compulsive liar. He had to come up with something more convincing than the portraits, which in themselves would probably have convinced anyone less sceptical. He had to persuade her differently, otherwise her tentative acceptance of him into her life would never develop and the electrifying pleasure of her company would be lost forever.

"Sorry I'm so late!" Bonnie announced, arriving flushed and out of breath, as if she had run the distance to get there. "I had a puncture on the top road which took some time to fix." She displayed the dirt on her hands. "I need to wash this grime off before I get any on my dress."

"There's an outdoor tap on the other side of the balustrade," he answered, getting to his feet, by which time the girl was already peering over to where he had indicated.

"I can't see anything!" she said, as he joined her and peered into the wilderness of what had once been Madeline's herbaceous border.

"Ah, no wonder," he mused, scouring the wall beneath them. "That's where it must be, along there, near the steps."

"I still don't see anything," she responded. He vaulted on to the stone capping and balanced on the top. "Do be careful, you were so terribly ill yesterday!"

"I'm much better now I'm here," he answered and dropped down the other side into a jungle of shoulder-high weeds. He trampled them underfoot as he tugged away a swathe of thick ivy and uncovered the tap he had indicated. Turning this on with considerable effort, he had to jump aside quickly as he tried, unsuccessfully, to avoid being saturated in the spray. They laughed and any tension between them disappeared as he turned off the water.

"When you've quite finished!" he said boyishly. She flushed and averted her eyes briefly. "Would you open the cupboard you'll find somewhere up there, behind you. I think it's beside the buttress..." his voice trailed away as he glanced into her lovely shy eyes. He felt a strong impulse to remain where he was and stare at her. But, in a heartbeat, she had disappeared.

She reappeared almost immediately. "I've found it, but it's impossible to open. I think it's stuck fast."

"Er, did you unlock it?"

"You didn't mention it might be locked. Anyway, I didn't see any evidence of a key."

Once the shock of being showered with icy water had worn off, he began to feel the cold dampness of the shirt clinging against him like a second skin. His shoe squelched as he moved back from the dripping foliage. "If you feel underneath the box, it should be hanging on a hook close to the wall." For a moment he thought she was about to laugh as he shook off some of the water that was dripping from his hair.

"Now you tell me," she responded good-naturedly, unable to restrain her amusement.

"Sorry, I'd forgotten Foxy kept it locked."

Briefly their eyes locked when she didn't respond immediately. It was as if she was trying to see into his mind.

"What is it you want me to get from there when it's open?" she asked quietly.

"There should be a red hosepipe inside on a reel. If you pass one end over, I'll connect it to the tap. There's no way you can get down here to rinse your hands wearing a dress, without it getting torn," he called after her. A few moments later, she dangled the rubber hosepipe over the balustrade.

"I've never seen one this colour in years," she said.

He attached the connection and smiled at the fond memory of Ralph's ulterior motive in keeping a small selection of gardening tools locked away inside the unit. "I need these kept away from those inquisitive little hands!" he used to say, when the boy wasn't looking but was well within earshot. In fact, he'd been taking the precaution of locking away his tools from Dora's obsessive pruning back of plants, sometimes severely, when taking cuttings for Mrs Jennings' retirement cottage.

"The hosepipe was a treasured possession," Jack continued, concentrating on attaching the stiff connection to the tap which he then turned on. "Foxy said it was Victorian and would never wear out. After all these years, it looks as if he was right."

He hastily reduced the volume of water after a squeal of surprise issued from the terrace.

"You can turn it off now, thank you. My hands are wet enough," Bonnie cried out, laughing. "And so is my hair! I'd swear you did that on purpose. I'm almost as wet as you."

They had been sitting on the terrace steps, drying out in the sun, when he decided to reopen 'the issue'. It would, he knew, inevitably have her disecting every one of his explanations. However, much to his surprise, she seemed prepared to listen. In fact, her attitude towards him had altered considerably. "Did you manage to talk to Mrs Jennings?" he asked cautiously.

"She was resting. I didn't want to disturb her." Bonnie altered her position on the steps so that she could see him better. "Anyway, I doubt that she would have remembered something as obscure as a nickname. Her memory's not what it used to be."

"Then you didn't get the information?"

"I didn't say that. I did ask my aunt too, as you suggested, but she had no idea. Which is unusual, considering she remembers every scrap of village gossip."

"Then we're back where we started."

"Not quite. I asked Dora instead. She gave me the answer."

"And was it satisfactory?" he asked rather impatiently.

"Well, that depends. When I arrived here today I wasn't at all convinced you could be telling the truth. You can't blame anyone for being suspicious of you, if you expect them to accept such a bizarre tale at face value. Would you, in my position?"

"I suppose not."

"To be perfectly frank, I can't help but be sceptical."

Contrary to what she was saying, he noticed the change in her attitude towards him and, for the first time she appeared more relaxed. "If uncovering the portraits didn't convince you that I'm sincere, then I confess you have me stumped. Anyone could see how they'd been stored!"

"I know that but... they could have been tampered with," she said, almost apologetically. "I'm sorry if that offends you. But to be brutally honest, I'm scared what you're telling me might just possibly be the truth and if it is, I'm way out of my depth. I need something more... tangible."

"The portrait of Eleanor McKenzie wearing the green dress couldn't convince you?"

"Very few dresses are made as a one-off. Others probably manufactured just like it."

"You actually believe that?" he asked spontaneously, which made her flush scarlet.

"Not totally, no, but you must admit it is a possibility."

"And what about the other painting? What about that? It was painted years ago. Anyone could see that!"

"You're right, of course, but it could be one of your ancestors. If you did inherit the farm, as you suggest, then you would have family connections in Dungellen. I'm sorry, these things alone can't convince me," she added.

"Then I'm sorry too. If you're not convinced now, there is nothing else I can come up with that might encourage you to believe me."

"Incredible as it might seem, Andrew believes what you told him, combined with his examination. I'm only sorry I can't be as accommodating. To be perfectly honest, I'll be glad when the new college term begins and I can distance myself and begin teaching again. At least there, the level of madness in the classroom is more acceptable than it is here."

"You can't mean that? Anyone can see at a glance you love this place."

"I do, more than anything, particularly on the estate, but I need to get away."

It was clear she was deeply troubled by his claims, and he felt great sympathy with her struggle against logic.

"It's obvious we will never resolve this. Not now. However, I would like to hear what Dora had to say about Ralph's nickname for the boy," he said. This caused much finger twining of the glorious red hair, and an unnecessary application of lipstick. Jack enjoyed this, and smiled.

"Turnip Head' is what she said. Dora was quite adamant about it," she answered dismissively. She handed him the brown carrier bag she had brought with her. "I brought these with me, which I think you ought to see." Together they unfolded the plans for the projected development.

"Where are these from?" he asked, with a combination of anger and astonishment.

"Clare took them from Edmund's car soon after... Jack McKenzie arrived in Dungellen."

He looked at her directly. "You mean the woman who behaved like a hyena in your aunt's store!" he stated, rather than asked. Together they studied the plans. "How can anyone but a raging lunatic propose building this hideous monstrosity here? It mustn't be allowed to go ahead." His eyes were blazing. "This must be stopped whatever the cost. With the exception of Moorcroft Farm and your aunt's property, every inch of this land belongs to the estate. It's Duncan's by right!"

"Actually, all of it belongs to the estate. My aunt's store and the Cap are both leasehold. As, I imagine is Moorcroft Farm. But none of it will be safe next month."

"How do you know all of this?"

"My aunt! Apparently there was a codicil incorporated into Madeline's will on the night of the fire which Auntie Helen notarised, which in effect, meant the Kincaids were unable to inherit. Not unless Duncan didn't return to claim his inheritance."

"Was there a time limit applied to this?"

"Yes. It must happen before his thirtieth birthday."

"He must be getting close to that age by now?"

"When I worked at the office, Mrs McNair mentioned Blake-Courtney was planning a transfer of ownership on the tenth of October, which is Duncan's birthday."

"That's only three weeks away! We must prevent this ghastly project from going ahead at all costs, Bonnie. We have to find him."

"We can't… that's impossible. He died in the fire. Everyone knows that!"

"He was alive when I last saw him on that night, and the blaze was well under control. You might have believed the scaremongering if you were only a child at the time," he said intensely. But Ralph would never have been convinced. I know him well enough to be sure that he would never give up on Duncan. I'm right, aren't I? He didn't believe the rumours, did he?"

"No. He never would. Contrary to my aunt's conviction that he's wrong," she admitted. He folded away the plans, returning them to the carrier bag, and picked up a rusted tin box from against the buttress where he had been sitting. Without resistance, she allowed him to take her hand and lead her along the terrace, stopping immediately before a pair of tall French windows. "What are you up to now?" she asked, as he crouched down and removed an object from the tin box.

"You'll need this if I'm to convince you I was here that night."

"Oh no, not all that again!" she protested. But her curiosity got the better of her as he produced the silver penknife from amongst the rotting folds of the material.

"This belonged to Duncan. It was a gift from his father which he wanted me to have. I couldn't accept it at the time."

"Then why do you have it now?" she asked.

"Because it was the only piece of tangible evidence I could think of, before you arrived, which I hoped might convince you I was telling the truth," he answered wryly. "It was buried in a hiding place near the boathouse, which I wanted you to unearth once I'd shown you where it was hidden."

"Then why didn't you wait until I got here before you dug it up?" she asked, as he brushed off some of the damp earth before handing her the tin box.

"Anticipating your reaction, I suppose," he answered lamely, watching closely as she examined the rusted lid.

"And what would that have been?"

"I got to thinking that it would have made sense if you'd thought I'd buried it myself before you got here."

"You must have had problems getting the lid off," she observed with interest. "It's completely rusted."

"I had to force it off with a bent nail and a penny," he answered. He took out of his pocket a rusted, cut nail of the old-fashioned variety, along with a bent coin, marrying them both against the scratch marks and grooves on the tin box.

"And what am I expected to do with the knife?" she asked curiously as he paced cautiously in front of the boarded-up doors.

"I'm certain this is where Duncan tripped up and dropped his pencil box the afternoon I took sick," he said. He examined the thick growth of moss between the flagstones, gauging an approximate distance from the doors with great care before he got to his knees, indicating a specific area. "If you probe around in here you might find something from that incident which fell between the cracks," he said, offering her the opened knife.

"Are you serious about this?" she asked, crouching against him.

"Never more so."

"You can't be certain about that. All these slabs look the same. What if you're wrong? No one could know what's under here," she said adamantly, testing the springy moss with the knife.

"I'm prepared to risk it. That's where you'll find something from his box."

"Such as?" she asked, unearthing a section of moss which produced nothing.

"You mightn't find any pencils. We collected most of those up. But I remember a lot of pen nibs being scattered," he said, as she unearthed a crumbling yellow crayon.

"How extraordinary. I can scarcely believe this is here," she murmured, unearthing another section of moss, beneath which she produced a cluster of pen nibs, rusted together into a clump. "This is remarkable!" she said, wide-eyed. "How could you? How could anyone have identified this spot so accurately?"

"I remember every inch of the grooves in this particular flagstone. Later on, when I became ill and could scarcely breathe, I collapsed and this carving was in my vision just before I passed out." He indicated the worn indentations cut into the surface where someone, years earlier, had carved the initials J.M. "It couldn't have been anywhere else along the terrace. This is where Ralph came to my assistance and carried me inside. He must have taken off his watch that afternoon and put it with my cufflinks for safekeeping. That's where I found them," he said, gesturing to the specific area against the buttress. "I know this watch meant a great deal to him, and that's why you must have it," he concluded, removing the gold-link bracelet from his wrist and handing her the watch.

There were tears forming in her eyes as she examined the timepiece in great detail. "Why have you been wearing it all this time? You wore it the first day I saw you here."

"I was keeping it safe. I didn't know then that Foxy was related to you."

Bonnie turned her head away to examine the inscription on the reverse before she confronted him. "His name isn't inscribed on the back... how could you know it belonged to my dad? This watch could have belonged to anyone."

"Because I've seen him wearing it often enough!"

She handed back the silver penknife.

Just then the osprey circled above them and alighted in a flurry of feathers on the balustrade a short distance away. The draught of its wings ruffled the folds of her dress.

"Don't be alarmed by the bird. It's around here all the time." Jack said, in an effort to regain a semblance of normality between them.

"I'm not. I don't think I'll be surprised by anything ever again," she responded with an enigmatic smile, handing back the watch. "I think it would be better if you kept this safe until I need it. I would hate it to get lost again," she said.

"Thank you," he answered, uncertain of what had caused her to react so generously. "I'll keep it safe, I can promise you that."

"I'm sure you will." She stretched lazily. "It's such a glorious afternoon. I feel like walking. It's too hot sitting here in the sun."

"I would like to see Mrs Jennings and Dora and ask them about that night. They might know something about what happened to the boy. If these plans are genuine, we need to find him more than ever," he said.

"I'm afraid that won't be possible."

"Why ever not?"

"They don't encourage visitors. Not any more. Mrs Jennings now sleeps for most of the day, and Dora? Well for her, it's more through choice. She doesn't like strangers."

"I'm hardly that and I would still like to visit them," he said firmly, and in such a way that she found it impossible to resist.

Mrs Jennings' cottage was located well away from the others that had once been occupied by lower-ranking employees on the estate, situated close to the north gate that opened into a lane running parallel to the cricket field.

Their cottage was set in an idyllic position beyond an meadow ankle deep in lush grass and flecked with wild flowers. After the meadow, the lane passed through a cluster of drooping willows, then narrowed to a footbridge from where a path led to the cottage.

The property had an old world charm, unaltered in years. It had two dormer windows set into the slate roof. On the left, there was a row of low outbuildings. On the right, a long wooden shed, and a brick-built privy. A low granite wall surrounded the ample grounds and the cottage itself was reached by a gently rising path, leading to a latched wooden gate.

On either side of the walkway were the gardens, choked with an array of flowers of every description. He remembered Ralph's comments on Dora's keen interest in getting the gardens "nice" for Mrs Jennings. Beyond the eye-catching floral display was a small orchard of gnarled fruit trees and a garden shed. Amongst the trees, a goat and two sheep were busily chomping the grass. Amid the noisy flurry of scattering fowl, an aged, arthritic sheepdog plodded towards them along the path, its bark, barely audible from a worn-out larynx. Leaving the old dog to the canine ritual of circling Jack's dog, they knocked on the cottage door.

"There's bound to be someone at home," Bonnie said, when they got no answer. From the corner of his eye Jack registered the edge of a net curtain twitching back into place in the room next to him, but he chose not to turn and look in case it was Dora, who might panic at the sight of him waiting there. And he presumed she had, since no one came to receive them at all, thus prompting Bonnie to enter the cottage and go into the sitting room, where they found Mrs Jennings asleep in a chair.

It was extraordinary for him to be suddenly presented, not with the jolly, comforting woman he remembered so fondly from just a few days earlier but instead to be staring at someone so drastically altered that she was barely recognisable. Transformed from the sturdy, homely creature who had concocted such miraculous food in the kitchen, a woman with glowing cheeks and radiating health, to a person shrunken to the point of emaciation. Her skin was dry and dusty, the texture of chalk. Her shape, even while sitting, was bent double in the chair.

Not wanting to startle her when she awoke, he crouched against her as she opened her eyes and stared into his own in the way he remembered. "How nice of you to call by the house," she said, smiling into his face as he took hold of her hand. "It's so good to see you looking so well. Is Eleanor with you today?" she asked, dashing his hope that she had remembered him. Soon after, she drifted into the comfort zone of sleep, and began snoring.

To prevent Bonnie seeing how the distressing alteration of Mrs Jennings had affected him, he avoided looking in her direction and, removing a handkerchief from his pocket, blew his nose as he wandered about the comfortable sitting room. He examined the nostalgia of a bygone age in the many Victorian prints, amongst which he came across a sepia photograph of the Hall the way he preferred to remember it. He took it down from the wall to examine it more closely.

"It was you, wasn't it? You were there with that white dog. Out in the gardens that night." A reedy voice stated accusingly, making him turn.

272

Fortunately, the alteration in Dora's appearance was not so drastic as that of Mrs Jennings. It was apparent she had aged, being no longer the young woman he remembered, but he recognised her immediately and, given the manner of her greeting, he recollected how old Ross had muttered that Dora "saw things", apparently things which no one else could see.

"I was there, yes, with my dog."

Removing the framed photograph from his hand, she too, gazed lovingly into the captured image. "It's supposed to be like that again – if someone cares enough," Dora said, tugging at his arm urgently. "If you go back again, take Mrs Jennings with you. Please!" she whispered to his reflection in the picture glass.

"You mean, they're expecting I should go back?" he asked curiously.

Instead of answering, Dora shook her head and changed the subject, and thereafter ignored Jack's presence amongst them. She inquired shyly after Bonnie's father, and less shyly about Hettie's collection of dressmaking patterns whilst she brought out a tray of tea things and a plate of fresh scones.

"I wish I had learnt the art of baking like the missus here. She was a wonderful cook, was Mrs Jennings. Everything she made turned out to perfection."

"These scones are delicious, Dora," Bonnie said, brushing away the stray crumbs from her skirt. "She must have taught you how to make these?"

But Dora shook her head. "The missus never cooked another morsel after the fire. Always kept saying the next thing she would make would have to be a rice pudding for the young master. If he ever came back!"

After the tea and scones, Dora herded the arthritic collie into the kitchen. All this time, Jack's dog had been lying quietly by the door, and as they prepared to leave he showed no interest in moving. He finally took the dog by the collar and held on to it until they were well clear of the orchard and beyond the garden gate. Only then would it follow them, albeit somewhat reluctantly.

There was a silence between them as they returned to the Hall by the same route they had come, and it wasn't until they had crossed the narrow bridge and the meadow that she posed the question.

"You liked him a lot, didn't you?" she asked, without lowering the intensity of her gaze.

"Who couldn't have liked a boy like that? He was unique."

"I meant Ralph... my father."

"Then you believe me?" he responded with startled incredulity.

"Yes, Jack, I do. You couldn't have known what I would find buried on the terrace. Or how much my dad cared about that watch. Not unless you'd witnessed those things for yourself."

Although he felt he should answer, he chose not to, deeply moved by her unexpected sincerity. They continued the rest of the journey in silence. When they had reached the winter gardens, and Jack was watering the dried earth of the beds, examining each plant for any sign of new growth, she posed another question.

"Will any of your family be joining you at the farm, once you are settled?" she asked.

"I don't have any. Not any more. There was an older brother who was killed along with my dad in an accident down the pit. My mother died eight years later. I've been on my own since then."

"How old were you?"

"Fourteen," he answered, very matter of fact.

"I'm sorry," she responded, before she ventured into an area of her own past which had been clearly troubling her. "What was my dad like when you knew him?"

"Where do I begin?" he responded with an infectious smile. "Everyone here adored him. It would have been impossible not to!"

"And what about Duncan? Did he feel the same?"

"Your father was his shining light. He worshipped the man. Ralph was the perfect hero for any fatherless child. He involved him in the workings of the estate in preparation for when he came of age. Taught him to play chess. In fact, he encouraged him to be creative in anything at all, to prevent him from becoming lonely."

"My aunt and my dad loved coming here. He brought me with him a few times, but it was so long ago, it's hard to remember exactly. What else?"

"Ralph sang quite a lot when he was happy. Show tunes, most of the time, and a bit of opera, although I've no idea what. He whistled too when he was preoccupied. A tune he'd composed for the boy when he was ill," Jack answered, as he cleared an area away from the dais where the grand piano had once stood. "Duncan would curl up here with Spud, listening to Ralph whistle while he tended this marvellous indoor garden." When he glanced again in her direction he could see that she was clearly distressed by the line of conversation, and probably on the verge of tears. "I'm sorry. It wasn't my intention to upset you."

"It's my own fault for asking the question I suppose. I barely remember any of this, except for a lullaby and yes, the whistling. It always made me stop what I was doing and listen. He never sang or whistled a note after the fire."

For a moment he imagined she had unburdened her thoughts, but not, it would seem, her innermost fear.

"I often wondered… if he would have altered as much, if Duncan hadn't been killed in such a horrible way," she said, wiping her eyes with the handkerchief he provided. "He searched every inch of the gutted tower and the estate. Every day for months after. He was like a man possessed, my aunt once said.

"It makes sense that it would affect him badly if Duncan was missing. Ralph thought the world of that boy."

Her face was bleached white, her mouth trembling badly as the delicate hands clenched tightly together. "But not me, it would seem!"

"What are you talking about? Were you missing too?"

"Of course not. I'm only questioning why he would take me away from a place where I was idyllically happy, and marry a horrible woman like Connie."

"That's rubbish, and you know it. How could you even think that about him?" he exclaimed unsympathetically. "Ralph adored you, and hardly made conversation without you being mentioned… at least once. He loathed the idea of uprooting you from this place. He talked about it more than once, but what option was there for a single parent? He had to earn a living and, since your aunt was finding it difficult to cope…" He broke off, unable to complete the sentence at the first hint of a smile as she looked up.

"You mean with a headstrong girl like me? But why sacrifice everything he had achieved up here to go away and marry?" she concluded.

"So you would have a mother's guidance."

"I wish I'd known all of this before now!"

"He couldn't have told your aunt the reason for taking you away. She wouldn't have allowed you to leave if he had."

He was about to say more when the noise of the first gunshot rang out. An explosive sound, which had them both scurrying outside just as the second shot rang out from the Cap. At the sound of a man's cry from the edge of the spinney, Jack raced towards the noise, keeping pace with the white dog, with Bonnie following a few paces behind, ignoring his calls to stay back.

Ahead of him, the osprey swooped above the trees, where it then hovered until he got closer. Then it alighted on the bough of a tree at the edge of the spinney. The inert figure of a man lay on the narrow track that led up towards the Cap.

"I know this man," Jack announced as he crouched against him, examining the gash at the side of his head. "Thank God he's not dead," he said peering into Phillip's face as Bonnie got down on her knees to help. "I don't think he's been shot; the bullet's probably embedded in that tree," Jack said, indicating a savage gash in the trunk at head height. "This chap's had a lucky escape."

"I'd better go and get help."

"No. It's better if I go. You stay with him, and keep out of sight," Jack said. "It isn't safe if you are exposed to whoever's out there!"

Squeezing his arm affectionately, Bonnie shook her head as she got to her feet. "There's no need for concern. I won't take chances with these poachers about. I'll be safe enough. I know these woods like the back of my hand. There's only a narrow field to cross once I get clear of the trees, then I can reach the road opposite my aunt's store. It won't take long before I'm back with the car."

Realising her suggestion made sense, Jack refrained from any further protest. "I'm sure I know this man," he repeated.

"It's Phillip Ramsey. He's staying with my cousin Andrew," she answered.

"I didn't know you were related; well, not for sure anyway."

"I thought you knew. It's inevitable in a village as remote as Dungellen. If you delve deep enough!" She stopped talking as he caught hold of her arm, listening intently. A car engine had started up nearby, where it had been concealed amongst trees close to the main approach to the Hall.

"They're getting away," Jack announced angrily, as Phillip stirred, groaning.

"Why would they use a car?"

"Well, they're not poachers, that's for sure. This chap was their target. What was he doing out here, dressed like this?" Jack said, indicating his vest, shorts and black plimsolls. "I thought you once said no locals ever ventured on to the estate?"

"Phillip goes running every day to keep fit," she said, peering through the trees, shielding her eyes from the glaring reflection of the sun. She watched the sleek bodywork of the Sunbeam Talbot as it swept past, accelerating fast.

"Were you able to make out who was driving?" Jack asked, unable to see anything himself as he was supporting Phillip as he began to come round.

"I'm sorry... the glare was too strong."

"You'd better get off to the store and collect the car. At least it will be safe out there now."

"Should I get Andrew?"

"You'd better come straight back. We can take him there together."

She held back at this suggestion, expressing her concern. "You'd better not. You know how you were affected being away from the Cap. I'll take him to Andrew's myself."

She returned less than half an hour later in the shooting brake. She then drove off with Phillip, telling Jack she would call at the farm on her return.

Two hours later, Bonnie and Andrew were at the store. In the back parlour, Hettie was busy with her darning and Bonnie had avoided the likely threat of an interrogation from her aunt by excusing herself to get changed. She left her cousin to deflect any awkward questions on his own.

"Another shooting, and after that incident involving poor Eleanor. These poachers should be outlawed. It's quite scandalous. The country's becoming more like America every day. Have you informed the constable about what happened?" Hettie asked.

"Well naturally. As soon as I'd taken care of the wound."

"Was the young man hurt badly?" she asked and was relieved when Andrew shook his head.

"Fortunately, he's suffering from nothing more than a thumping headache."

"It couldn't have been intentional, could it? Not the way Bonnie implied? Something must be done! Who knows what could happen next with such indiscriminate shooting."

"While I was there, I had a look at where the tree had taken both hits. If the shots had got him, his head would have been blown clean off! That was no accident, Hettie. It was a calculated shot. Who the devil could have done it? I've seen no strangers about."

"Years ago, a shot would never have been fired out of season, and then only on the estate."

"Mother was never convinced the shooting on the Cap which killed Eleanor was an accident," Andrew answered, thoughtfully.

"Helen was very close to Eleanor. She was bound to think that, if the police couldn't find who was responsible."

"You must admit though, it does make you wonder, considering the events which followed; the Laird falling to his death a few years later and that fire which killed their only son and heir?"

"Well, there have been some odd happenings in Dungellen these past weeks," Hettie said absently, contemplating a hole in a lisle stocking.

"I wouldn't mind taking a look at some of the police reports. Get a more informed idea of what did happen. I can't remember much about it… except the fire."

Hettie peered at him over her spectacles. "Well, that will never happen! However, I do have a few local newspapers I saved from that period. You might find something in them of interest."

"Where are they?" Andrew asked, getting to his feet.

"Not now, dear. They're in one of the suitcases, stored in the loft. If you call by tomorrow I'll show you where they are."

Jack finished bringing stuff from the barn, perhaps more than he could accommodate inside the farmhouse, including some of the paintings, bronzes and window hangings. He set the portrait of Eleanor McKenzie in an alcove alongside the inglenook fireplace and stood the other painting, of his doppelgänger, against a nearby wall, both of which he intended to hang in the daylight when he could position them better.

That night, his sleep was haunted by the vision of himself stepping out of the portrait. The first time he awoke with a start, to discover the man staring at him intently from the window seat, his back pressed against the shutter, his knees drawn up against his chest and his arms gathered around them. As Jack sat up in bed, the moon emerged from behind a cloud, and the image of the man melted away into a haze of silvery light.

The second time he awoke, the man was seated at the foot of the four-poster bed with the white dog curled up against him. However, unlike his own face and that of the portrait, there were signs of stubble around his jaw. Other than that there was no difference between them. This time the image didn't dissolve immediately, but continued to stare back until Jack sat up. Only then did the ghostly figure stand up and, stepping back, became silvery in the shafts of moonlight, before vanishing.

Unable to contain his curiosity, Jack got out of bed. He felt the warm indentation in the bedspread where the white dog lay sleeping and where he discovered Duncan's worn teddy bear, which he had last seen in the boy's bedroom on the night of the fire.

Throughout the remainder of the night he slept fitfully, waking the following morning with a splitting headache. It was barely dawn when he went for a swim in the bay. It did very little to ease the throbbing pain which was centred immediately behind his eyes, but nevertheless, he returned to the farm infinitely more refreshed.

Inland, the night sky above the rugged hilltops was lightening, the air sweetened with night-dew and honeysuckle. As he was about to enter the farmhouse, he glanced towards the darkened area of the Cap where he saw an unnatural glow, isolated above the craggy heights, over Dungellen Hall.

After swallowing a couple of aspirins, Jack went back outside to be greeted by the new day, which obliterated any trace of the earlier glow from the Cap. Something was out there, he was certain of that, but he had no inclination to venture up there to investigate. Instead he returned to his bedroom where he lay on the bed, intending only to close his eyes until his headache eased. He awoke two hours later to the sound of Bonnie's voice, calling from the stairs.

"Jack? Are you up there?"

"I'll be down in a minute!" he answered, struggling to get dressed. The pain in his head was now little more than a dull throb.

"The paintings look nice there," she said, as he joined her in the living room.

"They do, don't they? Why didn't I think of hanging them together over there?" He was staring at the painting of Eleanor McKenzie which had been placed next to the portrait of his lookalike, hanging on the main wall. "Is Andrew with you?"

"No, he's coming here later. Why?"

"Then who hung the pictures there?"

At this, she laughed awkwardly. "You did of course. Who else is here?"

"No one. I don't know why I asked that. But to be honest, I can't remember hanging them either," he shrugged. In the quietness that followed, he filled up the kettle and put it on the stove.

"Did you like my dad?" she asked, posing a question which made him laugh.

"Like' barely scratches the surface of my regard for him," he mused, pouring boiling water into the teapot and mulling over the perplexing issues which had arisen in his initial meeting with Ralph.

"Something's troubling you, Jack. What is it?"

"I'm certain that one day I'll wake up on a psychiatrist's couch, analysing the crazy notions I had the first time I met him."

"You say the oddest things."

He took time to consider.

"To begin with, I hadn't a clue what had happened, when you consider the improbability of someone travelling through time, to realise then…" he faltered, unable to continue as he experienced an unpleasant wave of nausea. He could hear her speaking, her voice was clear enough, but fainter than before and gradually receding. Unable to speak, he thrust open the window, his mouth agape as he inhaled deeply and desperately, certain he was going to pass out as his mind started to swirl in ever-increasing waves of darkness.

"You were saying?"

Clenching his hands, he dug the fingernails deep into each palm, as he continued with the conversation, attempting to remain focused. "I was shocked when I saw Ralph that first day," he said, feeling less nauseous and rolling back the sleeve of his shirt, exposing the gooseflesh along his forearm. "This happens every time I think about that day."

"Why? You couldn't have been scared of him? No one could."

"And I wasn't. It's difficult to explain properly how I felt. What troubles me is, how could someone actually recognise a man they'd never set eyes on before? And yet I knew him, instantly. I was convinced of it!" he said, clearly troubled.

"You're implying… you've been even further back? That time wasn't the first?"

"I honestly don't know. If I did… I can't remember anything about it. All I can tell you is that I recognised him. I knew even before he spoke what his voice would sound like. How perplexing is that?" he said weakly, his breathing noticeably shallower and laboured. The tone of his voice was rasping.

"You're shivering," Bonnie said, wrapping a blanket about his shoulders, which he pulled tight around him. "Come away from the window. Please. You're unwell. You should be in hospital, Jack, not here in the middle of nowhere."

His head started to throb again as the draught of cool air dried up. A searing pain flared at the back of his eyes as he attempted to focus on the Cap. "If I'm dying, I don't want to be anywhere else," he answered simply. He regretted his words instantly as she turned away abruptly, tears welling up in her eyes.

"I really need air!" he gasped, lurching against the wall. He would have fallen if he hadn't held on to the dresser by the kitchen door. "There's something happening out on the Cap," he attempted to say, but the words fused together and came out in a slur. He winced as shooting pains raged inside his head. He was unable to focus through double vision, but even so the activity on the Cap was clear enough.

A heavy mist had begun seething around the base. At the top, a seemingly impenetrable fog obliterated the familiar contours of the peak, from the centre of which an explosive shower of blinding flashes was being flung high in the air, as if the top of the mound was about to erupt.

Turning away from this mesmerising sight, he saw Bonnie approach him, voicing words he couldn't hear. When he reached out his right hand to take hold of her, only a ghostly shape of his arm appeared to rise; the solidity of his right hand was still grasped on to the dresser. When he looked for her again, she had disappeared. "Bonnie! Where are you?" he called out, stumbling past her without seeing. "You must get away from here. You're in grave danger!"

"I'm here, Jack, standing next to you." She reached out to take hold of his arm, only to grasp at thin air as the limb passed through her own hand as if she were dreaming.

His face felt scorched by the heat from the Cap. It was as if he was being seared alive. All the time his nausea increased. The horrific noise in his head increased tenfold, screeching like fingernails scraped across a blackboard. Despite his pain, he had to find her, and groped about the room unseeing and disorientated, suffering agonies as he blundered on.

Try as he might, he couldn't ignore his distorted vision, worsening as he stumbled into the kitchen. He careered into an enamel-topped table, displacing a pile of crockery and sending the plates crashing to the ground. To prevent himself from toppling over, he gripped tightly on to the doorframe as the flagstones beneath his feet began to vibrate, lurching up at obscure angles as though by the force of an earthquake. He staggered across the heaving, uneven surface, believing Bonnie would be outside, but she was nowhere to be seen.

Outside the farmhouse, the previously rusted tourer was unrecognisable in its current, immaculate state. The impeccable enamel of the bodywork and high polish of the chromium radiator grille and headlamps glistened in the unnaturally harsh glare of sun.

Curled up against the windscreen was his old cat, which stretched in preparation to greet him. Mewing loudly as it came towards him, the image began to dissolve into a heat haze. Likewise, the white-walled tyres on the vehicle dissolved like paste, leaving only the rusted spokes of the wheels as both images distorted, then disappeared. Jack's nausea increased.

Supporting himself against the wall he began to retch uncontrollably. Not normal vomit, but shards of yellow crystal flecked with crimson with every uncontrollable spasm. By now, the pain in his head was excruciating, as if it were clamped in a band of steel, ever-tightening with each retching motion.

He felt more physically drained than at any other time in his entire life and was frighteningly aware that his body couldn't take much more. The pain was occurring with such agonising frequency he thought death might be a welcome release.

Just as he felt he couldn't stand the pain any longer, he became aware of the softness of her body supporting him as his legs began to buckle beneath him.

"Thank God you came back... I thought I'd lost you!" Bonnie said with emotion.

He could tell by the quiver in her voice that she was really upset, but he was too exhausted to see her clearly as she cleaned the yellow saliva from his mouth with a handkerchief. She supported him away from the stench of the vomit, and eased him on to the running board of the rusted tourer, where he leant back exhausted.

"Was there much damage from the earthquake?" he asked eventually, not looking at her, but into the cloudless sky. The osprey could be seen hovering above the Cap, seemingly fixed in one position without any movement. "The house was shaking. I couldn't find you anywhere in all that chaos. I'm sorry. Are you hurt?"

"Not at all... Jack, there's been no earthquake. Nothing happened. Nothing at all."

He leant forward, resting his head wearily in the palms of his hands. "What? You didn't see anything? You didn't experience any of it! I couldn't have imagined it."

Moving closer, she put an arm about his shoulders. "There's no need to convince me that you experienced that. I saw what you went through... I know you're not lying."

"But how could you, if you didn't see anything?"

She stroked the downturned head reassuringly. "You were disappearing into another time, and then you came back; that was enough. Thank God you weren't taken all the way."

"Then nothing's been changed here?" he asked.

"Not inside the house, except for the broken crockery when you fell against the kitchen table."

"Something must have happened… or is about to," he said wearily, wanting nothing more than to lie down and sleep. "There is a reason for everything that happens here. There must be an explanation for what I saw. There has to be!" He swayed unsteadily as he attempted to stand, and sat down again rapidly. "I saw my old cat barely moments ago, for the first time since I came back."

"A cat? I didn't know you had one?"

"The last time I saw it was the night of the fire. Dora had it with her. The barrier must have opened again. It's the only explanation for what happened." He motioned her to keep silent as he listened intently. "Do you notice the stillness here? There's not a bird singing anywhere!" he concluded, struggling to his feet. His focus was fixed firmly on the osprey, which continued to hover over the high peak of the Cap with the same, unnatural stillness, and appeared to be staring directly at him.

He knew he was expected to climb to where it was hovering, and he staggered away from the rusty car, and from Bonnie's protests, towards a little track which veered away from the steeper, rugged route and gave a swifter access the top. When he looked back, he expected to see Bonnie at the farmhouse, but she was following close behind, with the white dog at her heel.

"Go back, please!" he shouted, grasping a clump of heather to prevent himself from falling, and gasping for breath.

"You can't attempt this climb alone, Jack. What are you thinking of?"

"Please go back, Bonnie. I need to reach the top on my own," he cried.

"Don't be so damned idiotic… I've climbed every inch of the Cap since I was a girl. You need me with you. You could easily fall if you take this route!" she said in exasperation as he resumed the arduous climb.

He reached the top exhausted and barely able to feel any sensation in the fingers of his left hand as he gripped tightly on to the dog's collar. "Do you see that?" he asked, but she could see nothing of the simple floral tribute of fresh flowers which had been placed against the outer railings of the shrine. Nearby, folded neatly on a rock, was a tweed jacket, woven in an unusual design, with neat elbow patches stitched on the sleeves. Above him the osprey still hovered as though painted into the sky, with not a feather tip moving.

"You see? There's nothing up here, Jack. When you've rested, I insist we go back to the farmhouse, but this time taking the path."

"I can't go back. Not yet," he resisted. He realised that, if she stayed, nothing would happen and the reason for his being there, not to mention the tortuous climb, would have accounted for nothing. "I promise I'll come down soon, but please… you mustn't stay here any longer. If you do, nothing will happen. I was brought here for a purpose," he said, sinking on to the rock against the folded jacket.

"I can't leave you here in such an exposed position. You could tumble over the edge in your condition."

"Spud will stay with me. I'll be safe enough," he said, in a valiant attempt to appear normal, fondling the silken ears of the white dog as it nestled up against him. "He won't let anything bad happen."

"Very well, I'll go, but promise me you'll not to go anywhere near the cliff edge. This section of the Cap is notoriously treacherous. Promise me that?"

With great difficulty, he raised an arm to give a reassuring wave as she set off along the path, wondering if he would ever see her again. He knew he was ill, maybe dying, barely able to draw breath. He knew there was no way he could get back to the farmhouse unassisted.

Wanting to see the old Hall, perhaps for the last time, he grabbed on to the railings of the shrine to gain higher access up the rock where he could get a clear view of the estate. He shielded his eyes from the glare of the sun reflecting across the bay. It enabled him to make out the gaunt shape of the tower which, unlike when he had visited it the previous day, had thin columns of smoke wisping lazily from the blackened granite, and no ivy or briar smothering the building.

From what he could make out of the terrace, this also appeared transformed. The balustrade was hugged by sprawling roses and beyond, none of the windows or doors seemed to have been boarded over. The gardens, as much as he could make out in the glare, appeared exactly as he remembered from the time he worked there. Staring intently, he could make out the clear shape of the dovecote which had crumbled underfoot the last time he had returned. The barn roof appeared perfectly restored. However, with such a glare, it was impossible to see if the boathouse had been returned to its original state, but he felt certain it had.

Without warning, Jack felt his knees buckle beneath him and a sickening thud as his head connected with rock as he tumbled head first to the ground, where his fall was cushioned by the banks of heather. For a time he lay perfectly still, not wanting to move, inhaling the scent of heather mixed with damp earth. But the intensity of the sun was making his head pound. He found a perfect place to rest against the jacket, where his burning face could be soothed by a cool sea breeze.

He had been seated there for only a short time when he sensed someone was standing behind him. "I wondered if you would come," Jack said, as a shadow fell across him.

"I come here every day in the pretence of having forgotten my jacket," Ralph replied, his voice nothing more than a rush of wind, but a sound clear enough for Jack to distinguish every word. "I prayed you'd come here so that I could find you."

"Is it really you, Foxy?"

"Only in spirit," he answered with a laugh, causing a gust of air to gather up the dust from the rocky surface and swirl glittering particles between them as Jack turned around to face him.

"You haven't altered at all. Not a bit!" Jack cried with astonishment, scrutinising every inch of Ralph's dear face.

"None of us have. Not in our own minds."

"You're talking in riddles," Jack replied, struggling to his feet with Ralph's help. "How did you get here without being seen?" He was aware that his vision was becoming more distorted. He stared at Ralph intently, noticing how translucent his shape had become.

"This is where I belong, so I come here in my dreams, hoping one day to give you the proof that Duncan got away from here alive!"

"Why was I selected for this task? Why me?" he asked shakily, convinced he would have fallen over if Ralph hadn't caught hold of him and placed a cooling hand on his forehead. The gentle touch steadied his vision and quelled his nausea.

"Because you have been willing to accept what you can't understand means that you will find him again. Perhaps you already have, but can't see it."

"I don't understand you. Not any of it!" he cried, attempting to stem the flow of tears on the sleeve of his shirt. "I swear I can't take much more of this."

Instead of responding, Ralph pointed out to sea, where a small red boat was drifting towards the horizon.

"He's out there, injured. You must find him quickly. Time's running out for you both. You should never have been summoned back again. Travelling the journey back once is risky for anyone. Having got this far for the second time is very hard for you. What you must understand is that Madeline had no alternative. Without your sacrifice, Dungellen will disappear for ever, and that mustn't be allowed to happen," he said this with great force, causing a blast of wind to billow out Jack's shirt, lashing his hair wildly about his face.

Soon after the MG had arrived at the farmhouse, Andrew entered the living room with a stack of yellowed newspapers.

"I called at Hettie's on the way here and collected these, which I promised to return, under the threat of death if I didn't!" he said with a grin. "You'd think I was ransoming gold bullion when I asked to bring them away. What in God's name is she saving these for anyway?"

"I don't know," Bonnie responded, twisting a coil of hair with vexation.

"What is it, Red? Something's up, I can tell. Is it Jack? Has he got worse?"

"There was a slight improvement to begin with."

"Go on. I'm listening," he said with interest, depositing the papers on a chair. "What happened?"

"Oh, Andrew, it was awful. I thought he was going to fall over, and reached out to stop him when my hand passed right through him as though I'd been dreaming."

Andrew removed his spectacles and polished the lenses before he responded. "You're kidding me, right?"

"It's not the sort of thing I would joke about, is it?"

For a moment he seemed uncertain of how to continue. "Perhaps not. But you must admit, it's a bit of tall order, expecting me…"

"What on earth would induce me to tell such a lie, if that's what you think!" she responded with blazing eyes.

"I didn't say that, Red. It took me a bit by surprise, that's all. Did Ralph ever mention… anything happening to him like this?"

"Not a thing, why?"

"Hettie did comment once, quite unintentionally, that he had a talent to see things which no one else could. After that, she clammed up and wouldn't say another word on the subject. Perhaps you have inherited the same gift?"

"Let me stop you right there. I wasn't 'seeing things', as you put it. Not at all! Jack was as real as you are now. What happened was over in moments. He passed through a shaft of sunlight…"

Her voice trailed away.

"You could have misjudged it, Red. If the sun was blinding enough, it's possible."

"That wasn't what happened at all. I know you're being logical, I'd be the same, but you can't explain this away so easily."

"Then tell me everything you can about what happened, and don't leave anything out."

It was some time before she was able to relate how the sequence of events had taken place as she had seen them. But she then inserted Jack's alternative interpretation. "Everything that happened seemed real enough to him."

"Did his shape dissolve completely?" he asked, with a degree of uncertainty.

"You are taking this seriously, aren't you? You do believe he was telling the truth about having travelled back in time?"

"Mother told me tales about some inexplicable happenings at the Hall when I was a boy. Back then, that's exactly what I thought they were, just stories. I'm thinking differently now, since Jack arrived here."

"Do you remember seeing him on the night of the fire?"

"I can't be certain of that. It's too long ago, but anything's possible. After all, Red, this is Dungellen."

For a moment Bonnie wouldn't look at him; instead she stared at the Cap where she had left Jack alone. "He's got this notion he's going to die very soon. Please do something to help him," she said, unable to conceal her distress.

"I'll do anything I can, that goes without saying, but I can't promise anything. I've never come across this before. I don't think anyone else has either. Jack's incredibly fit, possibly more than other men of his age. But he's only human. His body can't keep taking such punishment. Re-regulating the time difference is probably what's affecting him so badly. In my opinion, he could stand a chance of making a recovery having travelled once, but twice?"

"What will happen to him if he does go back again?" she asked tentatively. She felt very tearful.

"I must be honest, Red. I don't know. He's already taken a fearful battering. Where is he, in bed?"

Too upset to answer, Bonnie pointed to the grey mound of the Cap where the dense mist had descended, obliterating every crag and hollow.

"How could you let him go out there? He shouldn't be climbing! He shouldn't even be out! Have you no sense?"

"You imagine I had any choice in the matter! He has a mind of his own, and I could do nothing to stop him," she retorted angrily.

She was concentrating on a specific area of the Cap where a small, but clearer, patch of the mist was glowing, and moving gradually towards the farmhouse. "Andrew! Come here and look at this."

"What the hell is that?" he asked, craning his neck to see better as the image got nearer.

"Look. It's Jack! We must help him down. He might fall!" she shouted, trying to pull away as Andrew restrained her.

"No, we can't. Neither of us can be any part of what's happening out there."

"Let me go, Andrew. He needs help," Bonnie said, tugging to get free.

"Don't you understand? We can't do anything! He's not in our time. Look at him! Look at that brightness. If we went out there now, it could all go horribly wrong. He might never get back here. Not alive at least."

"How can you think that?"

"That's how Mother disappeared. She was out there, talking with Eleanor, on the night she vanished."

"Impossible. Eleanor died years before," Bonnie retorted, not taking her eyes off the descending figure on the Cap.

"I saw them together. As clearly as we can see Jack now. She would be here now if my dad hadn't interfered. He had no time for any of the legends about Dungellen, and neither did I. Not until he went outside to bring her back."

"What happened?"

"I never saw either of them again," he said, relaxing his grip on her arm.

"Andrew, look!" she said, catching her breath as Jack stumbled and pitched forward, slithering towards a sheer incline where his fall ended abruptly, his arm outstretched and yanked tight. "There's someone with him."

"I can't see anyone," Andrew answered, watching open-mouthed as Jack continued the difficult descent. "How in God's name did he manage that without help?" he asked, when Jack was apparently lowered down the sheer section of rock. "You're right. There is someone there. I saw the sleeve of a jacket, but only for a second. Red. Why are you smiling. You saw the same, didn't you? Was it Duncan with him?"

"It wasn't a boy I saw. It was the arm of a young man. I couldn't see his face, but I did recognise Daddy's old jacket," she said, refusing to comment further as Jack reached the final section of the Cap.

"You're saying Ralph is out there helping him?" he asked, with a shake of his head and adjusting his spectacles. "That's impossible. I spoke with him less than an hour ago, in Edinburgh."

"Then who is it?" she asked, as the ghostly figure assisted Jack to safety. "It's the same jacket he always wore. I just know it is."

"It could be anyone. Connie threw that coat away years ago," he said, but with less certainty than before, as the man reappeared, grasping Jack's wrist to steady the final but difficult descent.

At the base of the Cap, Jack stumbled to retain his balance as his helper released his hold. "Thank you," he said weakly, wanting to ask more questions before the apparition retreated into the blanket of mist. He heard only Ralph's soft voice urging him on.

"Find him, lad. Do it for all of us. Only you can bring him here, and prevent the ruination of Dungellen."

After that, the cloud lifted sufficiently to reveal the dark silhouette of the farmhouse. With grim determination he stumbled towards the building until his legs buckled beneath him, and he slumped exhausted against Andrew as he opened the door.

"Steady on, old chap," Andrew said, supporting the dead weight until Bonnie helped get him into the living room.

"Jack? Can you hear me?" she asked urgently as his head lolled to one side. "Andrew! Can't you do something?"

In moments, her cousin had forced open Jack's eyelids to peer into his bloodshot eyes. "Come on back, sport, I need you to stay awake. You mustn't fall asleep. You've got to be checked over thoroughly. Not by me. By someone with more experience."

"I won't go to any hospital!" Jack croaked hoarsely, as he attempted to stand.

"Listen to him, Jack. Andrew wouldn't suggest anything if it wasn't for the best."

But Jack held firm and, after a lengthy altercation, Andrew had to conform to his decision.

"What can I do to help?" Bonnie asked.

"Run him a hot bath while I get him out of these saturated clothes. His body's ice cold. If we don't get some warmth into these limbs, we'll lose the poor chap before the day's out!"

An hour later, Jack was cocooned in a blanket, and seated in front of a blazing fire in the living room, staring into the flames. "Duncan was alive after the fire. He got away in the red boat."

"Do you know this for sure?" Bonnie asked.

"I saw what happened after I got away. He was drifting out to sea. We have to find him," he said, struggling weakly to get out of the chair.

"You're not going anywhere in this state, Jack. You need total rest."

"You don't understand. It's imperative that I find him. And soon!"

"And we can help," Bonnie said, indicating the stack of yellowed newspapers which Andrew had brought with him.

For the remainder of the day, he had a disjointed sleep in the chair, being woken religiously every hour for a quick examination, after which he slept again. Meanwhile, Andrew and Bonnie began the lengthy task of scouring every news article in the pile of crumbling newspapers, some of which were complete, others not. Eventually, it was Bonnie who came across the first important item.

"This has got to be him, Andrew. Listen to this. 'On Thursday afternoon, a young boy was discovered unconscious in a small boat drifting in rough waters, two miles out from Lochenbrae. It was noticed by Mr James Campbell from Edinburgh, a keen ornithologist who had been observing a rare sighting of a huge osprey from the heights of Tippet's Crag. The police were immediately informed, and the boat was subsequently towed into the harbour by the trawler, *Braemar Abbey*."

"That's got to be him," Andrew responded eagerly. "What date have you got?"

"There isn't a front page on this one."

"Damn it. Then we'll just have to continue with the system and check every one," he said.

"What time is it? It's getting dark already," she asked, crossing to draw the curtains.

"Crikey, it's half past seven already. You'd better get off, Bonnie, or you'll never get back before nightfall."

After a heated discussion which lasted a good ten minutes, she eventually agreed to go back to the store and return early the following morning, leaving her cousin to stay with Jack through the night.

"It makes sense, Bonnie. If he takes a turn for the worse, I can get him to the Infirmary in the car. I'll catch up on some sleep in the morning."

"But what about the surgery? Your patients will be expecting you."

"I'll pull it in. I've managed on a couple of hours' sleep before."

Once they had Jack comfortable for the night, Andrew settled down into a wing armchair to watch over him, and Bonnie reluctantly departed.

When she returned the following morning, Bonnie discovered Andrew sound asleep, with Jack in the kitchen making tea.

"You shouldn't be doing that,!" Bonnie exclaimed.

"I feel OK," he responded, the grey tinge of his skin and the lifeless glaze in his eyes stating otherwise. As he poured out the tea his hand was shaking noticeably, splashing more of the liquid on to the table than into the cups.

"Here. Let me do that before you get scalded," she offered, deftly removing the teapot from his hand without any resistance. "How long ago did you make this?" she asked, feeling the teapot, which was stone cold.

"What's that?" he asked vaguely, leaning on the table for support. "What was I doing just then?" he pondered aloud, as she led him back to the living room. "I was going to make some tea. Would you like one?"

"I'd love one. I'll make some in a moment," she answered when he was seated. She shook her cousin. "Andrew, wake up! You'll be late for the surgery."

In need of a shave, he made a hasty visit to the bathroom. He departed soon after in a borrowed shirt from the ample supply of Dungellen linen in Jack's closet, crunching on a piece of toast, a cup of tea in his hand, before driving away from Moorcroft Farm in his MG amid a squeal of tyres.

When Andrew returned that afternoon, Jack was propped up in the four-poster bed with the windows wide open and a vase of wild flowers on the table next to him.

"How did you get him up here, Bonnie?"

"Phillip called in on his way out and offered to help."

"Was he OK? I didn't expect him to be doing anything today."

"He was worried that you hadn't been home last night," she answered, which brought a flicker of amusement to Andrew's tired features.

"Did he say where he was off to?"

"I assumed he was looking for the house again. He didn't say."

"I see you've been busy tidying up downstairs," he commented absently, whilst making an examination of the invalid. "There's not much improvement here, I'm afraid."

"He's no worse though, is he?" she asked with alarm.

"No, fortunately not. I think it's safe to leave him alone for now. I'll come up again after I've seen you off."

Bonnie went ahead of him into the living room, indicating a selection of the old newspapers on the dresser. "I went through the rest of Auntie's newspapers and got more information," she said.

"What, the entire stack? That must have taken hours!"

"It kept me occupied while he was sleeping. I took a few up with me at a time."

"What did you find? Anything interesting?" he asked, as she opened out three issues at the relevant pages.

"There were two reports in the *Lochenbrae Post*," she answered, reading from the first paper. "The police are seeking information on an injured boy found drifting alone in a small boat on Thursday afternoon beyond Tippet's Crag. Anyone with any information should contact the local constabulary on Lochenbrae 235."

"What else? Any clue where he was taken?" he asked, prompting her to select another article.

"This one does. Dated a week later," she answered, skimming through the text until she came to the relevant section. "The boy has since been released from the Royal Infirmary where he had been treated for extensive wounds and exposure." Bonnie put the opened-out news sheet on the table before she sat opposite, removing another paper from the stack. "It's a terrifying account when you consider what a child of that age must have endured before anyone found him. Do you think we'll find him alive?"

"I see what you mean. I've got my doubts. It's difficult to imagine how he could have survived such trauma, from what these papers are saying."

"Provided the reports are accurate."

"I agree, but it seems to me there's hope if the osprey was there, watching over him."

"What makes you think that?"

"An osprey is prominent in the de Beaufort coat of arms."

Bonnie was immediately more relaxed. "And because one's never been sighted in this area of the coast since the last century." Bonnie opened out the remaining newspaper article.

"Quite!"

"According to this article, there was a sighting twenty-five years ago!"

"My point exactly. And yet I've never heard a report of one since. Have you?"

"Not until the night of the storm."

"What else does the article say?" he asked, scrutinising the paper.

"The child has since been released from hospital, and placed into temporary foster care at a local boarding establishment, whilst the police await further information on the boy's identity. Failing that, a decision about his future will be decided at the next council meeting, scheduled in three weeks."

"This is grim news indeed. I'm only glad Jack's upstairs where he can't read this," he said.

"He knows. I'm sorry, Andrew, but he insisted on helping me go through the papers. It gave him a purpose, I suppose."

"And he read them all?"

"The first two, yes. Fortunately he was asleep when I came across this last article," she said, removing a final newspaper from the stack which she read aloud. "A decision was taken at the recent council meeting with regard to a boy found adrift in a red boat on open waters four weeks ago beyond Tippet's Crag, which we quote: 'It would be in the child's best interests that he is lodged under expert supervision at the Greer orphanage in Kenmere. Any requests for further information should be made there, and not with the local constabulary at Lochenbrae.'"

"Expert supervision!" Andrew exclaimed. "The poor little blighter. That place should have been pulled down years ago! It's a bloody asylum. No child should have been subjected to that!"

Chapter Eleven

At seven o'clock that evening, just as Bonnie was about to set off for the store, Phillip Ramsey arrived, flushed and short of breath.

"I thought I'd drop by and help out with the night shift," he said, removing his backpack.

"Your timing couldn't be better. Andrew can hardly keep his eyes open. I doubt if he'll still be awake in an hour," Bonnie answered as they heard him coming down the stairs.

"He's breathing easier now, and was asking for you," Andrew said, catching her by the arm as she went to go upstairs.

"Don't worry, I won't stay long, and neither should you. Go home and get a good night's rest. Phillip's here."

"I saw. Any luck with the search?" he asked.

Phillip shrugged, non-committal. "I'm not sure if I did. I couldn't get inside the place. It's boarded up. It's quite near here," he said, indicating the Cap, but Andrew was yawning and otherwise engaged with filling the kettle from a noisy tap.

"Fancy a cup when I've brewed up?" he asked, stretching his limbs as he returned from the kitchen. "So you had a good day?"

"More or less. By the way, I passed a bulldozer and a demolition truck, parked up on the top road. What the devil are they doing out here, in the middle of nowhere? It doesn't look as if anything has altered in these parts in years," he said, leaning against the sink.

"On the top road you say? Whereabouts exactly?" Andrew asked, suddenly alert with renewed interest.

"Not far actually. They're parked up near the entrance to a big estate. Between here and the village."

Bonnie leant her bicycle against the estate wall to an admiring chorus of wolf whistles from two of the younger men, and approached another workman who was occupied cutting away a thicket of brambles from the decorative iron gates.

"What are you doing here? This is private property," she stated, rather than asked.

"Cutting back, miss. I'm only doing as I was ordered."

"Who's in charge here?"

"I am. Who's asking?" an older man responded, peering at her from the far side of the wall. "We're not selling off any materials from the old house. Not until next week," he said, slicking back his hair as he took stock of his pretty opponent. "I could take you on a guided tour if you like, miss?" the man suggested, tongue in cheek. "I've got the house keys in my pocket."

"The law of trespass may not apply in Scotland, but breaking and entering does," she responded icily.

"There's no need to take on so, miss. It was only a bit of fun."

Returning to her bicycle, she tied away the tumbling red hair from her face. "I don't find the prospect of anyone razing Dungellen Hall to the ground the least bit amusing."

"Steady on, miss. There's no call for you to sound off like this. We're only doing our job!"

"Not on private property, you're not. If you're not out of those grounds before I leave here, I shall call the local constable and have you all arrested."

At the mention of the law, his attitude altered immediately from the debonair to one of practicality. "There's no need for any of that, miss. We've no intention of breaking the law."

"Then what were you doing over there?" she asked angrily. "That estate is private property."

"Idle hands I suppose, miss," he responded, attempting to clamber over the wall, and less athletically than anticipated, snagging his trousers on the spiked railings. "We were clearing the gates to get them open. The northern entrance in the village is only wide enough for a car. It's virtually impossible to get the bulldozers through."

"And by whose authority has this demolition work been ordered?" she demanded, barely able to absorb the revelation of what was being proposed.

Searching through a jacket pocket, he produced a signed document which he offered for her to inspect and which she read carefully. "This is all perfectly legal, miss. We've been contracted by a law firm in Lochenbrae."

"McNair, Courtney and Fife?"

"It says so at the top."

"I can see that Mr Blake-Courtney is responsible for authorising this outrage,. How could anyone consider such an indecent proposal? That building is a historic monument. It dates back centuries. Demolishing the Hall indeed! What is the man thinking?" she exclaimed, examining the proposed date of operation which was the tenth of October.

"Is that clear enough, miss?" he asked, as Bonnie mounted her bicycle.

"There are ten days left before this document becomes valid. Until then, I would advise you and your workforce not to set foot on this property or the constable will be informed immediately!"

Returning to the farm the following day, Bonnie reported the incident to Andrew, who seemed quite mystified by the information.

"I heard there were demolition vehicles in Dungellen. What's going on, Bonnie?" he asked, as she unfolded Edmund's plans on the table.

"These are what Clare took from Edmund's car on the night she ran away from him."

"And are quite possibly the reason why their apartment was ransacked," he said thoughtfully, examining each plan and elevation at some length. "It's unthinkable that anyone in their right mind would contemplate this ruination. There will be nothing left of Dungellen if this goes ahead, Is that Kincaid fellow behind this?"

"He and other members of his family, and the obnoxious Blake-Courtney. He's got a hand in this too."

"Angus McNair's new partner?"

"Yes, which means the plans will become legal by the tenth of this month."

"This has to be stopped. It would be disastrous for this community," he said, poring over each detail. "When does this have the go-ahead?"

"At midday, nine days from today, that is unless Duncan lays claim to the inheritance."

Removing his spectacles to clean the lenses with a handkerchief, he grimaced across at her. "I doubt there's much chance of that happening."

*

By the next afternoon, and eight days from the deadline, Jack was showing no sign of improvement. Throughout this time, the white dog hadn't moved away from the bedside. Outside, the osprey had been like a sentinel, perched on the weathervane attached to the barn roof, hunched, staring for hours on end at the invalid who had barely moved in the grand four-poster bed.

On the following evening, Jack's illness followed a similar pattern, throughout which time Bonnie, Andrew and Phillip each split the day into shifts, with one of them being constantly at his bedside.

"There's not been much change," Phillip said, when Andrew quietly entered the bedroom.

"No improvement at all?" he responded, examining the fresh bed linen.

"He was very sick after I fed him the concoction you left out in the kitchen. What is wrong with him? You never did say."

"I don't know myself, and that's the truth. I should have preferred it if you'd waited until I got here before changing the bed."

"I couldn't leave it stinking. I washed him down while I was at it, and changed his pyjamas."

"You're becoming a dab hand at this sort of thing," Andrew said wryly. "If you don't mind me asking, how did you manage to get him into the bathroom?"

This brought a flicker of a smile to Phillip's face. "As a matter of fact I didn't. I came across an old hip bath in the barn which I filled with tepid seawater and managed like that."

"Good idea! Seawater's good. It might help. Better than what I brought back from the surgery."

"Is he in some kind of coma? He hasn't spoken all day."

"Not exactly. We just need to make certain he doesn't drift off into one, otherwise we'll lose him completely."

"If it's that serious, why isn't he in hospital?"

Uncertain how best to respond, Andrew hesitated. "Jack's a special case. It would be unwise to move him away from here."

With six days to go until the deadline, Jack's breathing had become faster and had deepened from the shallow rasp it had been.

"What's going on here, Andrew?" Phillip asked. "I know there's something. What is it you and Bonnie are excluding me from? Like that bird, for instance." He indicated the osprey. "It never looks anywhere else but into this room. The only time it shifted is when I got Jack out of the bed and bathed him."

"It's a bird, for God's sake! Why should that bother you?"

Phillip squared himself up and stared back into Andrew's unconvincing eyes. "A bird, yes, but nothing like I've ever seen before other than the one carved into the crest on that gatehouse along the top road."

"Anything else?" he asked.

"Well, yes, there is, since you ask! What about this dog here?" Phillip said, fondling the animal's ears. "It won't eat. It doesn't sleep. All it does is stare at Jack in the bed."

"Animals do that," Andrew said.

"OK then." Phillip paused. "How could someone's naked body become transparent? It happened before my eyes. That is, until I doused him over with water from the bath. Before that, I couldn't grasp hold of him."

Andrew laughed with forced amusement. "The man's ill."

"Don't pass me off as anybody's fool. Please? I want what answers you can give me, like how the hell could my hand have passed through his? And don't say I'm imagining it, because I'm not!"

There was no choice but for Andrew to inform him of everything he knew about the events as they'd happened. After which he added, "Bonnie probably knows more about what happened than I do, but that's all I know myself."

There was a long silence. Then Phillip said, "As weird as all that sounds, I believe it could happen, and I'll tell you something else. The first time I met him at the garage I was sure that he knew me, and I thought there was something familiar about him too. Nothing I could pinpoint exactly, but there was definitely something."

*

On the fifth day Bonnie purposely rode past the gated approach to the estate, where she discovered two additional bulldozers and three ex-military tipper trucks parked in preparation for the proposed demolition work.

"If Jack doesn't wake soon, this village is done for," she announced on arrival at the farm.

"What the devil are these people up to?" Phillip asked.

"I meant to bring these along to show you before this," she said, opening out the plans of the proposed development. "I've been trying to reach my dad to see if he can help put a stop to it going ahead. I've left messages at the council office, but he's not getting back to me."

"Ralph would have a fit if he knew what was going on. These plans are bloody outrageous!" Andrew exclaimed, folding away the plans with deliberation. "Since Jack's breathing is more normal today, I might take a run over to Kenmere in the morning and see if I can piece together some information on what might have happened after Duncan was sent to the orphanage."

"What are you thinking? You can't go and leave Jack behind. He's an integral part of all this. More so than you or I," Bonnie said.

"I understand that. But time's running out. We must act now before it's too late."

"There's nothing we can do, except wait. You said that yourself. Jack needs to come out of this sickness naturally, otherwise anything could happen."

"I have to do something. You can't expect me to sit on my backside and do nothing!"

"You must." Bonnie was desperate.

"Is there no chance of asking Angus for an extension on the deadline?"

"I've tried that, but his hands are tied. Blake-Courtney's got every option covered in red tape."

With four days to go, there was a marked improvement in Jack's health. It wasn't yet daylight when he opened his eyes and pulled back the sheets, stumbling over the white dog in the dark as he got out of bed.

"What are you doing?" Andrew shouted, getting out of the chair to grab him.

"I can't stay in bed any longer," Jack answered, pulling on his clothes.

"Hey… steady on. You're in no state to go downstairs. Not yet."

"I've got to find Duncan. It's important," he said, taking Andrew's arm for support as he tentatively made his way down the stairs.

"You can't do anything in this state, old chap. Look at you. You can barely stand!" He helped Jack into the sitting room. "You've been out of it for days."

"Days? How many exactly?" he asked anxiously.

"This will be the sixth actually… if you include today."

"WHAT? That leaves me no time at all."

"Listen, Jack, you're in no state to go anywhere," he said, looking at the long-case clock. "I can drive to Kenmere by ten. Who knows what I'll find in a day?"

"Kenmere?"

"That's where Duncan was taken," he answered, handing Jack a selection of Hettie's newspapers where the relevant information had been marked. "If you read these articles, you'll understand what happened." He went to the kitchen and busied himself by spooning out some porridge oats into a pan of simmering water. Jack followed him in.

"Why was he taken there?"

"The council placed him in an orphanage. I know of it by reputation, but I'm not exactly sure where it's located. It's on the outskirts of the town. What are you doing now?" he asked, as Jack went back for his jacket.

"I'm going there, of course."

"You're not going anywhere," Andrew insisted firmly, as he regulated the heat under the porridge. "It's imperative you stay indoors. At least for the time being. You need to rest, Jack, otherwise God knows what might happen. You've been seriously ill, and you're in no state to handle that motorbike."

"If I can drive from Eastmoor to here after being beaten up and with a bloody hangover, I'm damned sure an attack of the flu won't stop me driving on these roads up here. There's never anything else about!"

"If it had been an attack of the flu I might agree, but it wasn't. In fact, it was anything but."

"Well, whatever it was, I'm over it now," he answered unsteadily, offering no resistance as Andrew forced him back into a chair.

"Now listen to me, sport. If you continue with this madness, you'll probably be dead before nightfall. Is that what you want?" he snapped angrily. "You can't subject your body to any more stress than it's been through already. Quite frankly, it's a miracle you're still alive. Time travel, for God's sake!"

"You believe it happened then?" he asked, incredulously.

"I'm Dungellen born and bred. Yes, I believe it happened!" Andrew snorted, then smiled, the frostiness in his attitude gone as he contemplated the next question. "I was meaning to ask," he began hesitantly. "Did you see my mother this time?"

"I didn't go back all the way, to the Hall. I only got as far as the Cap. I saw some people on the terrace, but I wasn't close enough to identify anyone."

"You saw Ralph, though, didn't you?" Andrew asked, stirring the porridge into a glutinous consistency.

"How do you know that?"

"We saw him helping you down that last section of the Cap," he said, indicating the area through the window.

"We?"

"Bonnie was here too."

"You both saw him?" he asked curiously.

"Well, not him exactly. Ralph couldn't have been there... could he? I know that he's in Edinburgh. It was his jacket that Bonnie recognised," he said, spooning the steaming mass into two dishes. "Do you want salt with your porridge?"

"You recognised Foxy's jacket?"

Andrew smiled knowingly. "That, and his watch. We could see both, quite clearly," he said, as Jack felt clumsily to see if Ralph's watch was still on his wrist. "Bonnie told me all about it. It's identical to the one you're wearing."

"This is getting weirder by the minute," Jack said.

"Welcome to the mysteries of Dungellen, my friend. So, what will it be? Salt or syrup on your porridge?"

"Syrup. It's the way we had it back home."

"Then eat up before it gets cold," Andrew said. He prised the lid off the tin, which he put between them, and pulled up a chair opposite. "Any idea how you were related to Eleanor McKenzie?" he asked.

"I haven't a clue," Jack responded, staring at the trail of golden syrup from his spoon into the bowl. "My dad was killed down the pit when I was a boy. Mam never mentioned a word about Dungellen, or that we had any relatives in Scotland. It was the biggest shock ever when I got the information about the inheritance."

"And there was no mention of the connection in the will?"

"That bloke didn't mention anything."

"You didn't see the will?"

Jack looked away, clearing his dish of the food. "I didn't think to ask. Inheriting this farm was too much of a shock, I suppose. And he put it back into the safe moments after, so if I'd thought of it he wouldn't have shown it to me. Anyway, I couldn't speak, my face was all beaten up."

"I'll get out my mother's copy of the family tree when I get time. She was a McKenzie too. There's got to be some connection there with Yorkshire," he said, spooning out some of the syrup for himself.

"I thought you were having salt?" Jack challenged.

"Are you kidding? I can't bear the stuff on porridge. It's a barbaric custom if you ask me." He checked the time. "If you're still set on going to the orphanage, we'll go together in the car. That way I can keep an eye on you."

312

"I'm almost back to normal," he answered, with a weak attempt at a smile, rubbing the stubble which only now was beginning to form on his chin after more than a week. "You see? This proves it."

"Almost... doesn't mean you can take chances, Jack," he said. He looked up as Bonnie appeared outside the kitchen window, leaning her bicycle against it to remove some groceries from the basket attached to the handlebars. "It's a good job we waited a bit longer before setting off. Red would have been furious if we'd gone without her."

After turning onto the road towards Kenmere, they travelled north, leaving behind the spectacular range of hills surrounding and almost concealing the village, cove and the extensive estate of Dungellen. Throughout the arduous journey, Jack would catch an occasional but reassuring sighting of the osprey swooping, terrifyingly low across the craggy rocks of the coastal road as the scenery became bleaker and less inviting. Soon after the road veered inland, Andrew began to accelerate hard, urging his car towards a mountain pass, where the edge of the road sheered away on the left at an alarming angle.

"Is there anything following?" Andrew asked Bonnie, consulting the rear-view mirror.

"I thought there was earlier. But now I see nothing," she responded, more concerned with Jack's ashen appearance than anything else.

Jack would have looked back through the rear window himself, except the further they were distanced from the Cap, the more uncomfortable he felt. His eyes became less focused and his breathing was noticeably shallower with the drastic alteration of altitude.

Once the sturdy MG saloon had reached the top of the pass, the droning of its laboured engine began to run normally again. After a couple of miles they passed through a region of barren scenery where the mountains dropped away to reveal a valley beyond, and Andrew announced they were less than five miles away from Kenmere.

The MG pulled up the brow of a steep hill and drove onto a hard standing where the council had dumped piles of grit in preparation for bad weather. It was a lay-by that gave a clear view of a narrow loch and cluster of houses which made up the small town of Kenmere. From their vantage point, the road continued, sloping away out of view beyond a clump of pine trees. It emerged again at a lower level to then snake along beneath them until it eventually narrowed at a stone bridge, which must have been more than half a mile long and which, in parts, seemed barely wide enough to accommodate even a single vehicle. Beyond this bridge the road intersected a dirt track, which deviated from the direction of the town towards the end of the loch, terminating in an expanse of rough, marshy ground.

When Andrew helped the invalid out of the car, Jack didn't flinch as he felt the rush of air above his head.

"Where the hell did that come from?" Andrew exclaimed, ducking as the tips of the osprey's flight feathers brushed his cheek.

"It's been following us since we set off," Bonnie said as they helped Jack to stand.

"Sorry. It took me unawares," he answered warily. Jack shook off Andrew's restraining hand and lurched away from his grasp. He didn't take his eyes off the giant bird as it skimmed gracefully along the air currents, the great breadth of its wingspan barely moving as it glided towards the loch.

"That's got to be the place, down there," Jack said, and he indicated a gaunt building on the side of the loch. "That's where we'll find the answers!"

"I don't see anything. Only trees," Andrew said with exasperation. "It's got to be on the other side of town. It's freezing up here. Get back in the car, Jack. You too Red. We're not dressed for this climate up here." Andrew felt anxious as he strong-armed Jack towards the parked MG.

"Wait, Andy, this is important," Bonnie intervened. "What can you see, Jack?" she asked, shading her eyes from the sun to squint at the loch beyond the trees.

"It's down there at the water's edge. Follow the flight of the osprey," he answered weakly, struggling to stay conscious.

It was difficult to discern the building distinctly, set at the water's edge in a small clearing amongst the trees. However, it was just possible to pick it out at the side of the loch, where the thread of a track continued beyond a hump-backed bridge, a solitary barn, two farm cottages and a public house.

"And the council placed children in there!" Bonnie exclaimed with a shudder.

"That must be the place, sure enough," Andrew commented. "Thank God it was shut down at the onset of the war and taken over by the military."

"It's closed down?" Jack asked anxiously. "You mean this has been a wasted journey?"

"Not in the least," Andrew said. "It's a starting point. Look, there's smoke coming from the chimney."

"Even so, it doesn't mean they'll know anything," Jack responded.

"Andrew's right, Jack," Bonnie said, taking his arm comfortingly. "If it is occupied, the owners might know something about where the children were moved on to from here."

"Knowing the way the military operate, they wouldn't have dumped any official paperwork when they took over. It's quite likely it was stored. And with a bit of luck, maybe down there," the doctor announced, assisting Jack into the car. "The best thing we can do is to get down there and find out."

*

On their arrival at the orphanage, it was apparent that an attempt had been made to convert the grim structure into something more appealing, adding window boxes overflowing with blooms, which in fact did very little to detract from the gaunt, unwelcoming architecture. The entrance was reached by a short flight of steps, fitted with utilitarian handrails which ended either side of a wide institutional door that had been painted blue and fitted with a brass knocker and a modern brass door handle, both of which were much too small in proportion for a door of that size, but both of which had been polished until they gleamed. Attached to the wall beside the door was a brass plaque inset with black letters that stated simply 'Boarding Establishment'.

Before they had reached the top step, the corpulent figure of Elizabeth McBride had opened the door to receive them. "I saw you driving up from the upstairs window. I was busy airing the rooms for your arrival," she said. The ample flesh of her upper arms quivered as she adjusted the ties on her capacious pinafore. "Which of you gentlemen is Mr Foster?"

"Neither, I'm afraid," Andrew responded, producing his card. "We are here purely for information, and if possible to look around. I do apologise for any inconvenience caused by not having an appointment. Mrs?"

"Elizabeth McBride," she replied, accepting Andrew's offer of identification. "I must inform you, doctor, it's our policy not to allow pets inside," she announced at the sight of the white dog as it jumped out from the back seat of the car. "We've had new carpets fitted throughout," she explained. She opened the door on to a wide hallway carpeted in a nightmarish floral design of vibrant colours.

Having no choice but to leave the white dog outside, they were allowed to follow her along another corridor, fitted with the same psychedelic carpet. They continued up two flights of stairs, on to a landing which then ended abruptly at narrow door to the upper landing.

"I do apologise for this," Elizabeth McBride said as she struggled for a time to unlock this door. It opened onto a worn flight of narrow, uncarpeted stairs. The stairway reeked with the dank, airless stench of a mausoleum. "This place hasn't been used since the army moved out. Lord knows what you'll find up there. Giant spiders, I would imagine!" Mrs McBride shuddered as she caught hold of the doorframe to peer anxiously up the dusty, wooden treads. Her feet remained firmly on the vibrant carpet. "We never go up there," she said, in a hushed voice. "That's where the orphanage kept the more difficult children as a punishment. Sometimes they were locked away for days at time. Alfred – that's my husband – heard talk that one of the boys was left up there until he died, although it was never proved. Which is probably for the best," she concluded nervously, stepping aside to allow them a passage through.

"Are there any records from the orphanage up there?" Bonnie asked.

"It's hard to remember. I only ventured up once. To be perfectly candid, we would never have contemplated buying this property if we'd known about the goings-on here. Now of course it's too late."

The stairway was indeed very narrow and the treads were layered in dust. The walls, painted long ago in a high gloss, were lit by a skylight of wired glass. They felt damp to the touch, either by association from the comments of the owner or from the dank and musty air, it was hard to distinguish. But regardless, the atmosphere reeked of immense suffering.

On the top floor there was a second, wider skylight of wired glass. This allowed them to see better the clutter of stacked chairs and bundles of roller-blinds stacked amongst a mound of cardboard boxes, each bulging with paperwork. And there was yet another door.

"Let's hope to God we don't have to search through that lot, or we'll be here all week!" Andrew announced, moving some of the boxes to clear a passageway through to the door.

"What's happening?" Bonnie called nervously as the daylight was momentarily darkened by the osprey's wings as it alighted on the roof and peered down at them through the skylight.

"This is too bloody weird!" her cousin retorted, adjusting his spectacles. He struggled to open the door, which had swollen with damp. Neither of them was aware of the alteration in Jack's appearance as Andrew eventually tugged the door free of the frame with a jolt.

"I can't go in there," Jack protested hoarsely, gasping for breath. Wrenching open the top of his shirt, he stumbled forward, losing his balance, crashing into the chairs as he fell to his knees.

In moments Bonnie was kneeling at his side, removing a handkerchief from the pocket of her cardigan to wipe the streaming perspiration from his face. "You don't have to go inside," she said. "Andrew and I can do that. We'll bring out anything we find for you to see. I promise."

"What's going on up there?" Elizabeth McBride shouted from the bottom of the stairs.

"I'm sorry," Andrew responded icily as he also knelt beside Jack. "I knocked over a chair opening the door. It was stuck fast with the damp up here."

"Oh, was that all? Remember, you can't stay up there too long. I have guests arriving here soon. I don't want any dust being trampled on to this carpet."

"We'll be down as quick as we can," Andrew called back somewhat inattentively as he attended to Jack, whose bloodshot eyes stared not at him but at the head of the staircase as though hypnotised.

"Madeline came here," Jack whispered.

"What are you saying? How could she have known about this place?" Andrew said.

"You think she was here?" Bonnie asked.

"I saw them both at the top of the stairs. Standing over there," he answered, continuing to stare at the same spot.

"You saw 'them', Jack?" Bonnie asked, looking not in the direction he was staring but directly into his eyes as he turned his face to her. "Who else did you see, Jack?"

"No, she came with my mother!" he answered as though hypnotised, re-focusing on the stairs. His mouth gaped as he sucked in lungfuls of the dust-filled air. Overhead, the osprey screeched wildly. Jack looked upwards and away from the stairs. His breathing became more normal as he straightened up.

"What the devil's this! There's blood on your shirt," Andrew said, unbuttoning it fast until it was open wide, exposing the scar on his chest.

"Don't look, Bonnie, please. It's so ugly," Jack urged her, averting his face from hers, as if by doing so she wouldn't be subjected to the sight of the exposed wound. Fortunately, Andrew shielded her from the appalling mess.

"He's right, Red. Don't get too close. It isn't a pleasant sight, and I don't want him more upset than he is already."

"Tell me what I can do to help. I feel so utterly useless. There must be something?"

"Ask that woman downstairs for some brandy. Tell her we have an emergency up here. And don't take no for an answer!" He was examining the scar with tentative fingers. Bonnie went down the narrow stairs, two at a time.

"Don't let her see this, Andrew," Jack pleaded, his features ashen and his eyes rolling with agony as he attempted to suppress the pain.

"What in God's name is this about, Jack? I can't make any sense of what's happening. It isn't logical for any old scar to begin weeping blood. After a week maybe, but not an old wound like yours." Andrew sat back on his heels and took stock of his own fingers with amazement. "And why, for Pete's sake, isn't there any blood on my own hands? By rights they should be smothered with the blasted stuff!"

When Bonnie returned, she couldn't see the jagged wound as her cousin was crouching beside Jack, staring blankly at him. "How is he?" she asked, but received no response. "I've got the brandy like you asked. I persuaded Mrs McBride to give me the whole bottle," she said faintly, horrified by the extent of so much blood pooling on the floor. "Andrew! Why aren't you doing something? For God's sake, help him!"

"I can't Bonnie, no one can," he said, placing the palm of his hand on the open wound. Jack groaned in agony.

"I didn't say make it worse," she cried, tugging his hand away from Jack's chest.

In quick response, Andrew displayed the palm of his hand, which showed no trace of blood. "I'm at a loss, Bonnie. I don't know what to do for the best."

"You have to do something. You're a doctor."

"How can I do anything, Red? Not if this comes from his mind. Don't you see? It isn't really happening."

For Bonnie, there was no logic in what he was saying. For a moment she hesitated before reaching out, laying the fingers of one hand lightly on Jack's skin to make contact. Not on the wound itself, but on a dribble of seeping blood. "This isn't possible, Andrew. It isn't real!" she whispered in disbelief as she examined the unblemished tips of her fingers. "Can't we get him to a hospital?"

"There's no point, is there? I confess, I'm flummoxed by the entire situation!"

"What about this brandy? Should I give him some?" she asked tentatively.

"It can't do any harm, given the circumstances. When you've done, pass the bottle over. I could do with a swig myself."

"We should get him away from here as soon as we can, Andrew. This place is awful!"

"Not until we've found what we came for," he answered calmly, removing the bottle from her hand. He took a long draught as Bonnie looked on in amazement.

"Are you mad? What are you thinking? You can't leave him here to suffer like this," she retorted, just as Jack began to revive.

"You've seen it for yourself, Red!" Andrew answered, deliberately fingering the bloodied area and displaying his clean hands. "None of this is happening. Not for real. It's all in his mind. If you won't listen to me, then ask him yourself. He won't leave here until he gets answers. Not after going through everything he's been experiencing. I certainly wouldn't. Would you?"

"What's happening?" Jack asked groggily as Bonnie buttoned up what she could of the shirt. "Andrew's going into the room to make a thorough search for anything that's connected with the orphanage. He'll bring anything he thinks is important."

"I have to go in there too!" he responded weakly, struggling to his feet.

"You're going nowhere, sport," Andrew said, but not firmly enough.

"It could destroy me if I don't go. It's already begun," he urged, when he saw the saturation of blood on his shirt.

"For goodness' sake, see sense. You can hardly stand," Andrew said. "Leave this to me. If there's anything in there which is relevant, trust me, I'll find it."

"I must go inside with you, and lay these ghosts to rest."

"You can see something?" Bonnie asked anxiously.

"Not yet, but they're in there, waiting. They've been in there all the time."

"Don't go inside, Jack, please," she begged him, close to tears. "Something dreadful might happen. I could lose you for ever if you go into that room!"

322

"I gave my word I would find him, and I shall!" he said, catching hold of the doorframe to steady himself before they entered the room. The room from which Jack McKenzie would never return.

Chapter Twelve

Beyond the door there was a heap of displaced furniture and the remnants of a wartime operations room that had remained untouched, gathering layers of dust since it had been abandoned years earlier.

The attic was a spacious area which ran the full width and half the length of the building and which had the advantage of two good-sized sash windows. There were three utilitarian wooden desks on which were two abandoned typewriters and a damaged military radio exposing three broken valves. The microphone, with exposed wires and no longer attached, had been left on a scattering of manila envelopes and paperwork. Attached to the wall were four green-baize noticeboards. Immediately in front of these were four linoleum-topped tables, positioned end to end. At right angles to the wall at the far end of the attic were six deep bookshelves, wedged between the exposed brick of two chimneystacks. The aisles between them were barely wide enough for a person to gain access to the myriad of files, journals and volumes crammed on to the shelves.

From the moment Jack had crossed the threshold he had stopped trembling as the germ of an idea took hold and what initially had begun as an absurd thought gained momentum. "Was I actually in the room, watching him?"

He held his breath in expectation. The osprey swooped into view, soaring high above the treetops. Neither Bonnie nor Andrew seemed aware of any changes in his mood in the scurry to get the operation under way. Wanting the idea to develop naturally, he chose to say nothing but helped Bonnie move chairs and clear a space on the map table for the pile of ledgers that Andrew had been manhandling from the shelves.

"Cripes, it's dusty in here," he said, dumping a grim pile of orphanage volumes into the cleared space. "Let's get one of these windows open. I can hardly breathe back there!" He coughed and wafted the air in a futile effort to clear the swirling mass of dust.

Outside, the osprey had perched nearby in a tree and stared intently at Jack as he struggled to lift one of the sash windows.

"Jack! What are you thinking?" Bonnie called out with alarm. "You mustn't do anything too strenuous. Andrew, for goodness' sake tell him, can't you?"

Instead of answering, Andrew strode across to the struggling figure to help, only to stop in amazement. "Well I'm blowed... I say, Red! Take a look at this," he said, turning Jack to face her. On his shirt the bloodstains had become much less evident and appeared to be fading.

After a few unsuccessful attempts to open that particular window, they caused a nasty crack across the glass. The two men gave up in exasperation when it wouldn't budge. At the second window, Andrew hooked a finger under one of the lifts and jerked lightly on it, expecting that this one too wouldn't budge, but this time the lower half shot upwards to its fullest extent with a crash.

"Wouldn't you know it!" he exclaimed in Jack's direction, then paused. "I must say, Jack, you look a damned sight better than you did earlier." The remark gave Bonnie more enthusiasm for the project in hand.

"Where should I begin with these?" she asked through a cloud of dust, as she opened a large volume.

"Check the dates on the first and last pages first," Andrew said, brushing off the dust from his own book, before opening the volume. "We're only interested in anything recorded from 1933 onwards. Nothing prior to that date would be of interest."

"Shouldn't the dates be recorded on the spines?" Jack asked, selecting three volumes for himself as he sat away from the others, near the open window where he began to breathe deeply as the stale, dank air was replaced. When he opened the first page of the second volume, he sat back in the chair thoughtfully and gripped the table as he pushed his chair back on two legs, closing his eyes momentarily.

"Jack?" Bonnie asked anxiously, getting to her feet. "Are you feeling worse? Let me help you outside. It's much too stuffy in here for you."

"I'll be fine. I'm just waiting."

"Waiting for what?"

"I don't know exactly," he answered with a smile for, in that moment, he realised I had to be here waiting for an all-important discovery which would free me after those interminable years of hiding.

After what seemed like an age of intense searching, it was Bonnie who came up with the first trace. "I've found something. This has to be him!" she exclaimed, looking from one to the other. "He's listed here as case file number 235. The date of birth and the names of both parents are unknown, and it says: 'Over a period of three months, the mute has given no early signs of responding to any recommended treatment. Added to which, doses of the prescribed medication are being increased and administered on a regular basis, again without indication of improvement. The boy is scheduled for re-assessment in three months.'"

When Bonnie had estimated an approximate date they systematically examined the stack of ledgers until Andrew located what he thought was the appropriate volume, but which ended a week prior to the date needed.

"I must have missed that volume. There's nothing else here which follows on!" he announced. He forced another passage through the cramped isles between the bookshelves, and soon returned with two more volumes and a stack of journals. "I found a couple more, mixed in amongst these medical records."

"Will they be of any use?" Bonnie asked.

"Since they put him on medication, they could well be," he answered, flicking through the brittle pages with keen interest. "What was the number of the case file you quoted?"

"It was 235," she answered. "Have you found something?"

"I'm not sure if it's connected. But Mother was here."

"Aunt Helen? That's impossible, Andrew. You must have misread it."

"Not in the least. I remember a period when she travelled a lot. For about three months... she was doing two jobs; taking her own surgery, whilst covering another position until the vacancy was filled. That must have been here. I honestly thought the job was in Lochenbrae," he said. Bonnie opened her own volume and scanned quickly through until she found a page with the pertinent entry.

"Dear God, this is awful!" she said anxiously, twisting her hair away from her face before reading: 'After three months of careful evaluation, our findings on the mute boy, file code 235, indicate that any improvement is negligible and, contrary to our expectations, he is becoming more unbalanced daily. We have to conclude that with age the imbalance of his mental health will deteriorate more until he becomes a danger to society. Therefore, unless drastic measures are taken to prevent this madness from developing further, it is crucial for his own protection that he is placed under stricter supervision than we are able to provide at this facility. On the advice of the medical officer, it is suggested this boy be transferred at the earliest date possible to a secure Mental Institution, where electrical treatment for the insane is available. Applications for the relevant paperwork needed have been filed with the appropriate governmental department at Westminster."

"What? That can't be right, let me read that!" he said, taking the book from her. "In my opinion, and Mother's too, to propose such a drastic course of treatment for an adult in this enlightened age would be an outrage. But for a child… it doesn't bear thinking about. He would never survive!"

"I couldn't agree more, but what doesn't make sense is that Helen must have approved the order to have Duncan committed. How could that be?"

Returning the volume to the table, Andrew contemplated the medical journal he had reviewed previously. "What date have you got there, Red?"

"The twentieth of December, 1934."

With much relief Andrew sat back in his chair and removed his spectacles. "Mother didn't take over the position until January 1935," he said, cleaning the lenses methodically.

"Which means Duncan would have been packed off by then," she said glancing towards Jack, who was examining another journal with interest.

"The orphanage wouldn't close to celebrate Christmas," Andrew said, "but Westminster most certainly would. There would have been no response to that request until the end of January at the very earliest."

Looking up from his own book, Jack opened out the relevant page. "If you take a look at this entry here, it shows he was still here a month after that, in March '35. That's when Madeline must have come." Jack said, sliding the open volume over for Bonnie's appraisal.

"Does it mention her?" she asked eagerly.

"Not specifically. Only that two visitors requested visiting rights. I saw them outside this room as clearly as I see both of you now. Helen must have told her what was happening. I could see it in her face. Madeline knew he'd been locked away from the other children in this room!"

"How could she have known he was in the building, let alone imprisoned up here?" Bonnie asked warily.

"It makes perfect sense. Mother would have recognised Duncan immediately," Andrew said. He made a hasty review of the medical pages until he located the entry relating to his mother. "Here's one of her case notes. It says here: 'In the interest of the mute child, case 235, I would strongly urge the panel to abandon its previous recommendation for submitting the boy to any course of electrode treatment which, in my professional opinion, would have disastrous consequences for any child in this badly traumatised state.'"

"Is there anything else?" Bonnie asked anxiously.

"Not here, there isn't," he answered, taking care not to skim over the pages. "There must be a follow-up of her assessment. Mother wouldn't leave his future hanging in the balance like this. She couldn't have rested until that barbaric decision had been overturned," he concluded. Bonnie removed a slim volume from the stack next to her and handed it to him.

"You might find something relevant in this," she responded, returning to the yellowed page of Jack's dusty journal. "The handwriting in this journal is so faded I can barely make anything out," she complained. She clicked on a table lamp, which to her great surprise, flickered momentarily and stayed alight, allowing her to study the writing in greater detail. She was oblivious to the action about her, as Andrew's own concentration intensified on the slimmer volume. Jack got up from the table and stared through the open window with clouded eyes.

"Here's more on Mother's assessment of Duncan," Andrew announced. "'Having reviewed case file 235 at great length the child is, as Doctor

Fisher suggested, suffering from complete memory loss through the severe injuries sustained. However, my own opinion is that the trauma of his experiences will undoubtedly have contributed to his wayward behaviour. I consider that it is imperative this child is no longer subjected to the isolation of solitary confinement, as is currently imposed, and the prospect of any electrode treatment must be abandoned forthwith before irreparable damage is caused. I propose that the child would respond better to the affection given by loving foster parents in the caring environment of a family home. Over a period of time, this could introduce the return of any lost memory, and the ability of speech.'"

"Good for Aunt Helen!" Bonnie said, momentarily breaking her concentration.

"If that is what happened, The only problem is, where the hell was he placed?"

"It's in this volume. His case number's here but it's very hard to make any sense of the handwriting. Can you read this, Jack?" she asked.

*

Instead of answering, Jack continued to stare outside, more specifically at the osprey, which all at once issued a chilling shriek. It was a sound which vibrated through every inch of the attic as the huge bird swept low towards Jack, where it then hovered, motionless, with only its feathers shifting slightly with the breeze. The coal black of its intelligent, unblinking eyes bore deep into Jack's own and with such intensity that Jack barely noticed the thread of light that had begun to emerge from his own stomach. He glanced back into the attic room, where, although he was enclosed in a sphere of light, the daylight had not only dimmed but both Bonnie and Andrew were frozen in mid-action, as if captured on film.

Between the motionless wings of the osprey he saw a gathering spiral of wind moving towards him, which coincided with a sickening tug at his innards. Looking down he saw the thread of light tightening as it stretched ethereally out through the window until the end was embedded into the underbelly of the osprey. The connection energised the next sequence of events in a dreamy state of slow motion.

The pain in his stomach became almost unbearable as he was yanked bodily forward, vainly attempting to grab hold of anything to prevent himself from sliding closer to the open window. Unable to prevent the inevitable as the electric-blue thread sparked fiercely between them, Jack was jolted clean off his feet as the osprey flew, tugging him out through the open window and into the spiral of rushing air.

Any giddiness he experienced at the onset of the flight soon stabilised when he was drawn into the soft down of the bird's underbelly, allowing him to relax as they travelled beyond the valley and flew higher. They soared above the chilling heights of the mountain pass, beyond which they followed the irregular coastline of the ocean until the glorious sight of the Purple Cap appeared in the distance.

As they got closer, dark storm clouds were gathering over the village and as they neared the estate, savage gusts of gale-force wind raged around them as they swept above the cricket pitch on the approach to the northern gate.

In Mrs Jennings' cottage garden, Dora paused from taking the washing from the line to urge the arthritic collie into the house. She picked up two black and white pups, small replicas of their mother, which she placed in the peg-bag along with a smaller white bundle which writhed in her arms until it was able to look directly at Jack, hovering overhead. The iridescence of its coat seemed to glow in the eerie, pre-storm light.

When they neared the northern entrance to the estate, rain was pouring down in a torrent, but only in that isolated area, where raindrops en masse thundered onto the roof of the Sunbeam Talbot like a waterfall, drenching the cluster of men gathered about the gate who were attempting to take shelter beneath the arch.

"Get on and do what you're being paid handsomely for!" a woman shouted through the lowered window of the car.

"The documents aren't legal until the tenth, Mrs Kincaid." The foreman of the demolition team attempted to reason with her. "If we do anything before that date, we'll be had up in court."

"It's either get on with it, or find yourselves alternative employment!" she concluded, winding up the window as the wind began to blow the rain sideways, rocking the car with the full wrath of the freak storm.

"Come on, lads, let's get a move on before we get drowned," the foreman urged as he fired up one of the bulldozers, waiting until his companion had the motor running on the other machine and the remainder of his crew were ready to move out in the four trucks, all fitted with side and tail boards to accommodate a mountain of rubble.

"I want to see evidence you've made some progress when we come back in an hour," Edmund shouted through a gap in the steamed-up window as he switched on the ignition. "Make a start and be quick about it. Bulldoze what you can. Any blasted thing will do. I want rid of those bloody ghosts before they get rid of us. If you haven't made a start when we get back, then I'll torch the place!" He drove off in a flurry of splattered mud from the spinning wheels, the car skidding to avoid the demolition vehicles as it spun out of control.

The wind howled in a fury as Edmund struggled to regain control of his car. The laden clouds released a downpour of lashing rain as the first of the bulldozers surged forward, its inadequate wiper blade struggling weakly against the force of the gale, unable to clear the splattered mud smeared on the windscreen, distorting the driver's already grossly impaired vision.

Inevitably, the inferior grip of the abused caterpillar tracks on the machine began to skid on the slurry. Unable to get a firm hold on the soft ground, the driver, in a state of panic, pressed hard on the accelerator pedal instead of the brake, which slewed the bulldozer at speed towards the north gate, where it crashed violently into the arch at a very oblique angle. The entire left side of the arch toppled, causing a catastrophic shudder which resulted in the entire assembly crashing down, burying the bulldozer and one of the trucks in a mound of dust and rubble.

As the bird hovered above the incident, Jack witnessed the prompt action of the other men, scrambling to clear the rubble from the trapped workers, and although he was impatient to lend a hand, being attached to the osprey at such a height there was nothing he could do. He was carried away from the disaster. The storm eased off as they passed over the grounds, becoming mist as they approached the Hall.

*

The osprey hovered over the long terrace before gliding lower above the gardens. Jack's vision was greatly impaired by the mist, but although the lovely gardens were partially concealed he could make out the recognisable shape of Eleanor McKenzie walking arm in arm with Madeline, exactly the way he had remembered them.

"Have they found where he is?" Eleanor called anxiously to John de Beaufort, as he emerged through the mist on the long terrace.

"They're trying their best. I only hope it isn't too late when they do."

"There must be something we can do to help," she said, as her husband vaulted the balustrade to reach them.

"We've done all we can, Eleanor," he answered, taking her hand before he looked up and stared directly into Jack's eyes. "All our boy has to do is to remember exactly what happened that night. Then he will come home to us."

Having absorbed every word, Jack then felt the osprey wheel about and fly deliberately higher into dense cloud.

Now he could hear the demolition crew calling to each other amid the scrambling of hobnailed boots as they heaved away some of the stones. There were intermittent faint cries from the trapped men beneath the rubble.

He was carried away further, until they came to a break in the cloud immediately above Mrs Jennings' cottage, greeted by the barking of the arthritic collie. Beneath them, the black and white pups scattered, yelping, as the shadow of the bird drifted over them, leaving only the solitary white pup to gaze up with calm eyes as they passed overhead.

Flying onwards, the lessening clouds dissipated as they cleared the mountain pass and the gaunt structure of the orphanage came in sight. When they came closer to this grim building, the bird slowed down. Jack was aware of a blue light illuminating the facade of the building on their approach. Not sunlight, but nevertheless it was a blaze of light, crackling energy which got ever brighter until the bird was hovering outside the attic window. Jack was quite unprepared for sight of the motionless figure of himself standing at the window, looking out. Inside, in the dim light of the interior, his two companions had remained frozen in the same positions he last remembered them in.

The osprey became still, remaining in a constant position in mid-air. Jack experienced a repeat of the strange tugging at his abdomen as the thread of blue light snaked away from where he was suspended, to spear his frozen image in the stomach. In moments, a radiating glow pulsated through every part of his immobile shape. Jack was suddenly tugged away from the belly of the osprey, a sickening wrench, then drawn by the blue thread as it became disconnected from the bird. Whipping free, it snapped him through the air to re-enter his own body and jolt his frozen image into life.

Squaring his shoulders, he shifted position, twitching the ends of his fingers as the sensation of life began to recirculate. He stared at the osprey, whose previously motionless wings suddenly swept into flight. It flew purposely towards the open sash window where Jack was standing. It seemed inevitable the bird would crash headlong into the attic. Jack could only watch, showing no sign of fear of the impending disaster that could seriously injure or even kill him. Nor did he flinch when the fearsome talons scraped lightly across the panes of glass on the half-open window in front of him, the huge wings temporarily blocking out every chink of light before the bird veered sharply upwards and disappeared from view.

Jack at last began to understand why he had been transported back to Dungellen, and could now acknowledge the importance of his own connection with Duncan. It clarified exactly where 'I' had been kept in hiding during those interminable years.

"What the bloody hell was that?" Andrew exclaimed, looking up from a journal as the osprey swerved past.

Jack faced them with a slow, glorious smile, as he embraced the knowledge of what had happened in that room so many years ago. It allowed 'me' to re-enter his life after many long years of banishment. With a long intake of breath, I prepared myself for the questions that were bound to be asked. My shoulders straightened as the clouds cleared from my eyes. It was perfectly obvious that neither of my companions had an inkling of the change which had occurred, which wasn't that surprising when I considered that I hadn't known myself... until now.

"Jack, why are you smiling like that?" asked Bonnie, who until then had been scrutinising the open page of the volume before her.

"Have you found anything?" I asked, casually enough, savouring the sound of my own voice.

"I'm not sure. The writing is barely legible on this page. It's very faded," she answered, angling the page towards the light. It's difficult from this to decipher exactly who adopted him... or where he was taken."

"The names would be Ruth and George Hardwick," I said, information which made her concentrate harder until she looked up again, smiling.

"That's absolutely right. How on earth did you manage to work that out from this scribble?" she asked, then resumed her concentration on the following information. "From what I can make out, the address here is somewhere in... Yorkshire," she faltered.

"Go on."

"I can't. The writing is barely legible."

"If you look harder, you will find the address is 33 St Luke's Road. That's in Eastmoor... where the Hardwicks lived."

"How did you work that out?" Andrew asked incredulously.

"We needn't waste any more time here," she answered, angling the volume towards Andrew. "Jack's right again. Read it for yourself, Andrew. We can go!"

"You know where he is. Don't you?" Andrew said. "Is he still living at that address?"

"No. No, he isn't!" I answered cautiously.

Bonnie was staring at me. "33 St Luke's Road, Eastmoor," she said.

Andrew looked at Bonnie, then at me. "What are you saying? Jack? Bonnie?" His eyes were questioning, then realisation began to dawn, slowly but very uncertainly.

I took hold of Bonnie's hand. She was quite silent. I tried to explain.

"When I first saw the orphanage from the pass, I had this dread of coming here and of what we might unearth. I honestly thought Duncan was dead. Now I understand why I blocked out every memory of this wretched place. If my adopted parents hadn't taken me away from here, I would never have survived another year."

There was a moment's silence.

"You are Duncan, aren't you?" Bonnie said quietly.

"Yes. Yes I am," I began, finding it hard not to smile. "Case number 235, which is how I would have been remembered if hadn't been for Andrew's mother. The tragedy is that I didn't recognise her, nor Madeline when they visited."

"Why on earth wouldn't she have taken you home?" Bonnie asked, expressing her confusion.

"I wouldn't have been safe in Dungellen. That's why they must have devised the plan to keep me out of harm's way in Eastmoor, presumably as a temporary solution. But as a precaution, in case my memory failed to return, Madeline must have insisted the Hardwicks fostered me as Jack McKenzie so I would eventually inherit Moorcroft Farm and return home."

"Then everything makes sense," Bonnie said, but with less enthusiasm than I would have expected. "The reason you look like the man in the portrait is because John de Beaufort was your father."

"And Eleanor McKenzie was my mother."

"Then what do I call you?" she asked tentatively, withdrawing her hand.

"Jack, I suppose. I haven't changed. What's in a name?"

"Everything," Bonnie answered. "You were becoming… a good friend, and now I don't know you any more!" She was clearly upset, and ready to bolt unless I could prevent it.

"I had hoped we were becoming more than just that. Or was I mistaken?"

She looked away tearfully. "You know what I mean. Now everything has been turned upside down. Your ancestral home is Dungellen Hall. You're the Laird. An important figure in our community."

"Nothing's changed in my feelings for you. After all that's happened, don't let this come between us. Not now. Please."

Smiling through her tears, she took hold of my outstretched hand, shyly. "You mean that?"

"More than life itself. I couldn't bear to lose you," I confessed. I wanted to continue, but the timing wasn't appropriate. Not with Andrew there.

Chapter Thirteen

We said our goodbyes to Elizabeth McBride, but the white dog was nowhere to be found. After an exhaustive search of the lane, I found him snared in a thicket of brambles and it took half an hour to release him.

During the journey back, I touched lightly on the details of my spiritual flight with the osprey, expressing grave concern about what we might discover on reaching the north gate of the estate. Then the conversation centred briefly on the wellbeing of the dog, which seemed strangely lethargic. It gave me cause for concern, but we travelled the best part of the journey in silence, which allowed me, and my companions, time to fully grasp the implications of my true identity.

"The north gate's coming up now," Andrew said as we passed the duck pond, turning right into the potholed lane parallel to the cricket pavilion. "You were right. That looks like trouble ahead," he continued, seeing the mound of rubble around which there was frantic activity. The workmen were struggling to heave off a section of the broken pediment from the bulldozer to enable them to the haul the driver clear. Grabbing his medical bag from the boot of the car, Andrew pushed through the cluster of men to inspect the injured driver as he was lowered to the ground.

"When you're done here, there's another over there, mate," a man said hoarsely, close to his ear. "That one looks like he's a goner. He took a right wallop to the head," he concluded, prompting Andrew to examine the figure lying on the muddy bank beyond the mound of rubble.

"Has it been raining here?" Andrew asked the man peering over his shoulder, as he began a rapid examination.

"It's been chuckin' it down, mate," he responded, lighting up a cigarette and inhaling deeply.

Ignoring the man at his shoulder, Andrew instructed Bonnie to bring over a rug from the boot, and then to take his car and ring the hospital for an ambulance, calling them from her aunt's store. "Lend a hand, Jack. I need to get this chap off this wet ground before he gets pneumonia."

"How is he?" I asked.

"Both legs are broken, I think in more than two places, and God knows what else," he answered, above the man's groans, as he injected him with morphine. After that, I assisted him to strap an improvised splint onto his legs while Bonnie fired up the engine on the MG and roared off along the lane.

"What happened to the Kincaids?" I asked the man with the hoarse voice who was wreathed in a cloud of cigarette smoke, observing all that was going on.

"I haven't set eyes on them. Not since the storm."

"Have you any idea where they went?"

"They were shouting threats," he answered, grimacing at the groans of his workmate, "but nobody was paying much attention in that freak wind. If that dozy twat hadn't driven away from here like a madman, none of this would have happened."

"And you've no idea where they were going?" I repeated.

"No, and I don't care either!" he answered, wafting away another exhaled cloud of cigarette smoke in order to see better.

"Do you need me here any more?" I asked Andrew, who appeared to have everything under control as he tended the injured men.

"There's nothing else you can do here, old chap," he said, as I made a swift calculation of how to get through the blocked entrance and into the estate.

"Why? Where are you going?" he called after me as I walked away from the group with the white dog close at heel.

"There's something happening up there," I answered, pointing to an area of the Cap where I knew the shrine to be, and where the osprey was hovering.

"You know I'd come with you if I could, but I can't leave here until the ambulance arrives," Andrew said.

"And nor would I expect you too. I'll check out the Hall on my way to make sure the Kincaids aren't holed up there. God knows what they'll be up to if they are."

"That posh chap threatened to torch the place if we hadn't started when they got back," the man with the hoarse voice said, lighting up another cigarette.

"See what I mean?" I called to Andrew as I set off. "If I don't get there fast, there might be nothing left of the Hall. Not if the Kincaids have their way."

With as much speed as I could muster, I made my way along the top road following the drystone wall. In my weakened condition, I knew I would not be able to scale the nine-foot-high wall, nor would the dog be able to scrabble over. I continued further until we reached a difficult but surmountable section of the wall that had been damaged by an enormous branch that had fallen from one of the estate's Redwoods. I could only assume it had come down during a storm.

Encountering some difficulty with the wilderness of brambles on the far side, we made slow progress, forcing a passage through snagging, thorny coils which caused multiple lacerations to the exposed areas of my hands and forearms, tearing my shirt repeatedly as I struggled free. Once inside the estate I had travelled barely a hundred yards when I heard the howl of tortured metal which I knew had to be the east gates being forced open. An exhausting sprint ensued, with the dog pacing its run more easily than I might have expected in view of its earlier condition. I was urged on by the sound of a powerful car revving up before it surged forward. From my position, I could see nothing of the car or the passengers as it roared through the grounds. It was subsequently hidden from sight along the leafy avenue of limes edging the full length of the drive until it dropped from sight down the slope towards the Hall.

From a glance towards the gate it was quite apparent how difficult it must have been to open the decorative ironwork that hadn't been disturbed in years, allowing only the narrowest gap. Knowing it must have been Edmund Kincaid's Sunbeam Talbot, I couldn't resist a smile, imagining how the immaculate paintwork would have suffered making such a difficult entry. Added to which, there was a flimsy piece of black material caught on one of the iron gates and fluttering in the gusting breeze, macabre in its isolation.

Increasing my stride, I set off down the slope at a run when I saw a billowing cloud of acrid smoke rise up beyond the far side of the Hall. Gasping for breath, I made my way to the long terrace where I discovered a piled-high mound of smouldering wood that hadn't properly ignited. I stamped out and kicked the smoking embers well away from the building, assuming the Kincaids would have fled the scene, until I caught the flash of reflected light from the damaged bodywork of the Sunbeam Talbot, barely concealed in trees a short distance away.

Seeing a movement inside the car, I made my way cautiously towards the vehicle, keeping myself well hidden. On arrival, I discovered not one but two people inside. Lying tied-up on the back seat, struggling with her bonds, was Hettie, tearful with frustration. In the front passenger seat was a badly scarred man. His unseeing eyes stared at nothing as I opened the door. His shrivelled body was pathetic, badly attired in a suit at least one size too large. His plus fours were of a bygone era, the bright check of the cloth more in keeping with the outfit of a clown.

"What the hell do you want?" the voice snarled as I opened the rear door to assist Hettie outside. The unpleasant discord of his voice triggered childhood memories, which even so, were hard for me to readily associate with this pathetic figure, staring about with sightless, milky white eyes. His emaciated figure was so alien to the Hamish Kincaid I'd fought with on the night of the fire. I shuddered as I relived the moment I saw him leap in flames from the blazing tower, fluttering wildly through the darkness like a firebird.

Once Hettie was out of the car, she stared at me for some time without uttering a word. This, considering her reputation, was in itself quite remarkable, and it wasn't until the bindings were untied that she blurted out the chilling account of what had happened, and thrust an envelope into my hand.

"You must stop them from hurting Bonnie, whatever the cost!" she cried. "Edmund Kincaid was quite specific in his instructions."

"Tell me exactly what happened!" I urged, with more reassurance than I actually felt once I realised that Bonnie was in danger.

"He forced me to sign over the store... and the Cap. If I hadn't gone along with their threats, that Phyllis woman would have killed Bonnie without a second's thought."

"Where have they taken her?" I asked urgently. Her look of wild desperation was tempered with sparkling eyes.

"Nowhere. She got away in the confusion."

"What happened?" I urged, seeing her wince at the recollection.

"During the struggle, when he tried to bind up her wrists, she wrenched off the metal ashtray from inside the car and hit him square in the face. The sound of the splintering bone was awful when his nose shattered, but he gets no sympathy from me. It's what he deserved. The blood splattered everywhere!" She indicated the bloody smears on the paintwork of the vehicle.

"And where is Bonnie now?" I asked anxiously.

"Up there on the Cap. No one knows the cliff tops better than my Bonnie. It's the only place she will be safe for now. That woman went after her like someone demented. She has a gun, and has every intention of using it!"

"I'm going after them. God knows what they'll do if they catch her."

"She isn't alone up there. Andrew's friend is there too. He was out running, and stopped to wait when he saw her."

"Even so, these people are desperate. They'll stop at nothing until they own all of Dungellen. Two unarmed people will stand no chance against them," I answered, impatient to be off.

"Wait!" Hettie called after me. "There's something else. They knew you would come here when Bonnie didn't return with Andrew's car."

"Did she have time to place the call to the hospital?" I asked, evaluating the situation.

"Only just. She'd barely replaced the receiver when they burst into the kitchen."

"Anything else?" I asked, endeavouring not to convey my concern at our exposed position.

"They expect you to be here at twelve o'clock precisely to sign a document to renounce any claim you have to Moorcroft Farm."

"And what if I refuse?"

I thought she might burst into tears before she answered, but she responded, unsteadily. "You can't. If you aren't here when they said, they will hunt Bonnie down, and..." she faltered tearfully and handed me a large, crumpled manila envelope. "I was told to give you this to read through and sign," she said, allowing the extent of her distress to finally show as I reviewed the contents of the envelope.

"They'll hunt her down anyway," I said when I'd finished reading. "In their haste to get after Bonnie they gave you the wrong package. This document has your own signature and details your relinquishment of ownership of the Purple Cap and your store." I put aside the envelope, knowing that I must find Bonnie before they killed her.

Leaving Hamish to contemplate the scraps of information he might have heard through the open window, trapped in his own darkness, I assisted Hettie away from our exposed position and onto the long terrace where she might be made comfortable and benefit from the seclusion, allowing me to set off on my search, which was uppermost in my mind. I became alerted to the familiar cry of the osprey as it wheeled above the Cap, its magnificent shape dark against the orb of the sun. I looked away and to my immense surprise I saw my old cat jump down from the balustrade and come towards me.

When I bent down to caress the familiar shape, my hand passed directly through, forewarning me that the events linking to my past remained unfinished. As I bent down to the cat, I had failed to hear the crack of the rifle as a shot was fired, but I registered well enough the exploding fragments of masonry around me as a section of granite, close to where my head had been moments earlier, was fractured by the first blast.

Urging Hettie to take immediate cover, I vaulted the balustrade and landed sprawling amongst the shrubbery just as the second shot whistled through my hair, grazing my scalp. I took good advantage of my concealment in the laurel whilst my would-be assassin reloaded. Fortunately, I had seen the flash of the second shot, which had been fired from a high ridge on the Cap and which, I thought, must be close to the shrine and, quite possibly to where Bonnie might be in hiding.

Making my way stealthily through the bushes I was able to emerge from the laurel at a run, but where I gauged the marksman wouldn't have a trace on my exit. Therefore, with the white dog close by, I made the difficult ascent to the heights of the Cap until I reached the rock that served as the roof of my parents' shrine. From my vantage position on the uppermost section, I mistakenly thought Edmund was alone, prowling close to the edge of the cliff top like a predator, a bloodied handkerchief pressed against his nose. The handgun in his pocket bulged noticeably as he paced a short distance along the cliff edge, his lank, fair hair lashing about in the wind like the tentacles of a sea monster.

"Do be careful, darling!" The seductive resonance of his mother's voice sounded anxious from her hiding place beneath me. Leaning forward cautiously to observe her, I caught sight of Phillip Ramsey's bloodied shape, sprawled, groaning, against a rock. I could see nothing which might indicate that Bonnie was, or had been with him.

While Phyllis was busy examining her rifle, I was able to scramble away from my vantage point, hoping the white dog would keep out of sight, and more importantly, not follow. I began the precarious decent, where one false move would have sent me hurtling on to the jagged rocks at the base of the cliff where the foaming waves crashed with an intense ferocity as the wind gusted up around me, ballooning my shirt free so that it lashed me. I gripped onto the rock face with barely a hand or foothold, cautiously inching my way down. With limpet-like movements I traversed a particularly dangerous section from where, sliding down blind, I was lucky enough to locate a foothold on a narrow ledge and subsequently reached the stability of the cliff top. From there, I was able to circumnavigate the shrine without attracting any unwanted attention.

With nerves jangling, I quelled the impulse to charge into the open, which would have done nothing to help Bonnie or get Phillip away from Edmund's witch of a mother. With my thoughts focused on how best I might take advantage of the situation and get hold of the rifle, I edged my way to the entrance to the shrine. Goose pimples crawled the length of both arms as I caught sight of the dark-haired woman sheltering in a shadowy cleft of rock, next to Ralph's carved dedication, at the back of the shrine. Her dark figure blended so well against the darkness of the rock, it would have been difficult for anyone to notice someone standing there but, with the heightening of my own senses, I was able to observe what others might not. Stupidly, I allowed my attention to wander as Eleanor McKenzie appeared and turned to face me, revealing those painfully exquisite features I had been starved of for the best part of my life. Being so transfixed by that ghostly vision, I failed to hear Edmund Kincaid as he came up behind me. I had only partially turned when the butt of his revolver clumped hard against the side of my head.

I awoke with the side of my face pressed hard against the cold, damp rock of the shrine floor, and with a thumping headache. Although dazed, I had enough presence of mind to lie perfectly still and listen to every sound that might help me to assess my predicament. Considering Phillip Ramsey's bloodied, unconscious situation, I attempted to reconstruct what might have happened before my arrival.

Staring hard as my eyes began to refocus through a swirling grey haze, I was able to make out Edmund's slouching figure at the cliff edge, when the dark outline of Phyllis Kincaid stepped in front of me, blocking my vision, and standing near enough for me to grab her ankle.

"What the hell were you thinking, Edmund?" she called out. "What use is this rifle without any bullets? Do you expect me to perform miracles?" she asked icily, lowering the barrel into my line of vision. "How many bullets do you have left in the revolver?"

"Two, I think... maybe three, or four... No more than that."

"Then make certain every one of them counts," she answered, as he continued his search of the cliff top. "Are you quite certain that redhead had the document with her?" Phyllis asked, stepping towards him, and well out of my reach.

At the mention of Bonnie my skin turned cold. Even so, I forced myself to remain perfectly still and quelled my impatience to get to my feet without alerting them.

"I saw it flutter from her hand," Edmund responded, staring suspiciously in my direction. "Are you certain he's out cold?"

Hearing this, I fully expected to feel Phyllis's wrath inflicted on my skull with the butt of the rifle, which she now held loosely in the fashion of a club.

"For the time being... fortunately your enthusiasm with the revolver didn't finish him off. It is imperative he signs over his part of the estate before tomorrow."

"And what then?" he asked with a shrug. "He's bound to contest ownership."

"He might... if he is still alive to do so," she answered, as Edmund stooped at a rock near where the path crumbled away, and stood up victorious with a flapping document grasped tightly in his hand.

"I've found it, Mother! It's safe," he called back, his voice thin and reedy against the force of the wind.

Squinting against a sudden flurry of dust which swirled into the cave, I saw the flapping of her skirt as she moved forward. I had to remain motionless until the opportunity came for me to stand when, hardly daring to breathe, I noticed a slight movement. Eleanor McKenzie was edging cautiously towards the entrance and, although I knew it was impossible to think my mother was still alive, it was hard to imagine anyone less ghost-like as she passed into a shaft of sunlight, all the time edging nearer to the cliff edge, but keeping well back in the shadow of the rock, and ensuring that Phyllis and Edmund remained oblivious to her presence.

"Then come away from the edge, darling," she answered, just as Phillip Ramsey groaned piteously as he struggled to right himself. This stopped Phyllis in her tracks as she was about to walk past him. At such an angle it was impossible for me to see her evil features, concealed beneath the veil of her ridiculous hat, which she was having difficulty restraining in the wind. In her right she swung the barrel of the rifle with surprising force, and gave a vicious thump with the butt hard onto Phillip's head, which felled him back onto the rock like a sack of grain.

At that precise moment my mother gained access to a higher section of the cliff top, where she got to her knees and peered over the crumbling edge of the path, calling down the cliff face. It was an action that made the hairs on my neck shiver when I realised Bonnie must have been forced over the edge. If still alive, she was in considerable danger. Unfortunately, Phyllis was alerted to my mother's presence as she was telling Bonnie to hold tight, and grasping her wrist before the narrow ledge, barely supporting the girl, crumbled away from beneath her.

With my head spinning, I struggled to my feet and stumbled after her, regardless of Edmund who purposefully raised the revolver and aimed in my direction. Continuing on regardless, I braced myself for the inevitable, but heard neither the shot above the force of the gale nor the ferocious growl of the white dog as it launched at Edmund from the top of the shrine, shuddering in mid-air as the first bullet struck it squarely in the chest. The second, fired in rapid succession, felled my dear friend in a motionless heap beside my feet. The sight of this caused me to charge at him in a blind fury, regardless of the gun barrel pointing directly into my face. He calmly squeezed the trigger, blissfully ignoring Phyllis's volatile instructions as she temporarily diverted her attention away from my mother.

"Don't, you bloody fool! You'll ruin everything if you shoot him before the document's signed!" she cried out, wielding the rifle at me to great effect. It brought me crashing to the ground with a hefty wallop in the back of the knees, Edmund's bullet now cleaving through my hair instead of being a few inches lower.

When I struggled up on my elbows, I saw a mass of dark hair uncoiling from the nape of my mother's neck as she knelt at the cliff edge as though in preparation for an execution. The alabaster purity of her uncovered arm, reaching down to clasp tightly around Bonnie's wrist to help her back to safety, the light fabric of the green dress fluttering wildly, her dark hair cascading over her shoulders when she turned to look up, not startled, as I expected, when Phyllis's dark shadow loomed menacingly over her.

I cried out in my inability to reach her in time, my swollen knees barely able to move, failing miserably to support my weight after the crippling blow. There was no alternative other than to crawl forward on my elbows with a rock clasped in my hand in readiness to hurl it at the hideous creature if I could but get that close. But I was well aware that even had I been able to run, I would never have reached the cliff edge to prevent the inevitable. In such despair, I had crawled barely a yard when I heard the terrifying screech of the osprey as it appeared, not from the sky, but as it swept up from beneath the cliff face a few feet away from my mother in its readiness to launch a fearsome attack. The blood-chilling sound, together with an intimidating display of arched talons ready to lacerate and impale, caused Edmund to squeal like a child as he dodged aside, the sudden movement causing blood to stream from his broken nose as he fired blindly at the huge bird, missing it completely as it swooped high above us before wheeling about to make its turn.

With the immediate threat of danger gone, Edmund deliberately trained the revolver in my direction. His expression was calculating as he squeezed down on the trigger.

Phyllis, preoccupied with the ultimate destruction of Eleanor McKenzie, wielded the rifle high above her head, the macabre glitter from her many rings flashing erratically as her fingers clenched tightly around the barrel in readiness for the final blow.

Harrowing as it was, I was transfixed by the sequence of events and wondered if, in spite of all the supernatural events that had prompted the return of my memory, this was to be the end of the de Beaufort family. During what I had assumed were the final moments of our lives, in my subconscious I registered the repeated click of the firing pin on Edmund's revolver as it hammered on each of the empty chambers in succession. The osprey, screeching wildly, swooped towards him, the sight of its immense talons presenting a terrifying prospect to its intended prey.

Facing the imminent threat, cut off from any semblance of cover, and yards away from the shrine, Edmund backed away from the horrifying sight, protecting his face as the talons slashed into his flesh, carrying him, struggling and screaming, above me as they wheeled high above the shrine, lifted on the rush of wind that dispersed Edmund's hysterical cries high above the Cap.

Unaware of Edmund's plight, Phyllis presented a formidable sight as she was caught in the updraft. The folds of her fluttering black dress became like a flurry of roosting bats as the rifle commenced its downward swing. My normal stream of vision altered to become a montage of images, enacted in slow motion.

It was then that my mother turned to face me and smiled reassuringly, exactly as she had done when I was a child, and I knew everything would be all right. Impossible as it seemed, at the crucial moment, when the crushing weight of the rifle ought to have made contact with her, instead the momentum continued, passing through her body as if she didn't exist. Instead of releasing her grasp of the barrel, Phyllis gripped even harder, but somehow managed to regain her balance. She turned as she became aware of Edmund's terrified screams for help, just as the osprey swooped above her, its talons releasing him at speed. He crashed into his mother, propelling them both away from the cliff top amid piercing screams as he plummeted after her. Her dress twitched about her as though plucked by a thousand demonic fingers as she twisted towards her death with a remarkable, balletic grace, her hat and veil drifting slowly after her.

When I reached the crumbling edge of the cliff in less than a heartbeat, with the help of my mother I hauled Bonnie to safety. I observed the final moments of Phyllis and Edmund as they thudded, in quick succession, broken and impaled on the jagged rocks. They were lashed and lifted by the incoming tide and carried away from the cliffs where they sank out of sight.

For a long time I couldn't allow myself to let go of Bonnie. At last, I felt the trembling warmth of her body subside and she eased herself gently away from the pressure of my arms, which were enfolded about her so tightly it must have been hard for her to breathe.

"I'm all right, Jack. Honestly," she said, glancing about her. She focused on the slender figure of my mother as she walked away. "She's Eleanor McKenzie... isn't she?" she whispered. I nodded in reply. "Why didn't she stay?" she asked.

Eleanor McKenzie walked towards the shrine and, as she passed the still body of the white dog, she urged it to follow. It struggled to its feet as if it had been sleeping. As it did, the two bullets clattered one after the other onto the rocky ground, as if supported by nothing but vapour. For a moment my cherished companion turned to me, his dark eyes soft and happy, then he trotted away towards my mother. They walked into the sunlight and dematerialised into the brightness of the sun until nothing of them remained.

Yesterday, we arrived at the offices of McNair, Courtney & Fife in good time to witness a protesting William Blake-Courtney, handcuffed and frog-marched to a Black Maria, a police constable grasping him firmly on either side, as Andrew pulled up in the town square.

I could barely contain my emotion as I assisted Bonnie from the MG. For a sense of occasion she had chosen to wear the green dress. Her appearance attracted many admiring glances and indeed left few heads unturned as she took my arm. Phillip was managing on his crutches. He had the appearance of a casualty of war with a plaster cast on one leg and a seriously bandaged head.

"It's OK, Jack. Leave him to me," Andrew said with a smile, taking over.

When I entered the office, ushering Bonnie before me, I needed no introduction to the man who stared back at me with unbridled amazement as he greeted his daughter. Although his once flaming red hair was now glacier white, and his dear face was roughened by the passage of time and an unfortunate marriage, Ralph was unmistakeable.

"Is it really you, Turnip?" he greeted me, striding over to hug me until I thought every bone in my body would shatter. "I had this dream…" he began, but stopped when he saw in my eyes that I understood, and he knew I had been there too.

In reality, it was hard to express how much I had missed being with him throughout the lost years, and yet, even as the thought passed through my mind, as he held me at arm's length, grinning, I realised that he knew my every thought. Then we began to discuss the complexities associated with the estate of Dungellen.

Once the documents had been signed, Dungellen Hall was finally mine. The remainder of the meeting proved most satisfactory. Ralph agreed to come back as estate manager and to take on Phillip Ramsey as an assistant, once he was fully recovered.

It was after this, when we were alone, that Phillip voiced what had been troubling him since we first met.

"Kenmere? You were there, at the orphanage?" he exclaimed, staring at me with fresh insight. "So was I. I thought there was something familiar about you when I looked after your dog at the garage."

"I can't understand how," I responded, remembering my injuries and how swollen my face would have been.

"It was the unusual colour of your eyes which got me thinking. That's what I remembered most when I met you as a boy, with that terrible scar, who couldn't speak!"

Some time later, I removed the watch from my wrist and offered it to Ralph, but instead of taking it from me, he ruffled my hair and told me to keep it safe for my heir. "I left it deliberately, hoping that when you came back to Dungellen, it might help you remember me."

After that, when Lorna had served tea, I noticed him grinning like a boy. Then I realised my arm was placed comfortably about his daughter's waist and, although nothing was mentioned about our future together, I could see in his eyes that he knew of our intentions. It brought tears of happiness to Bonnie's eyes when she heard her father's light tread as he left the room, whistling.

This morning, with Foxy's help, we removed all the cladding which had boarded up the long windows, and as we opened the door, I could swear I heard the old house give an immense sigh of relief as the pure sweet air of Dungellen wafted through the dusty interior, and the morning sun illuminated each of the neglected rooms. I had returned home, and with Bonnie at my side. We each carried vases of wild flowers as a token of the happiness our union would bring to that lovely place.

Later in the afternoon, when I returned alone to wander the estate and contemplate a revival of the house and gardens, to restore them to their former glory, I saw the osprey swoop low over the derelict tower and alight on the balustrade of the long terrace. The beating of its enormous wings created a cloud of glittering dust that formed itself into the ghostly shape of Eleanor McKenzie, who then spoke to the bird.

"Did you see her, John?" she asked, as the shape of the osprey began to transform into my father, John de Beaufort.

"Yes, I did. She is the perfect choice. My greatest fear is that she will not accept our being here. Not the way our son does."

"She has the gift, John. If she hadn't believed in my appearance on the cliffs, she would never have been able to catch hold of my hand."

"Then they will be happy together," he answered, encircling his arm about her waist.

"My thoughts exactly."

Now, I wait with my arms resting on the old balustrade of the long terrace to enjoy the warmth of the sea breeze rustling the delicate leaves on the nearby willows. The peace is pleasantly disturbed after Dora's unexpected gift was delivered earlier today. A lovely white pup now occupied wrestling with the lace of my left shoe as I wait for Bonnie to rejoin me in what will soon become our home. This is where I first began to recount the details of my life and I consider myself to be among the most fortunate of men.

END

Printed in Great Britain
by Amazon